# Praise for The Temple of Doubt

"*The Temple of Doubt* launches a powerful new voice in teen fantasy fiction. Anne Boles Levy brings serious game with her first novel. Expect great things!"

—Jonathan Maberry, *New York Times* bestselling author of *Rot & Ruin* and *The Nightsiders*

"Levy shines brightest in her potent descriptions of settings and her imaginative scenes."

—*Kirkus Reviews*

"In a society where going against the grain can bring shame, punishment, and even death, being different is dangerous. But Hadara's differences are what make her special and Hadara's struggles to defend her family, her world, and her soul against the Temple's meddling make for a gripping adventure. *The Temple of Doubt*'s inventive and richly realized world will have readers immersed from the start and eager for the sequel."

—Sarah Jamila Stevenson, author of *The Latte Rebellion*, *Underneath*, and *The Truth Against the World*

"*The Temple of Doubt* fascinated me. With a determined heroine who forges her own path, intricate worldbuilding, and a tantalizing plot that hints at more intriguing revelations to come, Anne Boles Levy shows herself to be a promising new writer. I can't wait to see where Hadara's journey takes her next."

—Eilis O'Neal, author of *The False Princess*

"Hadara may think of herself as a bad student and a wavering believer, but in truth, she is brave, strong, and often hilarious as she struggles to protect her family and find a place for herself within a culture that devalues her. Levy has a knack for exposing the ridiculousness of rigid belief while highlighting the real power that doubt has to transform a society."

—Sara Holmes, author of *Letters from Rapunzel* and *Operation Yes*

"A thrilling fantasy introducing an exceptional new heroine whose fearless challenges to authority and adventurous spirit could make or break her entire world. *The Temple of Doubt* captivates page after page, twist after twist. Clever Hadara is in danger from all sides, from the invading army, the compelling soldier Valeo who tears her city apart, and the secretive and devious Azwans who sacrifice innocents to serve their powerful god. Yet something more powerful than these has fallen from the sky—something alien and shining that is meant only for her."

—Janet Lee Carey, award-winning author of *In the Time of Dragon Moon*

"Fiercely original with a capable and plucky heroine, *The Temple of Doubt* rips open a door to a fresh new fantasy world. With a gorgeously written narrative and its intricate world building, fantasy readers are in for a treat. Hadara is a compelling heroine whose misadventures and missteps will only make you love her more."

—Amalie Howard, author of the Aquarathi series, the Almost Girl series, and *Alpha Goddess*

"What a wonderful heroine and wonderful world Anne Boles Levy has given us in this beautiful debut novel—one I certainly wish had been around when my daughters were young. They'd have fallen in love with Hadara as much as I have. Can't wait for Book II!"

—Bruce McAllister, author of *The Village Sang to the Sea: A Memoir of Magic*

# THE
# WELL
## of
# PRAYERS

Also by Anne Boles Levy

*The Temple of Doubt*

# THE
# WELL
## of
# PRAYERS

**BOOK II OF THE TEMPLE OF DOUBT SERIES**

## ANNE BOLES LEVY

Sky Pony Press
New York

Sky Pony Press books may be purchased in bulk at special discounts for sales promotion, corporate gifts, fund-raising, or educational purposes. Special editions can also be created to specifications. For details, contact the Special Sales Department, Sky Pony Press, 307 West 36th Street, 11th Floor, New York, NY 10018 or info@skyhorsepublishing.com.

Sky Pony® is a registered trademark of Skyhorse Publishing, Inc.®, a Delaware corporation.

Visit our website at www.skyponypress.com.

10 9 8 7 6 5 4 3 2 1

Library of Congress Cataloging-in-Publication Data is available on file.

Cover design by Rain Saukas

Print ISBN: 978-1-63450-193-4
Ebook ISBN: 978-1-63450-625-0

Printed in the United States of America

*To Brett*

*You see no purpose in traveling among the galaxies and taking their measure, you are content to watch life unfold on planets whose air you will never breathe. I cannot bear such sameness, each eon unfolding as the last. Let me journey, let me stray, let me see how no day on one world shall dawn the same as on another. I am brave enough to face whatever comes, assured that the worst danger is the one yet to come, on a day still several days away.*

*You are content to stand still and remain unnamed. I am not made this way.*

—*From Verisimilitudes 9,* The Book of Unease

I

*Your soul must come to me, clean and unblemished,
purged by fire of sin and fleshly weakness. From
the fire shall your soul be released, and your ashes
scattered that your sins do not stick to one place
and curse it.*
　　—From *Oblations 3,* The Book of Unease

It was my task to clean up after the drunks, sobered by
having their heads split open, huddling in corners, puking,
looking unsure how they'd gotten there. A mop became
my best friend as I swabbed away piss and blood and worse
things. The gore wasn't much different than the muck and
mires I'd waded through, and a mop handle was lighter
than an herb basket. I threw myself into my job, the more
mindless the better, happy for any distraction.

　It'd been a fortnight since I'd begun my apprenticeship as a healer for Ward Sapphire, reporting each morning to the main room of the sick ward, which consisted of
two large rooms—one lined with benches for people who

1

could be healed immediately, and one with cots for those who couldn't. By breakfast, the rows had already filled with the woozy and the wounded. They looked more fidgety and anxious than usual that morning, glancing around suspiciously, even narrowing their gaze at others, as though they'd each appointed themselves magistrate over others' misfortunes and were sitting in judgment over every clot or bruise.

Today had begun as always: bandages needed rolling, bedpans needed cleaning. I had sheets to lug to the laundry and rows of cots to make up, with blanket corners folded and tucked. A healer would inspect my work, rip out the neat little $y$ at the bed corners, and make me start over. But there was a new tension in the air, a terseness with the way healers snapped orders, even at patients.

Healer Mistress Leba Mara, a big woman with a voice to match, worked the line herself, her sturdy frame squeezing between the rows, using magical incantations to heal cracked ribs and the shallower stab wounds. I hated to watch the spellcasting: it created a jarring shock of electricity that only I could see, and a metallic taste that only I could sense. This was one of many secrets I kept, and one more reason I should've kept my head down and bent on minor tasks. But I never could. I was always looking up and butting in. I didn't aspire to be an orderly, after all. I wanted to do what Leba Mara and the other healers did—but without all the irritating magic.

All I had to do was figure out a way.

Leba Mara did triage as she went, sending the severely injured inside to cots, with me following along to sop up any trail of blood. Orderlies carried the injured to and fro on stretchers that never looked empty. I hustled from one room to the next, darting around busy people, my hands trembling only partly from fatigue.

I had to find a way. All this magic—it belonged to Nihil, and it should've stayed with him.

"You should do me first," a shopkeeper shouted out, waving his swollen and obviously broken wrist. "I'm the only one that's legitimate."

He cradled the injured wrist in his good hand as Leba Mara gave him a disapproving up and down glance.

"Well, it's true," he persisted, his haughty air crumbling into a working-class accent. "I just got mine's with a fall. Tripped over my own clumsy feet, is all. These others . . . huh. Guards had to drag 'em out of doorways and knock 'em sober. They're pyre fuel for sure."

I had to wedge myself between a suddenly very awake and angry drunk and the shopkeeper. I received a face full of stale, boozy breath and my smock became dotted with blood as the man wobbled into me. I propped him back up, but he swayed like a buoy at high tide. Soon, I thought I'd get dizzy, too. This, too, was part of my job.

"Tripped and fell, by Nihil's scrawny buttocks, you did," the drunk man said, waving his fists. "The guards was settling accounts with you again, wasn't they?"

Leba Mara cut in with a harsh, "Gentlemen!"

"Don't know what you're saying, you souse," said the shopkeeper. "Sober up and shut up."

But the drunk wasn't letting up, shouting past my shoulder at the other man. "Tipping your scales again? We'll see who ends up in an ash heap."

An orderly and I pinned the drunk's arms to his side and walked him back to a bench while Leba Mara held a meaty hand over the shopkeeper's mouth.

"You've both said enough," she said. "Nobody's going to the pyre today. Seal those lips or I'll sew them up."

She looked like she could do it, too; she was bigger than both men combined, and most of that heft was muscle. Added to that was her infamous Glare of Doom, and both men soon settled into a terse truce.

"Worse than usual," muttered the orderly who'd helped me, a stocky man named Til. "This place is getting crazy."

I shook my head but didn't argue. To my mind, all the crazy was being marched right out of us. Port Sapphire was a busy way station between continents, and we'd been a prosperous port until the Temple of Doubt sent us two Azwans and four hundred guards to hunt down a demon. They'd stuck around longer than anyone had wanted. Far longer. The throngs, the shouting, the hustle and bustle and daily messiness of living in the middle of the map had steadily seeped away last summer, replaced by a wary silence, empty canals, and orderly streets.

Somehow, the Temple had gotten sixty thousand stubborn, willful, wayward people to behave themselves and suddenly find religion. How awful. All my favorite shops closed early, and, even when open, people were too polite, too restrained. No one argued or haggled anymore, though no one could remember anyone banning it, either. It was as though we all knew we'd been naughty children, and now we filed obediently, heads down, onto ferries instead of paddling ourselves home every which way. No one bothered telling us what, exactly, we'd done, and we were all trying to guess what good behavior looked like after so many years of getting it wrong.

The gloom added to my own sadness, the storm cloud that had gathered over my heart and wouldn't stop raining self-pity. If I didn't have that mop to distract me, I'd be wallowing in grief over, ironically enough, one of the very guards everyone feared and hated and yet couldn't figure out how they'd ever gotten along without. Valeo, his name had been. He was dead, and I had my duties to help me forget.

"What's all this talk of the pyres?" I whispered to Til.

"Dunno," Til said. "They're all jabbering about it this morning."

"Well, let's go see," I said.

He shrugged. "Should tell a healer, I suppose."

The healer we asked insisted on coming with us and said he knew a way onto our roof. It involved me hitching up my skirt and clambering up the narrowest flight of steps I'd ever seen, only to find myself sitting precariously on the roof's terra-cotta tiles. I had to dig my sandals into a groove to keep myself from sliding down, but I loved the feeling that I was doing something vaguely forbidden, even though several other people were already around. We all squeezed shoulder to shoulder and peered northward, where smoke drifted lazily out to sea.

The funeral pyres usually burned far north of Port Sapphire on a stretch of solid ground, too far away to leach any of the smoke or stench into the city. Pyres were a normal thing: all of us could expect to be burned after we died so our souls could be freed from our bodies and fly to the Eternal Tree if we were found worthy of such redemption. At least, if you believed all that, which I didn't.

I followed everyone's stare to the place where thick, gray plumes lifted above the line of thatched rooftops. The smoke looked thicker and more robust than usual. The last time there'd been that much smoke had been when Ward Sapphire held funerals for all the fallen guards. They'd battled the fierce Gek in the swamps, and Valeo had been one of the men felled by poison darts. Measly, lousy, tiny little darts.

And I'd never forgive myself for it.

I'd been brooding angrily about his death for three six-days—ever since I'd heard the news from one of the Azwans. I'd stared at the horizon a few times, wondering which puff of smoke would contain the last cinders of his bronzed skin or stately frame, the ropes of muscle or the hard angles of his scarred and rugged face.

But where were all these new bodies coming from? I hadn't remembered any sort of plague, and while the guards were gleefully breaking open heads, no one had told me of any sudden killing spree.

"This is just since this morning?" I asked.

The people around me shrugged. No one said anything, so I kept asking questions. Who are they burning? Who died? Does anyone know anything?

I received only uncomfortable silence, a few coughs, cleared throats, and faraway looks until a familiar woman's voice bellowed from below us.

"Well, blast you all to the Soul's Forge," shouted Leba Mara. "Is my entire staff taking a Sabbath? What's going on up there?"

One of the healers shouted down to her about the billowing smoke, prompting her to crane her neck as she struggled to make out the distant plumes. All she did was shake a fist at us.

"Beat on my doubting behind, then," she said. "Get down here, all of you."

We clambered down, most looking more defiant than chastened. The healer who'd escorted me folded his arms across his chest and huffed at the Healer Mistress.

"If you know what this is about, we sure wouldn't mind the explanation," he said. "A lot of scared folks on those benches today."

"Yes, but not many on the roof, is there?" she snapped right back at him. "While you're talking, people are hurting."

The healer held his ground. "Ah, right, then we'll just watch them all hang, one by one, for a bunch of doodads and whatsits the Azwans decided weren't worthy enough. That's what this is, isn't it?"

"Then pray they don't find anything of yours in that pile. I hear it's all sitting in a warehouse right outside the Customs House, anyway. Right where a certain Lord Portreeve might see it."

The small group looked at me. She was talking about my father. My jaw flapped open and closed. No sound came out.

"Me?"

My voice squeaked.

"A big warehouse holding all our little heretical items," Leba Mara said. "Practically out your babba's back door, stuffed to the rafters with all our contraband."

Heretical items? Contraband? I caught my breath, unwilling to believe what I was hearing. Every time I thought the worst was over, the Temple returned with something new.

When they'd first arrived, the Temple Guards had raided our homes and seized anything with even the faintest taint of sacrilege to it. Even my two younger sisters had had items taken: a scrap of needlework and an old doll. And here we'd thought everyone would be safe and fine with the Azwans on their way back to the far-away Temple compound now that the demon business was all over. Apparently, the many tokens of our doubtfulness were keeping them busy.

I let out a small sigh, and Leba Mara must've guessed my thoughts, picking up the thread of my anxiety and weaving it into something fiercer. She scanned the horizon for the smoke and shook her head.

"Of all the unambiguous nonsense," Leba Mara fumed. "I'd of just burned those little whatnots, not the people who made them. And how do they know what belongs to whom? By all Nihil's incarnations, the Temple folk aren't like our local priests. Can't leave a single doubting soul alone, can they?"

The other healer scratched his chin. "So, you're no wiser about this than the rest of us."

"Wiser? I'm wise enough to keep myself to the certain path," Leba Mara chuffed. "We're to doubt our merits and be sure of Nihil's. If there's more reasons you want, you'll find them on the benches inside. Off, now, and do what the worthy priests pay you for."

The other healer sighed, defeated. He held a hand to his heart. "Nihil's ambiguities are the best salves."

"That's more like it," Leba Mara said, patting her own chest.

I bit back any response I might've wanted to give. My days of defiance were also over. I might not believe a word of it, but I kept that to myself. I just wanted to heal people, that's it—if it could be done without magic. And if I had to do that under the protection of the hated Temple, well, so be it. There was nothing I could do about any of this anyway; just one person, a girl at that, and a lowly apprentice. I had rid myself of anyone's expectations of me but my own.

We filed back inside, or at least everyone else did. Leba Mara waved me over.

I thought she meant to ask me more about my father and whatever connection he may have to the sudden increase in pyre smoke. Instead, she adjusted the blue uniform scarf that wrapped my waist-length curls in a high pile atop my head. A few wayward strands had flown loose atop the roof.

A guard stationed by the doorway kept his eyes on my head wrap, despite people coming and going around us, as though he'd zeroed in on an archery target, taking careful aim. Like his comrades, he was a good two or three heads taller than human men and stared down his long nose in a way that was both condescending and cruel.

I fumbled to fasten my scarf even with Leba Mara's help, my breathing coming more rapidly. My fingers couldn't seem to make the knot, and I finally gave up and let Leba Mara fix it. It wasn't perfect, but I had no mirror and however it looked would have to do. The guard gave a short nod at Leba Mara and turned his attention to the flow of wounded and sickly moving through our doors.

"You're lucky," she said, her voice a whisper. "They've been cutting off women's hair right on the spot, whipping out daggers at the first stray lock. You can't even let a pretty little curl or two show."

"Yes, and now the pyres," I said, shuddering. "What *is* going on? I'm sure my father doesn't know."

*If he did, would he have said anything to me?* I wondered.

"I'm just as sure he does," she said. "Even if he knows no more than I do, it's still plenty. And he has pull that even I don't have."

"He's only a civilian though," I said, which drew a sharp scowl from Leba Mara. For all her brashness, she didn't tolerate a sharp tongue from subordinates. "With all due respect, Healer Mistress. He is secular. Anything he says to the Azwans wouldn't be the same as coming from a priest or, surely, a healer?"

"Ah, but his eldest daughter is the Temple of Doubt's new favorite, no? Surely, there's something to be made of that, especially if that daughter should ask her father to intervene on our poor little city's behalf? Maybe ask them to spare a few of us, or find out when they intend to return to our Great Numen's side, where I'm sure our Kindly Master has more need of them?"

I hesitated. I understood the hint she was dropping; it couldn't have been more obvious if she'd embroidered it on my smock. But Babba hadn't mentioned my almost-sacrifice since my Keeping Day, like there was some sort of taboo against it. It also felt wrong to use my father's new position to wheedle him into helping. He'd been made Lord Portreeve, head of the civil government, a position the Azwans had wanted him to have as a sort of repayment.

And, yes, the Temple owed us a lot. More than a lot. Reyhim, the Azwan of Ambiguity, had said as much the night he took me to the altar to be sacrificed, which hadn't worked out the way anyone had expected. But if anyone could make anything happen in the secular world outside of the Temple's sphere of influence, it would be Babba. The warehouses were all in the commercial district, so they would fall under Babba's jurisdiction, right?

At least, that seemed to be where Leba Mara was headed with this. Maybe she was right. I might be only a junior apprentice, and still a little out of my depth in the working world, but Babba would know what to do. I had absolute faith in my father's ability to make it happen. Even so, it didn't pay to over-promise.

"I'll try," I said with as much unconcern as I could fake. "I can't promise my father has any more pull than anyone here."

"It'll have to do, then."

We went inside after that, under the careful eye of the guard, who gave me a disapproving once-over as we passed.

*Seek out the healer who would cure you of aches and pains: go to her before you seek some spell for your every complaint. Though the healer is a witch who combines nature and theurgy for her craft, she spares me from squandering my power on toothaches and ulcers.*
—From *Oblations 13,* The Book of Unease

The bustle of the busy ward usually kept me from dwelling on the events that had hit with cyclone force this summer past. My routine, until this morning, had been to keep busy enough so I might forget what had happened to me. The demon that had drawn the Azwans to our island was gone, but the Azwans remained, and my fate was inextricably tied up with theirs, at least until they chose to leave—as unlikely as that was beginning to seem.

What was the demon? The Azwans said it was the opposite of the numen who'd made himself our god. Such soul-stealing monsters occasionally dropped from the stars to war on him, and the last one had landed here on my island, New Meridian.

That demon had been destroyed, and I'd been at the altar when it happened. It wasn't a role I'd asked for, and that idea had been running around my head even before today, when everything had soured so ominously. After all, this trouble had all begun with and was supposed to have ended with me. I had some role in everyone's misery and my mop wasn't helping me escape it. I pushed at it a little harder, making sweeping strokes across the tile floor, but every knot of dust looked like a plume of smoke.

I'd been called—more like dragged—to the altar as a sacrifice to our god, Nihil, to protect him from the demon, and instead of dying as planned, I'd wound up with some tiny shreds of the creature within me. Yes, floating around in my head were demon-bits, sort of like the spiritual equivalent of a few toenail clippings and a lock of hair, but invisible.

No one was supposed to know about the demon toenails—except the Azwan of Uncertainty, S'ami, that is—but he'd kept his distance in recent six-days, and I was all too happy to give him wide berth. Neither of us sought out the other, and I was fine with that. I was supposed to alert him if the nasty demon-bits grew into something more substantial, and I wasn't exactly eager for that to happen.

The question I had to ask myself, over and over again, was this: *am I me?* The question wasn't to find out if I was feeling out of sorts or maybe lacking a little confidence. No, the question had become *am I still Hadara of Rimonil when I gaze out at the world or hear things?* Lately, I'd heard many things that made me think I'm more than out of sorts, possibly addled, or even all-three-moons crazy.

For example, seeing magic.

Today was a perfect case, especially with the activity ratcheted up to a frenzy. As Leba Mara worked her way down the benches, she dangled a gold weight from a short length of chain. The weight itself was no bigger than her thumbprint in the shape of a broken shield. It was her personal totem, taken from one of the constellations, because, as she said, "In a proper sick ward, it's always a fight to the death." The broken shield vibrated over injuries and I'd brace for the sparks and the odor and acrid taste that flowed through her and out into her patients.

I tried to detect patterns, or ebbs and flows, or at least subtle changes in hues as spells were cast. The shopkeeper with the broken wrist—his spells looked mostly crimson, which ought to suggest blood, when I'd have expected shades of black and blue. He walked out of the sick ward, waggling his fingers cheerily, convinced he'd been magically cured and praising Nihil for it, but the spell lingered like a memory around the allegedly healed spot. It clung like bark on tree, sealed against the skin and bone it had mended.

If only I had someone I could talk to about what it meant, about how such spells really worked, about what went into magic and how I wasn't convinced in the same way as the shopkeeper. Was it all just a giant placebo, a fake cure that only worked because people were thoroughly convinced of it?

Another commotion interrupted my thoughts. A prostitute, her hair chopped short around her ears, was sobbing onto Leba Mara's shoulder. That's what we did to women of loose virtue—forced them to wear their hair short and

THE WELL OF PRAYERS

uncovered to let the world know their shame. Only this woman seemed a little younger than myself and couldn't possibly be old enough to ply a trade like hers. She was holding a bloody rag to her nose, her eyes swollen shut after what must've been a nasty beating.

"Guards?" Leba Mara asked.

The girl nodded and sobbed. "Just one. He didn't want to pay."

I turned away. I didn't want the girl to see my face, as I'm sure it registered pure disgust. Not all the guards were vermin. One had been good, or mostly so. Valeo would have something to say about this girl, I was sure of it.

*I don't take what isn't freely given.*

He'd said that. I hadn't quite understood it then. But I did now, when it was too late.

The girl sobbed something about being hanged that I didn't quite catch, but I didn't need to. It was everyone's thought today.

Leba Mara patted her heart with her hand, the other arm still draped around the girl. "May no doubts remain in your soul, Nihil bless me, you won't go to that pyre. At least not for this, alright?"

"So be it," echoed others. They all patted their hearts, as if that alone might spare them the noose or a slit throat. Nihil likely wasn't scrying from our sanctuary these days and was far away again. He hadn't seen their heart-patting and I doubted he'd care.

And there it was, the big lie: I was a doubter. A skeptical, sarcastic doubter. And the hypocrisy of it all—I'd heard Nihil's voice through the scrying mirror. How many people would give all they had for the chance to hear that beautiful tenor radiating around them? Only me, doubtful me, had heard it, not counting the Azwans and high priest, who probably hear him all the time.

I believed in Nihil. He was a real numen inside a borrowed human body. So what didn't I believe?

His goodness, I suppose. Or maybe I doubted his wisdom making us dependent upon the magic that sometimes worked and sometimes didn't, leaving everyone to guess if that was deliberate.

Maybe I didn't believe in belief. Maybe lack of faith was the only thing I knew for sure.

But I doubted. I'd thought that would make me strong, but it just made me different.

My mood improved, though, as I resumed my chores. Babba could set things right. With his big promotion, my family wouldn't have to fear the gallows, and maybe no one else would, either. Amaniel's screams and accusations still rang in my ear over her lost stitching. She'd sewn a picture of one of Nihil's incarnations. The soldiers—my soldier—had seized it, along with little Rishi's white-haired doll. It looked too much like Nihil's current body, I suppose. Who really knew anymore?

The only good to have come of that day was meeting Valeo. He was gone, but he'd given me purpose I'd never had. There'd be no more Valeos if I could help it. Just like Leba Mara, I was determined to make people live if I had to drag them back from the Soul's Forge myself—if I even knew where such a place was. It was where the unredeemed went to have their souls remelted into someone new.

I'd been a terrible student in school because I seemed to have an allergic reaction at any mention of doctrine, and probably couldn't find the Soul's Forge if Amaniel took me there and shoved me into it. Ah, well, it only convinced me further that I belonged here, where I could make myself useful. I was learning to push a mop well enough, and I worked hard that day, blind to whether I was scrubbing my way through the floor altogether and halfway to the bottom of Kuldor. After this came the Sabbath and a full day home with my family. I had something to look forward to.

"Try not to take too much to heart," Leba Mara's voice jolted me back to reality. "That's my Hadara, a real soft spot for the afflicted. No one should've told you about those pyres. I bet you've thought of nothing else."

"It wouldn't have changed anything," I said. "I will ask my father to help. Just let me finish this part of the floor."

"An orderly can finish up. I've got something more important for my shiny, new apprentice."

Leba Mara guided me by the elbow across the ward to her office, hardly more than a hidey-hole that probably once held brooms. She'd somehow managed to squeeze a table and stool in there along with the day's duty rosters.

"I see your dedication, Hadara, but you know, not everything has to be drudge work," she said. "I've been meaning to lend you this."

She plunked a book into my hands. Books were rare commodities here, since all the engravers and typesetters were on the mainland. I ran my fingers along its worn spine and leather cover, looking for a title. The cover was blank; it had likely been rebound more than once, judging by its yellowed pages.

The first page announced, HUMAN AND FEROXI ANATOMY.

I glanced up, wondering if she really meant for me to have this and if it wasn't somehow heretical. She was trusting me with something more valuable than all the goldweights in the Temple's possession. I had a book, a book full of medicine and natural wonders.

"Thank you, Healer Mistress. I don't know what to say."

"Oral quiz is after Second Workday next week." Leba Mara poked me in the ribs. "Study hard. I take only the best."

I grinned and tucked the book under my arm.

Only the best! A book!

I couldn't do much, but I could do this.

I don't recall saying my parting goodmoons to everyone as I wandered out the door, my nose already planted in my new treasure. The pages gave off a musty odor that I inhaled like perfume, and my arms cradled the book as if it might start to wail or fuss if I treated it too roughly.

A few casual flips of the page and my surroundings dissolved. Cross sections of the human heart jumped out in crimson, followed by diagrams of muscles and joints and their assembly points. They gave way to a spread of cutaway views of a baby in the womb. Here were facts, not philosophies, and it was easily as miraculous as anything I'd witnessed in the sanctuary; the book cast its enchantment over me. How many nights had I sat up with Amaniel, trying to memorize Nihil's incarnations when the most important story in the world was unfolding on these lovingly preserved pages?

What, in my short life, could I possibly have found more important than the curved sweep of this hunched form, with its tiny fists clutched to its chest, its sealed eyes waiting for its first glimpse of the world?

3

*The woman who would serve me best is one who
knows her place among her people. If I had meant
for any woman to achieve more, I would have let
her be born somewhere or sometime else, or as a
man.*
　　　　—*from Oblations 18,* The Book of Unease

I stumbled out the door, blindly following all the other
bodies threading along Ward Sapphire's footpaths. My steps
fell in line as I plodded along, my nose deep in illustrations
of Feroxi limbs, then the human digestive tract, and even a
diagram of a hair follicle. How could anyone chart something so tiny?

I paused on the chapter headed, "Comparative Genitalia,
Feroxi and Human Males." Pious girls from proper homes
didn't even discuss such things, let alone look at pictures. I
was sixteen and old enough to be married, but I was supposed to wait until my wedding night for Mami to give
me The Talk About Sex that anyone who grew up by a

dockside already knew in great detail. Sailors and long-shoreman weren't exactly shy about educating passersby on how it all worked.

This was different, I told myself. It was a textbook and for medical purposes. Only the best, Leba Mara had said. Study hard.

Besides, I ought to know where babies came from, right? Right.

I turned the page.

And immediately started giggling.

I slammed the book shut in case anyone saw me. How juvenile had I just been? Giggling over anatomy. Was I sixteen or six?

Still, I'd never seen a real one, unless I counted all the times I'd had to change a baby boy's soil cloth. No, those didn't count. At all. I crinkled my nose just remembering the rivers of toddler pee my many little cousins alone must have contributed to the world.

People jostled past me on their way toward the Ward's wide, iron gates and the pavilion beyond. I opened the book to a different, safer, page on tendons and, once again, my feet strayed off course, my mind too busy turning over the diagrams as I turned the pages. I felt a tug at my sleeve and glanced up to see Amaniel in her gray school uniform.

"Wasn't school over at high heat?" I said, irritated at the distraction.

"No, staying late again."

"How much tutoring could you possibly need? You're their best student."

"That's why."

"Well, if you can stand the schoolmistress all that time ..."
I had a fading memory of my wrists getting slapped with
her pointer.

"It's not with her."

"Then who?"

Amaniel smiled. "It's a secret."

"Please don't tell me with an Azwan."

Amaniel's smile broadened. "I could be a high priestess
someday."

I blinked a few times, expecting my crazy sister would be
replaced with someone saner. Then again, she was the one
the priests usually loved, and I was the one they'd pointed
to as the bad example. "That's ... great. Yes, great. You'd be a
very, um, special priestess. A nice one, too, I hope."

"I'd be as nice as people deserved, yes?" Amaniel stuck
her nose in the air. "And no more."

Our pace slowed as we passed through the main courtyard beneath its swaying trees and giant planters brimming
with tropical blossoms that were only just now fruiting
over and dropping their petals. Autumn, such as it existed,
came late to our island and meant only days of endless
sun and sea breezes. It was a gorgeous day, but it had been
a long time since I'd noticed whether days were good or
bad. They'd all begun to run together.

I sighed and shook my head. "Forget being nice, then.
At least try not to be so haughty. I need your help."

"From Scriptures? A prayer you haven't memorized
yet? A tricky spell the healers can't cast? I could probably
help." The smug look on Amaniel's face would ordinarily
set my brain spinning, but I let it pass. I had to ask her ...
but then what she'd just said hit me.

"Spells?" I nearly gagged. A scene of my sister waving a gold totem popped into mind, and I squeezed my eyes shut against it to no avail. I opened them to see her gloating. "No. Absolutely not. Never."

That smug look again. "Yes. Spells," she said. "I have Nihil's blessings on me too, it seems, even if it's not a special one like you, but maybe by *my* Keeping Day there'll be a special blessing for me too. I aim to try."

My jaw must've dropped because I felt a sudden dryness inside my mouth. She was still jealous about my Keeping Day celebration, when the Azwans recited a blessing Nihil had composed for me. Something about my willing, worthy soul and whatnot. Amaniel was jealous, and no matter what cruelty the Temple got up to, Amaniel would always see the world through the prism of her being the Not-Hadara, for better or worse.

And this was worse—so much worse. I thought of the shopkeeper again, so convinced he'd been fixed up and made right, thanks to some nonsensical hocus-pocus, waving his arm like new. Maybe he had been cured, and maybe, like many, he'd be back in a few days, complaining of aches and swelling all over again and wondering what he'd done to deserve Nihil's ire this time.

Would I ever be able to rip the Temple out of our lives? Or cram any sense into Amaniel?

But what good did it do to argue? She had her mind fixed on this. I wouldn't dissuade her by yelling at her.

"Well, isn't that grand," I said. "Don't hex anyone."

Amaniel scoffed. "That's such an obscene waste of Nihil's theurgy."

"And what isn't? Look, what do you know about that warehouse where they keep all our contraband? The items the soldiers seized?"

A wide, wild-animal look on Amaniel's face told me she likely knew even less than I did. "They kept it all? All that stupid, useless stuff? I'd have thought they'd burned it."

"Me too. They're calling people to accounts for it all. Hanging people." I pointed to a wisp of smoke on the horizon. The pyres were dying out for the day and didn't seem like much any longer. I'd hoped she could imagine it being much, much worse. "See?"

"That's the price for perfidy, Hadara, as well you know. Nihil sows doubt and reaps . . ."

"What about your needlework? They have it locked up somewhere. Didn't the high priest himself tell you it was a graven image?"

I cherished the shocked look on Amaniel's face, but her reaction turned weirdly sour. She scowled and turned away. "I'm hardly in the same category as those people. You should hear some of the things I've learned about."

"Then you know about all this?"

She shrugged. "A little. The Azwan says it's his sacred duty to go over our contraband, item by item. I just didn't think he meant it literally."

"Oh, like he could've meant it metaphorically? Honestly, Amaniel." But I had a sudden hope. "Then you can work on changing Reyhim's mind, while I get Babba to close the warehouse or something."

"Not if Nihil lives a million years," she said. "We aren't worthy to intervene with the Azwans. And no, that doesn't mean I like it. It's just . . . just that . . ."

"It's just that you want to join the people who kill people because they don't like a few pictures?"

"Stop, Hadara. Stop. I . . . I need to think." Amaniel chewed her lower lip and glanced back at the horizon. "The convicted are getting a proper funeral, at least. They'll go back to the Soul's Forge if it's really that bad. Won't they?"

The Soul's Forge. Where the unworthy went for reclamation, or whatever myth was current.

I gaped. Not one word came from my open mouth. What words could even exist? My sister was absolutely fine with the idea of a pyre burning for much of the day.

She shook her head, pursing her lips. "Oh! You. You! Are making me doubt. Stop that! You're not supposed to have these doubts either; you'd promised Babba and everyone else who'd listen."

She had me on that one. "Alright! I'll stop doubting." *For now,* I told myself. I needed to get out of here, I needed to change the topic, I needed to forget much of today had happened.

"Anyway, I have something very certain and factual and truthful to show you," I said. "But we have to get it past the guards. Are you going to turn me in and send me to a pyre?"

Her eyes rested on my text, still tucked under my arm.

"Why do you have that?" she asked. "It looks very big and impressive. Is it from the Customs House? Did a merchant bring it? Babba must've loaned it to you. Why you? Is it poetry? I love poetry, too, you know. And it wouldn't get you sent to the pyre, unless it was heretical. That was a joke, right?"

Her words came rapid-fire, as if she were trying to assess the danger aloud, until she ended dismissively: "Besides, I know you, you don't care about religion enough to be heretical."

"Shh . . . it's anatomy," I countered. "From Leba Mara. It's completely sanctified, but maybe not the sort of thing the guards might appreciate." I glanced up toward the many sentries and wondered if I should sneak it up my dress. That would likely only spark more attention, not less. "I'll show you once we're on the other side of the gate. It's beautiful, it's . . . I can't describe it. Anyway, there couldn't be anything in that warehouse worth dying for, understand? This is all about that precious Reyhim of yours wanting to show everyone he's the big boss."

She didn't—couldn't—know Reyhim might also be her grandfather. That was another secret I had to keep, this one under Mami's orders.

Amaniel frowned. "What if I told the Azwan you said that?"

"You're horrid, you know that? You're going to help me with Reyhim, and you're going to help me get this book past the guards so I can show it to you."

"Why should I? And why are you bossing me about?"

My breathing got all raggedy, and I rubbed sweaty palms on my work smock, which I'd forgotten to remove. I was taking too much out on Amaniel, and it was backfiring. Why should she help me? She had nothing to gain from helping me sneak a possibly naughty book past the Temple's humorless enforcers. Once again, I hit up against the stubborn reality that her ambition to be a priestess was a normal one to have; my opposition, however well-intended, would only ever be seen as misguided, at least by most people, including our parents. I sighed.

"I've only ever wanted to be useful," I said at last. It was true. "And you've only ever wanted to be the best. Can't you trust me this one time?"

"I've always trusted you."

I blinked. "Really?"

"Yes. You do always want to help people. It's going to be your downfall, I think. It's why you go out into those Nihil-forsaken swamps. Or used to. And I think you're going to make the best healer our city's ever seen, if you don't get yourself arrested. So, alright, I'll help. And I cannot wait to see what's in your book, even if it's *not* poetry."

Amaniel accepted the challenge with a smirk and slid her arm into the crook of my elbow, as if that would somehow hide my bulky cargo. "There's a way through. By the gates there's that one guard."

I looked toward the gates and shrugged. "What one?"

"The half-human one," she said. "Don't tell me you've forgotten."

Half . . . human?

That couldn't be. There'd been only one. I'd called him a half-brow, a slur, like calling him some sort of mongrel between human and Feroxi. The man who belonged to that term was dead of a Gek poison, which he'd gotten while in the swamps trying to protect me. I turned, time itself slowing while my eyes honed in on the target, his helmet gleaming above the crowds jamming through the Ward gates. He was just a bit shorter than the other guards, the helmet peaking just a little less in front, the skin on his arms bronze instead of pale.

"How can that be?" I breathed.

I gripped Amaniel's shoulder, suddenly unsure of my knees. The whole courtyard spun. How was he alive?

One of the Azwans had told me he was dead. Valeo's comrades had confirmed it. He was dead.

But he wasn't dead. He was standing there, grim-faced, at the gate.

Not in a shroud on a pyre in flames. Not ashes scattered to the winds. Not a distant memory of a man who'd said we couldn't have been friends in any case, and then agreed we were.

Who had lied?

**4**

*This isn't love,*
*It's a hard, gray rain,*
*On a broken, brown land;*
*Everything bright is dark today.*

*This isn't love,*
*It's a long campaign,*
*And a bitter last stand;*
*Everything won is lost today.*

*This isn't love*
*It's a slow, dull pain*
*With no healing at hand*
*Any good feeling has bled away.*
*        —from "This isn't love," a popular song*

Valeo was as broad and massive and imposing as I remembered. Every pore on my body seemed to come alive at once, as if the air raced through every part of me and I were a sieve, full of holes through which the wind could blow, feeling every speck of dust, every jot of moisture, nerves on fire, prickling with a mix of joy and terror and pure fury.

I wheeled on Amaniel.

"You knew, didn't you?" I shouted. So much for trust and helpfulness and all that. "You kept this from me."

"Kept what from you? That some big, thick-skulled guard was standing there, like all the other big, thick-skulled guards?"

"That he's alive! Valeo's alive!"

Amaniel held a hand to her eyes and peered over at him from across the courtyard. "Why, yes, he is that. So you remembered he has a name besides 'half-brow'?"

"You! This. I don't. Oh!" I was so angry, I couldn't speak. There was room only for rage. "You have no idea, do you?"

She shot me a quizzical look. "Well, now I guess I have an idea. But it's you who never told me—your sister! You had feelings for him. I tell *you* everything."

That was true. I'd kept one secret too many, perhaps. I shook my head and my anger, at least toward Amaniel, dissolved. "I'm sorry. I've missed him so much."

"Well, there he is," she said, nodding in his direction. "Just don't forget to hide your book . . ."

But I didn't hear her. I was off. My lungs struggled to keep pace with my feet as I took off without even thinking of what I was doing, where I was going. I tugged Amaniel behind me and executed one of the clumsiest curtsy-bows I'd ever performed without toppling over, the book tucked under my arm. "Your Highness."

Why hadn't he tried to find me? Why hadn't I known he was alive?

Would it be immodest to hug him? Or hit him?

I was so happy! And frustrated. Who'd kept his not-being-dead from me? S'ami? Valeo's comrades? How many people were in on this conspiracy? And why?

Valeo only glowered at me through the slots in his helmet. His deep voice carried an icy tone. "Hadara of Rimonil."

"You're alive." I almost reeled from a whole new set of emotions ripping across me. With all that had already happened, plus the heat that suddenly seared across my face and down deep into me, I felt as though I'd been turned upside down and shaken. My common sense dropped right out of my head. "I can't believe it! You're alive."

"Have been for some time," he said. "All my life, in fact."

"You're not dead. You're very, very alive." The day's earlier horrors were already forgotten. What else could crowd the sight of the bloody sick ward from my head?

"Good of you to notice. Move along, please."

"I've thought of you." My heart must have been loud enough to hear across the bay. "I'd heard you were dead. I heard the tonic didn't reach you in time."

His gaze narrowed and he lowered his face to eye level with mine. I stared, terrified, into the two fierce, brown dots that had become his eyes. "You heard wrong."

His icy tone was cooling me off quickly. I'd been telling myself for two six-days that I was too busy to mourn a man I'd barely known. And here, all I wanted was to dance around him, and all he wanted was for me to move along. I was more confused than angry, and suddenly embarrassed. How many people had seen me flinging myself at him? I'd just made a complete idiot of myself.

Oh, but he was alive!

Amaniel performed a much lovelier version of the curtsy. "Please, great guardian of—"

"Move." Valeo cut her off and waved us past.

A stream of people filed behind us, moving us halfway across the square in front of the gates. I slowed then and Amaniel stopped to ask what was wrong.

"I don't understand," I said. "How did I offend him? Why didn't I know he lived? Amaniel, how come he didn't come find me?"

Maybe he hadn't known that I'd lived. He'd been on his deathbed—correction, sickbed—the night I'd been taken to the altar for sacrifice. Maybe he'd never heard . . . oh, nonsense. The whole island knew. How could he not know?

Amaniel waved a hand as though my unhappiness was a mist she could dispel.

"It's just poor upbringing," she said. "Not all the guards are decent men, obviously. Anyway, don't waste another thought on him. I'm still annoyed you didn't tell me you liked him. That's so not like you! Especially when I can fix you up with someone so much better. I'm meeting lots of handsome seminary students who are wife-hunting."

Oh, how awful—seminary students. I couldn't imagine a worse fate, except maybe being tied up with rocks and tossed in the bay. "I don't want anyone—"

Amaniel scowled at me. "Hadara, he ransacked our house and was rude to us. I mean, after you insulted him, but still. And he made me angry with you, so that Babba smacked me. Remember? It was always his fault, you know. Are you just being contrary? You're like that sometimes."

"Amaniel! I thought he was dead. And he's not!"

"HAH. *Da*. Raaaaah." Amaniel got that annoyed tone in her voice she reserved for when I was being extra stupid in school. "Hoorah, he's alive. He's still a thug. And only half human! I could ask the Azwan of Ambiguity to make some proper introductions to the right sort of men, but you have to be a lot nicer to me. A *lot* nicer."

"So I should forget that Reyhim was the one who ordered our homes ransacked?"

Normally, the sight of my sister's face darkening would make my day. But I didn't have much fight in me right then. I needed a laugh the way some folks need a cool drink. My insides fluttered and flitted until up was down and inside out. Besides, I'd pushed her far enough for one day—and myself, too.

"Never mind," I said. I pulled her aside and opened the book. "Take a look."

I found the page with the part of a man's anatomy I wasn't supposed to know about until The Talk. I wondered if Valeo's looked like the one in the book—hairy and ugly. I'd seen him in a loincloth and that had nearly sent me reeling, even though he'd been feeble and dying.

Amaniel took one glance and threw both hands over her mouth with a squeal. "Oh, you can't possibly think Babba has one of those. It's disgusting."

I grinned. "It looks like a crane's neck, only all plucked."

"The poor crane."

That brought fresh peals of giggles from both of us.

A shadow fell over the book. A walking tree must be behind us, from the size of it. A familiar voice growled from the tree-man shadow. "Is that the proper respect for what makes a man, a man?"

I snapped the book shut on Valeo's hand as he reached for it. "I'm going to be a healer," I said. "Besides, it takes more than that to make a man. You have to be nice to ladies."

"I will when I find one. Give it over."

We'd stopped, and a sea of people parted around us, continuing on their way toward the bridge. He was as I remembered him, glaring and beady-eyed even from deep within his jut-browed helmet. I stood my ground.

He'd lived and hadn't told me, hadn't contacted me or sent word or anything. I hated him every bit as much as I'd once nearly panted at the thought of him. Obviously, I'd been misled about his dying, and he'd probably wanted it that way. What else could I assume? He had so much to apologize for.

"It's perfectly chaste," I said. "I got it from the sick ward."

His meaty hand didn't budge from within the thick book. "Give it over or I'll rip it in half."

I let go. Valeo whipped it open and glanced back and forth between the offending page and the two of us. I feigned indifference. Hairy and ugly. Just like the rest of him. "I'm really glad to see you're well, Your Highness."

"I'm First Guardsman Valeo and nothing else," he said. He waggled the book under my chin. "I could arrest you for this."

"I swear I haven't done anything."

"You possess contraband."

"It's as I told you."

"You're not a healer yet. It's therefore forbidden. You want to argue the point before an Azwan?"

"Oh, please." I was on firm ground on this one. "My sister just came from an Azwan's side and this is all fine by him."

Which, in a way, wasn't totally a lie, since the Azwans had arranged my apprenticeship.

A big shoulder edged in front of me, about two or three fingers-width from my nose. I could bite Valeo, he was so close. I might have to if he didn't give my text back. How could I have mourned him for even half a moment?

Valeo grunted at me. "You're bluffing," he said.

"You're annoying." I should be afraid of this big baby and his pointy toys. His daggers and swords remained sheathed, however, and his neck was turning a brownish red as he frowned, his chin crinkling. The heat in my own cheeks gave away the flush I knew was creeping over me, as well. But I'd seen Valeo's same look on Babba whenever he was losing an argument with Mami. So I did as she did: I planted my feet, dug my fists into my hips, pursed my lips, and waited.

I was going to get that apology.

"You listen." Valeo hovered over me, malice emanating from every finger-length of his oversized frame. "I'm doing you a favor. You thought you could just stroll past the sentries with that thing?"

"It's called a book."

"My people were writing books while yours were splotching handprints on cave walls."

"Touchy, touchy."

Amaniel piped up from behind me. "Please, pious Guardian of Nihil's Person. We're so grateful for your vigilance, we swear."

I turned around one tiny, furious, barely controlled step at a time, hoping I could keep my hands from wrapping around her neck. What did Amaniel think she was doing?

She kept on: "Perhaps you've forgotten, mighty warrior, that all doubts have been removed from my sister's name? Her textbook will help her healing skills. It's chaste, as she says."

The book was back in my arms a moment later, and the brute actually apologized—to Amaniel. To me, Valeo only said: "Keep moving."

I narrowed my eyes and hugged the book to my chest. I also didn't move. I had a brief moment of the purest, sweetest pleasure watching his face contort in rage. He turned bright red somewhere beneath that bronze bucket he wore over his head. I hadn't believed for a moment that my life might be in danger. Something had changed in him, something I sensed I could exploit, though I wasn't sure how, or what I was after, exactly. I'd stopped him cold, which was a power I hadn't known I had.

I gave him my sweetest I-hate-you smile as I spoke: "Happy Sabbath, First Guardsman Valeo and Nothing Else."

"Nihil's balls! You little—" he said.

"Language, please!" I feigned shock.

"What, with that book of yours, don't you know all about a man's unmentionables by now? Maybe you need someone to teach you how they work."

This was when growing up by the docks came in handy. I'd heard replies to this kind of talk before. "*You* teach me how *your* unmentionables work? Well, I can't imagine that would take long. It'd probably take longer to find them."

An out-and-out guffaw came from Amaniel's direction. I grabbed her arm and the two of us strode off. Never mind the apology. Humiliating him was working well for me, too.

Amaniel glanced over her shoulder. "He's following."

Valeo overtook us in a few angry strides and planted himself between us and the bridge. I stood my ground and braced for a stream of obscenities. It never came.

He shook his head. "You're not doing this to me."

"I'm not doing anything to you."

"I don't care at all about you. I've watched you come and go from here for days already, like I'm invisible to you. I wouldn't give Nihil's toe fungus for you."

Had he really been watching for me? And I'd walked right past him, not seeing him alive and well and glowering at me?

The bottom fell out of my day. It had been a bad day so far, and I ought to feel worse about people dying. But this man had been alive, and I'd been oblivious. I was worse than an idiot; I was livestock, bleating and stupid and following the herd with my head bent and my eyes lowered.

"I could have my pick of Feroxi warrior brides," he said.

"Congratulations." A bitter tone crept into my voice.

"They have lands and armies. You have only a vulgar book and a blessing from the Temple."

Amaniel shot a quizzical look at me. It dawned on me that Valeo and I were having two separate conversations. I was defending my book; I couldn't figure out what he was defending. Why was he being this way? It's not like

I'd been deliberately avoiding him, and he still hadn't ever bothered to point out his state of not-being-dead to me.

"You don't like me," I said.

"That, I know."

"I thought about you and grieved for you and hated myself for not getting that tonic made in time. Of all the things that happened to me that night—and ever since— not saving you was the one that ate at me the most. So you just listen."

Somewhere inside my brain, all foggy with rage, his new expression vaguely registered as amazement.

"You're going to escort my sister and me home and be pleasant about it, or at least not so grumpy. And then you're going to forget the admittedly tiny part I may have played in saving your life and start thinking about some gigantic, beetle-browed warrior bride."

"With hairy legs," said Amaniel. Nihil's navel, how I love my sister.

"And a big, cold castle," I added.

Amaniel lowered her voice. "I hear they wear their armor to bed."

"How adorable," I said. "You and her and all that matching bronze."

Valeo folded his arms across his massive chest and scowled. "I don't like where this is going."

I shrugged. "Well, we're going home. You coming?"

He stepped aside to let us pass, then stomped along behind us. Amaniel kept turning her head to narrate Valeo's progress as we made our way across the bridge and beyond. I shrugged, pretending he was no more than an annoying street vendor hassling me to buy useless junk.

"I thought you hated him?" I said after Amaniel's fourth update.

"It's still a huge honor to have a Temple Guard escorting us," she said. "Besides, I think he likes you."

I chuffed. "Reyhim's passed his gold totem over your brain too many times."

She elbowed me in response. I snuck my own peeks over my shoulder as we strode along, half out of disbelief and half out of grudging pride that I'd managed, once again, not to get myself arrested or killed. But the disbelief part was winning. Valeo, a prince, was following me home. But I'd liked him, sort of, before I knew that. No, I hated him, even now. But he was following me home.

I snuck another glance to make sure. He kept his mean, brooding face on and added a scowl for extra emphasis.

This was too good to let the moment pass. I wanted to have him trail me all over the city until I wore out the soles of my sandals. Instead, we led Valeo to a quiet side street off the main market square, lined with merchants' homes painted in eye-scorching hues, with window boxes and potted flowers in a riot of colors. It was the only street of homes in the commercial area, and the nicest address in the city. The three of us paused outside the portreeve's official residence, a statelier place than our last house, with a gated entrance. Off to the side was Mami's private hearth, where a cook and a serving man were hard at work.

I sent Amaniel in ahead of me, hoping to have a word with Valeo, or maybe a few hundred words.

All he said, however, was, "I have returned you in all pious trust," and turned to go.

"Wait," I said. "You can't just leave."

Could he? I still hadn't gotten my apology. Then it occurred to me that was the smallest part of what I wanted from him.

"You asked for an escort," he said. "And I provided it. I have duties elsewhere."

"Your Highness, wait."

At that, he turned. "I am First Guardsman Valeo Uterlune of the Second Uncertain Unit of the Unsleeping Vigil over the Great Numen's Borrowed Personage. I am not His Highness, not to you, not to anyone on this wretched island."

I blinked back tears, my fake indifference crumbling. "I have no idea what you just said. Your Commander made a point to call you a prince."

"I am a prince, but I am First Guardsman—"

"Yes, yes, I got all that. Sort of. Don't ask me to memorize it though." Maybe I should've just let him go. Feeling all this contempt from him was worse than thinking him dead.

"You're crying."

"I never cry." I sniffled and inhaled a hiccup. "I'm just confused why you're so angry with me. Don't you have heretics to hang?"

He took several abrupt strides forward until he was once again using his superior height to make a point. "You find that funny, yes? That Nihil is crushing your backward little city under the heel of his boot? I never took you for shallow."

"Nihil's navel, no! I mean, I didn't, you . . . I was angry with you. For being angry with me." I sounded like a complete fool. Honestly, sometimes I feel like every word that ever came out of my mouth should be painted vivid green like our plague banners, so people would know to avoid them.

"You've no reason to be angry with me," he said. "I will, however, show you what you should be angry about. You, of all people, making light of Nihil's ire. You, of all people, when you have the most power to help."

"Ire? Me? Help?" What had I done? What power would I have?

If he'd said I could fly or make the world spin backwards, I'd have believed him sooner than the idea that there was something I could do about the Azwans' or Nihil's ire or the plumes of smoke. If I could do something, I'd like to think I would've thought of it by now.

"Meet me in front of the Ward gates on First Workday before you report to the sick ward."

Then he was gone, striding up the narrow street as though he owned it, thumb resting on his sword hilt, turning the corner without looking back. I watched him without tearing my gaze away until long after there was nothing left to see. It finally occurred to me to shut my wide-open mouth and stop stammering excuses and miserable replies to the empty air.

I pushed open our gate, feeling its squeaks and groans like I'd uttered them myself.

5

*A gracious hostess opens her mind as well as her hearth.*

—*Sapphiran proverb*

Babba anticipated a crowded Sabbath eve by our hearth. Two sea captains with ships in port were making a courtesy call, and a few merchants and their wives had sent word they'd like to sample the new lord and lady's hospitality. They rowed up to our private dock on the Grand Concourse, where the women of House Rimonil greeted them in our finest dresses, as Babba told us we were to do every Sabbath, our hair wrapped in colorful lace, a new strand of perfectly matched pearls dangling from Mami's slender neck.

We were keeping a tradition that stretched back before anyone knew to write down such things, before laws and rules and codes of conduct. Back then, a stranger showing up uninvited must've presented every kind of danger and no promise of reward. Breaking bread together created a bond of trust between guest and host; it was a singular stamp of civilization, and the household of the newest Lord Portreeve would see it honored.

All these lofty thoughts circled in my head as I helped the cook with this platter and that bowl, elevating our simple meal in my imagination to great historical importance, made all the more urgent by the thought of those funeral pyres. I would make sure there would be one civilized spot in this city tonight—one place that was safe, if only for a short while—even if I had to struggle with a whorl of madness in my head over a living Valeo and his invitation. What did he mean, I had power? Over what or whom? What is it he wanted me to see?

Never mind. I needed to distract myself. Too much was riding on this dinner and the mood it would set. Babba had to be convinced to do what no one else could, to use his newfound position to stand up for our city and persuade the Azwans to leave us be, and that was easier to do over wine and food and lively company.

Dinner tonight was Babba's favorite; lentil stews spiced to sear the palate, piping-hot flatbreads to eat them with, and a poached fish as long as the span of Babba's arms. I had to slap Rishi's sticky hands away more than once, until I saw Babba dipping a finger into the fruit relish and scowled at him. He flashed a guilty grin and snuck away.

From around the front of the house, the gate rattled. A nod from Mami meant I should go answer. The air seeped out of my lungs. For a brief moment, I thought it might be Valeo, and then realized how utterly illogical that would be. Even so, my heart beat faster, and I caught myself mentally rehearsing something to say to him.

As I rounded the front of the house, a newborn's wail pierced the quiet street, along with a familiar woman's voice shushing it. I peered through the iron lattice toward the dusky street. "Dina?"

"Let us in, it's not just the baby who's hungry," Dina said with a laugh. My cousin's red-faced baby boy wailed from inside a sling across her bosom.

"You're quite the howler!" I said, jiggling the gate open. "An opinion on everything, I take it."

Dina's husband peered over her shoulder. Faddar was chubby and barely out of his teens, his beard only a sparse crop of dark strands. I chuckled. "He looks like you, Faddar."

His wife poked him in the side. "It's the baby fat," Dina said. Faddar flashed a lopsided grin and shrugged.

"Your cousin feeds me too well," he chuckled.

*This is what happiness looks like,* I told myself. *Remember this when you're picking through those red-ribboned scrolls.* The courting notes were streaming in now that I'd turned sixteen, but my sudden value as a future wife owed more to Babba's new position. I wasn't sure I wanted to marry someone who saw me as a plank in his career path, or whose parents saw an alliance with House Rimonil as a safe harbor in a storm of trouble.

Yet I couldn't help browsing through the scrolls with Mami and my sisters, even if it turned my stomach to hear them sighing and giggling. Mami couldn't resist doting on the florid pleadings of this or that third cousin or his shy best friend. Maybe I should marry one of them, she'd suggest with all the subtlety of a windstorm. No, the one with the handsome beard who used to tease me in school, Amaniel would insist. Not him. This other one is halfway to his first fortune at the Customs House. Yes, he'd do, they'd agree. Or maybe not. And then they'd start all over again.

I refused to even think about a husband. I'd turned sixteen only a half-season ago, and even if the notes piqued my curiosity, it was only to see who'd written and if I knew him. I pictured none of them by my side, day or night. I could practice kissing my pillow with my eyes closed, but what good was that? When I opened them, it was time to don my blue smock and head to the sick ward. And the only men I saw there were battered or hungover.

I led Dina and her family around to the dining patio.

"Word's out that two merchants are looking you over tonight, Hadara," Dina said, lowering her voice. "Though, careful, it's their wives you want to impress."

"Looking me over? Am I for sale?"

"In a way, yes. They've got eligible sons."

Oh! Nihil save me from Eligible Sons.

"I don't think I'm ready," is all I said.

"You'll be ready if your Babba says so. Anyway, mind what I tell you. The fathers just want to see that you're good-looking and sweet. But your prospective mother-in-law? She'll be sharpening knives for you."

"Knives? Meaning what, exactly?" I had enough to worry about besides possibly murderous future in-laws.

"Ever wonder why the sons aren't present while Dearest Mami makes your acquaintance?"

"No, not really, I—"

"Dina, love!" Mami was there to greet us, and all conversation stopped while she and the guests swore up and down the baby was the most adorable thing ever, and

Nihil's blessings were surely on the new parents, and may he bestow many such blessings in the future.

But it was just as Dina had said. The two merchants' wives kissed the baby's head and then immediately looked over to see my reaction. *What do you think of your new little cousin?* asked one. *You must love children, don't you, Hadara?* asked the other. *How is working at the sick ward? Are you afraid of getting ill yourself? You do take good care of yourself, yes?* I found myself going 'round and 'round with the questions until Babba motioned me away. I bowed to the ladies and made a prompt escape.

I joined Mami and Amaniel as Babba leaned in to whisper instructions. "No matter how the conversation turns, I want smiles, yes? No tragedy, no politics, at least not from us. Smiles of welcome."

I knew he wasn't talking about the nosy wives, but Mami gave him one of her cross looks. "We hardly need lessons in hospitality, Rim."

"Actually, we do," he shot back, his voice still a whisper. "Every moment of this meal is a test. Make sure the new Lord Portreeve and his family pass inspection."

She gave him a peck on the cheek by way of an answer. "Girls, go help the cook. And Hadara, I know it'll be hard, but make yourself as unnoticeable as possible, please. You're the hostess tonight, not the main course."

Unnoticeable? I'd happily crawl under our house, even if it lacked the stilts of our old one, for the chance to go unnoticed. But one glance at Babba's stern nod at Mami's instructions and I figured it was better to just perform another curtsy-bow and grab a platter. After I'd been handed a wine jug, I realized how utterly I was going to fail at Mami's instructions. I had to ask Babba about intervening; Leba Mara was counting on me to convince him. How was I going to broach such a delicate subject while having to smile until my cheeks hurt?

The longer the evening dragged on, the harder it became to keep that Smile of Welcome pasted on. Thunderous conversations rumbled from every corner of the long table. Speculation ran high that the Azwans would leave soon, or they'd stay forever, or the Temple was taking over or would leave us alone. Both ship captains had heard my story in other ports of call, but I didn't match what they'd imagined: a "wild girl" ought to sport twigs in her unkempt hair and a crazy gleam in her eye. I politely poured the wine from a fluted pitcher, asked after their ships, and demurred most conversation. That was my role, and I fell into it with unusual vigor, even for me.

I had to stay focused before I tipped the wine into someone's lap. Babba couldn't have anything to criticize before I got to ask about the warehouse.

Mostly the men talked politics, which meant loud appraisals of the border war between Feroxi and humans on the mainland. Both races fought to control cargo routes and croplands. That much I'd gathered from a score of similar wine-fueled debates, even before all the troubles with the Azwan. It'd been going on for years.

"It's spilled over to here," said one of the merchants, an overfed, jowly man with a permanent frown. "We've got our own Feroxi troubles these days."

"You've got nothing," said a sea captain. "A few broken skulls and missing men? Where are the slaves they've taken

or the razed villages? Where's the cropland they've seeded
with salt or the orchards they've axed?"

The merchant pressed his case. "You're saying we
should wait until then? Until our whole island looks like
the borderlands, like one giant boneyard? We should act."

His wife patted his arm. "Maybe not so fast. Don't be
in a hurry to volunteer men younger than yourself. They
might have their own ideas for their future." At that, the
woman nodded toward me. Of course, she was one of the
ones with a son my age. She wouldn't want him getting
speared before she could seal a deal with House Rimonil.
I refixed my Smile of Welcome and refilled her husband's
cup. He meant to continue his argument, but Babba interrupted with a wave of his hand.

"You forget, friend, these particular Feroxi aren't land-
grabbers," Babba said. "They're Nihil's guard, or mercenar-
ies, or call them what you will. They leave the boot-stamp
of the Temple. Unless you want to take Nihil on, that is."

"No, Nihil forbid it," said the merchant. "You can make
them back off, at any rate."

"Meaning?"

The merchant pointed straight at me. "You've got a
weapon. Use it."

I froze in my spot, the wine jug tilted at a dangerous
angle.

"My daughter isn't a weapon." Babba's tone was quiet
and purposeful.

The merchant took the pointed finger and jabbed the
table with it. "She's got Nihil's blessing. An official one. Not
just us and our prayers and wishful thinking. How many
people on the mainland can say that?" He stared around

the table. The ships' captains shook their heads. Not many, apparently, or they didn't know. I wanted to tell them I'd paid too high a price for it.

The merchant jabbed at the table again. "Use her to get at the Temple. You're her father. Get them to back off."

Dina piped up from the corner where she'd nestled with her son. "I've come from the street merchants to ask you to intervene, too. You know, because Hadara's my cousin, so they picked me. Sorry, cuz, but we're getting desperate. Two stalls've been smashed in the past six-day, and we'd barely recovered from their raid."

It was my turn to wade into the thicket. I'd been looking for a chance, and here it was, big as a fish platter. "I wasn't going to say anything, but Leba Mara's request sounds like these others," I fixed the fat merchant with a stare. "She's worried too many people are headed to the funeral pyres."

One of the sea captains shrugged. "As I say, you don't have the problems they do on the mainland."

Babba shook his head. "This is the Azwans' business. You cannot expect me to have sway where the priests do not."

The fat merchant wouldn't stop. "We have a portreeve who's new and untested and we're under Feroxi siege from within. What are you doing about it?"

"I believe you mistake me, friend," Babba said, his tone cooler. "Some good men have died here in recent days, including the former occupant of this house, my friend and mentor and as fine a lord as ever guarded this port."

The fat merchant leaned back as if getting a better view of us all. "I repeat. And you're doing what about it, exactly?"

"Again, what can I do that the priests haven't already tried?"

The merchant spoke up quietly, his voice low and serious. "The priests aren't in a position to ask."

"I won't grovel," Babba said. "And I won't send Hadara."

"How about Amaniel?"

"She's fourteen, for Nihil's sake."

"Perfect. Nihil likes them young." The merchant tented stubby fingers in satisfaction. Amaniel didn't flinch beside me.

Babba reached across the table and grabbed the man's arm. "You don't take my hospitality and offer up my children. You can leave."

The fat, sweaty merchant stared bug-eyed at Babba's tight grip. "Remember who put you in this fine house, *Lord* Rimonil—and who can take you out."

All I heard after that was a din of angry voices. Shouting here, pounding the table there, a number of wagging fingers from the wives. In other words, it was perfect for hatching a conspiracy. Sapphirans love to argue; it's like a sport. The winner's the one who gets the last word, or maybe the loudest word—it can be hard to tell. Babba can hold his own against anyone, and if they really made him feel cornered, I half-expected him to march them all down to the Ward before dessert. Just to show them.

Getting Babba's back up was all part of my strategy, such as it was. The angrier he got with the others, the more he'd listen to me—or so I hoped.

At first, it looked like I was right. The threat to unseat Babba didn't come to anything. The other merchants took Babba's side against the fat one. They were all in the

Merchants Guild that had made Babba their portreeve. The dispute, though, made me suddenly curious about what Valeo had wanted to show me, and what power he thought I might have.

I couldn't shout like they could. How could I ever hope to get heard? It just seemed best to let the arguers do what they did best—give Babba grief, and then give in.

I'd pick up the subject later, of course. Poor Babba would get no peace tonight.

A wooden spoon banged on a tin platter for everyone's attention. We turned shocked faces to Amaniel, who held the spoon aloft as though it were the schoolmistress's pointer.

"It wouldn't help," Amaniel said. "Sacrificing me, it wouldn't help your cause at all."

I thought I'd been brave breaking protocol to speak up, but Amaniel was outright brazen. That wasn't like her at all. She continued, her voice trembling.

"The Azwans are determined to bring Port Sapphire under closer scrutiny. We are a proud people, and pride brings certainty in ourselves. The Azwans will return us to the certain path, but it will cost us. If the city could've gotten off with the sacrifice of a single virgin, it would've been done already." Amaniel leaned back, clearly satisfied at her speech.

A sea captain shook his head. "The curse of a pious household."

The fat merchant smirked. "When we master our doubts, our faith will be certain, eh, Amaniel?"

"You'll not question my daughter's piety," Babba said. "If there is nothing the priests can do, there is nothing I can do. And that is all we shall discuss on the matter."

If I could've stuffed my unhelpful sister into a wine jug and tossed her into the Grand Concourse, I would've done so. She'd just made my task about a thousand times harder.

One of the wives leaned forward, her voice a loud whisper, as if worried the Azwans might be under the table, listening in. She tugged on my sleeve.

"But *you* know what to ask, don't you?" she said. "I mean, specifically, about what they're up to. The Azwans."

I spoke up without thinking. "The warehouse?"

The merchant chuckled, which I despised hearing. He wasn't worth feigning my best behavior for. "Since when do the host's daughters command the conversation?"

Mami swooped in and shooed both of us away. "Hadara, Amaniel, inside."

We curtsy-bowed and left, my ears hot with indignation. Once inside, Mami put arms around us both. "My brave, outspoken girls. Of course, I was mortified from head to toe."

"Sorry, Mami," I said.

"I spoke the truth," Amaniel said. Her chin quivered. "God's truth is greater than any household custom."

Mami shook a finger at Amaniel. "You're a hostess. You hold your tongue when your father entertains."

Forget the Smiles of Welcome. My eyes did the Roll of Disbelief. Once, Mami had been a smuggler, stealing out into the fens with me beyond town. We'd picked rare herbs that we sold as medicine, something strictly banned by the Temple. We'd taken such secret pleasure in our apostasy, Mami and me. Now, she was just another rich man's wife, fussing over platters and manners and things that didn't matter at all.

"You educated us at the Ward, Mami," I said, sticking up for Amaniel. "What did you think the schoolmistress talks about when she's not whacking girls with her pointer?"

Mami drew a deep breath and held it. In the interval before she let loose, I caught Amaniel's hand and squeezed it. The haranguing that flew from Mami felt like it seared the hair off my scalp and curled my toes. Then Mami turned on her heels and was gone in a huff, back to refilling platters and making small talk with the wives or fussing over Dina's baby.

Amaniel and I flopped down on floor cushions in the spacious living quarters where the parties would move indoors in winter.

"Well, that was a disaster," I said.

"Mmmm." Amaniel shrugged and propped her elbows on her knees. "Next time, let's agree not to anger our parents before dessert."

"Why?"

"I don't know about you, but I barely ate a thing."

"Me too. All that serving."

"And hostessing."

"And smiling. How can we eat through a smile?"

"Carefully, I suppose."

I snickered. "So. No offending anyone before dessert."

She nodded and fluffed up a cushion before settling in. I did the same, and we waited for someone to send for us, or an all clear, or something to indicate Mami had relented and our exile was over.

In the meantime, my Stomach of Empty grumbled.

# 6

*The man who has never been humbled by his own
child is neither strong nor bold.*
                        *—Sapphiran proverb*

We hadn't been waiting long, just letting the voices rise and
fall from out on the patio, when a pair of luminous green
eyes peered around the corner at us. Babba never had to
order our not-so-secret houseguest to stay hidden—she
made herself scarce when strangers were about.

"It's okay, Bugsy," I said. We'd all adopted the pet name
Rishi had given the Gek girl. She'd come to live with us
after her swampy homeland had burned. She'd been the
one to snatch a tin box from my outreached hand, and in
that box had been the demon and everything it caused.

Amaniel motioned hello with a curl of her fingers.

"That's good," I said. "Who taught you that?"

"Bugsy. We talk when you're not around. I'm learning
her hand signals."

"I thought you hated her."

"Nihil loves us all."

"You *are* getting religious."

"Well, you were declared pious officially and all. Though sometimes I can't tell if you mean it."

I snickered. "I'm ambiguous about it. Or maybe uncertain."

That brought a smile to Amaniel. "The five Doctrines of Doubt, eh? Well, at least you're not incredulous, discordant, or irreverent."

"Oh, I'm definitely irreverent," I said. "Enough to make Azwan, I think."

I'm not sure what our parents would've thought if they'd walked in on us snickering, but at least the Gek was impressed. She nestled between us to steal some warmth for her clammy body.

"You're making your ha-ha noises," Bugsy said. "You're happy."

Bugsy didn't speak the human and Feroxi common tongue, not at all. Her lizard-mouth couldn't make word sounds as we did, but clicks, cackles, croaks—all of which developed as speech patterns the Gek—and I—would recognize. That was another weird gift from the destroyed demon. No matter how obscure the language, I could understand it. I could only speak the few languages I'd learned in childhood, but my ears caught every nuance of everything else.

I only regretted it when I stood on the docks and listened to sailors singing. Nihil's knuckles, the things they think about when at sea without women for too long.

I threw an arm around Bugsy. I rarely saw her, since the sick ward kept me busy until after sundown most workdays.

At least that meant fewer chances to betray myself in conversation with her. I couldn't risk anyone knowing I understood her speech. It raised too many questions I was afraid to answer.

I wanted to talk with her, seizing the rare opportunity. I wasn't sure what I wanted to ask, or how to phrase it, since she was convinced I was a piece of a star, just as the Azwan S'ami believed my mind held shards of a demon.

*I feel bad*, I signaled. *You're alone.*

From outside came Babba's deep voice saying something about Rishi that prompted laughter. Then came the high-pitched voice of my littlest sister as she sang a nonsensical rhyme she'd made up. Something about pickle berries. The adults laughed some more and clapped. They must be desperate for entertainment if this is the depths Babba went to.

Bugsy's bug eyes lit up and she began tapping her foot. I waved a hand in front of her face.

*Talk*, I signaled.

Amaniel eyed me sideways and listened for Rishi's voice.

Bugsy cocked her head to one side and then the other, surveying me. "Talk about what?"

I signaled to Bugsy. *Star.*

The star had fallen to Kuldor, but instead of a meteorite, the debris was shaped like an egg and contained a demonic spirit, at least, if you believed the Azwan's version. The demon didn't exist any longer, except it did in some form or other, and those were the demon toenails that scratched inside me, and I knew because I shouldn't be able to know how to speak to Gek.

But Bugsy was no help at all. "You understand me, so you must be the star. We talked about this. I even showed you the space in the sky where you were born, and where you are now missing."

Amaniel got up and began pacing, oblivious to us. She often did this when her head was stuck in some scriptural passage and she was imagining how her unique interpretation would make her the wisest mage—all the way up to Azwan, perhaps. We were all going to bow to her superior worthiness someday.

I shook my head and gave Bugsy a friendly squeeze. I signaled: *How did lizardfolk come by the fallen star?*

"The elders found it in the swamp. It talked to my mother. She was shaman." Bugsy's eyes began to well over again. She righted herself and took a gulp of air. "The shaman knew what the star wanted and why. Until the evil drabskin killed her."

That made me flinch. The evil drabskin had been Valeo. This conversation was about to take a wrong turn.

*"Why did it pick me?"* I signaled, keeping my fingers low on my lap so Amaniel wouldn't see, even if she did look over.

Bugsy shrugged. "You or your mother. You're the only ones we trusted. My mother said the star wanted the human who wanted *it*. That we would know. And then you came for it and you asked for it."

So I showed up and opened my mouth and got myself picked. Just superb. *"So why not a Gek?"*

"We aren't good enough vessels. I don't know why."

I stroked Bugsy's scaly head and scratched behind her earhole. The creature sighed.

"I wasn't allowed to be there when they spoke," she croaked. "But I know I didn't want the unnatural drabskin to have it. Did I do the right thing?"

She was talking about S'ami, the Azwan of Uncertainty, and his magic, which Gek saw as a violation of nature. Bugsy had taken a flying leap onto a roof to keep the box from him. It hadn't gone well for her. I sat her in my lap and put my arms around her. If there were a wound I could see, I could figure out some way to patch it up, but all my smarts were useless in the face of hurts that stung on the inside.

It seemed like that would be all I'd get out of the Gek. Eventually, we'd have to help her find her home. I wasn't sure how I'd do that safely, but I had promised her I'd try. We sat around, Amaniel, Bugsy, and myself, taking in the arguments from outside as the voices rose and fell. After what seemed a long time, Rishiel poked her head in. "They're serving dessert and Mami needs Amaniel to make tea."

Amaniel went to fetch a jar from a cupboard and I filed outside after my youngest sister. Our cook had made a sugary nectar from a succulent that grew just about everywhere, which she drizzled over a spongy pastry and fresh berries. If anyone remained angry with me after I served it, they were beyond hope.

Fortunately, anyone can be forgiven almost anything over dessert, especially after an evening of wine. Babba pulled me onto the cushion next to him and rested a hand on my shoulder. It was the closest he'd get to reconciliation in front of so many people.

"Tell me what you know of that warehouse," he said.

I told him what little I had learned from Leba Mara.

Babba drained his cup and set it aside. "They've been very businesslike about the whole thing. Very organized. They use the Ward priests as their clerks. I assume that's for added secrecy."

"Clerks? That means they have records, though."

Babba nodded.

"You can close it down though, right, Babba?"

No. He shook his head once. "There is no closing down something the Temple wants open."

"You can talk to the—"

"No one. There is no one to talk to on this matter."

"And there is no one else who can try? No one with your clout?" I hoped that would appeal to his sense of pride, at least. He gazed at me thoughtfully.

"I won't use you, Hadara. The Temple wouldn't appreciate it, for starters. They'd see right through it. And I think being willing to sacrifice you once should be the quota for any father."

I resisted the urge to hug him and kept my demeanor businesslike and calm. This was no time for sentiment. "I know you don't want to see me put in further danger. But everyone is in danger now."

He stroked my cheek with the back of his hand. "My eldest. My half-wild, stubborn, strong-willed, and utterly kind-hearted daughter. It's never mattered to you to get all those religious details right, so long as you are doing the right thing for people. You get that from your mother, you know. You get the stubbornness from me. The night the Azwan dragged you off was the worst of my life. No, I don't want to see you in danger ever again."

I should've soared at all the praise. Between Leba Mara and Babba, I was hearing all kinds of unfamiliar compliments. But my spirits flagged anyway. What if there really wasn't anything Babba could do? He had all these new responsibilities as the city's chief burgher. Whatever it is Valeo thought I could do would be pointless. As Amaniel had said earlier, I'd made promises. I intended to keep them.

The fat merchant cleared his throat but his tone was gentler, more conciliatory. "Lord Rimonil, none of us is accustomed to being under the Temple's thumb this way. Will I lose my life over a clumsy love poem I wrote for my wife?"

"A love poem, eh?" Babba raised an eyebrow. "They confiscated that?"

"I compared her to several of Nihil's dead wives."

Silence fell over the crowd. His wife stared down at her hands, neatly folded in her lap, and said nothing. I felt pity for the man, but more for his wife as her eyes teared over. Whether she was as beautiful or memorable as any of those sacred women, only her husband could say. That he shouldn't have committed it to parchment was only obvious if you ran a Temple that hanged people for lesser crimes than clumsily expressing your affection.

"I sincerely hope it doesn't come to that," I said.

"Me, too," the merchant emptied his cup and set it on the table. His wife patted his hand and flashed a tight smile at no one in particular.

Babba's cup also landed on the table with a decisive thud. His hand clamped down on my shoulder and gave it a gentle shake.

"If Hadara wants it, I'll talk to them," Babba said. "After the Sabbath. First thing. I pray it's enough."

"So be it," the merchant said.

Others around the table murmured their assent. "So be it."

They sounded so feeble, I wouldn't know they were the city's most powerful men outside the Ward.

Above us, Lunyo completed its nightly rise, the light from its lopsided, gibbous shape blotting out a corner of a nearby constellation. It was the Crippled Warrior, with his hunched form and broken spear, a sign of defeat, a lost cause, its scattered stars frail and twinkling.

7

*I will descend on those who turn from me. Look at your fields and imagine them charred. Look at your homes and see empty space, for even their foundations I would uproot.*
—*from Oblations 16,* The Book of Unease

I paced just outside the Ward gates, back and forth, furious with myself. It was First Workday, the day after the Sabbath, and I was at the appointed place at the appointed time. No Valeo.

He'd probably never meant to meet me. Maybe this was some sort of vengeful prank to repay me for not noticing him the times I'd walked right under his nose, thinking he was dead. Wasn't he a little old to have hurt feelings?

Idiot. Woolass. Beetle-browed thug. Ugly, hairy *thing.*

At least I'd arrived early enough that no one at the sick ward would be looking for me just yet. Though that was small consolation. I could be enjoying a hot breakfast instead of the day-old flatbread I'd gobbled down in a rush.

"You wearing a hole in the cobblestones?" Valeo's voice boomed behind me. "Or just lost?"

I wheeled around. "You're late."

"No, you're early. They're just getting started."

"They? Who is they?"

He was carrying his helmet under his arm, rather than wearing it, so I could see the curious expression he wore. He studied my face as if decoding some message written in my frown. "You're annoyed with me for having to wait a little. There are people who've run out of time altogether."

I shifted uncomfortably. I was relieved to see him. I wanted him to not be angry with me, but realized I had to start by not being angry with him. I didn't want to sink into all that painful sarcasm from the other day. It had left me exhausted and I wasn't ready for another battle. I exhaled, long and sad.

"You said something the other day about me being shallow," I said. "That hurt. I don't know why you'd say that."

"Take a walk with me."

Since that's why I'd met him there, I agreed, and followed him inside the Ward gates. It was only a quarter turn after Dawn Prayers, so most people were still at home. We'd only gotten halfway across the courtyard, however, when he motioned for me to sit on an ironwork bench with intricate scrolls. I hated those benches. My skirt flounces were always getting caught up in one of their spokes or curls. But I sat and rearranged my dress and waited for him to say something.

He sat next to me at a safe distance and leaned his elbow on his knee, giving me that studious look.

"What does the word *power* mean to you?" he said at last.

The question took me by surprise. I sensed, though, that if I gave my usual sarcastic reply, the conversation would go nowhere promptly.

"I suppose it means the ability to get people to do what you want," I said.

"And who wields power? And how?"

Wasn't it obvious? Maybe this was a trick question. The Temple was good at tripping people up with their own words. I had scars on my wrists from the times my old schoolmistress had whacked them for answers that didn't satisfy her. I rubbed them as I thought of how to reply to Valeo.

"The Azwans, through their magic, I suppose. People like my father, through the law and tariffs and taxes and such. Why?"

"I've been thinking about power lately," Valeo said. "What it is, exactly, and who wields it. Would you say I have power?"

I would've laughed, except for his sincerity. "You're a soldier. A Temple Guard! You have the power to enforce the Azwan's edicts, raid homes, terrify people. Kill them."

"The power to kill people," he repeated, his voice soft, almost regretful. "Yes, I suppose I do. I have killed."

At this his gaze seemed far away. I shifted, but whether it was the bench or the conversation causing me to stiffen, I wasn't sure. It didn't matter. I should be home, eating breakfast, not here.

Valeo noticed my discomfort. "Our conversation bothers you."

I nodded. "I'm learning to heal people, not do . . . what you do."

"What I do," Valeo said, his voice still soft, sounding alien and small to his big body. He twisted his fingers together in his lap, leaning over those big knees, his head still cocked so he could look at me. I tugged at my skirt flounces and rearranged myself for the dozenth time.

"What I do," he said, "is try to convey some sense of authority. I suppose that's different from power."

He waved one hand around vaguely, his eyes taking in the Ward grounds. "Here, I have no real power. A first guardsman is low in the ranks. But Nihil's guards are all Feroxi, and they look to me, their prince, even though they're not supposed to. The Commander knows that. The Azwans know that. They use it to their advantage. And so long as I follow orders and do as I'm told, the men look to me and think it's all as it should be."

"I'm not sure I understand," I said, suddenly fascinated. He was giving me some sort of glimpse inside his head, and it wasn't full of rocks, as I'd sometimes supposed. Funny, how my feelings about him darted like shore birds, depending on how deep his tides were running. But what was I fishing for? "You get some benefit from the men looking to you as prince, but you don't outrank them, and everybody's happy?"

He nodded.

"And what," I asked, "does this have to do with power?"

"What if everything isn't as it should be, Hadara? What if my role as some sort of leader-in-training of a nation runs up against my duties as a humble servant of our god?"

"Then you choose Nihil," I said. "That is the obvious answer. That is the one that keeps you and your men safe."

Our eyes connected and locked, an electric moment, as though the same static coursed through us both. I could feel it in the relief that welled up in his face, the way he nodded quickly, rapidly, his gaze still reaching deeply into mine. I knew. I understood. The Valeo in front of me was two separate men, and they were at war with one another. Maybe, while he was here, he could never be the prince he wanted to be, but he also couldn't hide his desire to serve our god and be good at it.

I took a deep breath. He had confided something heartfelt. "I'm sorry if you thought I was being shallow the other day. I'm sure you're in a difficult position."

He leaned in. "And what power would you say you have?"

The shift in conversation took me by surprise and annoyed me. We'd been doing so well, me learning all about his inner battles, only to have him turn the tables. I pursed my lips, folded my hands into my lap, and looked him straight in the eye. "You and I both know that no woman has any power that her father or husband doesn't allow her to have."

"Then you need to learn that you're wrong."

I shook my head. "I don't see how. Whether we're talking about power or authority or however you define it, I supposedly have none. I had a birthday party and a blessing and now I change soiled sheets for a living."

"The Azwan of Uncertainty says you're the most powerful person on this island, but you don't see it. I'd like to show you." He got up and offered me his hand. I took it and let him help me up. His hand was warm, unlike the last time I'd held it, when it had been clammy with fever.

I wasn't about to refuse. I couldn't imagine why an Azwan of all people would say something so disturbing. Why was an Azwan talking about me? S'ami knew about my ability to understand tongues, but did Valeo? How much would S'ami have shared with one of his guards? I squeezed Valeo's hand, and he squeezed back, and it was almost as if he were courting me, which only unsettled me further.

We didn't walk very far, only to the sanctuary's wide doors. Shouting reverberated from within, and I could make out Reyhim's distinct rasp mingling with S'ami's booming baritone. The two Azwans were at it again, unable to keep themselves from their furious and shockingly public rivalry.

Valeo pulled open the door for me. I began to remove my slippers in the vestibule.

"No need," he whispered.

I wondered if Nihil made an exception for his guards to the rule about being barefoot in the Great Numen's presence. That felt odd to me. Surely, I was still required to remove them? But Valeo shook his head and held a finger to his lips. The Azwans voices were moving farther away.

I should've turned myself around and gone toward the gates and home, refusing to follow Valeo, but my feet had brought me here and my ears were tempting me onward. Valeo held the double doors open and we tiptoed into the sanctuary proper.

The Azwans and a group of priests were ahead of us, leaving by a side door that led onto a stonework patio overlooking the bay. S'ami whirled around and shouted at Reyhim. "I cannot believe he just agreed to this. You talked to him without me. You didn't tell him what you intended, though, did you? If you'd gone through me first, he'd never have—"

Reyhim raised his voice above S'ami's. "I don't need the permission of *Nihil's Ear* to speak to him myself. Go shopping for more purple silk if you can't stomach doing your duty."

"What duty calls for killing old women and cripples? This was supposed to be a few examples to get the point across, not—"

They vanished onto the patio amid a throng of priests, taking S'ami's words with them as the distant doors clicked closed. I gave up tiptoeing—it was too slow—and followed Valeo's giant strides across the sanctuary, aware my slippers were thwacking against the tile floor. I shot a nervous glance toward the mirror but it simply glimmered back at me. If Nihil was scrying, he wasn't shouting at me to stop right there. So I kept going.

The side doors were thinner and less impressive than the main doors, and I could hear something that sounded like the wind moaning above the surf. Valeo and I pressed our ears to the crack between the two doors. What I thought was the moaning of wind against the breakers became more like weeping. Was I imagining it?

No, there it was again. Someone was sobbing. Or several people, men and women alike. Valeo cracked open the doors. The weeping and moaning grew louder and more distinct. I peered through and nearly dropped to my knees.

On the patio, the Temple had built a gallows.

I braced myself against Valeo's arm, hanging on, terrified, feeling my knees giving out beneath me. I steadied and looked out again.

Three nooses swung violently in the sea breeze. Beside the platform stood several guards in a rigid row, their backs to me. Between each of them, I could make out three people. One was a woman with a sack over her head and her shoulders stooped. Hers was the sobbing I'd heard. I could barely hear it above the crashing of waves on the breakers beneath the patio, but now that I knew what it was, I couldn't block it out. Nearby were two men with their heads similarly covered and their hands bound. One was missing a foot and a soldier was propping him up by his arm. The three condemned were waiting their turn to be led up some steps to the scaffolding, moaning, their words indistinct, swallowed up by the commotion around them.

The Ward never executed anyone like this that I could remember. The magistrate hanged murderers, but that was done far north of town where no one would see. This execution would be visible to ships out in the bay. Nihil never wanted to call attention to any soul he'd failed to redeem, or so the priests had always said. But there the clerics stood, in flapping sapphire-blue robes and long faces, like a flock of regretful birds. Some had their heads bowed or turned, unable to even look at the condemned.

So what was this spectacle, then? Not public enough for a crowd, but not hidden? I glanced around to see if the audience held a few clues. Only a few soldiers, the contingent of priests, and the three condemned.

And Babba.

He stood to one side, nervously fingering his beard, as upset as I'd ever seen him. He hunched his shoulders in a way he never did, as though to make himself small or invisible, as though he could shrink from the scene.

He had failed. I knew it. I could see it. I had counted on him. He'd promised. He was supposed to fix this, to fix everything. He was Lord Portreeve, the highest secular post, and he was going to say something and put an end to the funeral pyres. But he hadn't, that much was obvious. He'd let me down. He'd let everyone down.

My fury landed, silent and clouded, on Babba's cringing form. How dare he? Hate crept across my face and into my skull until I clamped a hand over my mouth as though I could stuff the screams back down, took a few ragged breaths, and watched, unable to break away.

"Old women and cripples," S'ami said again. He folded his arms across his chest and glared at Reyhim.

The woman next to the platform was indeed old. I could see her bending from age and not just fear. Her dark skirt and thick sandals looked familiar. Could that be Widow Reezen, our old neighbor? Her tiny, birdlike frame shuddered with sobs. What could Widow Reezen have done? She must be eighty. She never missed a dawn prayer even at her age. She went to the Ward every day. If she wasn't pious, no one was. Was the whole world going mad?

I sank back into the sanctuary's darkness, barely a handwidth from Valeo, as if his armor offered some protection to me as well. I was at a loss to understand what I was witnessing but unable to break away. The darkness hid me, and no one would see me as long as I could keep from shouting my fury.

I shuddered and closed the door. I'd seen enough.

# 8

*It took only a day to reclaim the rebel city and behead the heretics who'd seized it. But the villages and towns outside the capital were harder to reclaim. That required more time and skill and patience than even my guards possessed, and some of those felled by the guards were likely blameless. A warning to all who would rebel against me: that there is none truly innocent so long as untruths rest unchallenged.*

*—from Verisimilitudes 14,* The Book of Unease

"Why did you bring me here?" I whispered. I was alone in the dark with Valeo, too angry to know what to do, but too frustrated to stand around and do nothing.

"To see for yourself," he said.

I shoved him into the corner, my fist pummeling uselessly against his leather corselet. He backed away from me and took my feeble pounding with a few grunts but no sign of remorse.

"This ... this is your idea of power?" I asked hoarsely.

He grabbed both my arms and held me still until I stopped writhing and beating at him. I sank into him, my cheek against the clammy leather, panting. "I don't understand. Why would you bring me here? What is it you want from me?"

"Watch with me. Just watch. For now."

"And then what?"

"I think you'll know. The right thing always comes. It's what my own babba would say. The right thing comes to those who are prepared to do it."

Valeo had a father, too. Of course he did. A human father at that. Somehow that thought reassured me and I peered again through the doors at my own father. I waited for Babba to act or speak. Something. Maybe he was waiting for his chance. Maybe there'd be an opportunity for him still.

S'ami had begun pacing before the gallows, visibly angry. I hadn't thought he'd be the one to defend my poor city. What had we done?

"Give them another chance," S'ami said. "A chance to repent."

Reyhim folded his arms across his chest and said nothing.

The high priest stepped forward but I had to cup my ears to hear him. "Most Magical and Worthy Azwan, please reconsider. The items the guards collected were so trivial. Straw totems and brass charms and beads to ward off evil eyes and nonsense. Superstitious diversions, that's all."

Reyhim snorted. "Would they have such superstitions if you'd continued my work purging them? So everything I did here was forgotten in less than a generation?"

"Then execute me, Reyhim. Spare these people and punish me."

"This *is* your punishment."

A loud moan went up from the woman. "Please. Oh, please."

I recognized Widow Reezen's voice after all. I hugged my arms to my chest and squeezed my eyes shut. I could run out there and try to stop Reyhim, give up my sudden good graces with the Temple or appeal to him as my maybe-possible grandfather to stop this.

But he'd once killed the woman he loved, hadn't he? That woman had been my grandmother, his paramour. So what would ever warm his cold soul ever again? Anything? I cracked open my eyes as if I could slow the pace at which I was seeing this horror unfold.

S'ami cut in. "What's your hurry? Are you suddenly worried this tiny speck of a city is overpopulated? How many do you intend to round up, exactly? Have you discussed *that* with Nihil?"

Reyhim laughed. "Nihil won't miss them."

The group of priests suddenly broke apart and they milled around, murmuring in sharp but hushed tones, Babba among them.

S'ami once again took up my poor city's defense.

"I'm not saying this place is paradise but there's no spot on Kuldor that Nihil has said is superfluous. They're sinners and doubters all, every last one, to a degree I don't think any of us has ever seen. The sheer volume of all those little pagan items is staggering. But you're suggesting—"

"What I'm suggesting is nothing less than what you've said in turn," Reyhim said. "The enforcement of doctrine has gotten lax, did I not hear you say that? Or that maybe we should kill every last sinner?"

"Not seriously. Not ever." S'ami sounded resigned, which made me nervous for him—and for Port Sapphire.

"Well, I'm serious," Reyhim continued. "Nihil for his own, unfathomable reasons put you in charge of that demon. That's done with, and I thank you, but it's time for you to recall who is fourth Azwan out of five, and which of us is number one. And I shall order this island to return to abject piety or it will suffer the consequences. Not for nothing did we have the Guards record what they'd seized."

The priests and Babba became one crowd of angry faces, but no one spoke any longer. It occurred to me that no one would. If Babba had said anything to either Azwan, they either hadn't heard it or it hadn't mattered. I should've run off, but the part of me that had grown up hearing Widow Reezen's shaky alto singing lullabies and silly children's rhymes demanded I stay.

And Valeo had said I had a power.

And maybe it was a power I could use.

I ducked under his arm, swung the door open, and walked through. I wiped clammy hands on my skirt and tried to slow my breathing. I had only a vague idea of what I wanted to say, and no idea if anyone would hear me say it. My throat was too dry to even swallow, and I shivered in the sea breeze, as much from terror as the sudden chill. Yet turning back wasn't an option. This felt like the right thing to do, stepping out like this, just as Valeo had said. And I would do it.

It took a moment, but eventually several of the priests and guards noticed me just before the last of my courage could bleed away. I didn't look over at Babba, but I'm sure he saw me, too. I didn't want to look at him. I'd lose my nerve, instantly. No, better to pretend he wasn't there. Better to pretend he'd never bothered to step in at all than to realize he'd tried and failed.

The high priest shook his head at me. To him, I was still his schoolteacher wife's worst student, no matter how many blessings Nihil himself bestowed on me. So I turned to S'ami, who was suddenly my only hope in this mess.

"You can't do this," I said. I hoped I'd think of a reason why that didn't sound exactly like what S'ami had tried—in vain—to say. "You have to stop."

Of all the reactions I might have expected, had I thought about it, Reyhim's throaty chuckle wasn't one of them. But there it was, dry and chilling even above the wind and surf, or maybe I only imagined it to be the loudest sound, except perhaps for Widow Reezen's heartbreaking moans.

"Well, Blessed Hadara, here to teach us a thing or two about doctrine, perhaps?" Reyhim's smile was the ugliest I'd ever seen. I took several trembling steps forward despite my feet wanting to turn and run. "I don't believe I've ever heard anything good about your abilities."

"We need hope. Can't you give us hope? We were all so excited when you both came," I began. And we were. There'd been the days of scrubbing and whitewashing, the throngs on the pier, the lightning bolts of excitement at the sight of those red sails. I hadn't mustered much enthusiasm then, but I wanted Reyhim to feel it now. "We had hope then, that we were to get Nihil's brief attention, that we could be of some help to him, however meager."

That was a lie in my case, but I could feel the truth of it for others. I glanced at Widow Reezen, her head tilted to listen to me, and I raised my voice. I knew the truth of what I wanted to say. "We believe in Nihil and we believe in you. Can you not give us this one hope that we can do better, to *be* better? Can't you teach us to be the kind of people Nihil would accept and love? Instead of discarding us?"

*Instead of murdering us?* I didn't say that part. I kept my eyes on Reyhim and watched as skepticism replaced the merriment. I went to say more but he held up a hand. His voice held more than its usual harshness; I heard bitterness and contempt mixed in.

"Words wisely chosen. It is good to remember not to underestimate you. The answer: no. I cannot. I have done all that any holy man could here," he said. "You will never know in a hundred lifetimes what I have sacrificed for this wretched, sinful place and its people. And for nothing. So every lesson could be lost once I left? You will all pay dearly, and it won't ever be enough."

His words hung in the air, resounding off the patio stones and settling on everyone's faces like they'd all been slapped—hard. I was close enough to see veins in Reyhim's forehead throbbing, his jaw grinding, grinding, the spittle gathering at the corner of his mouth. He took two lurching steps toward me, the madness in his bulging eyes stripping away any remaining dignity.

As he leaned in, intent on my reply, all eyes turned to me. S'ami in particular cocked his head to gauge my reaction. He would know what I knew about Reyhim and my grandmother. And now I knew the full truth of it, but it came as no comfort to know that he'd loved her. She was still dead by his orders, no matter whom he blamed for it.

"I'm begging you," I said, my voice trembling.

"Then don't," Reyhim said. "Or you will regret who hangs next."

It was then that I looked over at Babba, who'd pushed his way to the front of the crowd. I was struck by a terrible thought that he'd only embarrass himself now, and wanted him to go away, to leave this be, to let me handle it, however feebly.

"You'd made us a promise, Worthy Azwan," said Babba. "That my family would suffer no further, and that the Temple would owe us for my daughter's sacrifice. We should be spared, Azwan. You vowed yourself."

"Ah, then it is for your family only that you speak now?" Reyhim's voice reeked of contempt. "Not terribly civic-minded of the Lord Portreeve."

"If you would listen to my entreaties on behalf of the citizens—"

Reyhim held up a hand, and Babba's voice fell silent. It was no use. If anything, I felt mortified by what Babba had said. He had fallen further. I stared at him in blank sorrow, unable to muster sympathy for him. Babba stared at his feet and said nothing, but I could see him swallow, again and again.

"Perhaps, Hadara, you have more lovely words to add to this occasion?" Reyhim said. "Not that it would make a difference. Nihil himself has decided."

I had hated Reyhim before this moment. Nothing would ever change that. Nothing.

S'ami came up beside me, placing a fatherly hand on my shoulder.

"He means it, Hadara," S'ami said. "Nihil has given him blanket permission to punish your people as he sees fit. The profane must be purged."

A triumphant smile crept across Reyhim's face, making my neck redden with more contempt than I'd ever felt for anyone, ever. He motioned to the guards and gave instructions I couldn't make out. The men stood unmoving, unyielding, as if they hadn't heard.

I stared out at a wall of men, uniform in height, all wearing the same stern, faraway look, as if they'd all been carved from the same block of stone.

No one moved. Even the restless crowd of priests fell silent, aware that something wasn't quite right.

"Are you deaf?" Reyhim shouted at the soldiers. "You have orders."

The three condemned twisted their heads around as though trying to see through the sacks over their eyes. Through the crack in the doors, where only I knew to look, Valeo stiffened, his fingers balling into fists and releasing. I glanced into his eyes, and for the second time today, felt the briefest moment of connection. His gaze was tortured.

Prince or guardsman?

I understood. He was also waiting for the right thing to do.

"You dare not refuse." Reyhim started sputtering and turned to another guard I recognized as Valeo's Commander, his ice-blue eyes glaring down at the Azwan. His gaze held uncertainty that seemed completely, utterly wrong for someone sworn to obey an Azwan's every word.

Was he refusing too? I had a newfound respect for the man.

For S'ami, too, who'd stopped pacing and was pointing to the Commander. "You see? You stretch their loyalty. Even the Feroxi have their limits. They didn't enlist to become executioners to the weak and defenseless. Their vows shouldn't extend to killing the lame and aged, and you defy their traditions to force them."

"They're fighters. They kill." Reyhim's rasp came at a high pitch. "What's the difference between a sword and a noose to them?"

The commander stiffened, on full alert, more than if he'd been at attention. "We will obey if the order comes from Nihil directly, Most Worthy."

"It comes directly through me, his Most Worthy servant, as shall the next order to plant your head on one of your precious pikes."

With that, Reyhim raised his gold totem and a blue-gray, ugly spray rose from it in a cloud over the commander's head. The commander's right hand jerked toward his sword, then stopped just over the scabbard, as he eyed the steamy cloud hovering over his head. The priests cowered and covered their faces. This was some dark, dreadful plague Reyhim had conjured, and it was aimed at the commander.

As it settled on him, a sweat beaded on his brow as it lowered toward his plume, searing it off as if ripped by acid. His chest rose and fell as the cloud crept ever lower. He brought his arm up slowly, achingly slow, for a soft chest-thump. It wasn't so much a salute as a surrender.

The cloud stopped its descent, and even rose ever so slightly to a safe hand-width above what was left of the plume, but it lingered like a bad dream, threatening to return.

I took a halting step forward, only to have two soldiers glide into place in front of me, partly blocking my view of the two Azwans. It had been decided. The moment of resistance had passed, for all of us. There was nothing more to say and nothing more I could do. But I could at least be the woman who wasn't going to let an old friend die alone. I looked from one soldier to the next and whispered, "I won't interfere. Just let me be there."

But they were looking over my shoulder to someone behind me.

Valeo.

I wondered what he had decided to do, just then, when there didn't seem to be anything left but to stand help-lessly while the last thread of trust unraveled between the Temple and its people.

Valeo nodded at the soldiers, and they parted so he could stand by the platform. He took it on himself to lead each of the three condemned in turn up the short steps to the scaffolding. I was confused. How could he do this ter-rible thing himself?

As the soldiers turned over each of the condemned to him, I thought I understood. Perhaps he was doing this odious, unthinkable task so they wouldn't have to. He was guardsman and prince both, a man who followed orders in a way that spared his comrades having to choose between their sacred vows or their sense of pride. At least, that's what I wanted desperately to believe as he propped the crippled man up by the elbows. The commander, embold-ened by Valeo's actions, leapt onto the platform, taking up position between the lever that worked the platform's drop and Widow Reezen, whose muffled weeping resumed, louder now than ever.

It was more than I could bear. I picked my way to the wooden scaffolding and up the steps, aware that all the speechifying and arguing had stopped. No one spoke, not even S'ami. Not Reyhim, not the commander, who glared ice and knives at me but stepped away from Widow Reezen and her muffled weeping.

I stroked her arm.

"Widow Reezen, it's me," I said. "I'm here."

"Hadara, such a sweet girl." The woman straightened. "Don't risk your life for me. I am an old woman and a sinner. Nihil is merciful, child, and he long ago sent my beloved husband to wait for me beneath the Eternal Tree."

My eyes welled up and I couldn't speak. So I stroked her arm, gently, slowly, and waited for someone to say she could go, that it was all wrong or a bad dream. I needed to hear something beautiful and kind.

"I'll be here, Widow Reezen," I said. "I won't go."

"Thank you, child. Nihil's blessings on you." She held herself straighter than I'd seen her do in years and turned away from me, a note of courage in her voice. "Husband, I come."

I took the hand S'ami extended, clambering down from the scaffolding to stand with S'ami and Babba flanking me. Babba kept his gaze on me, but I'm not sure why. Had I failed him? He had failed me, failed the city, and Widow Reezen was going to die.

S'ami tugged gently at my sleeve. "It's time to go, Hadara."

I shook my head and brushed his fingers away. I still had some fight in me. I began to hum the children's rhyme about the moons, about strong Lunyo and vain Qamra and sneaky Keth. She'd taught it to me and it was my tribute to her, even if it wasn't the sort of prayer the men around me would chant. I sang the childish words, loud enough for her to hear, as Valeo gently guided her to the spot where the floor would give way beneath her feet. My eyes welled and my voice faltered, but I kept up my singing.

When all three of the condemned were in place, S'ami began pacing, a jerky to-and-fro with no rhythm to it. He radiated fury, but I didn't know if came from a true pity for our people. Maybe he was sore he lost an important argument to Reyhim.

Reyhim nodded to the commander, who glanced up at the hideous cloud of steam still wafting just out of reach.

And then the deed was done.

The lever pulled, the trap doors sprung. The two condemned men dropped immediately and were quickly dead, dangling with their heads at mad angles. But Widow Reezen, too small and frail to weigh much, jerked about, writhing, popping like a cork, slowly asphyxiating. Too slowly. I stopped my ears to her death rasps.

"Do something!" I screamed. I shot a pleading look at Valeo. "Stop this! Help her. Oh, Nihil, help her!"

Valeo whipped out a dagger, but instead of cutting her down, he held her body steady and plunged the dagger into the side of her neck. She immediately went limp, blood streaming out of a slit in the sack.

The job done, Valeo withdrew the knife and glanced over at Reyhim, who narrowed his eyes and nodded.

I fled.

# 9

*A little girl believes her father has no equal: a young woman knows it to be true.*

*—Sapphiran proverb*

I ended up on a stretch of boardwalk close to our old house, watching a puddle of puke float away in the canal below. I seldom cry, so my stomach decided to take up the job of weeping. I had heaved and sobbed giant waves of air before coughing up the remains of stale flatbread and gobs of acidic goo.

I leaned against a railing, resting my head in my arms, hoping the strong breeze would cool off the steam that whirled in my head. My head scarf was askew, my curls escaping at wild angles, but I hardly cared. What did it matter, anyway? All I could see when I closed my eyes was Widow Reezen, again and again. I breathed in. Breathed out. My breath stank, my throat hurt.

I couldn't sob. So I just kept breathing. And seeing her dying, over and over—the twitching and writhing, the snap of the neck, the dagger going in, coming out, the body going limp.

Over and over.

"Hadara."

It was Babba. I didn't even look up.

He leaned over the railing with me and all the sobs I'd held back came bursting out at once until my entire body seemed to heave with them. I closed my eyes and let Babba pull me into his chest, but I couldn't return his hug. Instead, my arms fell uselessly by my side, and I wept into his shoulder.

He cried, too, after a fashion, in the way men do, and I could feel his chest against my face, the breath coming in short, shuddering bursts. When I looked up, his eyes were red and he stared out at the water, unable to meet my gaze.

"She was my mother's second cousin, did you know that?" His voice was ragged.

I nodded.

"She held us both as babies," he said. "And I couldn't . . . I didn't . . ."

His voice caught. He hung his head and drew me closer, clinging to me so tightly, I found it hard to catch my breath. This wasn't a father I recognized. This was some other man—some weak, needy thing, bent and maybe broken, who would blow away in the first storm.

After a long moment, I pulled away.

"You were supposed to talk to them," I said. "You're the Lord Portreeve. You were supposed to make them listen to you."

"I did. Or I tried to." Babba fished a handkerchief out of his sleeve and handed it to me. As I cleaned up, he leaned against the railing and looked out across the canal.

I looked, too. It seemed better than trying to talk. I slid my left arm into the crook of his right, and we gazed out at the water together and let time slip along with the silent current. I forgot all about being strong and never crying. I let the tears flow, and Babba didn't try to shush or comfort me.

"She's dead," I said after a while. "It's all so pointless. The whole Temple, everything. My sacrifice or blessing or whatever that was. It was supposed to make them go away."

Babba hung his head. "No, it was nothing you did. I failed. I made promises I was too much of a coward to keep. As if I could haggle with an Azwan. What by all Nihil's lives was I thinking? Of myself. Only of myself."

I wiped my eyes and looked up to see his face almost contorted beyond recognition. His expression lacked strength and his usual confidence and sternness. The man who looked down at me was punishing himself, the anguish in his eyes relaying a history he'd always kept hidden. The Babba who never showed weakness of any sort was simply another unhappy soul.

My anger at him dissolved into an awful, bottomless remorse.

"No, Babba, no. I did this," I said. "You could've said no when everyone else asked you. But you didn't want to say no to me. I asked too much."

"In a thousand lifetimes, you could not ask too much."

I sniffled and wiped my nose on the cloth he'd given me. I felt a degree of control returning as I thought about what could've gone differently. Was there something either Babba or I could've said or done that would have resulted in something other than us standing here, shocked and shaken like frail twigs?

"This is the part of my life like in all the old legends you used to tell us when we were small. There'd be this part when the hero realizes the king, his father, isn't perfect and the hero storms off. I guess I stormed off."

Babba didn't move even an eyelash. "Because you've discovered I'm simply human, like anyone else."

"At the end, the king always dies and they reconcile on his deathbed."

"Do you plan to wait that long to forgive me?" The question was an earnest one. Babba stared down at me, his eyes reddening again.

"I don't know how I'm supposed to feel. You're *my* father, and I'm a woman, not a hero, and I do love you. And I know, better than anyone, that what you said was all you could say."

Babba's voice came out strangled.

"You're wrong, Hadara, about being a hero. What *you* said back there was the most heroic thing I've ever heard. You may not believe your schooling ever did you any good, but those words came from somewhere."

It was my turn to get choked up. My thoughts came out in a flood, as if I'd been crying them as tears, all in a stream. "I just wanted to help. I'm going to be a healer. I wanted to heal this whole city, all at once, but I'm just one girl. S'ami told Valeo I was powerful, but I don't know what he meant; what power could I have?"

I had said Valeo's name, which conjured up the blood-ied dagger in his hand, something I could never un-see.

Babba took one of my hands in both of his and gazed out along the canal again. "Well, I don't know this Valeo. But if S'ami says you're powerful, then he would know. And I believe him."

"But I can't stop this. You couldn't stop it. No one can." My voice rose to a wail. "I can't stop anything."

Babba raised an eyebrow. "Then perhaps your power is to start something."

*Start something?* I sniffled. "Like what?"

Babba shrugged. "I expect you'll figure it out. You and your mother. You're the ones who always seem to know what needs doing."

The canal and its slow ripples caught our attention again for a few moments, our gaze wandering off into our own avenues of thoughts and distractions. A brass horn sounded from the far-away Ward, signaling a full turn since midmorn. If I lingered much longer, it'd be midday.

Yet I wasn't sure I could face Leba Mara and her sar-casm today. I straightened myself slowly and sighed.

"Duties," Babba said, glancing quizzically at me. "At the sick ward?"

I nodded. "Leba Mara won't be happy with me."

"Word will have reached her by now. She'll know. You won't have to say anything."

"I suppose." That sounded right, but I didn't want this moment to end. It wasn't that I was enjoying myself, it was just that I couldn't bear the idea of trudging back to Ward Sapphire and going about my day as though it had been any other day.

"Today is not off to a good start, but we must continue it, Hadara. We have duties, and we must do them, yes?"

I nodded, and we hugged and held onto each other until I could feel my heartbeat match his. He had me take his arm and we walked back to the Ward together in silence, me watching my feet as they reluctantly took me back, the planks of boardwalk disappearing one by one. I clutched the cloth he'd given me, which I twiddled between my fingers, occasionally wiping a stray tear or dabbing at my nose until we reached the familiar pavilion by those hideous iron gates. If we passed anyone, I never saw them, and Babba didn't acknowledge anyone with his usual solemn nod.

We parted with a final kiss on each cheek. I was alone with my thoughts. Only two things ran through my mind. The first, of course, was Widow Reezen dying.

This was the second: my father had called himself a coward.

That, too, felt like a death. I wanted a different ending for him, and for me.

# 10

*The first demon I let live among the people so that he might learn to love and be loved. Instead, the demon took a name, Ice-dust, and swore to destroy me. He pursued me to my Temple and threatened me upon my altar, cursing my name and answering my theurgy with flame and fury.*

*I am immune to your perversion of nature that you call magic, Ice-dust said. I knew then he had to die.*

*—from* Verisimilitudes 10, The Book of Unease

As Babba had predicted, Leba Mara had also heard about the executions and my presence there. But her not saying anything was worse than if she'd asked endlessly about it all. I kept anticipating and bracing for questions that never came, and instead had to contend with sad, pitying looks and sighing head-shakes that left me wondering if she wanted me to speak first or was dropping hints I should remain silent but strong.

Finally, Leba Mara motioned me aside.

"Y'need the rest of the day off?" she asked, her face pulled into a concerned look I didn't really want to notice.

"No," I said, looking away.

"Better to keep busy, I suppose."

I shrugged, staring at some blurred spot on the floor. "Sure."

"You young ones and your one-word answers! Girl, I'm trying to help here."

"I'm alright," I said, examining my feet with sudden interest.

"Look, I'm going to tell you something I never told anyone, not even your mother," Leba Mara said.

That caught my attention. What would she have ever withheld from Mami that was important? Something about herbs or medicines? I couldn't imagine, but I was intrigued.

"I had to witness your grandmami's hanging," she said, her shoulders giving an involuntary shudder as she recalled it. "I was a young healer then, just gotten my totem hardly a season earlier. Reyhim needed me to examine the body, make sure it was certain dead. Yes, we still do that. All three of today's hangings were in here already, freshly killed."

I put a fist to my mouth to keep from retching, unable to keep back memories of Widow Reezen's bloodied, broken corpse.

Leba Mara looked away.

"You get used to death," she said, her voice distant. "You can't be a proper healer if you don't. Doesn't matter how they die, corpses all look the same after a while. Only I hadn't seen a hanging before then, and I vomited on Reyhim's blue robes, I did. Nearly got myself hanged for it."

My jaw dropped open. "You puked all over the Azwan?"

"He wasn't Azwan then, just a stuck-up, mad-pious high priest with his sights on the Temple proper."

"You puked on him," I repeated. I wanted to laugh, in a sick, weird, unfunny sort of way.

"I puked all over those lovely blue robes and his fancy blue slippers," she said, looking me straight in the eye. "Proudest moment of my career."

And then I did laugh, a hoarse, hiccupy sound that mixed with a few dry sobs. I put a hand over my mouth, but any attempt at discretion died when Leba Mara joined in, her mouth cracked into an utterly wicked grin.

"That's a good girl," she said. "Look, with the respect due to him, Reyhim's become the Most Worthy of all Nihil's servants for a reason. You'd have to be mad-pious to want to make every last, stubborn disbeliever fall in line. He's good at what he does, may Nihil bless his hardened crust of a soul."

Part of me understood that Leba Mara had to enforce doctrine as our healer mistress. The other part of me wanted to stomp away in disgust. Just because this was what an Azwan decreed didn't make it right, and Reyhim needed no apologist. I wanted to believe that, and I mistrusted anyone—including Leba Mara—who was going to suggest otherwise.

I folded my arms across my chest and glared at Leba Mara. "How many more people will it take until the Azwan has filled his quota of disbelievers?"

Leba Mara shook her head. "No one can answer that, Hadara. All we can do is our best."

"Is that what Nihil expects of us?"

Leba Mara's tone hardened. "It's what we expect of ourselves. Never lose sight of that."

The guilt pang hit sharply, and I winced. "You're right, of course. I'm sorry. It's just hard."

We walked back into the main sick ward together, her arm around my shoulders, which felt comforting. Yes, she had to enforce rules—she couldn't be a healer without the Temple's say-so—but she did so on her own terms. Maybe that was the example I needed. I hugged my middle and imagined she was my grandmother, and she was old and wise enough to make me feel like I could get through today. Eventually, the tension seeped out of my shoulders.

"That's better, Hadara," she said once we were back among the throngs of healers and patients. "Can we find a speck of sunshine in all this?"

"Sunshine? You mean something good?" How could something good come out of this day?

"Who'd be that hard-hewn rock of a soldier come looking for you? Vanyo or Vaneo or something. Didn't seem to be on a mission, just wanted to check on you."

That Valeo had stopped by looking for me wasn't exactly a ray of sunshine on a dark day. He was hail and storm clouds and the last thing I needed was for Leba Mara to fish for new gossip at my expense. The sick ward could be as bad as the marketplace sometimes. "That would be Valeo. It's a private matter."

"Oh, alright then. Private Matter it is," Leba Mara said with a wink. It was so out of character I almost gasped. Valeo plus sunshine plus winking? What kind of crazy things did Leba Mara imagine about us?

"Time was when I had 'private matters' with a young gentleman." She was practically singing. I'd never seen her so cheerful.

I was horrified. Widow Reezen was dead. For all anyone knew, more people were being hanged as we spoke. And Leba Mara was reminiscing about her courting days.

"I should go get my mop." If I could keep from flinging it, I'd consider it an accomplishment.

"Not so fast, O young woman with the Private Matter." Leba Mara took out her broken shield totem and waved it overhead. "Training today."

"Training? In what?" I asked, clearly irritated. Maybe I should've agreed to a day off after all.

"Oho, annoyed I'm onto your little secret, are we?" Leba Mara turned pink with joy. She then waved to everyone around her. "Well, we won't tell anyone, right all?"

About thirty people, including patients, laughed aloud. Some secret. My face flushed. My whole body flushed. I couldn't hold my tongue any longer.

"They're hanging people," I blurted. "The Temple built a gallows on the patio behind the sanctuary."

That shut everyone up.

And got everyone staring at me.

Finally, a beggarman cradling his bloody hand spoke up.

"We know," he said. "The fishermen's all been saying it this morning. They's seen it from halfway outta harbor."

An orderly rolling bandages nodded. "The bodies have already been in for examining, didn't Leba Mara explain?"

"Yes," I mumbled at my feet. "I just don't see how you can be in a good mood about it."

Leba Mara turned back to me, fists on hips. "Don't go blaming folks for thinking young love is something to be cheery about in these dark days. Yes, alright, he's a Temple Guard. I'd have picked someone a bit, ah, more local, let's say. More attuned to our ways. Less . . . imposing. But it is what it is. Soldiers fall in love with local girls all the time, if the old legends tell it right."

I gulped and changed the subject. I didn't want to be any more of a local legend than I was already. Besides, I had other obsessions than romance. "My Babba tried, you know. He really did."

I wanted them to know it wasn't because Babba agreed with this. I needed them to know he hadn't failed them. Not really.

"He's a good man," Leba Mara sighed. "It wasn't much of a hope. But stop trying to change the subject. Young love is very serious. And who knows? You might do some good reforming one of them. Don't you go missing a lovely chance at happiness because you're too caught up in others' misery."

She waved her totem again overhead and began singing about young love and spring flowers and kissing and more love. Then she darted and wove the totem around me, casting sparks in a dozen shades of soothing green. The sparks became light waves, the hues becoming more subtle and varied. The more she waved it around, laughing, as if taunting me, the greener the air around me got.

"Feel anything?" Leba Mara asked.

I shook my head.

She lowered her arm and gave me a confused look. "That's the best I can do for a cheer-me-up spell. It sometimes works, sometimes doesn't."

"Sorry, no." I didn't feel any different. Not at all.

"Humph. Well, there's no helping self-pity. All you need is to return to work." She motioned me over to the beggarman with his injured arm. "Let's begin our training, then. Easiest there is. All we're doing is washing it off first to see how bad it is. So all we're going to do is conjure some moisture, just a few drops. Watch closely, and do as I do."

Magic. I ought to be dancing around with excitement. I should be leaning in, ready at a jump. Magic fascinated everyone I knew, but the Temple only let a miniscule number of people actually try it. If Nihil didn't deem you worthy of using his theurgy, you didn't. That simple. So Leba Mara was offering me one of the highest honors the Temple could bestow, something that had to be cleared with an Azwan. If this had been Amaniel, she'd be exploding with joy.

Except, of course, an Azwan already allowed Amaniel to study magic, and I'd come to my own ideas about its worth.

And I hated even the idea of it. I'd much rather heal people by washing their injuries, stitching them up, splinting broken bones, and whatnot. That's what it said in the text Leba Mara had given me to read. It made few mentions of magic, as if the authors meant for healers to be ready if the already unpredictable magic gave out on them.

And that was good enough for me.

That wasn't what Leba Mara had in mind. At the very least, I supposed I should know the truth about how easy or hard it was to conjure or spellcast or scry or curse or heal.

"With Nihil's blessing on you, love, this should be easy for you," she said. "You ought to be quite powerful, I'd think."

My back went rigid at that, and I forced a smile. Yes, I had Nihil's blessing, but it hadn't occurred to me that came with blanket permission to learn magic. Of course. How stupid could I be? The Azwans were likely expecting it.

Nihil's nose, I hoped that wasn't so.

Leba Mara had me hold my hand over hers so that we held her totem together. She waved it over the man's injured arm while she muttered some nonsensical words about water and waves and droplets of rain.

A sharp jolt went through my hand. I found myself on my bottom, staring up at Leba Mara, who was hopping around, shaking her empty hand. My heart seized up in my chest.

The altar. The egg. The flash of light and then nothing.

I closed my eyes and inhaled, deep and long. There is no altar. There are no Azwans. I pulled myself to my feet and stopped my reeling, found my center of gravity, and opened my eyes. See? The sick ward. No altar. I also didn't see any totem, but I did note a smoldering black scar on the wall over the beggarman's cot. He peered out from beneath the crook in his elbow, eyes wide in shock.

"Why, by all three moons," Leba Mara said.

The man just looked at us.

"Must not be working right today," she said, crinkling her brow.

An orderly picked up the totem and bounced it from hand to hand, then dunked it in a basin of water, where it landed with a blunt hiss. When it was cool enough to touch, he handed Leba Mara the totem again. She held it up to her eyes and squinted at it, then down at me. I rubbed my singed hand on my smock. It stung, and the hair on my neck pringled.

"Hadara, did you do anything?" She gave me her warning side-eye.

I shook my head and gulped. "I swear it."

She waved her totem over the man's arm to try again. This time she did so without me touching her—just to see if it works, she said—and immediately a light mist gently scoured the man's arm clean.

"Well, isn't that peculiar," she said. "Nihil's never deprived me of his theurgy before. I'll have to ask the high priest about it later."

The orderly patted her arm. "It's alrighty, Sister Mara. We all have days."

"Not me. Never." Leba Mara turned the gold totem over in her palm as if it had disappointed her. "Peculiar. Wonder what you have to do with it, Hadara."

I rubbed my palm on my dress again. It didn't sting any longer, but it had to be more than coincidence, didn't it? It was something about me. I could see magic when others couldn't. I understood languages. But what was this new thing I could or couldn't do?

"Maybe we shouldn't try anything," I said, "until after you speak with the priest?"

She scowled, but didn't argue.

After that, I made it a point simply to watch Leba Mara work. A few half-formed excuses floated in my brain, but I didn't need them. She was so rattled, she muttered to herself as we worked. She decided we'd start with small injuries—surface wounds and ingrown toenails and bad headaches and the like. I followed her around as she examined people, and that suited both of us. It's what I was really interested in, anyway, and I spent the day with my eyes bugged out and brain engaged. Questions poured from me. It felt good to be distracted, and I threw myself into learning everything I could without letting up for a moment. Because if I stopped, I would start thinking about this morning, and that felt like a dangerous thing to do.

"What part of the text are you up to?" Leba Mara asked.

"Digestive Tract."

"Skip to the skeleton. Most folks don't come in with stomach aches or diarrhea unless it's bad. But bones? Even an achy bone'll bring 'em in every time."

I nodded, making a mental note. Bones.

"Make sure you know it from cranium to phalanges, please."

Phalanges. Fingers and toes! I knew those.

But what was a cranium? A head. Of course. I could slap my cranium. It obviously wasn't working right if I didn't recognize such an obvious word.

Leba Mara had already moved on. "Skin ailments. There's a million, or maybe it just seems that way."

The skin patients had been lined up along the benches. Leba Mara pointed out rashes, burns, blisters, warts, cheloid scars, and so much more, and my own skin itched and burned in sympathy.

It went on for half the day like this, me examining pus and blood and swelling that Leba Mara would then make shrink or even disappear with a wave of her totem. It's not that I doubted her magic worked—but I knew the effects were temporary. Everyone knew. Leba Mara would be redoing these spells again tomorrow.

I didn't dare air that idea, though, and focused instead on the gore and guts as we made our rounds. Odd that such sights didn't make me feel queasy. Maybe that's why she'd had me work as an orderly for a few six-days; it certainly had gotten me over the worst of things. Not much bothered me anymore, even before this morning. I'd not only seen it all, I'd emptied buckets of it.

"Well, you'll never guess the time," Leba Mara asked.

"Past high heat, I expect," I said.

"Maybe so, but it's also time for your . . ." and here she leaned in and whispered loudly, "Private Matter."

And then she winked.

Sure enough, Valeo was standing all rigid and soldierly in the doorway. Heat washed over me.

"Would you excuse me, Leba Mara?" I asked.

"Take your time. It's dinner anyway. Come back after."

And then she strode off with a last wiggle of her wide hips, as if to mock me. "Private matter," she muttered again, then laughed.

I shook my head as she walked off. Perhaps it was an unintended compliment that I'd hid my distress so well, she thought I was more prone to flirting than fretting.

Valeo waited outside the sick ward doors for me. He looked me up and down, but I'd made sure to take off my smock. I didn't have anything gory or gross stuck to me.

"Thought I'd check on you," he said, shifting uncomfortably. "You know, in case you . . . if this morning . . . I mean . . ."

"I know I took off rather quickly," I said. "I'm sorry."

"For what? I'm the one who should apologize. In fact ..." he inhaled deeply and held it for a moment. "His Most Magical and Worthy Azwan, S'ami, Nihil's Ear, has ordered me to apologize to you."

The exhale was long, loud, and rather desperate sounding.

"Ordered. For showing me the truth? You'd accused me of being shallow. You could apologize for that. But never, ever for showing me the truth."

"I have my orders."

"Do I need to stomp all over your boots again?" I wasn't really angry. If he hadn't shown me those gallows, Widow Reezen would've died thinking she was alone. She hadn't even known Babba was there, and she'd held him as a baby. "There is no apology needed. You wanted me to see it. I saw it. I don't know what you thought I could do, but I'm trying to learn to save what people I can."

"You're thinking too small."

"What?" Once again, the flush raced up my neck. How was he always able to do that to me?

"The Azwan says he felt a sharp spasm in Nihil's theurgy around midday today. He is seeking an explanation." Once again, I met Valeo's searching stare, only this time, it was through the slits of his helmet.

I rubbed my palm on my dress again. Was it me? That was about the time Leba Mara and I had begun working together.

"I've no idea what that might mean," I lied.

"He has asked me to inquire."

"So you're not actually here to check on me? You're here under orders."

"Hadara, I . . . yes. I have orders. But, I . . . I don't want you to think I . . . I'm sorry. I don't know what I'm trying to say."

How I hated his helmet. It hid his expressions, so I couldn't read whatever it was he was hiding from me. All I knew was that I wasn't going to pretend he was my friend any longer. There was no such thing as friendship with this man now. I would always see him with that bloody dagger in hand.

"You appear to have carried out your orders," I said. "Thank you. You may go."

I spun on my heels and headed back to the sick ward.

A spasm in Nihil's theurgy? I didn't know what that meant. I didn't know how he'd known about the totem and the shock I'd gotten.

Was this the power S'ami thought I had?

I thought about that well into the evening until my shift ended. Leba Mara had decided my tutorial was over for the time being, and I promptly found myself with a mop and bucket again. That's how it would be, she said. A little learning, a lot of work.

I didn't mind. It gave me time to think. Once the horror of this morning had played itself out in my memory a few more times, I began recalling bits and pieces of what Reyhim had said. They'd recorded everything the soldiers had taken in their raids. I already knew it was all being held in a warehouse.

And that was key. I'm not a bureaucrat's daughter for nothing. I know exactly how merchants keep their records. I'd seen it countless times.

I knew exactly what I needed to do.

But first, there was someone who apparently wanted to know a few things about me, and I wanted answers, too.

# I I

*Ba'l replied; why would you care, Master, for the
daughter of nomads?*

*She was also my daughter, I said, and so is
her mother, who grieves. Her father is my son, who
builds her pyre. I made Ba'l bring me his youngest son and sacrifice him, too, that Ba'l should
know what the nomad felt for his daughter.*
—from "Death of the Nomad's Daughter,"
*Verisimilitudes 6*, The Book of Unease

Only a nagging, breath-stealing desperation could have
made me brave the network of leafy courtyards where
the Azwans were staying. I'd never dared go around the
back of the sanctuary and through the narrow alleys to
the tiled staircases that spiraled up to spacious apartments
with views far out to harbor and sea breezes that whistled
through the eaves. I hugged my shawl and shivered, my
chill owing more to a sudden case of nerves, not the mild
weather.

It was the Sabbath, a full five days after the Widow Reezen's death, which was the last day I'd spoken to Valeo. He'd kept his distance after that, nodding in my direction, and I answered with similarly curt nods. My thoughts whirled too quickly, but I'd forced myself to wait until a day when I knew even the Ward's side alleys would be quiet.

I didn't have to wait long.

S'ami was alone when he arrived, glancing over his shoulder as if expecting an ambush. He hustled me up a flight of steps, slid open a brightly painted doorway, and ushered me into a sunlit parlor as wide as my parents' new patio, filled with a tidy array of floor cushions and low tables, plus several hefty trunks, the tops stacked with scrolls and books. I'd never seen so many books in one place and wondered why he'd bother lugging them across the sea—as surely that's why the trunks were there.

I had to let the wonder of such riches settle on me until S'ami cleared his throat.

I whirled around, fearing I'd already upset him, but he had relaxed his stance and eyed me with simple curiosity. Earlier, I'd managed to sidle up to him after Sabbath prayers as others filed past on the way out. Could I see him? Urgently? He'd murmured to wait a full turn, meet him at his quarters, come alone.

So here I was, swallowing back my jitters, saying nothing, my bravery seeping out the wide windows. They overlooked the courtyard where we'd just met and were open to the world. Only the sanctuary had real glass on its windows—every other place including this one had only slatted shutters for when it rained. Who could overhear us, in this place where what I had to say could cost me my life?

A heaviness settled on me, and a tinkling, buzzing feeling skittered across my skin in waves. The room went suddenly still, with even the distant sea and its breezes hushing. No sounds leaked through the windows. The room was silent, without so much as a bird twitter or leaf rustle from outside.

"Is that a spell? The quiet?" I asked.

S'ami cocked his head and held up his gold totem, the wisdom knot. "Fascinating. You can tell I cast a spell of muting just now? It's a habit of mine. Privacy, of course."

I nodded. I knew I needed to see him alone, but something else nagged at me. The first time I'd seen S'ami had been on a pier, when he'd publicly shamed me with this same magic. I hugged my arms to my chest and clamped my legs and backside tight, locking out the memory of that violation.

"I . . . I am not really comfortable being alone with you," I said, looking away. Those books again. I could stare at the books and wonder, and not have to feel anything else. "That spell you cast at me on the pier that day. . ."

"Is irrelevant now," he said. "Unless you want me to say I wouldn't have cast it had I known you better, which is something I cannot say at all. However, I will work no magic on you now. This I promise."

"Is it too much to ask for an apology?"

His face hardened. "Is that really what you came for?"

I shook my head, still avoiding eye contact, and headed for a floor cushion by the nearest table. I'd already lost my first skirmish of the day with him. I'd done better on my sickbed after I'd awakened from my ordeal at the altar, and that encounter was the one bringing me here today. I needed to ask him questions, and we'd forged an odd alliance, one that I was about to test.

I sidled behind a low table staring at a stack of books. S'ami seated himself across from me, and I began setting the books to one side. Was it ruder to touch the books or to not see my host? The indecision threatened to paralyze me, but he only leaned back and watched me impassively.

So I moved the books.

Then there was an inkwell and some pens, some blank parchment, and blotting paper. I nudged those aside, too, in case I elbowed it, or it got in his way, or anyone's way, or a breeze lifted it. Anything, really. Anything to calm myself down and buy a moment or two to regain my courage.

My fingers trembled, and I reached for a jeweled carafe filled with water and pringlement leaves. I poured two cups and slid one toward him. He left it there and drummed his fingers on the table, clearly annoyed.

"Are you practicing to be a barmaid?" he asked. "Tell me why you're here. If I need water, I'll call a servant."

"You invited me. If I had questions, I mean."

"And do you?"

I nodded and stared into the cup I clutched to keep my fidgety hands at peace. The cup was wooden. I wondered why it wasn't glass, like the carafe. I wondered why I was wondering that and why I didn't just leave.

"I suppose I shall have to start," S'ami said. "Because whatever it is you have to say is too terrible to broach?"

I squeezed my eyelids shut.

"And yet you trust me," he continued, his tone thoughtful, not damning, as I'd expected. "After everything that has passed between us, you are here, trusting me with your honor, your secrets, possibly your life. What misery must have led you to this."

I hung my head. I had no answer that felt true, and I couldn't lie.

He sighed. "Well, this question of trust is in the air for both of us."

My eyelids fluttered open in shock. "Trust . . . me? But, I don't . . ."

He kept going. "Have you heard a voice in your head?"

"No."

"Have your limbs moved without you wanting them to?"

"By Nihil! No." I looked up. He was frowning.

"Do strange words pop out of your mouth?"

I rolled my eyes. "All the time!"

A corner of his mouth lifted into a sly grin, and it looked genuine enough. He slid over to a cushion next to me, his demeanor suddenly open and relaxed. "You really can't master formalities, can you? Ah, well, that's all I can glean from Scriptures. There was only one man, a giant, who was partially possessed."

"May I ask what became of him?" If S'ami had dropped his usual vigilance over formalities, I was going to ask whatever I needed.

"It's in Verisimilitudes, look it up." He sipped from the glass I had poured, which I took for an unexpected sign that something approaching trust had passed between us. I could almost relax.

"I'm a horrible student." I didn't smile.

"I heard. Believe me."

"I swear I'm not illiterate. In fact, I have a lot of knowledge."

I eyed the piles of books with renewed envy. S'ami picked up a scroll that had strayed and plopped it back onto a stack.

"I didn't say you were illiterate. But we're not here to discuss your favorite poetry."

"My apprenticeship."

"Is there a problem with it?" He raised an eyebrow. "I'd heard only good reports so far."

That meant he was checking up on me, which was all the encouragement I needed.

"Earlier this week, Leba Mara had me touch her hand while she spellcast. Her totem blasted out of reach, like a lightning bolt. You felt that?"

"Then you understand very little. Why should I care about a healer's feeble ministrations?"

He was testing me. I sighed and closed my eyes again.

"In prayers today I could see your spellcasting," I said. "You tossed out rainbow hues but all incandescent. Not like that first day you arrived on our pier. You were showing off then and *wanted* us to see your magic."

"So how was this different?"

"I could see it forming, straight from when it first came from your mind, down to your fingertips, out your totem. It was like the threads on a loom, weaving and unweaving, only like lightning, too. As if you could control lightning, paint it colors, and send it out, humming and vibrating, to blanket us."

I opened my eyes. S'ami was leaning forward, just finger widths from my face, poring over my every feature as if memorizing them. "Go on."

"The high priest's are beautiful, deep reds and ambers. He can do greens, too, but they're muted, and he has trouble with blue. His blues are weak. Reyhim's are pale, wobbly blues and grays, mostly slate. I could barely make them out except he was wearing white and it showed up against his robes."

S'ami clasped my hands in his, turning them over and over, his voice terse. "Tell me you aren't wearing gold today. No gold rings or bracelets or toe rings, anything."

I tensed and yanked my hands back. His grip held firm, his palms moist and hot.

"The Ward confiscates gold," I said.

"Of course it does. So no fool can teach himself to cast spells."

"Azwan, what did I see?"

He dropped my hands and reached for my face, and I instinctively pulled away.

"Remain still," he ordered.

His hands pressed hard against the side of my head, but I kept still and steady and made no threatening moves against this predator, even as he turned my face this way and that, the way Leba Mara checks a sore throat or black eye, except he kept his eyes locked on mine, and I kept my focus on not moving a muscle, the dread tamped down deep within me until I thought it would burst from my chest.

His voice rose. "I wanted you dead. I wanted this power for myself. The power of a god. That death throw was the strongest I'd ever cast. I stood over your body waiting for what was left of the demon to pass to *me*. If only you hadn't touched . . . ah, it's no use." His hands dropped to his lap. "My plan was no better than yours, who had no plan."

I shriveled in place, shrinking into the cushions, head tucking behind a tower of books, my dread tightening into knots of tension in my fingers, my stomach, my every muscle. I ordered myself to stay calm and alert, as I did whenever I ventured into the swamp. That's kept me alive more than once. I kept my voice gentle and singsong, barely above a whisper. Calm the beast, even in the man, so the saying goes. Inside, however, an entire acrobatic troupe tumbled in my stomach. I'd be lucky not to throw up on S'ami's fine vestments, much as Leba Mara had once done to Reyhim.

But which was more frightening—S'ami's despair or the demon remnants drifting inside me like dust?

"You can have it, whatever it is," I said. "Take it. I don't want anything to do with the Temple. I want no demon in me."

"The star comes to you as you come to it." For the first time since I'd met him, he hesitated. "That night at the altar, you talked of your dead grandmother, a heretic. I don't think she had anything to do with this. Did the Gek even know of her? The Gek chose you. They were waiting for you to step forward and agree."

"I didn't agree," I said. I hadn't. How many times had I already told myself this? Did I even believe it anymore?

He was echoing what Bugsy had said—what I didn't want to hear. I hadn't agreed to this at all. The day we'd gone to the swamp and I'd found myself surrounded, I'd wanted whatever it was they'd found so that I could see it, too. I'd envisioned a conversation with it, mostly. I'd wanted answers. I still hadn't gotten them, only more questions.

"You ordered them to bring what they'd found to you," he said. "I saw you pounding out those hand signals."

I thought about that. "Did the Gek or the demon choose me?"

S'ami paused for a long moment. "We're not sure. We debated exactly that question, but we don't know enough about those creatures or how they talked to the demon. Did you ask that Gek who lives with you?"

Why drag Bugsy into this? There was no reason to trust him with anything Bugsy had said.

"She's a child. She doesn't know much. Please, I want to give back this, this, talent or whatever it is." I want to be strange, swampy Hadara again. How many other girls wanted to be me? None. Until a few six-days ago, I hadn't wanted to be me, either. "I want to be done with all of this."

Instead of an answer, S'ami fished out his gold totem from his vestments. The wisdom knot shape fit comfortably in his palm. He whispered a few words in Tengali—a string of nonsense phrases about breath and wind.

I perked up and glanced around. Nothing in the room moved, and there was still no sound. But a gentle breeze filtered through the shuttered windows. Pages flapped on an open book. Needing something to do with my hands, I closed the book. I placed it atop another stack.

When I was good and ready, I gave his wisdom knot a sidelong glance, not trusting it or its owner.

"Pale blue," I said, watching the thin array of sparks rise.

He nodded, and chanted about snow in winter. The room grew chillier, and the sparks brightened. My eyes didn't lift from his totem.

"Cerulean, or maybe sea blue," I said.

His intent wasn't difficult to figure out. He went on this way, changing incantations, changing the hue of his magic, his eyes never leaving the gold weight in his hand. I could've lied or pretended I didn't see anything, but I answered my best, even as the spells grew more complex and colors mixed together, becoming ever more subtle shades. S'ami had stumbled on the one way to keep me cooperating—give me a problem no one else can solve. I wonder if I wore that particular weakness like a hair scarf, but wrapped around my entire being.

"We should stop," he said at last. "Nihil, I'm sure, has already detected my casting. He will wonder what I'm up to."

"What will you tell him?"

He shrugged. "Entertaining children. Or amusing myself."

"He'd believe that?" I was a terrible liar, and I had trouble understanding how anyone else could be good at it.

"Nihil believes many lies, including his own."

That wasn't the answer I was expecting.

"Azwan?"

"What if the first spell was someone's younger sister?" he asked. "What if the more complex ones were a family? What if, by casting those spells, I silenced forever someone's deep laugh, or halted a love song, mid-verse?"

"I'm . . . I'm not sure I understand."

"I think, deep down, you do."

I shook my head. No. I did not. At all.

"The Gek, the demon, this talk of being an undoer," he said, waving vaguely around. "It seems you've been given a task from people in two separate worlds. And I join them in wanting you to complete it."

Two worlds? What two worlds? And he'd said that hated word.

"Undoer." A chill crept down my spine as I spoke it. "I wish to be a healer. You made the arrangements yourself."

He reached across for his water cup and raised it toward me, as if toasting me. "Of course. You were a model of compassion and decency with the soldiers after they were poisoned. And a quick study, too. As I said, reports from the sick ward are indeed satisfactory, so far."

No one had ever praised me like that. I was Hadara the wild girl, the lazy student, the bad influence on Amaniel. I had trouble reconciling that Hadara with what I was hearing. Was he flattering me? But Leba Mara did indeed call me her best apprentice. And, yes, Babba had said I was heroic, but parents are supposed to say things to cheer you up. But a model of compassion and decency? I was compassionate and decent and had a monster in my head, maybe. And the man raising his cup to me knew that better than anyone.

My shoulders straightened as S'ami leaned in close again until his mouth was scarcely a finger's width from my ear. He murmured, distinct but low. "You'll heal what Nihil has harmed and undo nearly two millennia of tyranny and perversion."

"I'm to do *what?*" I shivered at the heat of his breath.

"Don't be coy. You love Nihil?"

"Yes, yes of course I do, Azwan." I was emphatic enough to sound convincing, I hoped. I was frantic to figure out what he wanted from me.

"Then you're the only one." He gave me a self-satisfied look, but I only gaped back at him.

I felt utterly lost. I had no compass to find my way out of this conversation or this room. I might have been a dreadful student, but these were uncertainties I'd never heard promoted as theology before. "But, I—"

"No one loves him. Fear, yes. But not love. He's a demon."

I kept sputtering in confusion. "He's a what? No, no, he's the Great Numen. A god. Is this a test? I did learn this in school, I—"

Maybe one of these books held answers to this. No, no, they didn't. I was pretty sure there was nothing anywhere about Nihil being a demon. Was there?

"He is a demon, Hadara. You know it," S'ami said. "You know sacrifices to him are nothing more than sanctioned rapes. He killed my daughter. She was twelve. Twelve! Just because he put her on an altar first doesn't lessen the crime."

I didn't need a conversational compass; I needed a map. I couldn't navigate the wilderness of this man's anger and grief, and I was all turned around by it.

"Then this is about you," I said, a bolt of understanding ripping through me. "About your loss, and your child. But what does this have to do with me?"

Stupid question. It had everything to do with me. S'ami only said, "You tell me."

"You want me to use whatever powers you think I have. For you."

"For all Kuldor. Let's be rid of that narcissistic pestilence once and for all. Join me."

Join him? He'd gone mad. Yes, that had to be it. His intensity gave it away with a sudden, fierce gleam in his eye. And who exactly ever had so many books? What was in them? So, yes, madness.

Wasn't it? Madness wasn't in my anatomy text. Could a mind be broken?

"This is blasphemy, isn't it?" I said, keeping my voice measured, calm, rational. "I mean, if you really mean all this."

"Oh, it's blasphemy, alright. And I mean every word."

I leaped to my feet. My thoughts were in a thousand places at once, from the sick ward to the warehouse to Nihil and S'ami and everything he'd said and back again, around and around. The stretch between the doorway and me looked a thousand body-lengths wide. I wanted to run the whole way.

My thigh hit a stack of scrolls, which spilled onto the floor. My words tumbled with them.

"You're his priest. His highest priest. So this is just a test and I'm failing. And that's fine."

I headed toward the too-far-away door, but he was on his feet faster, the scrolls kicked out of range. He lunged, intent on his point, his voice a throaty growl. His fingers wrapped around my upper arm, but I held my ground. He wasn't going to hurt or kill me, not when there was some chance of winning me over.

Which there wasn't.

"Nihil comes from the same distant realm as the demons," he fumed. "Another world entirely, but they can't take physical shape. That's why they try to steal ours when they get here. They're just minds, free-floating; souls adrift in the vast universe."

This—wasn't what I'd expected. I let it sink in a moment, this idea of a free, unattached soul, finding its way to a man's body and becoming Nihil. Finding its way to me and becoming … what? A thought bubbled free from deep inside my head, where I'd been afraid to think it. I'd come here seeking reassurances, not answers. I'd wanted the Azwan, the one who was supposed to know everything there was on the subject of demons, to tell me I was fine, that I was within some otherwise normal range of weird. I wanted to leave here feeling happily, cheerfully different, not damned.

I plopped back onto a cushion, afraid to meet his gaze and his suddenly smug look.

"Demons come from the stars," I said, as flatly as I could manage. "I'm quite sure that's in one of these books. Maybe all of them."

"A simple explanation for simple minds. Which yours isn't."

Nihil blast that man for flattering me again. No one in the Temple hierarchy would ever suggest I might be smart. Except him. I let him pace in front of me, mentally measuring how I could duck around him and flee, if needed, even as I felt the will to do so seeping from me. A free-floating soul in my head? I still hadn't gotten used to the one I was born with.

"Alright, then, what are they?" I said. "How do they live without bodies?"

He nodded, smiling, clearly pleased with my questions, but kept up his pacing. "They're fine in their realm, as best I can tell. They only need one when they fall to Kuldor."

"And that's in these books?"

He paused in his pacing and rummaged through a stack, tugging out a thick, leather-bound volume. "My father is the greatest astrologer who ever lived. If there had been evidence, it would've been in here."

The volume landed with a thud back on the table. Its title, in Tengali letters, meant nothing to me. Apparently, I could only understand other tongues when spoken. The written word only yielded its meaning in my native language.

"Nihil must've shown them how, as they're the same species," he continued. "He steals one of ours, and we lovingly call it an incarnation. He's been walking around in the current body for, oh, about a hundred and eighty years and yet it looks fresh-picked. Not a day over forty. The man who first inhabited that flesh and animated those limbs? Long dead. But the body, Nihil's appearance—if you could see it—is flawless. Ever wonder how he does that?"

"You're going to tell me that magic is the simple answer."

"You're learning."

"So the right answer is?"

"He steals the power for it. Which you must know. Tell me you know this."

"What power? You mean magic itself?"

The S'ami who answered was a different man—not the smooth, arrogant one I remembered. This one was a raging river barely concealed behind a stone dam, the controlled tone holding back roiling whitecaps of contempt. "How they must hate him. He's a parasite. He sucks up their life-force for his magic. Every time I cast a spell it harms these invisible creatures. You can't blame them for trying to stop him."

"So his magic has a source." My mind raced, brimming with questions. "And it's these, these spirit people?"

"It's one source. Not the only one. The other sources are irrelevant. This is the one that eats at me. If they are anything like Nihil, but his opposite, then they're a magnificent race. Powerful, knowing, true. And good—which he is not."

His anger was real, then. S'ami was really blaspheming. I wasn't ready to absorb it. The ghosts of all those welts on my wrists cautioned me against believing anything the Temple said too readily. Traps and lies; this was the Temple of Doubt's currency, with which they bought obedience.

"How do you know this?" I asked. "At the altar, you said the demon can't be trusted."

"I spoke true. The demon didn't come to help *us.*"

"I knew that, Azwan, I did. But how do *you* know any of it?"

Some of the tension eased out of him and the sorrow returned to his face as he stopped pacing. "You are entirely too clever. And I've let you slip into impertinence again. The question of trust, you see. How do I know what I know? I'm unlucky enough to be one of the better mathematicians to ever curate the Boundless Repository. Nihil's earliest diaries are written in code. Very early, before he learned to lie even to himself."

"Who commits such terrible deeds to parchment?" Wonder had overcome my fear.

S'ami scowled. "Look, this is the wrong approach with you, as I suspected. You have already seen with your own eyes what trouble Nihil causes. It's no different anywhere he reaches. It is the price of the magic I wield on his behalf. When you don't just see it, but understand it, you'll beg to join me."

"Join you in what?"

"You will have to imagine that answer for yourself. Now leave me be. I've said my piece for the day and I need time to myself."

He turned away at that, shoulders hunched, all the animation suddenly evaporating.

"You're dismissing me? You tell me all this and I'm supposed to go and, what, have a lovely Sabbath? After this?"

I went to stammer something, anything, but S'ami waved vaguely toward the door and spoke. "Yes, do have a lovely Sabbath. It's a magnificent day."

"Azwan . . ."

He shrugged and gave me a nasty sidelong glare. "Look, do what you always seem to do. Gather your family around their hearth and gossip. The mad Azwan ought to be a lively tale. Don't leave out the part about you being partly possessed."

My heart began pounding again, my tongue thick in my throat. "You said I wasn't."

"I said no such thing."

"Azwan—"

He cut me off. "Show up on time for your training and do as the healers ask. Be sure to tell me any other unusual talents you develop. And if you should think of some way to help your people, be sure it's prudent and doesn't leave a mess. I hear you're handy with a mop."

## 12

*I shall tend for you a garden of fragrant blooms and fruit always ripened, that you may pluck from any tree and find succor, and expend yourself in delights unknown in life. These you shall find in death.*

*There shall blossom in my garden a shade tree beyond all others that shall cast its cool shadow upon all who seek refuge beneath its perfumed boughs. There you shall rejoin loved ones and friends and people of virtue you once knew, that you may enjoy their company with no constraints of time or rivalry.*

*All that is knowable shall be known; all that is doable shall be done. For my garden shall be your paradise, that you shall know a life of ease without end.*

*—from Oblations 3,* The Book of Unease

I was going to have anything but a magnificent day.

It was the Sabbath, the market stalls along Caller's Wharf were all shuttered, and I found myself weaving around them aimlessly, sometimes stopping to lean against one, trying to ward off a sense of dizziness.

Nihil, a demon.

No. How?

S'ami had told me how: our numen was another race's demon.

The meant every time Leba Mara healed someone, Nihil robbed some creature of its life-force. Nihil the demon.

I thought I was alone in suspecting Nihil had limitations and that he couldn't do everything he claimed. Perhaps a part of me had clung to the idea that all his little lies were in service to some higher truth—some noble, ultimate purpose. But S'ami didn't believe even the doctrine he was preaching. And what S'ami had revealed meant he'd gone far, far beyond the blasphemy of doubting and into furious rebellion. Should I believe him?

I gave my whole head a quick shake, as though dust had landed on me.

How could I know what to believe any longer?

After avoiding the question for so long, I was staring into the dark pit where all my faith used to be.

Nihil, the demon—who wasn't a god. And if Nihil wasn't a god, then none of the rest of it was true. There was no Eternal Tree and no afterlife, not for anyone. No reason to pray or pat my heart or make the vomit-hands or any other pious sign. It wasn't simply that the Temple of Doubt spouted lies; it was built on one.

My surroundings blurred.

It was all a lie.

All the welts I'd gotten studying Scriptures that, for all I knew, were total fiction.

My grandmother had been hanged—martyr to a lie. How far had her own doubts taken her? To the gallows. Just like Widow Reezen.

And no hereafter; no reward or redemption or everlasting bliss for loyalty to Nihil, the spirit-thief. Only the unending blackness of death, for us and for those spirit creatures he killed one spell at a time. That couldn't be. How could it?

I leaned against a kiosk. The force knocked a gourd loose from a strand of them hanging overhead. It fell with a hollow thud and rolled at my feet. I gave the fist-sized squash a solid kick, sending it spiraling away, chips of its flesh flying in every direction as it bounced against cobblestones until it smacked against the corner of another kiosk and wedged there.

I'd just destroyed a piece of someone's inventory. Did I feel better now? No.

Maybe I wasn't ready to toss away all my most cherished beliefs. Nihil had to be god, even if he was only our god and nobody else's, just the god of Kuldor and not the whole universe. Maybe it was a matter of perspective. He was a demon to his enemies; and they were demons to us. Yes, that must be it.

I wasn't ready for my personal abyss to be real.

My legs wobbled and I clutched the side of the stall, my head against my hands. I expected my stomach to upend, but it didn't even flutter. It wasn't fear overtaking me, then. Something else, a mix of feelings I couldn't sift through and pick out by name. Questions and ideas jumbled in my head, but mostly about S'ami, at the heart of this whole mess, one of the Temple's most powerful people but plotting Nihil's overthrow. Why do it this way, recruiting an ordinary teenager on a faraway island?

But he hadn't hired me on—the Gek had.

*The star comes to you as you come to it.*

The Gek chieftain had told me this. I'd gone out to the swamps to guide S'ami to the Gek. The lizardfolk had retrieved a glowing egg that held the demon. No one knew that then. All anyone knew was that a falling star had crashed into the marshes, and the Gek had gotten there first. And whatever they'd found, they'd put in that tin box.

They had a much bigger task in mind than getting the Azwans back on their ship to the mainland. That's all I'd wanted: for everything to go back the way it was and for people to look at me as someone who knew a few things, as someone who could muster a little respect from the Ward and my sister and everyone else.

But knowing what I did, could I settle for that? Living my entire life under the shadow of an untruth?

*You know to undo what must be undone.*

They'd said that, too, the Gek. Nihil's earlobes, I'd only turned sixteen a half-season ago. Why was all this landing on my narrow shoulders? I didn't want to be anyone's undoer. It sounded like it should be capitalized: The Undoer. Take on the Temple of Doubt, overthrow Nihil, make the planet rotate backward, double the stars in the night sky, flatten the entire universe. Anything else on the Gek's or S'ami's list? Maybe unravel the calendar scroll and bring back S'ami's daughter. Yes, that might do, I thought wryly. Or maybe nothing would be good enough.

And the whole time I brooded, Nihil's gorgeous tenor rang in my ears, the voice from the mirror. I'd been awed by that voice. If I could've kissed it, I would've, it'd been so musical, so flawless and thrilling. I remember how I'd felt: that I was truly in the presence of a god.

I couldn't trust my gut on this one. I had no idea what feelings were true or where my thoughts were leading me. My feet, though, had led me in a maze around the city until I realized I was no longer getting any sense of relief from walking. My dissatisfaction had only grown, along with my confusion which gnawed and nibbled at my sense of balance, at everything that kept my life and my thoughts in equilibrium—the good, but skeptical girl, the unmagical healer—until I didn't know where to go or what to do with myself or what to think.

Without having any real purpose, large or small, or any sense of direction, here or in my soul (if I had one), I focused on only the smallest tasks I could manage. I could put one foot in front of another. I could breathe the autumn air. In. Out. Crisp and fine. Breezes don't know gods from demons. I could appreciate that.

I could tug the shawl around my shoulders, adjust my head scarf, tuck in yet another stray strand, and turn toward home.

I 3

*The difference between love and warfare is that love requires thicker armor, sharper weapons, and less pity.*
*—from Lady Infikta of Ferokor's Manual of*
*Love Stratagems*

He was at the end of my street, watching my house. It took me a few moments to recognize the tall man pacing in front of our gateway, clad in simple broadcloth in the dark colors of the mainland and not his usual armor. By the time I recognized the banged-up, scarred features and shoulder-length mane of black hair, he'd noticed me and had begun striding my way, filled with sudden purpose, even if he bore his customary frown.

I have to admit, I hadn't missed Valeo keeping his silent vigil in front of my doorway. It reminded me of all the most unpleasant reasons for seeing the Temple Guards here: them watching us for signs of blasphemy or even the faintest misstep. Valeo'd watched over our old house by himself, day and night, and he'd succeeded in seriously unnerving me.

It had been a big obstacle to overcome in learning to like him. And then, just when I had, I'd watched him end my neighbor's life, and I'd forever see his bloodied hand and that dagger and Widow Reezen's hooded, limp form. Even if I thought I understood why he'd done it, I couldn't ever wash the stain of it away.

Did he know he was upholding a faith built on lies? That every order he carried out was done for a demon?

But then he had his own doubts, and that already made him different than most people I knew. I would never have known about Widow Reezen otherwise or about his own conflicting halves. His skepticism became, at that instant, the standard I knew I'd use to judge every person I'd meet from that day forward. If you believed without question, you and I would have nothing in common. The certain path led nowhere.

So while I was less than comfortable seeing him at his old post in front of our new house, even out of uniform, I would at least see what he wanted. Besides, his midnight blue surcoat looked rather smart on him, even if it was large enough to wrap a woolass in, but his ballooning trousers in their gray and maroon stripes hid what I knew were fiercely muscular legs. A pity he hid them.

I checked my sudden heavy breathing and ordered my heart to stop pounding.

Amazing how my body betrays me at every turn, as if this were anywhere near a proper time to be having improper thoughts. I stopped moving as I took in the full sight of his civilian self, with his many cabochon rings, bangles clattering against his wrists, and rows of silver hoops in each ear. I suppose one can't wear those under a helmet. That was a pity, too.

So he was wealthy. Well, he was a prince, after all. I'm not sure why I should be surprised. Maybe I'd gotten so used to seeing him in pretty much the same armor as all the other lump-headed guards that it was a shock to realize he was, indeed, not like the others. Should I be impressed? I felt like I should be. I let him amble up the narrow street to me until he stopped and gave me a courtesy bow of his head and shoulders. I gave the appropriate curtsy-bow in reply, glad to be wearing one of my prettier Sabbath dresses with its embroidered border. Odd, the things I find myself obsessing over. Why should I care what I look like? Nihil was a demon and a spirit-thief. Valeo was a prince and a killer. What would my wardrobe ever change?

Then again, some things did not have to change, and one of them was the way I was raised. I wasn't some wild thing living in the swamps. I was a lady's daughter. It wasn't much, but it was something.

"Mistress Hadara of Rimonil," Valeo said. "A word, if I may?"

So it was going to be all formal, was it? I could do that too. "First Guardsman Valeo Uterlune of the something-something unit of the something else, yes. You may."

Alright, so I was lousy at formalities. At least I was consistent.

Even without his helmet, his expression was unreadable. He didn't laugh, though, and that wasn't a promising sign.

I tried again and gestured toward my gate. "We have a nice patio by our hearth."

"I was hoping for someplace private," he said.

Mami had warned me about men who want Someplace Private with a woman. That's how women usually ended up in trouble. And I was all about playing it safe today. I'd had enough turmoil for one day, maybe for a lifetime. I hadn't forgotten all the promises I'd made my family, either. No more trouble for the wild girl who grew up following Mami into the swamps for herbs and roots. Mami had made a similar promise to Babba, to be dutiful and pious. I had Nihil's blessing, which meant about as much as a hiccup or a sneeze. But it meant everything to my family, and they meant everything to me.

I led him to the end of our street to a small park, hardly more than a square with a few palm trees and a shady place beneath a citrine tree that was first blooming. I often sat and read on a carved stone seat beneath that tree, but it didn't look like it would hold two humans, let alone a half-giant and a human. But Valeo brushed petals off the seat and we sat down, each gingerly perched on an opposite corner, no skin or clothes touching, facing the Grand Canal. Very public, very chaste, yet no one could overhear us. And in public, I'd find it easier to resist any temptation to cry or shout or pound his chest in fury. Perfect—if a bit precarious.

Plus, we had the perfume of all those citrine buds to lighten up the air and our mood. But I couldn't sit back without brushing shoulders. He had massive shoulders, which filled out his surcoat in a way that only an idiot wouldn't notice. He coughed once and shifted at an angle, as if trying to figure out a chaste way to sit. I did the same until half of me hung over one edge.

"Are you here under orders?" I asked, keeping my voice cool.

"No, it's just me this time."

I glanced up and he inhaled, sharp and quick, as if nervous.

"The Azwan of Uncertainty confirmed he led you to believe I was dead." The air seeped out of his lungs. "That clearly isn't the case. It caused a misunderstanding. And then I led you to those the gallows. I'm not sure I can explain my actions . . ."

"You were in a difficult position," I said. "I understand that, I do. But can I be honest?"

I may as well get right down to it. The poor man had obviously been stewing about this since I last saw him. He nodded grimly.

"It's hard, when I close my eyes, not to see you on that platform," I said. "But I'm trying. I feel I owe you that."

"You don't owe me anything. I did what I had to do, and so did you." His gaze was solemn, and so desperately sad.

I sighed. "You came to apologize for something that now seems like it was a century ago, instead of days."

"My timing is poor, then."

"Why would the Azwan let me think you were dead, anyway?" Then again, why not? Nothing either man did ever made sense to me. And all the things he'd said about Nihil, about demons, reeled in my brain, even as I sat there with Valeo. The day shouldn't be so sunny, I decided. It should thunder and crash lightning and rain torrents of misery. The day you unseat your god in your heart should have storms.

Valeo was somewhere trapped inside some other conversation, however, that had to do with such tiny, unimportant concerns as our feelings for each other.

"It's as I once told you," Valeo said. "Nothing can ever come of any friendship between us."

"And yet you're here." I wanted to tell him how sad, how insignificant, our friendship was to the world, maybe the universe. What did anything matter anymore?

"Yet I'm here."

"And have you been back to the gallows?"

He shook his head. "No. The Azwans found a civilian to pull the lever. They just need a couple guards on hand to keep order. They should've done that in the first place."

"What about not hanging people in the first place?" My lower lip jutted out. It was not the conversation Valeo had come for, but it was the one he needed to have.

"Alright. There's that." He gave a slow nod.

"You agree with me?" I was more than a little surprised.

"It's getting out of hand, is all. I've defended the tithe caravans en route to the Temple city. People would outright steal if we didn't. They deserve what they get. I'm no longer sure your people do, but I'm not willing to disobey and die in their stead."

"Well, that's succinct, at least." I had to admit I didn't have much pity for thieves and outlaws, either. On that, a portreeve's daughter and a Temple soldier could agree. Valeo's candor also felt like a crisp breeze, bringing a sharp crack of cool reality. He could be counted on to be honest, and that, too, was a relief.

"I just came from the Azwan," I said.

"S'ami? He's been curious about your powers."

I nodded. "He wants me to keep developing them and report back to him."

"Seems wise."

Valeo obviously wasn't going to take the opening I was giving him; he just sat there, self-absorbed and silent. I wanted to tell him more, so much more, but I was also aware that I was talking to a man charged with upholding Nihil's doctrine with a spear who harbored no doubts about whom he'd choose if it came to his life versus mine.

"The Azwan told me some things," I said, trying again.

"I trust him more than any other person in the world," Valeo said, meeting my gaze head on. "Whatever he told you, I have absolute faith in him. Absolute."

I let silence settle over us. There was nothing else on the subject I dared say.

But Valeo had plenty on his mind. "Why did that make you nervous?" he asked. "You're quiet all of a sudden. I meant only that he'll take care of you."

Did I need taking care of? I wondered what about me said *helpless*. Then again, maybe I should try and enjoy the kindness behind his statement instead of dissecting it like the dead little frogs Leba Mara had me cut up for practice. I was overthinking everything.

"He told me you were dead," I said.

"Just now?" Valeo raised an eyebrow.

"No, you know what I mean. Why would he do that? How is that taking care of me? How can your faith be so absolute in someone who lies?"

"He thought we'd be gone by now," Valeo said. "He didn't know we'd be sticking around until running into each other was inevitable. Would've happened sooner if—"

"Yes, I know, I know, if I had actually noticed you," I said, frowning. "But this raises more questions than it answers. How come—"

"He was trying to protect us both."

"From what? Each other?"

Just then, our knees bumped together, requiring yet another adjustment and balance shift. What difference did it make if a completely random and innocent part of our bodies brushed? Why couldn't we just have a lovely day together? Bumped knees and all? And forget all this talk of doctrine and faith and protection?

By way of an answer, Valeo rubbed his hands together and followed my gaze to the many boats floating by. None of them carried goods, as it was the Sabbath, but families were out enjoying a breezy autumn day, picnicking in the mild weather, children's laughter and singing carrying over to us and mixing with the citrusy aroma. It was a day for being carefree, undisturbed by pyres and gallows that were also resting, at least for a day—a day when even Valeo could relax and prop his elbows on his knees and let the tension release from his shoulders.

I straightened my own posture and folded my hands in my lap in my best imitation of modesty and waited for him to say something. After all, this had been his idea. Then I remembered who was guest and who was hostess and decided a speck of graciousness couldn't hurt.

"I like having you here," I said at last. "You're like my rock. Very little seems to bother you, and right now, maybe that's something I need."

"I can be strong, but I'm not a rock, Hadara," he said, stiffening. "I'm not unfeeling. Not entirely."

I couldn't have been more astonished if he'd told me he was indeed carved from stone. "How is it that you can misconstrue that?"

"I admit I want contradictory things," he said at last. "I want you not to care that I'm a nobleman, but when I thought you didn't care at all, I didn't want that either. And now I have no idea what to think. A rock? Am I?"

"You. Are solid and dependable. That's all I meant," I said, my voice soft, pleading. "And if I'm supposed to notice only the parts of you that you want me to notice, then please give me a list so I get it right for once."

I stared at his shoulders, then caught myself and looked down at my hands. My fingers had begun twiddling a piece of fringe.

He chuckled and shook his head. "A list. Alright. Please notice how hard I'm trying to apologize for being a dense rock. You forgive me?"

How could I help but smile at that? I'd have to be as frozen as the Crystal Desert to stay angry. "Of course. Am I also forgiven for being so obtuse and self-absorbed that I could walk right under your nose every day and not see you? Or that you could ever see me as shallow?"

I'd forgotten how deeply he could laugh as he nodded yes. He leaned back and put one arm against the tree—and around me. But not touching. His arm hovered somewhere over and in back of me, brushing against bark rather than skin. He wasn't going to give into any temptation being near me, and that settled matters for me. Yes, he was strong and well built, but we were friends.

And that made me both relieved and disappointed. All I said, though, was: "It's a magnificent day."

That's what S'ami had said to do—to enjoy my magnificent day—even if everything felt wrong and upsidedown. Seeing Valeo was only a hiatus before it all heated up again. I could enjoy this all I wanted, but that warehouse was only closed for the day, and all the items that Valeo and his comrades had seized weren't going to gather dust for long.

The gallows would start up again, and there would be another body or three or six, as there had been every day since the start.

The whole notion of that warehouse had been nagging at me. I'd even gone to see the building a few days ago, sneaking out of work under the pretense of meeting Babba. We'd walked home together, with him joking about his adult daughter escorting him. I hadn't seen much, except to note where it was.

It wasn't anywhere near where Valeo and I sat, silently and awkwardly enjoying our day, but it was near in my thoughts. If I didn't believe in Nihil as a god, or even as someone good, what difference did it make what I did with that warehouse?

Suddenly it hit me. Warehouse. Valeo. It all added up. He could be there—I knew I wanted him to be. I needed my rock to lean on. I wanted to hug him and jump for joy. I had the beginning of a plan, almost. Babba had said to start something, hadn't he? Maybe those weren't his exact words; it'd been something along those lines, though.

Start something.

I turned to Valeo. "This doesn't have to be so awkward, you know."

"Am I awkward? I guess I'm not a conversationalist."

"Me neither. But we're friends, right? You're going to marry a Feroxi warrior bride with lands and armies."

"You already made me regret mentioning that."

"And I'm going to become a healer and marry some merchant or other."

"Why are we having this conversation, then?"

"Because we're friends. So you don't have to sit here thinking how much I get under that thick skin of yours, S'ami doesn't have to pretend either of us is dead, and I don't have to worry that I'm being unchaste sitting by myself with First Guardsman Valeo and Nothing More."

What little I knew about flirting I'd learned watching Dina and other young women with their husbands. Valeo, I was sure, was even worse at it. It made sense to drop the entire pretense and go for less subtle forms of manipulating him into place.

Because I had a plan. And I had . . . power? No, that wasn't it.

I just had to make sure I had Valeo.

"You don't get under my skin, thick or otherwise," he said, grumbling. "And you're awfully lighthearted all of a sudden."

I thought about that a moment, wondering if I'd made a wrong turn.

"I've always gotten under your skin," I said. "From that time you looted our home, even."

"I was under orders. And as I recall, I nearly cut you down where you stood."

"Empty threats," I said with a shrug. "You like it when I make you angry."

"I hate it when you make me angry."

"But I *can* make you angry. I bet most women can't say that."

He threw up his hands in mock despair. "This is your idea of friendship?"

"Are we being honest? Neither of us is the cuddly sort. I think this works."

"No sooner do I figure out where I stand with you, then you change the rules on me." He looked genuinely irritated. "You should worry about how that seems."

"You nearly died, and I was there to see it," I said. "Do you know how that seemed to me? Like I was going to lose the one person in the whole Temple of Doubt who mattered to me."

The lumpy bit that all men have on their throats—the textbook called it a laryngeal prominence—rose and fell several times. Hard.

Then he reached over and fingered a stray curl that had fallen loose from my head wrap. He twirled it absently while staring into my eyes. I didn't shy away at the gesture, though probably there was some rule saying I should.

"I know what you did for me," he said. "I remember everything."

"You do?"

He nodded. "You held my hand, you stayed with me."

"I was losing you. Other Feroxi didn't make it." I bit my trembling lip.

"Then maybe it was the human half of me that proved too stubborn to die."

I punched his sleeve, even though I felt like crying. "You! We shouldn't be friends. You raided my home. You dragged me to a gallows. You stabbed my neighbor! You're everything I ought to fear."

"I know. I am all of those things. And I get under your skin." It was his turn.

"What? No. Of course not," I lied. "Not usually. Just . . . sometimes."

"Often."

"Never."

"Always."

"Are we haggling? You're impossible."

He stood and held out a hand to help me up, which I took.

"I have what I came for, I think," he said.

"And what's that? Bringing me to the point of utter confusion?"

"No, I came seeking clarity. I have it now."

"And what's so clear?"

"We're friends, Hadara. I have a lot of comrades, buddies, mates, whatever you wish to call them. But I don't have many friends. You don't see the prince, you see me. Me! And that makes me happy. If our fates would let us have more, I would go to your father right now. But this is what we can have, and it'll have to do."

Anything I could've said just then fell back into the lump in my throat. I gave his hand a short squeeze but didn't drop it, my eyes welling. He wanted more. I wanted more. And yet we'd gone as far as we could without angering our families. If I could see him just one more time, and make my plan work, if I could somehow pull this little act of disobedience off, I could settle for friendship. Couldn't I?

We walked the short distance back to my gate, hand in hand, whispering with our heads close. I told him when and where to meet me later, much later, but not why. He was on full alert, not for any danger, but for every word I spoke, every movement of my lips or eyelids, the crook of my head, the lifting of my chin. His eyes followed all of it, as if he were mentally mapping my face and its contours.

My plan was the worst idea ever. I'd made it on the fly while distracted by Valeo's regal self. My plan relied on a constellation of events aligning perfectly: my parents being asleep at their usual time, Valeo being in place, and nothing going wrong, which never happened. Once I had whatever I needed from the warehouse . . . and . . . and . . . oh my.

Another piece of the puzzle fell into place. I had yet another someone to talk to— another to goad and coax and cajole and likely argue with—who was also vital to all this. Bugsy. The Gek had a role to play, and a rather large one, come to think of it. Because if I got what I thought I needed—some sort of record, a ledger book, a stack of papers, something—then how to get it all back out? Oh, there were too many pieces of this plan!

And my hand felt so right in his.

Stay on the path, Hadara. It wasn't the certain path— more like the crazy path. Starting something was tough. I'd never planned anything other than dinner before, and my brain was reeling.

But other people were dying for Nihil, and Nihil was a demon, and as long as those things were possibly true, nothing I tried could be worse than doing nothing.

He walked with such deliberate slowness, my only thought was the appointed time would arrive before I walked the short block home.

"I'll be there early," he said. "Just in case."

I forced myself to stay put and not jump around with glee. I kept my voice to a murmur, reminding him of the details I'd only just invented. Valeo's expression didn't change from one of studied concentration.

When I finished, he leaned in close. I jerked my head back in case he decided to kiss me. "My father's inside."

"You're in no danger," he said. Then his voice dropped low, almost to a growl. "Golden eyes."

I tensed. I remembered the last time he'd called me that—in his delirium.

"Golden eyes," he said again. "The face scores of men saw in their visions."

I didn't feel terribly flattered to know that. After all, their visions had been nightmares. "You'll come alone?"

Valeo nodded again and dropped my hand, which felt endlessly empty now. He backed away and gave a slow, sweet chest-thump, as if he were saluting me very, very politely, and turned down the dusky alley.

# 14

*A nestling never forgets the smell of home.*
—Gek saying

"Look out!"

I dodged in time before a wooden bowl dropped on me. I looked up to see Bugsy stuck to our ceiling, cradling a dozen kitchen utensils. She was flushed a brilliant shade of crimson. She was also flinging things. A mixing spoon nearly clipped Mami's forehead. Mami had been the one to shout the warning.

Behind Mami, Amaniel and Rishi sought cover behind a divan. Rishi had a pillow over her head.

At least I didn't have to explain where I'd been, or with whom.

"Dare I ask what's going on?" I said, ducking a ladle.

"You ask her!" Mami said. "She won't talk to any of us."

"Where's Babba?"

"He's barricaded himself in the cupboard so she can't reload. At least she's down to utensils now. We've lost a few urns. "

I stared around our sitting room, littered as it was with spoons, bowls, a frying pan, pottery shards, even a broken glass or two.

Ouch!

A soup spoon hit the back of my head.

"She won't say what's wrong?"

"Like I said, daughter, she's not speaking. Her hands have been full of missiles, mind you, so there's not much in the way of signals happening. You're welcome to try."

I shooed everyone from the room. Bugsy skittered across the stucco ceiling to a far corner and hissed at me.

I signaled back. "Is there something I can get you?"

"HOME," she howled. It came out sounding more like a mash cat than a lizard.

Ah. Yes. Well, she'd been with us since mid-summer, and it was early autumn outside. I'd be homesick, too.

I signaled back. "Why now? Yesterday, you were fine."

"Yesterday, I didn't smell them."

"Smell who?" I sniffed several corners of the room, but all I smelled was oily wood polish.

Bugsy dropped to the floor, turned a rainbow set of colors, all clashing and mismatched, and cowered behind a floor cushion.

"Smell who?" I repeated. "Is there something dead in the house? Or outside?"

"No! It is best you don't know."

"Best for whom?"

"Best." She scrambled up the wall and across the ceiling again. "You have to let me go."

"We let you go every day. You yourself do not wish to pass our gate."

"You have to come with me."

"Come where? And why?"

"You're the undoer. You have to undo."

Undoer again. Did she speak with S'ami? No, that was impossible.

I picked up the ladle. I waggled it in her direction instead of replying. Maybe she'd understand my extreme annoyance. I wasn't the undoer, not for Bugsy, not for the Azwan. I was a good girl from a pious home with an important apprenticeship. I was no longer the girl who followed her beautiful rebel of a mother out into the wilds. Mami was no longer a beautiful rebel. She was a loyal wife and seemed fine with it. Rebellion for anyone in our family was out of the question.

Undoer. Never!

Even if Nihil wasn't a god, I wasn't one either. I had one simple—alright, complicated—plan to put in place and then I was done interfering with the Temple of Doubt and its wicked god. And to make it all happen, I needed this half-grown lizard-child to stop throwing things at me. I had some haggling to do, apparently.

It took time. A long time. I'd already slid all the doors closed, but I didn't know how long before someone got too curious or simply wanted the sitting room back. I must've been struggling with a weepy, croaky, hissing Bugsy for a full turn. At last, we seemed to have come to an understanding. She'd clambered down and crouched beside me as I sat cross-legged on a cushion. I reached over to stroke her head.

*Bam! Bang! Clangety clang!*

I jumped.

Bugsy fled.

A metal spoon pounded against a copper pot. Babba burst through the door, using the pot as a drum, sending Bugsy scurrying up the wall, out the open door, and to some faraway corner of the house—all in the time it takes to blink.

"What by all three moons are you doing?" I shouted, fingers plugging my ears.

"Rescuing you," he said. "She didn't bite you or anything?"

I rolled my eyes. Of all the idiotic ideas and terrible timing. Babba was trying to play the drums just when the last piece of my plan was lurching fitfully into place.

But poor Babba! He just wanted to be my hero. It was pathetic, to be sure, but also kind of sweet. How awful that I was going to betray his trust tonight. A queasiness rose up in my throat, as it always did when I was anxious. I was risking all kinds of trouble.

It was for the best.

No, it wasn't. How could I risk something so flagrant when Babba had done nothing but try to defend me? Because I was the only one with Nihil's blessing, the only one with all doubts removed from my name, the only one who might get away with defying the Temple just this once. That blessing meant nothing more than that—a chance to do something without getting myself hanged.

I had to get to the warehouse.

Just a few more turns of the sun, then of the moons, and I'd be on my way, for better or worse.

I plucked the metal spoon from his grip.

He shrugged. "Your Mami thinks that creature is going through puberty. I've already lived with two girls going through the life change, thank you, and that's more than any man ought to endure."

"She wants to go home."

"I won't argue. You'll recall I didn't want her here to begin with. Though she did have to pick the cook's day off for her tantrum. Cookie has the best luck with her."

Why did my father have to be so exasperating? Then again, at least he was being honest, unlike his eldest daughter.

My spirits sunk to somewhere around my feet. How could I sneak off like some common hoodlum with Babba making jokes and scaring off Bugsy to save me? He'd be furious with me. I'd be putting myself in danger, and I'd put him through enough already. I felt like the rottenest child in world history. Here was Babba with all his new responsibilities and his endangered city and his would-be thief of a daughter. This wouldn't do at all.

I sighed. Valeo would be waiting alone in the dark tonight. That made me feel awful as well, but what could I do? Poor Valeo. Poor me! I wouldn't get to see those shoulders. No! No! I wouldn't get to put my plan in place. Yes, that's it. Plan. Not shoulders. I'd have to think of something else. Plan-wise, that is.

"If you're sure she's bent on leaving, then open the gate for her," Babba said. "I don't want her sticky footprints all over our wall. She can come and go like anyone else."

Oh? We rarely left the gate open. Here was a chance, my only chance. If I didn't take it, when would be the next time I could go? He didn't know the invitation he'd just extended. If only my plan weren't so complicated. If only I knew for sure it would work. How was I to pull it all off, anyway? It was a terrible, terrible plan.

There was only one thing to do.

I did as I was told and opened the gate.

# 15

*It is one of the great ironies of love that rarely does one set out intentionally to steal a man's heart. You may purloin his affections with so much stealth that even you do not realize a crime has occurred until the victim confesses the deed.*
—*from Lady Infikta of Ferokor's*
*Manual of Love Stratagems*

My cloth slippers made only a mild shushing sound as I crept out. I'd decided if Amaniel or Rishi had trouble sleeping—we all had our own beds now—I'd stay inside tonight. That was all the incentive I needed to change my mind back to being a good, pious daughter. But my sisters slept like stones. So I got dressed slowly. If I couldn't find my best Sabbath dress in the dark, I wouldn't go meet Valeo and set my plan in motion. But the dress was atop a pile of folded clothes, right where I'd left it. If the small satchel I'd packed earlier made a clanking noise, I'd set it down and creep back to bed. But it made only a mute thud against my side.

If my parents' door was open even a hair, I didn't dare try and tiptoe past. That would be the end of my sneaking around. The door was firmly shuttered. I was hoping the house would be completely soundless so I couldn't risk making any noise getting out. But Babba's snoring could deafen anyone, so there went that excuse.

My last hope was the creaky iron gate, which I'd left ajar as Babba had asked. Maybe a breeze had shut it. The gate was still open, waiting for skinny me to slip through. Now all I needed was to spot a constable or a drunk or someone strange looking and I'd turn right around and march back to my room.

Callers Wharf was entirely empty.

I peered around shuttered stalls looking for Valeo, but he was nowhere to be seen. Well, that did it. I was going home. I'd been stood up, right? I decided to make sure and did a hasty survey of the square, right and left, around corners, down alleys, and then toward Pilgrim Bridge. There he was, leaning against the end of the bridge, arms folded against his chest, staring at me.

I paused. Valeo wasn't wearing his armor, of course, but I'd assumed he'd show up in the same clothes as earlier. I couldn't have been more alarmed if he'd shown up naked. Even by the light of the tallow lamps, I could see richly embroidered layers of silk. How much in the way of clothes did one soldier get to own? I felt a pang of self-consciousness. Maybe it wasn't too late to run home. All I had to do was get my knees to stop wobbling and I was sure I could make a run for it.

I should've worn my silk dress, the gift from S'ami. Instead, I'd worn the same dress as earlier, a dark shift I thought might camouflage me at night, and felt outclassed. A prince. I was standing on Callers Wharf with a prince in silk clothes and it was night and we were alone and why had I worn such a regularly nice dress instead of a spectacular one? Where was my head? I should've stayed in bed.

I wasn't supposed to care about him being a prince and his fancy clothes. So why had he worn them? We were friends. Who held hands. This wasn't getting any easier just standing around second-guessing myself. I'd been spotted, so I may as well make the best of it. I held my breath and strolled from my hiding spot as if I did this every night. He made no move to greet me.

"You made it," I said, feeling stupid for stating the obvious.

"You're not alone," Valeo said. He stared past me to where a pair of green eyes could be seen glimmering between two stalls. I hadn't forgotten about Bugsy. I was just hoping he had. Wrong. I'd promised to get her home all the way to the swamps in return for helping me tonight. It felt wrong to be tricking Valeo, and I had to hope that either he wouldn't mind, or he'd join in once he understood what I was really doing and why. All the pieces had to fall into place: Valeo going along with a plan he didn't yet know about, Bugsy playing her part, and me getting her back to the swamps. One more trip couldn't hurt, I suppose. Thinking that gave me the tiny copper-weight of confidence I needed. I had a promise to keep.

"That's Bugsy, my chaperone," I said.

"You have a Gek chaperone?"

"You've already met her, in fact. You killed her mother."

He gave a start and pulled back his left arm defensively. I could see the tip of a jagged scar on the skin, where Bugsy had once tried to gnaw free of his steely grip.

"I told her to keep her distance," I said.

"I don't like it. There's blood between us."

"Exactly. That's how I know you'll be a gentleman."

Valeo leaned in to study my face, and I studied his in return. By moonlight, the shadows cast his face into sharp relief. The prominent nose and deep-set eyes beneath that sharp brow ridge made his face look as if it'd been battered into rough shape with axes and picks and left to set that way. I worked at *not* noticing the strong jawline, noticeable even in the moonlight, or I'd never get farther than this bridge.

He grunted. "I'm not turning my back on that thing."

"She's unarmed."

He held up his scarred arm again. "She doesn't need weapons."

I put on my best "I'm sorry" face and said simply, "Please."

Valeo grunted. "I should've known better. Is there some particular power you have over me?"

"Why do you ask?"

"You didn't have anyone cast an enchantment on me, did you? A something-more-than-friends spell?"

Too bad he couldn't see me roll my eyes in the dark. "Don't be silly. I'm learning to heal hearts, not break them."

"I guess I should be relieved." The edge in his voice told me he was anything but.

"I am sorry. I'll tell her to go." I turned and made a signal to Bugsy, one she'd been waiting for. She scampered away, in the opposite direction from home. Valeo didn't have to know that.

He clamped a hand on my shoulder.

"Any other tricks?" he said.

I flinched and wriggled free from such a decidedly unchaste touch, but my drape got stuck under his hand and didn't move with me. My hair broke free of its linen prison, tumbling down my back as a sea breeze lifted lengths of curls and sent wisps flying behind me. Valeo caught his breath. His hand reached up and I felt his fingers lacing through my loosened locks. I didn't try to stop him. It occurred to me I probably should, but those fingers felt sweet entwined so gently in my hair, and it didn't seem like a threatening gesture. Just the opposite.

He whispered, deep and breathy. "Then again, this whole night will be worth it if only for this moment."

"Valeo, I . . ."

"Why do we ask women to hide one of Nihil's most dazzling gifts to them?" He bent over and nuzzled my locks. I closed my eyes, feeling his warm breath against the back of my neck. "You've lost your wild smell. I noticed it earlier."

"Pardon?" I smelled wild to him? I felt oddly flattered.

"That first time I saw you, you smelled like flowers and the outdoors and other stuff I can't even name. Exotic stuff," he said. "Now you don't."

"Oh." I mean, what am I supposed to say to that? "I'm sorry, I guess."

"I miss it."

"I . . . oh. I don't go to the fens anymore. Since, you know."

"Yes, I know. Too bad. I liked that smell a lot. I've dreamed about it."

Men dream about the way women smell? I was learning a lot tonight. "But the first time you smelled me, wouldn't that have been when you were ransacking—"

"This is the second time today you've mentioned that. You're holding that against me after all these six-days, are you? After everything we've been through together?"

"No, no, of course not, but you—"

"Once. Again. I was obeying orders. And I wouldn't have hurt you."

"I heard that other guards—"

"I'm not other guards."

"Yes, that I know. I wouldn't be here if you were. That's all I'm trying to say."

He ran his fingers through some of my curls. "It's a beautiful, moonlit night on a tropical island and I'm with the prettiest woman here. Let's walk." He offered me his elbow.

I took it, unable to speak for a moment. The prettiest woman? Really? So far, sneaking out had been a great idea. I'm the prettiest! I suspected the whole compliment was an outrageous lie, but it didn't matter one copper. I wanted him to keep saying it. "What happened to your Feroxi warrior brides?"

He laughed. "Another thing you keep bringing up. Yes, there is such a woman in my future. Though an arranged marriage didn't exactly work out for my parents. They're estranged."

That was a startling admission to make to a woman he barely knew. He'd once told me he had no family at all. I didn't point out the contradiction, since in his mind, perhaps there wasn't one. He was obviously beyond pretending his home life was normal. I decided I liked his candor. "How sad. For your parents, I mean. And for you."

"I think they're much happier without each other."

"And you?"

"This makes me happy." He reached for my hand and we strolled that way, our bodies close together, along the stretch of the Grand Concourse with its reflection of two crescent moons.

"We have no future together," I reminded him.

"Then we enjoy the present."

Valeo was pleasant company after all, describing how his mother had been elected queen by all the other noblewomen and acclaimed again just last year. He was proud of her, and he liked strong women. All Feroxi did, he said. No weak females in his race. He tried to get me to picture the vast halls of Ferokor and the fierce women who provisioned and defended them. I'd never seen stone fortresses, so I told him I could only picture stucco and thatching. That brought more deep laughter. That wouldn't last long, he'd said, against pitch and flaming shot.

He didn't say so, but I imagined those lady warriors defended themselves from humans. There must be another side to those border skirmishes that animated dinner conversations around Babba's table. However, Valeo dwelled mostly on his childhood in the Feroxi capital, Ironhills.

He didn't notice when I steered him away from the waterway to a spot behind the Customs House until he looked up and saw where we were. Either I worked up the courage to take the next step or I really did have to go home.

Valeo lifted his arm from my shoulder. His voice held a note of irritation. "Why'd you pick this place?"

"This place?" I blinked big eyes at him.

"You're one lousy liar. We wound up in the ugliest part of the city? Behind not just any warehouse, but this one?"

I didn't dare say anything. Let it play out, Mami always said.

Valeo went on, a disappointed tone creeping into his voice. "Well, I didn't think it was my good looks that made you notice me. But did you think I have a key? Or how did you expect to get in?"

I twisted out from under my satchel strap and emptied its contents on the cobblestones with a clatter. It wasn't much as tools go—a small metal nail file and some hair pins, a few nails, and a long skewer I'd lifted from the pantry. "Think any of these would work?"

Valeo's jaw dropped and he stared from the pile at me feet, up to me, and down again. "You had this all planned?"

"No. Not really. I mean, I did, but I didn't. I wasn't going to do it but then I thought I should at least try, don't you think?"

"Don't I think what? That it'd be a very romantic evening helping a lady burglar do a little looting?"

"How do you know that's what I'm here for?"

"Because you're not in front of a rotting warehouse to show off the city's architecture?"

"Well, if you were me, what would you do? While everyone you knew was afraid for their lives? While the Temple was executing people because of poetry scrolls and silly wooden dolls?" I sounded a lot more cross than I felt, but I couldn't help myself. It was all falling on me and I couldn't stand it another moment. Someone had to hear me out and understand.

"Silly wooden ... you're kidding," Valeo said. "Scriptures are clear on the subject of graven images. Paganism—"

"Is worth getting killed over?"

"Your people are in paradise compared to the mainland. Do you have any idea what Nihil's putting them through there? The ongoing war between Feroxi and humans that benefits only one man?"

No, I had no idea what was going on there or how it benefited Nihil. That was the only correct answer. I stood quietly instead, stunned. "I'm sorry. I'm not Feroxi but I'm trying to defend my people, too."

He snorted. "It won't help. And it's more foolish than brave."

There was only one thing left to do—beg for mercy. Modesty be damned. I flung myself at his chest, wrapping my arms around that narrow waist, pressing my cheek into the caressing silk of his shirt. I'd never hugged a man who wasn't Babba, though I'd thought about it just about every moment of every day lately. This wasn't Babba and his lanky frame. This was flesh wrapped around steel, all hard muscle that stiffened when I hugged him. Had I made a mistake? I closed my eyes and pleaded.

"You don't remember calling me an ignorant island girl, back when we first met? Maybe I just want to know why this is happening to us."

I felt his arms wrap around me, and thrilled at the rangy contours of his muscles under my own palms, warm and firm. He nuzzled my hair with his cheek, and there was a distinct note of sorrow in his voice. "You can't be beyond his reach. No one can. Everyone's tried. Everyone. Even the Feroxi."

"But you all help him. Willingly."

"It's to our advantage."

I remembered our teacher reaching for Amaniel's hand to strike instead of mine. Sister against sister; that was the Temple's way. I nodded. Valeo nudged me away and spun me around to face the warehouse's double doors. They were of splintered, weather-beaten wood, the latches bound by iron chain.

"No getting in," he said. "You could try. The moment you succeeded, I'd have to arrest you. Orders. Duty. Whatever you want to call it. But you could try."

I bent over and picked up a few of the tools. When I stood, I noticed Valeo had stayed behind me and fallen silent. "You alright?"

"Admiring the view," he said.

"You can see the water from here?"

"Never mind."

I had no idea what he was talking about. All I could see from where I stood were those ugly old warehouse doors. I walked over and tried to stick a hair pin in the bulky iron lock. Sparks flew up the pin and singed my finger tip. I leaped back with a cry.

Valeo peered at the lock. "Spells of warding, presumably."

"S'ami?"

"He's an Azwan. He'd outsmart you before breakfast, and twice more by lunch."

I reached toward the door without a pin. When I'd touched Leba Mara's gold totem, I'd been nearly burned, but it hadn't left a mark. Maybe I could safely handle magic on its own. I placed one hand on the lock. Sparks flew from the lock in a stream of colors that must be from S'ami's talented hand. The static has gathered under my palm but I didn't flinch. Without the steel pin there, it wasn't hurting. I let the fizzing and crackling build to a crescendo. I should have pulled away, but after a moment it tickled more than stung. The static kept building into a ball beneath my outstretched palm and then suddenly burst.

My hand tingled. I shook a few sparks free.

The lock fell open with a clank.

Valeo strode over and looked from the lock to me and back again. "How in all Kuldor did you do that?"

"I'm not sure." It had just happened, just like that. I hadn't known it would and I wasn't certain I could do it again—or *would* do it again. Simply holding my hand in place had taken all the courage I'd ever had. My skin smarted from it, and I rubbed it against my dress.

I looked up at Valeo. "What now?"

He shoved one of the double doors open and nodded toward the black interior. "Alright, I'll take the bait. After you. But touch nothing."

I edged sideways into the doorway.

"I mean it," Valeo said. "Touch nothing."

"Mmm, can't hear you," I muttered.

I was in.

# 16

*By their blood, I shall choose giants for my guards. Let them guard my Temple and my person, let them stand forever tall between my enemies and me as an unmovable wall.*
—*Verisimilitudes 10,* The Book of Unease

We slipped into the stifling darkness. I became aware of shelves piled high with black, bulging masses. I assumed they were sacks of people's belongings seized in the raids of their homes so many six-days ago. I took a few shaky steps forward and felt the jab of something sharp-cornered against my side. More shelving. Valeo's hand slipped under my left arm and held me in place.

"Let's wait. Our eyes will adjust," he said.

It took long moments for my eyes to focus, moments in which I let his arm wrap around my waist. I didn't want him to stop, but I didn't want him to get any braver, either. His hand slid toward my hip and I wondered if I should pull away. That would be the proper thing to do, but it wouldn't be the *fun* thing to do. So I stayed put and enjoyed my sudden giddiness while the fabric of my dress slid beneath his fingers. His breath grew heavier, deeper, more labored, and I wondered if he was tired. It was late.

But maybe men got all breathy for other reasons, I wasn't sure. I'd never thought to ask Mami and it didn't seem like the sort of conversation to have with Babba. I wanted to say a prayer thanking Nihil for the feel of man hands, and for Valeo's hot breath on my neck, but I didn't know if there was a pious man-hands, hot-breath meditation. That brought the schoolmistress' stern face popping into my memory and I braced for an imaginary whipping where Valeo's hand rested. Curse that old witch, anyway.

Maybe I should pray for help in the dark. Then it struck me that I'd be praying to Nihil for help defying him. Guilt flashed through me and I quietly prayed for forgiveness in advance, ignoring the small problem that I knew his benevolence to be a lie. The prayer eased my conscience not at all. Then I felt guilty for thinking I wasn't really repentant and ran out of prayers I could say with any degree of true feeling.

A gray shape slipped through the open doors. Bugsy flashed by in silhouette and vanished into the gloom. Valeo leaped away, his body tensed for a fight.

"That creature's here, isn't it." He was accusing, not asking.

I let the vast room's silence answer for me, taking in the stale, stinging smell of mildewing burlap and still air. Valeo pulled me by the waist close to him and drew his mouth close to my ear. There wasn't any affection in his voice.

"You can tell me what you're up to right now. You're putting me in a bad spot, Hadara, if anyone figures out I was here. Talk or walk. Your choice."

"I need only one thing, promise."

I did need only one thing. I'm a clerk's daughter. I've been in warehouses. A warehouse has an office. An office has records and one of those records must be the ledger or bookkeeping scroll or stack of papers I wanted, the one that listed every item the guards seized in the raids. I needed it. Without it, the Azwans wouldn't have any way to know which bundle of contraband belonged to whom. Then they couldn't execute anyone, since they'd have only sacks of junk with no clear owners.

Valeo shook my arm. "What one thing? Something of your family's? You'll never find it in this darkness, unless that Gek creature can smell it."

I shook my head, but he couldn't see it, so I whispered instead. "I need to find the office."

"For what?"

"Why? Losing your nerve?"

He dropped my arm and brushed past me. "Touch nothing."

Was he kidding? I wasn't here for a tour of the place.

All warehouses were laid out more or less the same, so I could feel my way along the front wall to the corner, where the cube-like office would be. Valeo followed a step behind me, a hulking presence, and every so often a patch of satin would brush against me. Even through my clothes, my skin felt more alive, more aware of his movement. I had to remind myself he was also part of the reason I was here, him and his thousand comrades and their brutish looting.

157

I found a doorway by listening for Bugsy's soft clicking.

"What's in here?" she asked. "All I see are your hemp-weaves for your writing."

Hemp-weaves? Ah, the hemp roll. Maybe she'd found the ledger. I stepped forward and she hissed. "He's here! It's him! You didn't tell me it'd be him!"

I tried to sign to her that I had, that I'd explained it all to her impatient self before we left. She'd been too eager to explore the wider world with me, too eager for a chance at going home afterward, and too stuck on the directions I'd given her. Or maybe I'd been too hasty. Could she see my hand motions in the dark?

Valeo bumped into me, and I thought I saw a cold glint of steel in one hand. He also hissed. "Where is that thing? If it comes near me . . ."

I couldn't see Bugsy leap so much as feel it. A clammy mass launched itself in our direction, knocked me aside with a sticky foot and landed, jaws snapping, on Valeo's chest. He batted it away with one hand, and I saw a metallic flash in the other. I was right. He was armed. It looked like a dagger, but the darkness swallowed it up again.

Bugsy squawked and darted out, Valeo behind her, cursing and vowing to finish her off. I froze. If anything happened to her—or him—I'd be responsible. Sneaking, thieving me. The whole weight of all the shelves filled with sacrilegious rubbish pressed down on my already shaky confidence. Maybe I should've waited for Babba to talk to the Azwans, for what good it would've done. Then again, no. I was the only one who stood even a slender chance of getting away with this. The Temple owed me something.

Around me in the darkness came crashing sounds, and Valeo stumbling, muttering curses, Bugsy croaking, "Shaman-killer! Nest burner!" and many other things Valeo was better off not knowing about. I had to make this quick before they drew a crowd or, worse, a constable.

I buried my face in my hands and shook my head. No tears came, but the pit in my stomach ached. The crashing sounds grew farther away but more frequent. They were wrecking the place. After a while, I could see a bit better, enough to make out a few battered desks and piles of papers. I felt along the desktops until my fingertips rested on top of a loosely bound book. I bent in close but couldn't make out a single scribble in the inky blackness. I could only hope this was it.

I crept out into the warehouse proper and softly called for Bugsy. A gray shape formed at my feet, hissing. "This is your fault."

I leaned down and waved the book. I managed to free a few fingers and form the word *please.* She grabbed it, and a small sob escaped her scaly slit of a mouth. Her tone changed to a wail. Bugsy was crying again. I put an arm around her and held her close, feeling her slender chest heaving against my shoulder. "I want to go home," she croaked in my ear. I held her tighter. I wanted to explain everything I regretted, and what she meant to me, and how I wished her beautiful forest hadn't burned that day. In the pitch-black, my hands were mute and useless.

She pulled away and looked up at me. "You kill him?"

I shook my head. Two eyes glinted just a finger's width from mine.

"Please?"

I shook my head again.

She peered over her shoulder into the blackness, where Valeo's form loomed not far away. He'd been watching us. Bugsy snarled at him, flicked her long tongue, and darted toward the doorway, the ledger tucked under an arm. A moment later, her shadowy form had flitted across a single beam of moonlight and was gone.

# 17

*If men were any more complicated, they'd be women.*

—*Feroxi proverb*

The powerful hand that clenched mine held it so tight my knuckles rubbed. Valeo's many rings dug into the skin on my fingers. He dragged me forward, faster than my long legs could keep up, an angry jolt to each of his giant strides. We were out on the wharf, crossing behind the warehouses toward the rows of brightly lit cantinas called Sag Town. Its rotting boardwalks jutted far into a shallow corner of the bay and did indeed sag under our feet. It was not the sort of place a man should take a pious woman. Not at all. As soon as I had realized he wasn't escorting me home, I tried to pull away. Valeo had jerked me forward by the hand until my left arm felt like it would pop from its socket.

"Where are we going?" I asked.

"To give me my alibi." His voice was a throaty growl.

"Meaning?"

Valeo halted, and I nearly plowed into his back. He spun on his heels, a snarl on his rugged face. "You have the Temple's blessing, I don't. Maybe you think you can use whomever you wish, maybe you think you're better than the Azwans at whatever game you're at. I don't have that luxury. If I'd known, Nihil's nuts, if I'd only known . . ."

"I'm sorry." I shrank under his glare. I'd no idea I could upset anyone this way. First Bugsy, now Valeo. I was ruining everyone's lives tonight and had no idea how to make it up to either of them. All I could do is mumble another apology.

"You're not the least sorry."

"My people . . ."

"Are going to be in ten times the trouble if the Azwans think there's anything missing from there. There isn't, is there?"

I stammered. The warehouse had obviously been too dark for him to see the ledger disappear along with Bugsy.

Even in the dark, I could see Valeo grimace as he spoke. "Nihil's damn nuts. What'd you take?"

"Stop swearing. Please." I wasn't so sure he wouldn't hurt me. I remembered how he'd reacted when I'd called him a half-brow—this was a hundred times worse. I'd used him and he knew it and I wanted to sink under the boardwalks in shame.

"And that creature." There was that scowl again.

"She's gone, I promise." Poor Bugsy.

"You promised earlier she was gone."

"This time I mean it."

"Who by all three moons do you think you are? Do you know who I am?"

My voice came out weak and wavering. "First Guardsman Valeo of the something-or-other unit? No different from anyone else?"

Valeo exhaled sharply and looked up and all around, as if the right thing to say were being carried toward him on a breeze. "Here I thought I was the luckiest man on the island because you don't seem to have any idea how beautiful you are to a Feroxi. Tall, willowy, strong, smart. I could go on. Nihil's nuts, I thought we were friends, even. But I could be prince of the sewer-sweeps for how you treat me. Yes, I know, I wanted you to not notice my rank and title and birthright and I don't know what else. If I wanted proof it wasn't an act, I have it now. And that bothers me too. Do I know what I do want? Not really. Maybe. A little. But I know what you're all about, at least. You really don't give a swamp rat's behind for me."

"Oh, but I do!" I could punch myself. I'd gone back and forth on my feelings for him all night, but I'd made up my mind too late. I realized that I adored him and his wise-cracking self and his childhood stories and even his short fuse and rough features. I wanted him to adore me, too, but I'd apparently missed my chance. Stupid, stupid me. "You're right, I don't care that you're a prince. Well, not exactly, though it is amazing. But I do care that I made a mistake and put you in danger and now you hate me enough to swear at me and say such awful things. Or nice things. They were kind of both, weren't they? You said nice, awful things. Oh, please shut me up or I'll babble like this all night."

He sighed. "I'm in this so damn deep right now, I don't even care if you did cast a love spell on me. At least tell me what I risked Nihil's wrath for tonight. What were you up to back there?"

"I was desperate," I said. "I figured you're a Temple Guard, no one would question you if they saw us together."

"So you needed some big, dopey dromedary of a man to maybe batter down a door and lug a few sacks for you," he said, his voice seeped in sarcasm. "Should I have spit like dromedaries do? Or placidly chewed my cud while I waited around for you?"

I shook my head, not trusting my voice to keep from breaking. "I've never seen a dromedary. And please don't spit. I've already said I'm sorry. Maybe you should just take me home."

Valeo shook his head. "Not until you've covered for me. There's a chance I could get us out of this, or at least me."

"Covered for you?"

"My company knows I took you out tonight. I need to be seen with you. It'll help your alibi too. This dopey dromedary has a few tricks of his own."

"Your company?" I peered around him toward the cantinas, where lanterns shone on people spilling onto rickety walkways, singing, waving bottles of spirits, weaving and wobbling and staggering off.

Valeo's hands slid from my shoulders down my back and pulled me closer. I brought my hands up in time to keep him from holding us chest to chest, only to find my arms pinned between us. The silk of his shirt slid beneath my fingertips, and the skin of my palms roused again to the hardness of the muscles beneath. A tremor seemed to go straight through my fingers up the length of my arms, settling around my breasts, the curves and slopes of my torso, all the way through me. I could melt into him and stay that way forever.

His voice sounded breathy in my ear. "Everyone. And they're expecting this."

I gazed up into his brown eyes, his pronounced brow no longer knit in anger. "Expecting what?"

"This." He pressed his lips on mine, sudden and firm. I pulled back. This wasn't what I'd pictured for a first kiss, and certainly not what I'd practiced against my pillow. I pushed against his chest, then angled my head away, expecting to see his frown. Instead, he seemed hesitant, unsure, his eyes roving my face as if waiting for my response. Without thinking, I leaned in again. Rough fingers entwined in my hair near the nape of my neck. His tongue parted my lips and I felt myself opening up to him.

He tasted of salt and sweet, of nectar and tisane—like silk would taste, I suppose, if you could glide your tongue around it. I took in his scent, a mannish mix of warm spices and the outdoors, of breezes carrying aromatic hints of forbidden things. Maybe it was a good first kiss, after all.

"Hadara of Rimonil, is that you?"

A male voice shattered my reverie and Valeo and I pulled apart. I turned toward a lantern held up in my face. I squinted into the sudden, painful light. Beyond it, I made out a yellow constable's uniform, garish even at night. You couldn't miss a constable in our city, ever: they were the color of citrines and could be just as tart. I recognized the constable as the one who'd flirted with me near the boat launch shortly after the Azwans arrived.

"Natanno, how nice to see you."

"I didn't think you were the sort to be out late at night. Does Lord Rimonil know you're here?"

Valeo took a small step forward. "Constable, Natanno, is it? Everything's fine here. I'll take the lady home soon. Promise."

Natanno bristled. I'd overheard at the sick ward that the port watches hated surrendering even a jot of authority to the Temple Guards. It was a kick in the stomach that they somehow couldn't be trusted to police their own turf. Natanno kept his eyes on me.

"I guess you didn't get my courting note, then."

Oh, that poor man. I would've tossed it even if I'd seen it. I suppose I should've sent a rejection note, all formal and apologetic, if I weren't busy breaking into warehouses and kissing soldiers.

"I'm sorry, Natanno. I'll look again for it."

"In the stack, you mean?" The knife's edge in Natanno's voice cut a few lengths from my size. He continued, his voice low and hurt. "I never pegged you for the mean sort, Hadara. But I guess you found someone you like better. What'll you do when his ship leaves? Sort through the stack again?"

Valeo broke in again. "Look, Nutyo, or whatever your name is, we'd love to chat about your love letters. But it's late, yes? And your job is to clear the streets. So if we go, you have no quarrel with us. Goodmoons to you, sir."

With that, Valeo grabbed my hand again and pulled me toward the nearest cantina. I glanced over my shoulder to see Natanno, the lamp held aloft, glaring at me. Valeo drew me closer to him.

"Cover your hair, Miss Meanie."

"What?"

"Mistress Heartbreaker, cover those Nihil-blessed tresses of yours."

I tugged my wrap back over my hair. I hadn't bothered with it since it had come loose. No wonder Natanno had been shocked—me with my hair uncovered, kissing a man, out late at night. I hoped he kept his mouth shut about it. I didn't think he would, and I wondered how long it would take until the first rumors got back to me. Nothing this night was going according to plan, but considering how hastily I'd made those plans, I shouldn't have been surprised. Dismayed was more like it.

That dismay turned to something much worse when Valeo held open the door to the cantina for me. I took one step in and realized I absolutely should've stayed home that night. Or gone anywhere else, like maybe back to the swamps or to one of the moons.

# 18

*Your good name is my gift to you. Defend it well. Build upon your name as the foundation of a house, and tend it as a fertile pasture, that what grows there shall be the virtues of a life well lived.*
—*"The Highest Oblation," Oblations 1,*
The Book of Unease

I walked into chaos: Feroxi everywhere in everyday clothes, all noise and raunchy singing and mugs raised. A few scraggy women danced with heads uncovered, revealing shorn hair that framed their gaunt faces. They wore ragged clothes that bared more flesh than I'd reveal in a bathhouse and gyrated around the men or sat in laps, heads bent toward their customers, whispering.

Prostitutes.

I turned to stomp right out, straight into the solid wall known as Valeo. He stopped me with those oversized paws of his, one on each shoulder, and spun me around again.

"Alibi, remember?" He had to shout in my ear to be heard.

"This isn't a fit place for a proper girl," I said, my voice almost a roar.

"And that wouldn't be you right now, would it?"

"This is wildly inappropriate. Besides, the constable already, and we don't even, not really, I mean and well, this . . . it's, it's . . ."

I wanted to elbow him, but he leaned over and patted my shoulder. "It's just for a bit. C'mon, my friends will love you."

Oh. So this was about his friends. Well, I guess I couldn't really object if he wanted to show me off to his friends, but he'd have to live up to his promise to make this short. Very short. Valeo was already steering me toward a table against a far wall. He'd pressed one hand against the small of my back, part navigator, part owner. I tensed and walked slower. I almost wanted to run outside and scream, but then I'd have to find my own way home with miserable Natanno lurking out there. Still, I didn't have to let Valeo get his way so easily.

I got the creeping sensation I'd been noticed. The noise was dying down and the musicians were setting down their pipes and string instruments. Faces flush with boozy cheer turned my way and fixed glazed stares at me. I lost my nerve again, spinning around to once again find myself blocked by my boulder-sized escort, who wrapped an arm around me protectively. Or maybe possessively. At least it offered a measure of comfort in this wicked place. I looked up at that unhandsome face, and it grinned back at me.

"They're staring at me," I said.

"Well, of course they are. That's the whole point."

"There are prostitutes."

"They're not the ones interested in you."

Honestly, the man made me fume. Maybe I should change my mind about him. Did he have to have a sarcastic reply for everything I said? Couldn't he just kiss me again and shut up? I didn't want to be kissed in front of this nasty bunch though. Just looking at them made me feel like I might catch something.

Valeo nodded to a few men in the crowd and the music picked up again. What a shame I'd never, ever be able to share this with Amaniel. I'd never know the instant comfort of her shocked look, or her words of shared outrage and sympathy. She'd be much too angry with me to pat my arm or reassure me how awful I must've had it. Maybe I would tell her anyway. The shocked look had to be worth it.

I glanced down at the rickety chair he'd led us to and wondered if it would snag a hole in my dress. Before I could move, Valeo had plunked himself into it and patted his lap. There didn't seem to be another chair anywhere, so with as many frowns and grimaces as I could muster in one small instant, I plopped into his lap and then did my best to ignore him. I pushed away the arms that wrapped around my middle, but he just laughed. What was so funny? I turned to scold him but he'd buried his face in my neck and was making soft "mmmm" noises. He gazed up at me with eyes that suddenly seemed much bigger and browner and rounder and—if I didn't know him any better—almost adoring.

Maybe he needed me to stomp his foot again. He seemed to sense my unease and held my head to his shoulder and murmured into my ear. "It's alright. My brave Hadara. My naughty, thieving, law-breaking girl."

I made a sad face and puckered my lower lip. "So have I made it up to you yet? We can go home now, right?"

Valeo chuckled. "Not even close," he joked. "Though you're on my good side for being the prettiest woman here."

I glanced around at the other women. "But they're all … you know."

I sighed. A lot of these women would be patients in the sick ward tomorrow with welts and bruises after their customers sobered up and got all pious again. I then had a thought that made my stomach do a somersault.

"You don't do this, do you?" I said. "Patronize these prostitutes? Send them to the sick ward?"

Valeo jerked back, his brow instantly crinkling darkly. "No. I don't. I'm with the company I prefer."

"And …"

"And let's try to enjoy ourselves."

"Can we go yet?"

Too late. A Feroxi threaded his way among the tables toward us. He pushed a man off a chair at the table next to us, dragged the seat to our table, and dropped into it. His graying blond hair framed a square-jawed face and cold blue eyes. I'd seen that stare before.

Valeo nodded toward the man. "Commander."

The commander called to a woman carrying a tray of bottles. "Over here."

Like that, it was done, and a lopsided bottle and three battered tin cups were set before us. I wondered if he ordered his own mother around like that. Probably.

He spoke in Fernai. I pretended not to understand.

"Make up your mind whether you love her or hate her," the commander said. He didn't even look at me. "I have fifty coppers riding on the outcome."

Valeo picked up the bottle, poured two cups, and handed one to the other man. "When I set my mind to something, you'll know."

He took a sip and leaned back. They were sizing each other up, that much I gathered, but why? Didn't they already know each other? Maybe men are such unknowable creatures that even other men can't figure them out.

The commander smirked and leaned toward us, speaking in a conspiratorial hush, still in Fernai. "She's trouble. I know it, you know it." He glared at me, as if daring me to contradict him. He couldn't know I understood his language, so I sat wordless and wide-eyed.

Valeo shifted under me to bring his own face close to the commander's and answered in Fernai as well. "Nihil has something of mine, and I have something of his. It's a fair trade, isn't it?"

I managed to keep the smile frozen on my face, glancing from one to another as they spoke, pretending my heart wasn't pounding in my ears. Pretending I was a sweet little thing who had no idea I was the subject of a chilling, under-the-breath chat. What did Nihil have of Valeo's? Maybe dragging him to the warehouse had put him in more danger than I realized.

The commander sipped from his cup and regarded me again. "She's not his, exactly. Though he could change his mind. Iana's dying, remember, and he won't save her. He'll be needing his next wife soon."

"He has thousands of willing women to pick from." Valeo drained his cup, which reeked of something strong and bitter, then refilled it. "Tens of thousands."

The commander shrugged and continued. "Or he could change his mind the other way and you could find yourself with a blasphemer on your lap. That'd be my preference, by Nihil's whims and wishes."

"I know your preference, with all due respect."

The commander narrowed his eyes at Valeo. "You didn't see yourself in that sick ward. Or the other men. My men. Drooling and pissing yourselves, raving about some golden-eyed prophetess."

"The Gek did that." Valeo's voice held firm. "Nihil's made everything right for once."

"Nihil's not here."

"But the Azwans are."

The commander kept quiet for a long moment, swirling his cup and staring from me to Valeo and back again. It was the same disapproving glare from when I'd first met him. Mami and I had helped the Azwans locate the meteorite in the swamp, where the cold-blooded Gek people were keeping it. I'd squished into his boat on the way back from the swamp and had squirmed under the ruthlessness of that same iron gaze.

"You're making her nervous," Valeo said in the common tongue.

"Yes, please, can we go now?" I braved a smile again and stroked Valeo's shoulder. Men liked that, right? Stroke, stroke.

Please take me home before I scream, I wanted to say.

173

Instead, he patted my lap. "My commander is unsure what to make of you. So, tell us, Hadara of Rimonil, why does Nihil like you so?"

I stared at Valeo like he'd suggested I undress in front of everyone. I began stammering something, anything, but nothing really came out. If I were them, I wouldn't have thought Nihil spent a fraction of a moment on me.

The commander shook that big, blond head and resumed talking in his native tongue, still unaware that I could understand every word. I tried not to stare as he spoke. "It's the Son of the Second Moon, praise that brilliant mind. He has something figured out that we don't. And the Fey One must like what he's heard."

Valeo scowled and replied back in Fernai as well. "Commander, you're not seeing. You can reprimand me tomorrow for this, but I'll say it. You heard what happened at the altar. Nihil did witness that. We didn't."

"Meaning?"

The two men leaned so close, their bulging foreheads nearly touched.

"Commander, you think god's gone soft? Or the Azwans? She's got . . . something. I don't know what."

"Whatever it is, our Master will likely want it for himself."

The commander leveled one of the more hateful stares I'd ever gotten and abruptly switched to the common tongue, likely so that I'd get both his spoken and any unspoken warnings. "You remember I warned you, Your Highness. This one's trouble. Worse than your mother, even."

"Leave my mother out of this."

"You're the one who talked of a fair trade. Ah well, you're right." The commander raised his cup in a sort of salute. "Nihil lift all doubts from our brave queen."

Others at nearby tables overheard and raised their cups and mugs and entire bottles. To my vast relief, they all used the common tongue, so I didn't have to figure out how to act ignorant any longer.

"To our brave queen," came the cries. "Thorns and thistles!"

Bottles and mugs started raised at all the other tables, as well, answered by a basso and boisterous rendition of "Thorns and Thistles," the song I'd heard on the wharf when their ship arrived.

*Thorn and thistle and brave men bristle*
*Lest flesh be torn to shred;*
*Thistle and thorn, the roses adorn*
*Be careful where you tread.*

Valeo stood and I hopped off his lap. He raised his cup and acknowledged their tipsy tribute. I know a forced smile when I saw one, but I didn't feel sorry for him exactly. He probably couldn't ever truly get away from his background, no matter how he tried. Valeo put an arm around me and spoke to the crowd in the common tongue.

"And to our un-doubtable hostess, the blessed Hadara of Rimonil."

"To Lord Rimonil and his beautiful daughters!" one man shouted.

Another added, "Human or not, I'll drink to that."

Somehow I didn't think that's the kind of compliment my father would want to hear. Nor had I realized they liked their Sapphiran hosts enough to learn our names. Like Valeo, I was also developing a talent for smiling through gritted teeth. If this kept up, I'd grind them down to nubs before the night was out.

Another Feroxi rose and bobbed unsteadily before us. "Hey, guardsman your highness Valeo, tell us how you do it. Eh? Holy and lucky and endowed and all that in every which way, brow to foot, you are."

Someone else added, "Especially where it counts."

That brought roars of laughter and jokes from every direction. I turned to go, dreading where this seemed to be going. The shouting came from every direction while I covered my ears.

"Not human at all, that."

"Not half-cocked, is he?"

"Guess blessed Hadara won't ever be doubtful in that regard."

"The royal family jewels is a quite the treasure, eh?"

More laughter and back-slapping and boorish grunts of approval followed their filthy talk.

I gripped Valeo's sleeve so hard I thought I'd rip the satin off it. He silenced the crowd with a wave of an arm, his tone genuinely irritated. "Is nothing sacred to you lot? This woman is sanctified. She offered up her own soul to save our Master. And this is the language you use? Show more respect."

The entire room rose unsteadily to their feet and the music stopped again. Cups and mugs waved in a toast. Valeo tried again. "To blessed Hadara."

The shouts came back: "Blessed Hadara of Rimonil."

"To House Rimonil."

"So be it."

They tossed back their drinks while I felt a blush creep the length of me, which no one could see under all my coverings.

He nodded. "Time to go."

"Yes, I think your friends have spotted me by now."

I pulled my wrap tighter around my hair and we were gone with a final wave to the crowd. Out in the street, I fumed and he whistled. His arm was around my shoulders, his step light and untroubled. He gazed up at the stars. "Not a bad night, after all."

"That was disgusting."

"I'm sorry. I guess I was still angry when I brought you there."

I sighed. "Alright. You were angry. Now I am, too."

"So no more kisses?"

I flashed him a dirty look, which he couldn't see by the dim torchlight of the alleyways. We slowed our pace.

"I have to sneak into my bedroom without waking anyone," I said at last.

"Oh." He sounded crestfallen.

I elbowed him. "It was a nice kiss, I suppose."

"You *suppose*?"

"I don't have any other kisses to compare it with."

There was that smirk again. "I can fix that."

This time, his lips tasted of that awful brew he'd been drinking, but I didn't mind. We had a few luscious moments before the hailstorm known as my parents broke around me. I could sense it coming, both from the lateness of the night and what I knew of my parents' sleeping habits.

That storm waited at the end of the row of pretty houses on our street, ready to lash me from every window and doorway. They were all lit up, every one, as though every torch and lantern we'd ever owned was in use. My house was one big, fat beacon.

Waiting.

For me.

# 19

*I am a restless creature who flouts the prudent course, who seeks shadows instead of light, then would reverse myself. This I want and then that, to take risks and then retreat, to settle down and then wander, to weave and then rend.*

*Do not begrudge me this urge or say that I am fickle. You are made this way yourself, after me.*
—*from Verisimilitudes 1,* The Book of Unease

I stopped for a long moment in front of my lit-up house, wondering if I should run off and hide out in the swamps forever and ever. That might be better than the tongue-lashing that awaited me. Valeo took a step sideways, away from me, as though we'd already been caught together.

"I've had bad luck with irate fathers," he said. His voice echoed down the street, ruffling the blanketing calm of early morning.

"I'm in this by myself?"

He shrugged. "Guess so."

"What about *my* alibi?"

"What'm I to say? Not to worry, my Lord Portreeve, we only broke into a warehouse together."

"You kissed me!"

"Oh, and I kissed her, too." Valeo cocked his head at me. "That'll help, I'm sure."

"Sarcasm. Nice."

"Just returning the favor, Mistress What-Gek-I-don't-see-a-Gek."

I didn't have time to retort before Babba stepped out into the entry courtyard, dressed in a simple longshirt and trousers, his arms crossed on his chest. He stared lightning at me. I'd be hearing thunder, too, judging by that look. I swallowed. Hard.

Babba's voice was quiet, like an earthquake is quiet before everything topples on you.

"Hadara."

"Babba. I can explain. I promise."

Valeo decided to chime in after all. "May I apologize, Lordship . . ."

"I believe you've done enough, guardsman." Babba scowled. "I'll be lodging a complaint with the Azwans in the morning. My daughter isn't included in your wages."

"Of course, sir." Valeo backed up as if to go. "Good-moons, sir."

That might've been that if Constable Natanno hadn't also stepped out of our house and folded *his* arms across his gaudy yellow uniform like he had Babba's same right to be angry. I gasped. Out of the corner of my eye, I could make out Valeo's features hardening into something much, much lower than contempt.

Babba nodded toward Natanno. "Thank you, Constable."

"Your Lordship." Natanno bent and retrieved his lantern from a bench near the gate. I recognized it only after he'd picked it up and wanted to kick myself. And him. I'd enjoy burning his courting note or sending it down the toilet hole in the bathhouse later.

Babba opened the gate for Natanno to exit, his eyes never leaving my face. Natanno slipped out, only to have Valeo grab his arm.

"Just a moment, Constable."

"Off me, Feroxi, or you'll be kissing the dirt floor of our jail next." The warble in Natanno's voice sounded less than convincing.

"And what law would you be upholding, exactly?" Valeo's face set even harder. A constable had no authority over him, and I could see in their faces both men knew it.

Babba interrupted. "Pious guardian of Nihil's person, I'm sure you won't mind if the constable escorts you to your ship, in case any other young women should tempt you from the certain path along the way. I hope that when I speak to the Azwans tomorrow they'll have your assurance I was being overcautious."

That would've silenced the entire cantina of randy guards. I'd never heard such a mix of sarcasm, flattery, and threat all in one. It was sublime. Did being a lord bestow amazing powers of eloquence? I wished he'd become lord earlier. I could've threatened every girl who'd ever snubbed me with a speech from him. I'd have had the most blissful girlhood in city history.

Then I remembered I was due for a private audience with the same newly made aristocrat. I slipped through the gate, my head bowed, and waited for Babba in the courtyard. The gate clanged shut on the two younger men. The slow, unsure retreat of their footsteps echoed on the cobblestones.

"Babba, you cannot believe a word of what Natanno—"

"Inside." Babba's voice was hard as a drumbeat.

I hesitated long enough for the sound of scuffling to carry from outside our gate. Natanno yelped in pain, followed by the distinct slap of fist meeting flesh and another shout. I didn't move so much as an eyelash—and wouldn't have even if Babba hadn't been holding a hand up for me to stay put. Babba went out the gate and disappeared down the street, leaving me alone in the courtyard, but not for long.

Mami poked her head through the doorway. "Where's your father?"

"Down the street with the constable," I said.

"Is that him I hear fighting?" She emerged in her night-dress, her face knit with worry. I shook my head.

The sounds of flesh-thumping ceased, followed by Babba's voice, his words indistinct but his tone unmistakable. Some men yell when they're angry; Babba lowers his voice to an undercurrent, slow and strong and impossible to fight. I would've liked to have heard what he was saying to the two men. (And to have been there to beam grateful rays of sunshine at Valeo. Imagining him pounding that constable into pebbles was going to get me through the rest of the night.)

The gate clanged shut behind Babba and the lightning stare returned. My smile vanished and horror, shame, guilt—pretty much every bad feeling I could name smashed into my head at once. I had to shake off feeling like a naughty eight-year-old. The Temple, the city, everyone considered me a fully grown woman. I had a right to come and go as I pleased.

Didn't I?

Babba's face dissolved into a fierce, twisted frown. "A Feroxi. And not just any Feroxi. *That* Feroxi. Have you forgotten Widow Reezen? Have you forgotten who raided our home?"

Mami cut him off. "Not here. Inside."

I tugged my wraps around me and pushed open the door to our home. Amaniel peered from a doorway, then withdrew. I wanted to snap at her, tell her to go jump in a canal. But I'd be doing the same as she if our situations were reversed. I felt worse when I realized I didn't see Bugsy or the ledger.

"I was trying to help the city, Babba," I said.

"Quiet," he said. "You'll speak when I tell you."

Babba clutched something in his hand he'd brought in from outdoors. I realized with a start it was a redbeam switch. I hadn't had my bottom swatted since I was Rishi's age. "You've no right to do that to me. I'm too old for that."

To my amazement, Babba nodded. "Your mother gets the honors."

Mami took the switch from him. "Bend over, Hadara."

"But Mami—"

She erupted. "Just because your father is an important man now doesn't mean you can run off as you please. I'll not have people saying I raised my daughter to be some wild, untamable creature. Bend over."

I took a huge breath and tried not to whine like a toddler. "I am sixteen and can——"

"You live in our house," Mami said. "And while you do so——"

"Mami!" Was she really going to give me the "you'll live by our rules" lecture? And then switch my bottom? Maybe I shouldn't have bothered to return at all. The swamp as a permanent home was sounding better by the moment. Where was that stupid Gek with the ledger?

"Listen to your mother," Babba said. "You have no idea what went through our heads with you missing."

*And rightly so,* I thought. If they knew what I'd really been up to . . . but my mind was already circling back to poor Bugsy. Was she lost? She was missing, too. Hadn't they noticed that? She couldn't find her way back to the swamps; all she knew was our home. What if she couldn't find her way back here through all those unfamiliar streets and canals? I pictured her flicking her tongue on the cobblestones, trying to find the scent of our home. That's what I really deserved the switching for—for losing Bugsy.

*Crack!* The switch hit my bottom. I still had my dress and underclothes on. The blow barely registered. Mami obviously needed lessons from my old schoolteacher on how to do this properly. What's more, Babba'd turned away and had his right hand tented over his eyes. Was I going to get the "this hurts me more than it hurts you" lecture, too?

This had to stop. I hadn't planned on telling them about the real reason I'd snuck out and my brief stint as a burglar just yet—I hadn't gotten that far in my planning. But it didn't look like I could delay any longer.

"Look," I said. I grabbed the switch from Mami's hand. "Bugsy and I got the ledger from the Azwans. We saved the city."

She tried to grab the switch back but I was taller. I held it over her head like I was taunting Rishi with a piece of candy.

Mami fumed. "How dare you. If you can behave like a child, you'll get treated like one."

This was turning into a festival of favorite scolds.

"Did you say *ledger?*" Babba had turned around and was giving me a quizzical look. Babba with his ear for business talk had heard me even though Mami had ignored me entirely. I wanted to hug him.

"It's a record of all the stuff the soldiers seized. They won't know whom to arrest without it."

He took a few steps forward and opened his mouth, but Mami took over in her there's-no-arguing-with-me voice. "Rimonil, we discussed this. She needs to learn—"

"Did you hear what she said, Lia? There's some sort of record of the evidence. Where is it?"

"Bugsy has it." I could tell from the looks they exchanged that this was going to need some explaining. "I broke into the warehouse, Babba. With Valeo. And Bugsy. We, I, got their ledger. I just owed Valeo a kiss. You know, for his help."

Mami gave me a hard, squinty stare. "Where did you learn to lie like this? Not from me."

"Babba, tell her." I turned to enlist Babba's help but his face was unreadable.

"I'll be in our room, Lia."

"Babba! You can't—"

He wheeled around. "Hadara, shut up when we tell you. Truly. And next time, think on what you owe your family's honor while you're doling out kisses to strangers."

Mami held out her hand for the switch and opened her mouth for what I was sure was a lengthy and loud lecture on our family's honor and what people thought of us and me being an untamable beast. I'm not really sure, as she never got to give it.

A shout came from outside. It was Natanno again, loud and insistent, rattling our gate like his life depended on breaking it down.

"Fire, Lord Portreeve," he shouted. "Fire on the wharf."

Babba raced from the bedroom and was outside before Natanno had finished. Mami and I peered through a slat in the window covers. A red glow lit the horizon south of us, distinct from the sunrise that would be breaking soon to the east. Natanno called again: "A warehouse, m'lord. Next to the Customs House."

A warehouse—my warehouse. I grabbed my wraps from a hook by the door and tossed them around me.

"Where do you think you're going?" Mami said.

"To prove my innocence."

"Innocence? You mean that? Then I'm coming, too."

I savored the confused look on her face that said she didn't know whether she believed me. She made me agree to wait while she dressed and gave a few quick instructions to a still-not-sleeping Amaniel, who gaped at us but didn't object. I knew my sister would be furious she was once again missing out on the excitement, but I'd give anything to be the pious, good girl who never made trouble, just for a few moments, and just to see what it felt like. Would it feel safe? I liked the sound of that. Safe. Unworried. Content.

But there was no time for contentment. Mami and I raced out the gate Babba had left open in his haste, toward where fierce curls of smoke lifted into the receding night.

20

*Surely the stars will sputter out and the sun extin-*
*guish before people turn from wickedness.*
—*from Verisimilitudes 5,* The Book of Unease

A fire horn blared in short, clear bursts as Mami and I sped along Callers Wharf toward the Customs House. Even from a distance, we could make out flames licking through the roof of the warehouse I'd left earlier that night. Hot ash stung my throat and I rewove my head wrap as a veil across my nose and mouth.

At the sound of the horn, men raced across Pilgrim Bridge holding wooden buckets brought from home. They formed hasty lines to fill and pass the buckets along to splash at the warehouse. I tried to plunge into the crowd toward where I thought Babba might be, Mami's hand in mine, but yellow-clad constables blocked our path and redirected us back to the pavilion. Once there, we had to scoot out of the way as Feroxi poured from the Azwans' ships moored beside us.

They didn't have buckets, but they were tall and could reach the spots the human men couldn't. For a time, it looked like humans and Feroxi together might succeed in getting the flames under control. Dawn was sending its first weak beams across the bay, and I began to feel unsure why I'd come. Mami wrapped an arm around my waist and whispered in my ear.

"Did you have anything to do with this?"

I shook my head.

"You swear?"

I nodded. "I left here ages ago."

"Tell me about this Feroxi of yours."

"I don't think he did this, either."

A small crowd of onlookers had gathered around us. I didn't want to have this conversation with so many people about. A rumble through the group turned my focus toward the wharf. Guards parted the crowd to make way for both Azwans. Their faces were stony and set on the warehouse roof.

S'ami hesitated as he swept past us, but otherwise didn't acknowledge that he'd seen the two women with golden eyes. Mami pulled me back from the crowd, which seamlessly filled our places.

"Alright," she said. "Your Feroxi."

"Mami, he didn't have anything to do with this."

"That wasn't my question."

I sighed. How could I possibly explain how I felt? My eyes burned from smoke and sleepiness. What was I supposed to say about Valeo and kisses that seemed a hundred days ago already?

"Well?" Mami shook my elbow. "Do you love him? Nihil help you if you do."

"I don't know, Mami. Do I know what love is?" I knew the corners of my mouth were turning down and I was tearing up. I drew a deep breath to keep a hiccup down.

I became aware of another sensation, but couldn't pinpoint it at first. I uncomfortably shifted when it hit me: some sort of music played at the edge of my awareness, like a soft chime. It vibrated within me in a way that felt all too familiar. This was S'ami's magic. I could sense it without seeing it, without having to stand where I could watch it flow from his fingertips. This was some new power, or a boost to my existing one. Either way, it was unwelcome.

"Do you hear that music?" I asked, on the off chance there was a more ordinary explanation.

Mami looked over her shoulder toward the warehouse, where the flames leaped to new heights. "Now? Where would there be music?"

I cursed my queer ability. I was feeling more foreign to myself every moment. "There's something wrong."

The fire wasn't going out, but up. Something S'ami was doing was making matters worse. I grabbed Mami's hand and tugged her along after me.

"Hadara, we can't go over there."

"We have to, Mami. There's something wrong." I felt it—a sour note in the music, a ferocity and anger to the magic that twanged to my awakening sense of it.

I pushed against the stubborn constables, shouting that I had to see the Azwan, right now, very important. Enough people recognized me to let us squeeze through to where the Azwans waved their arms above the bucket brigades. The water was going where they directed it, but stronger flames answered them. Sparks flew to other rooftops, including the Customs House. It was only a matter of time, maybe moments, before neighboring buildings caught fire, as well.

The closer I got, the better I could sense the other Azwan, Reyhim, also channeling in his weaker way. The beams of sparkling spells clashed in mid-air, the two magic users working at cross-purposes, fighting each other. Whether that was deliberate, I couldn't tell.

Mami leaned close to me. "I don't like getting this near to these men. What are you doing?"

"I'm going to help," I said. Though I wasn't sure how yet.

I pushed closer to S'ami, who turned his head to watch me. I reached one unsteady hand toward the flashes of colorful sparks that emanated from the wisdom knot, a rainbow of power that I knew only I could see. With Mami gently trying to tug me away, I managed to lay one hand atop the Azwan's. The same charge coursed through me as when I'd opened the lock on the same warehouse doors.

S'ami gave me a wary side-eye. "I trust you aren't holding my hand because you like me."

I held my hand steady, frowning, and waited. S'ami returned his attention to his spellcasting. I realized he was waiting for me to do something, anything. This was a test, then. The thought crept up that perhaps he'd started this fire, or made it worse, but I returned my focus to the static that flickered between the palm of my hand and the back of his. I didn't think anyone around us could see, except Mami, who was keeping her eyes trained on my hand against the Azwan's.

The pulsing from the totem grew stronger and more flames shot through the warehouse roof. He was adding to it, then. My emotional state was already too raw to take in this new fact—that one of the highest of all high priests could be endangering the city to make some sort of point or probe the limits of my weird talent. I flinched, distracted by my knot of irritation, as the flashes of magic ceased. They balled under my wrist and imploded, leaving behind only a tingling. The flames on the roof died down as the buckets of water finally reached their mark, helped along by an oblivious Reyhim's spellcasting. The brigades brought the flames under control again.

S'ami again eyed me sideways and gave the shortest of nods before withdrawing his hand from mine. "You were supposed to tell me when you developed any peculiar new powers."

"How did you know?"

"Don't undo any more warding spells of mine."

With that, he turned his back to me, leaving me with Mami all wide-eyed and clingy. "What new powers?"

"I'll explain later, Mami, please. Let's go."

"What did you just do?"

"I can't explain it exactly. I can undo some of the magic . . . not all, I don't think," I stammered. How could I ever explain to her, especially with her staring up at me with such a worried look? "This is the wrong place, Mami. I can't explain it here."

"But you wanted to come!" She scowled at my change of heart. "We should at least find your father. Then you can tell us both."

I nodded. Yes, Babba. Exhaustion caught up with me then, pounding between my ears, making my head nod and my lip quiver and my shoulders droop. I rested my cheek on Mami's shoulder and let her fold her arms around me. "Hadara, if something was going on with you, you should've told us. Were you afraid we wouldn't understand?"

I nodded, my cheek brushing the fabric on Mami's wrap. I never, ever cried, yet here I was, a sniffly, hiccupy mess, and this time dissolving in public, no less. I could only muster up enough dignity to let my mother dry my eyes and lead me toward where she thought Babba might be.

"There'll be an inquest," she said. "If you were in that warehouse, you'd best say so."

"I swear, I—"

"If your father doesn't make an example of you, he'll be accused of favoritism. Corruption, even."

"But Mami, I—"

"My instincts are never wrong on such things," she said, though not really to me any longer. She was focused on the crowds ahead, and on some distant spot where my father might be. "And then we must address this new talent. It must be related to your sacrifice. It is, isn't it? That's why the Azwan wasn't surprised. How complicated this makes things."

We both lapsed into silence, me sullen, Mami thoughtful, both of us worried. I didn't hear my name being called in the Gek tongue at first, a low croak that couldn't get its long, narrow tongue to hit the "d" in my name. The voice came from somewhere behind me, and I paused, tugging Mami's sleeve to stop.

"Do you see him?" she asked, meaning Babba.

193

"It's a Gek, Mami."

"What would a Gek be doing here?" She peered into an alley where we'd stopped. I couldn't see it either, and it didn't sound like Bugsy's frantic chitter. This was deeper, lower, more adult.

There. A pink tongue flicking in the shadows. I stepped forward, Mami beside me, the two of us peering into the grayness where the first rays of sun had yet to reach. It could probably see me standing in the twilight, so I signaled a greeting.

A Gek crept forward, crouching, flicking its tongue in every direction, its hide camouflaged a dusky gray. It held a large, brown package in its arms, which it shoved at me before darting back to the safety of the alley. It was a book, and not just any book.

The warehouse ledger had found its way back to me.

Before I could react, the Gek chirped from the shadows. "Shaman-daughter is with us. We come to show we can burn nests, too. Then the star will come back to *us*. It was a mistake to let you leave us."

I stared after it as it retreated to the safety of the alley, wondering how on all Kuldor I was supposed to warn everyone.

"Was that a Gek?" S'ami's voice boomed behind me. I nearly dropped the ledger.

S'ami peered into the alley. "What's it want? What did it hand you?"

Mami spoke up, and I wished she hadn't. "It gave Hadara this book of some sort."

A moment later it was in S'ami's hands, the pages flipping under his fingers, his eyebrows crinkling as he studied the contents. It snapped shut in my face as he spoke. "It would seem the warehouse isn't a total loss."

"We have to go," I said. "We have to leave here now."

S'ami kept staring at me. "What did the Gek say?"

Mami shook her head. "It didn't give us any signals, Most Worthy. It just shoved the book at Hadara, croaked at us, and ran."

I swallowed. "We have to go. All of us. Now."

S'ami nodded, slow, deliberate, understanding. "Then let's go."

He turned toward the crowd by the warehouse, the bucket brigades having disbanded to a loose gathering of sweaty, panting volunteers. "We're under attack. Guards, your weapons."

Men looked at S'ami in confusion.

Then flaming arrows rained on the surrounding rooftops, sparking a half-dozen small fires. The alleys and walls erupted with Gek and their crude weapons, unleashing sudden streams of human blood.

## 21

*The warrior's life is one of constant readiness, or it is his death.*

*—Feroxi proverb*

"Fall back! Fall back!" The commander's voice rang out from beyond the throng of men. Mami grabbed and pulled me toward the waterfront. People around us screamed, tripped over long skirts, women pulling children to their feet and scrambling together toward the Azwans' ships. There was nowhere else to go. The Gek popped up from what seemed like every rooftop in the commercial half of the city, backing us into the Grand Concourse with a hail of arrows and javelins.

The fire horn sounded again and the commander ran near me, shouting. "Stop that Nihil-blasted thing! It'll only bring more unarmed men. Don't you have a battle signal?"

The horn changed its call to a complex rhythm I didn't recognize. No one in Port Sapphire did. I whipped around to see a score of men racing across Pilgrim Bridge toward us, unarmed and unready. We'd never heard a battle horn here before. The crowd by the Grand Concourse waved them back, frantic, people pushing and shoving their way to the bridge.

An arc of blue light caught the corner of my eye. It shimmered above a crowd of men by the Customs House. S'ami and Reyhim had erected a shield of light, but I remembered from the swamp how it had singed everything it touched. It would be no help if it saved the Azwans but razed half the city.

I began weaving back through the crowd as Mami tugged at my dress. "What are you doing?"

"Something's wrong again."

"How would you know? Hadara, what kind of power are you supposed to have?"

I halted, the panicked crowds shoving me back, parting and dodging around me. I took in their panicked faces, the smell of sweat, the soot on damp foreheads, the trickles of blood on limping, staggering forms. These were my people in the only home I'd ever known. I couldn't bear the thought that the Gek had come here because of me. Had I brought this disaster on my own city? A part of me answered a solid *yes*.

Mami whirled me around and shook me by the shoulders. "Hadara, you're going into shock. Wake up. We have to go."

"Mami, no. It's the demon."

"What crazy talk is this? The demon's gone."

"It's not." I knew that had to be true, that everything S'ami had said and that the Gek had wished for was real. The Gek wouldn't be interested in taking over our warehouses.

This was about clearing a path back to the demon. To me. I knew that as certainly as I could see the fleeing forms around me, thrown into crisp relief by the sun's first rays. The Gek knew the star was within me—they'd intended that, and they wanted it back, with its human host intact, or else I couldn't explain why they'd warned me of their attack.

Mami shook me again. "Stop that. You're scaring me."

"The demon didn't die, Mami. Not completely. I need to find S'ami."

I let Mami's shock register for a moment before grabbing her again and pushing forward. I wasn't used to seeing her befuddled and it bothered me. I almost preferred the angry Mami with the switch to the lost Mami huddling against me as I forged a path with my elbows and shoulders against the tide of bodies. It took longer than it should've to go the dozen body lengths to where the Azwans had retreated beneath their shield of glowing cyan. The Feroxi were regrouping behind them, pouring off their ships with armor and weapons. The commander was everywhere at once, urging with his voice, his face reddened in fury.

"No snake defeats a Feroxi. No scaly vermin wins a second time against Nihil's own."

A familiar voice boomed beside us. Valeo dashed in front of us, fully armored, sword at his side. "Lady Lia, this is no place for women right now. Take your daughter across the bridge to the Ward."

Hearing her title stiffened Mami's back and she regained her bearing. She leveled a cool, detached gaze at Valeo. "My other children are behind enemy lines, it would seem, as is my husband. And you'll not tell me where to stand in my own city when it needs me most."

"You are needed at the Ward, Lady." Valeo didn't budge.

I put a hand up to stop him. "I need to get to the Azwans."

"You'll go no further."

The commander's voice interrupted us, blasting above the crowd. "Guardsman Valeo, get those women out of here and take up your position."

Valeo thumped his chest in salute. I saw my chance and darted around him, making a break for the flash of amethyst amid the crimson-clad soldiers. I dodged other soldiers as they scrambled into place behind the blue shield that covered much of the pavilion. Beyond it, the Gek warred on the merchant ships, a number of sails already ablaze, decks crawling with their lithe forms. The roofs of warehouses either sported scores of Gek or flames.

I wanted to scream at them that we should all be on the same side. We all wanted the same thing, Gek and human, swamp dweller or Sapphiran. We wanted the Temple out of our lives. But it was to the Temple I had to turn.

I reached S'ami out of breath just as Valeo lunged for my elbow and missed. "It's me they want, Azwan. If you give me to them, I think they'll go."

I was between both Azwans and both cocked their heads toward me. Reyhim spoke first, breaking off in the middle of a mumbled spell.

"And how would you know this?"

I turned to S'ami. I didn't know how much he'd ever told his colleague about me, given their rivalry. He stopped his musical chanting. "She knows, Reyhim. They've already approached her."

Reyhim shot me a quizzical look. "They hand-signaled you? Here? This morning?"

I nodded. That was mostly true, after all.

The two men continued their spellcasting for a moment. Valeo edged me aside. "My apologies, Son of the Second Moon. She got away from me."

S'ami didn't take his attention away from his task. "She'll go to the Ward. The healers will need her."

I shook free of Valeo. "No, please. Listen."

"You listen," S'ami was curt. "We are not surrendering you to the Gek for any reason."

Mami spoke up from behind me. "What is this about the demon being inside her?"

Reyhim whipped his head around. His section of the blue shield sputtered. "Who says this?"

"Hadara does, Most Worthy." Mami didn't change the tone of her voice. "I thought it was something you both knew and were keeping from her father and me."

A hail of javelins shot across the hole in the light shield, some clattering near us.

S'ami's voice cut off Reyhim's reaction. "Your spell-casting, brother."

Reyhim shifted his gaze to the shield and raised his totem, but his half of the blue sphere sputtered and sparked.

"A rather large detail to leave out of your reports to our Master," Reyhim said. "If it's true."

"We don't know that it is," S'ami said. He glared at Mami. She glared back. S'ami restarted his spells.

"Mami, please, tell them to listen to me."

"You heard these holy men, daughter," she said. "They're not surrendering you. Neither am I."

Behind us, the commander called for archers, more archers. He pointed to the silhouettes of Gek along the rooftops. "My cross-eyed great-granny could knock those scaly bastards off that roof. Positions!"

Screams and shouts came from north of us, along Callers Wharf. A voice called out, "They've seized the wharf, they've cut us off."

Another voice, "They're at the bridge."

The commander shouted them down. "Retake that wharf."

The Gek must have crept deep within our city before beginning their attack, and the fire had drawn men out of their homes unarmed and defenseless. My stomach churned just thinking about my unwitting role in all this. If I were a Gek leader and had to pick a target to burn, maybe I'd ask the shaman-daughter to point out which building the star-demon human had gone into. It all led back to me. I'd gotten my sisters and father in danger, and so many other people besides.

"Azwan, please," I begged. "I can't go to the Ward now, not with the bridge under attack. Let me go with the Gek and maybe they'll retreat."

S'ami's mouth tightened into a firm line. "By the blood of my own daughter, no."

So I was part of S'ami's plan to topple Nihil, whatever that was and whenever he swung it into action. He wasn't giving another race an advantage over him, even if it should've been obvious to him that he and the Gek hated Nihil alike. He'd made a vow on his dead daughter's memory. I listened to his chanting, my own resolve dissolving into a sense of futility.

The city would be just as ruined if I didn't move soon. And Babba was out there, maybe still alive, and I had to get past this magical shield to stop the Gek from harming him. It all made sense, didn't it? It all pointed to me joining up with the Gek, seeing what they wanted, helping them however they needed. And maybe they had answers about what was inside me. What did the Gek know of the star? I would get no answers from the Azwans, of course. The only answers lay beyond their shield.

I glanced around, frantic for a way to run past the Azwans and their rigid circle of guards. Reyhim shifted closer again. "Get that damned commander over here. What in Nihil's name is going on? We can't conjure this shield forever."

My heart nearly skipped a beat. Would it come down on its own?

The commander trotted over. "Archers are in position, Azwan. Guards from the Ward are defending the bridge but they can't hold it long."

Reyhim's hoarse voice roared in anger. "These vermin are tossing nothing but sticks and rocks. What do you mean you can't hold the bridge?"

The commander stiffened. "We'll hold the bridge, Azwan. With your help."

S'ami cut him off. "Where is the Lord Portreeve?"

Mami leaned in to hear the commander's reply, as did I.

"Last seen near the merchant ships with what was left of the bucket brigades, Azwan. They were tearing off warehouse doors for barricades. Clever, but I'm not sure how long they'll last."

"Can we split the men, get some of them to head toward the merchant vessels?"

The commander peered down at S'ami with a skeptical squint to his eyes. "The bridge to the Ward is the more strategic position."

S'ami didn't even glance at Mami and myself as he spoke. "Then fall back to the bridge."

They were just going to leave Babba and the bucket brigades to die.

I plunged forward, diving under arms before anyone could stop me. It didn't occur to me to expect arrows from my side of the shield until I'd reached it. They called for me to halt—the commander, S'ami, Mami—but I was there. The shield rose from my feet over my head in a long, continuous arc, blue light dancing in waves, static pouring off toward me, fizzing harmlessly around me. My hair began to stick out straight from the nape of my neck, beneath my wrap.

I raised my hand and watched the static leap from the wall of light to my outstretched fingers. I was in dangerous territory—I could tell from the tense, alert pose every man had taken and from how all those eyes peering from all those helmets burned through my back. They'd fallen silent, watching. So had the Gek. Thousands of eyes, human, Feroxi, and lizard, peered at me—anxious, expectant, poised.

Around me lay the ashes of scores of javelins and arrows that had disintegrated on contact. If this came down on anyone's head instead of dissolving, that person was dead. I'd seen what it did to the Gek in their swamp. If I touched it, would it reduce me to a pile of ashes, as well? There was only one way to find out. Babba would be worth this sacrifice in any case. Same with the merchants beyond. That's what a healer agrees to, anyway—to save lives, possibly at the expense of her own. I slapped at the shield, a harsh, back-handed sweep of my arm that sent an arc of sparks. A shock coursed through me, and I collapsed to my knees. I whipped my head up and around to stare straight into the bright, morning sky. Either the shield was gone, or it was less visible in the bright sun.

No, it was gone. I leaped to my feet, ready to run. Behind me, I didn't doubt for a second that guards waited for a signal to open fire on the Gek. It would come whether I was in the way or not. The commander likely didn't care either way.

Ahead of me, the Gek charged. A horn blasted from behind me. I stood directly between the two armies with no way out. I froze, unsure of where, exactly, to head. I aimed for one side, hoping it was the fastest way around. I took three, maybe four, hasty steps when my legs pulled out from under me. My ankles jerked up together, airborne, and my body slammed hard into the cobblestones. My right hand had shot out to break my fall. Pain tore up my crunched wrist. I cried out and writhed around to see my ankles bound with rope, a rock at either end. This was some weapon of the Gek's that they'd tossed like I was a mainland woolass being rounded up for shearing.

Shouting and roaring and the clatter of weapons came next. I curled in a fetal position, as though it could block the arrows and javelins crossing in midair above my head. They made an incessant whine, like the air itself protested. The dull crunch of steel arrowheads hitting walls sent an involuntary contraction through every muscle in my body. Without the magical shield in place, the battle had begun in earnest.

I had to get myself out of there. I could crawl a short ways, pulling knees to chest and extending my forearms along the cobblestones, caterpillar-like. Knees to chest again, arms extend. If I put no weight on my right wrist, I could manage the shocks of pain. I pushed and pulled myself closer, closer, to the Customs House doors. Booted legs thumped my way. I might make it after all.

Then from behind came a massive attack of sticky, clammy fingers. Scores of Gek hands hoisted me up, settled me on numerous narrow shoulders, and hauled me off like ants carrying a juicy bug. "Hold still," they chirped. "You're safe with lizards."

My wrist and ankles throbbed from being toppled when the battle first began. I didn't feel very safe. I couldn't use my injured hand to signal them to put me down, at least not until the pain dissipated. A dozen pairs of boots thundered into place around us and blood splashed onto me. It wasn't mine—Gek were falling all around me. I lurched as Gek stumbled and died until others slithered in and took their place. My stomach roiled, but I didn't have the time or the space for getting sick.

Finally, I landed on several Gek, who didn't move. And neither did I.

"Get your scrawny butt out of here." The voice was Valeo's, and he stood over me, one leg on either side of me. I did my best caterpillar crawl underneath the sea of legs and found myself pulled back by sticky fingers. The fingers let go—cut down by Valeo or his men—and I crawled again. A moment later, I was pulled to my feet by still more guards and carried like a child behind an uneven wall of shields.

I was deposited by the Azwans and teetered until an elbow steadied me. Valeo again. I leaned on his shoulder as he stooped to cut my ankle bonds. A quick glance around told me we were behind a solid wall of soldiers.

I was right back where I had started.

*I gathered all the peoples, human, giant, and lizard,
and told them they angered me. But we did not make
this war, said many in the crowd. You should blame
those who spilled blood and not the innocent, too.*

*No one is innocent, I replied.*
—*from Verisimilitudes 4,* The Book of Unease

Mami pushed my scarf back from where it had fallen over
my eyes and tenderly probed my injured wrist, momentarily becoming the same woman who'd fiercely insisted on
taking me to the swamps to pick herbs. With instinctive,
precise movements, she unwrapped her own head scarf
and wrapped it around my wrist, bandaging it as well as
any healer might. Her own hair remained tightly bundled
in a knot at the nape of her neck, with no apparent care for
the rules of modesty.

"You're a mess," she said, shouting over the din of battle
as she smoothed and tucked me back together. "What possessed you to do that?"

"I'm going to find Babba. And I'm going to see what the Gek want. It's the only way they'll leave us alone."

Reyhim interrupted. "They'll not have you. If we need to repeat that a few more times, you'll hear it in a jail cell."

I tried to mask my fury. "Most Worthy, I could talk to them. And my father's trapped back there."

He pointed across the pavilion. "Not any longer."

A procession of enormous wooden doors clattered and clunked into view from between the rows of warehouses. Some doors faced up, some forward or back or to the side. It looked like some sort of giant, upside-down ship thudding toward us or maybe the scales of a sea monster. Arrows and javelins rained down from every direction. Dozens of men crouched beneath those sooty, battered chunks of wood that they'd pulled off their tracks at warehouses up and down the wharf. They moved at a slow jog, keeping together, never losing their footing despite the drumbeat of missiles. They must have stripped every last warehouse of its doors for their moving barricade.

The Gek scattered to every side, jabbing at the giant, wooden, scaly beast and falling back again. I was watching the triumph of human ingenuity. A cheer went up among the Feroxi. I released a huge lungful of air, not realizing how long or how deeply I'd been holding my breath. Relief flooded through me like a salve for an aching heart as the front row of doors parted to reveal the grunting, heaving humans beneath. There was Babba, in the lead, staggering and lurching to a stop.

A hero.

Behind him, men carried their wounded on yet more of the doors.

The magical shield was gone, vaporized by my earlier effort, so the men only had to make it as far as the line of soldiers, which they did. The guards returned the Gek fire to either side of the wooden barricades and then fell in around them, until every last civilian was behind our lines, safe.

Reyhim extended his arms toward Babba and rasped, "I've never seen a braver thing in my life."

Mami raced up to Babba and held him close. His clothes were soaked in blood. I made to run toward Babba but a large hand held me by my shoulder. It was Valeo. "The Azwans wish for you to stay."

I took another deep breath and held it. On the far side of the pavilion, the Gek regrouped in the alleys and the firing stopped for a few moments, long enough to see the shadows cast behind them by a radiant morning sun. Between us and the Gek were scores of bodies of all three races: Gek, Feroxi, and human. I wondered when was the last time that had happened, if it had ever happened before, all three races on one battlefield.

A low, throaty chirp began among the Gek, beating a steady rhythm, calling and calling, beseeching.

Praying.

I covered my ears, tried not to make out the Geks' words, bit both lips hard and squeezed my eyelids tight. I wouldn't hear them. This wasn't what I'd expected at all. I fought the sudden urge to run. Suddenly, joining them seemed like the entirely wrong idea. Not if they were praying like this—to me. To the star.

My heart thudded in my chest and I couldn't breathe. I closed my eyes and focused on my right wrist, but it was already feeling better, so there wasn't much pain to drive out the incessant, throaty warbling. I felt sick and lightheaded and I expected my knees would give out. This wasn't happening. Everything I hated about Nihil, about the Temple—

"What are they saying?" S'ami asked. "Translate."

S'ami spun me around and grabbed my uninjured wrist. I wouldn't—couldn't—tell him. Not even when Reyhim expressed shock that their hisses, clicks, and croaks were words—and that I could understand them. He asked, "This another one of the girl's strange powers? Is she the demon?"

S'ami turned to me. "Are you?"

I shook and shook my head. "No, I'm not. I'm Hadara of Rimonil. I'm not the undoer, I haven't done or undone anything."

S'ami remained cool. "Is that what they're calling you? The Undoer?"

"I won't translate. It's all lies. I won't."

"Do you mean that?"

I pinched my lips together and kept my hands, even the not-quite injured one, over my ears. I wanted to hear nothing more, not one syllable, of their prayers and odes to me.

S'ami turned to Valeo. "It is time."

"As you wish, Azwan."

The soldier who'd given me my first kiss placed one paw on my right arm and led me away, off toward the Ward and a jail cell and an uncertain fate.

## 23

*Friends are not always the people you choose, but
the people who choose you.*

—*Tengali proverb*

I hated them all. Hated. I hated S'ami and Reyhim and
their clumsy magic and the suddenly worshipful, blood-
thirsty Gek, and even the solid lump of a guard who lugged
me along Callers Wharf. I struggled to match Valeo's long-
legged pace. My frustration found a target and I put the
meanest snarl in my voice I could muster. "So much for
that kiss. You're the worst form of hypocrite, you know
that?"

Valeo's mouth pressed into a single, thin line, but he
kept up his rapid stride, with two other guards falling in
behind us, as we made our way along the wharf behind
a thin row of soldiers. The Gek were still regrouping
and keeping back, sticking to the narrow alleys between
warehouses and the now-doorless doorways. Valeo kept
his eyes sweeping the way ahead of us and said nothing.

I yanked my arm away, hurt at his sudden change. "So, now you're all business again. I suppose last night was just pretend."

He whipped around. "Pretend? Look who's talking. What was our little outing last night but some pretense of yours?"

A few soldiers glanced over their shoulders at us and then whipped their heads back around. I could feel my ears redden. "Never mind. Let's just go."

He nodded. "We're bringing you to the Ward until this is over. Try and cooperate with the Azwans for once?"

"Or what?" Why did it have to always be about the Azwans? Why couldn't they—and Valeo—cooperate with me? It always came down to me being the bad girl, when I'd done nothing wrong.

Instead of answering, however, Valeo put a hand on my shoulder as though to guide me in the right direction, I yanked away, and he reached for my wrist instead—the bad one. I yelped.

He scowled. "I didn't hurt you."

"My wrist. From earlier. When I fell." I clutched my bad hand in my good one.

Strong arms folded around me and straightened me up, staying there until I steadied myself. I felt better leaning against him, and much of my irritation dissolved. I was being awfully hard on him. He was doing his job. I remembered the two Valeos and wondered if the warrior and the prince could ever be at peace within him. Why did it have to be like this?

His body was solid and strong, and that had a healing effect of its own. I'd never admit it to him, but it did. Valeo gently turned my wrist around to look at it. He touched a swollen spot and I winced.

"Sprained," he said. "I don't feel any break."

"It'll be fine. I'm alright, I promise."

Valeo looked up at the other guards. "To the sick ward first." The men nodded.

Well, that was totally unnecessary, and I was about to protest until it hit me: the sick ward, not Ward Sapphire. He'd just found an excuse not to arrest me. I bit back a smile, unless I gave his plan away. I took a good look around me, though, wondering at the sudden quiet. The Grand Concourse flowed before me, easing its way out to the bay, as calm and steady as ever. From behind the railing, two clear green eyes blinked at me.

"What is it?" Valeo said, following my gaze. "Damn them."

The men guarding me had their swords drawn and charged the railing, but the creature had slid into the water and vanished with a few ripples. Once again, I'd hesitated just a moment too long to act.

A voice carried across the water from Pilgrim Bridge. "Behind you!"

Arrows shot to the right and left of me, downing the other two guards, dead. The shafts stuck from their necks. I screamed.

The thin line of soldiers evaporated, men racing toward the pavilion or the bridge—whichever was closest. They'd spread themselves too thin along the narrow wharf, offering no protection from this new assault.

Valeo hustled me along, but I was slower than a Feroxi soldier and twice I stumbled over bodies that fell in my path. We gained some momentum until I slammed into Valeo's back—he'd halted mid-stride. The Gek formed a wide semi-circle, with the two of us dead center, our backs to the waterway.

Valeo thrust himself in front of me, both swords out, scanning the roofs of the kiosks, some of them smoldering, others with moving brown forms along their edges. Wrists flicked back to launch a score of javelins, bow arms flexed as a hundred arrows notched. If Valeo didn't know he was committing suicide, then it was up to me to stop him.

I darted in front of Valeo to face the Gek and I threw my arms open wide. "They're after me. They won't fire at me."

"Get behind me, dammit. I'm protecting *you*."

"You're arresting me, remember?"

I could make out more shadowy forms scuttling down the walls of kiosks and taking on a mottled gray to match the cobblestones. The Gek crept forward, shoulders low to the ground, weapons at the ready, visible only because I knew to look for them. They made no sound, no hissing or croaking or clicking, as they stole forward, stone by stone. But the arrow tips pointing from alleys and doorways didn't fly loose. They wanted me alive.

I knew that already, from their chanting. I drove that out of my mind. I wasn't their Undoer. I wasn't their anybody. I was only Hadara, who'd gotten herself into unimaginable trouble for being a tiny bit more rebellious than usual. I was infinitely sorry, I prayed silently in my head. I won't do this again, Nihil. I'll go back to believing in you. You can be god of all Kuldor or just this one wharf. I don't even need an Eternal Tree. I'll go back to school and memorize your jillion incarnations and your infinite list of long-dead wives and their names and character flaws and birthmarks and favorite tea blends. Just please leave me alone, leave my family alone, leave my entire beautiful, unruly, mish-mash of a city alone.

Valeo pushed my arm out of the way and sprang in front of me again. "I'll take care of them."

A half-dozen javelins soared toward us, missing by finger-widths.

An ugly thought jumped into my head: escaping would be easier if I let the Gek kill him. I hated the idea and hated myself for thinking it. I clenched my good fist and bobbed and weaved behind him, hoping the Gek would think twice before firing, lest they hit me. It worked, and the next volley of javelins was a thin, half-hearted effort that mostly landed wide of us.

Elsewhere, the battle raged as guards fought to get to us across Callers Wharf. Gek arrows flew in every direction, with the guards creeping forward behind walls of shields to either side of us. Valeo and I were alone on this stretch of wharf and utterly exposed. The next volley of missiles wouldn't miss. I ducked under his elbow and in front of him again.

"You can't take care of them. You're outnumbered." I put one foot ahead of the other, staggering my stance so I wouldn't budge when he tried to push me again. He edged me aside like a curtain.

"You're also outnumbered—and unarmed," he said, his broad back to me. His swords were useless here—and his shield was somewhere at the bottom of the swamp.

"They want me alive." I dodged to one side, faked him out, and ducked under his other side. I faced the Gek again, who'd paused on the cobblestones, watching. I panted, my pulse throbbing in my head, sweat trickling down my back.

"They can't have you." He elbowed his way ahead of me, working both swords in wide arcs, yet artfully missing slicing me in half.

"Nihil's earlobes, Valeo. This can't go on forever."

"Nihil's earlobes? That's how you curse?" He batted javelins away. I had never seen that before. I hadn't known it was possible, but he swatted them like sting flies. They split and splintered, ricocheting wide of us.

"I'm the only thing standing between you and the Eternal Tree." If there is one, I added silently. This was a lot of effort for a god I didn't believe in.

A gust of wind blasted my side, sweeping javelins and even arrows wide of us. The wind fizzled around me—magic. The wind hit hard at the Gek, and they fell back to regroup, giving us a moment's respite.

A shout came from the pavilion. It was S'ami, behind a wall of shields. "What are you doing, dancing? Get that woman to the Ward."

Valeo shouted back. "She won't go."

I had to speak up, too, even if no one believed me. "They won't harm me. His Highness won't let me protect him. I can be his shield; it'll work, I know it will."

If it didn't kill us both first.

From the corner of one eye, I could spy S'ami flailing his arms, exasperated. "We'll write ballads about your doomed love. Before we commemorate your tragic and untimely ends, however, do you think you can at least try to move away from the enemy, instead of toward them?"

From further back, Reyhim's gravelly voice carried across the wharf. "We've got wounded here. We need that wharf retaken."

Valeo lowered his voice to a growl. "Alright, then, you go in front."

I obliged, with a sense of triumph, but it was short-lived. The Gek resumed their forward creep. Behind me, Valeo muttered. "Now what?"

"Now we edge closer to the bridge together, with me in front."

We both stepped sideways, one tiny, crab-like move at a time, not daring to make a run for it with the Gek aiming at us from several directions at once. If Valeo and I separated, he was as good as dead.

And I couldn't let that happen, even if it defied all logic.

They rushed us. A thousand shadowy forms leapt to their feet at once, racing at speeds I didn't think any two-legged creature could achieve. Valeo grabbed my arm—hard—and made a run for it. I tried to match his pace, panting, lungs aching, as we raced for Pilgrim Bridge. The men at the bridge charged forward with shouts, echoed behind us from the pavilion. I looked up from pounding Valeo's back to see the guards storming the wharf from that direction as well.

Our long legs made short work of the wharf, but the Gek were faster. They formed a wedge that drove hard between the two halves of the Feroxi pincer, a band of them reaching us as the guards closed in. Then Gek were all over us, shoving us over the railing and into the Grand Concourse.

The waterway caught me sideways, knocking the wind from my lungs. I resurfaced sputtering and began treading water. I needed to get my bearings—quick. I had to get away from any crossfire. Valeo had lost his swords and fought bare-handed, pushing Gek away, grabbing their hands from his throat, trying to work a few swimming strokes in my direction. "Hadara, get out of the water. Get to the men."

I looked up. Guards fought at the edge of the wharf. Several broke free of the battle and were extending hands to us, but the Gek had already pulled us too far to reach. One called to me in a croaking voice. "Come with us, Undoer. We won't harm you."

First things first. I shook my head and tried to swim toward Valeo. He shot up out of the water and was pulled straight down with a look of surprise. The last I saw of him was his fingertips as he strove for safety. The Gek had him. They'd pulled him under.

I dove.

I dove and dove, desperate to see through the murky, green water, desperate to push boats and punts out of the way, knocking my wrist painfully against wooden prows, splashing and parting the water in front of me, toward where I thought he must be. I could make out the gyrations of water and bubbles being forced aside and around and a flash of limbs and boots. I hadn't known how well Gek could swim until I saw them swarming over Valeo underwater, anchoring him to them.

Drowning him.

They pulled at my arms and clothes, dragging me to the surface. "Undoer, leave these nest-burners," one called.

Another croaked. "You're safe with us."

I fought against them to dive again, but I was being pulled and dragged farther from the spot where the river rippled and burbled from Valeo's struggle. I turned toward the nearest Gek and made the sign for *mate*. It was all I could think of. I flashed it again and again. *Mate mate mate mate.*

Several Gek nodded and dived away. Others held me above the waterline and pulled toward where the Grand Concourse fed into Sapphire Bay. I was a strong swimmer, but I couldn't battle the choppy bay even on the best of days, which this clearly wasn't.

Valeo's head burst through the surface and he gasped and gagged. I thanked Nihil for those vast Feroxi lungs and screamed Valeo's name as loud as I've ever screamed anything in my life.

His long arms sliced through the water toward me, and the Gek cleared from his path. The distance between us vanished in a few quick strokes. Water streamed from the gaps in his leather armor. His helmet was still on, stuck over that un-handsome, bashed-up face I was so grateful to see. He sucked giant lungfuls of air as the water lapped against his armor, which sagged on him like a shell he'd outgrown. "I fought them off."

I blinked back tears. "No, you overgrown turtle. I told them you were my mate."

"And here I thought I was a hypocrite of the worst kind."

I drifted closer to him. I wanted to hug him or at least put my arms around him, wipe away the water streaming around his face, but all I could see was the leather and bronze of his armor. I reached my good hand up and brushed my knuckles against his cheek—it was the only part of him I could touch.

My chin quivered. "The Gek will probably take both of us now."

He shook his head, treading water around me, and gave a long, serious stare at the Gek paddling around us. "I can't let them do that."

"Because why? I have to go on some sort of rigged trial? Be made an example of? Like my grandmother?"

"You'll have to trust S'ami. He has it all figured out."

"Trust S'ami? Is this a joke?"

Instead of a reply, Valeo eased his helmet from his head and tapped the bulge in the forehead, the one only half as deep as his comrades' helms. "Had this made for me in Ironhills. Sorry to see it go."

It slid into the water and sank. He undid shoulder straps next, then the buckles along his sides, letting his leather corselet fall away and ease beneath the lapping waves. Two oversized boots bobbed to the surface and began drifting out to sea. "Much better. Ready to swim for it?"

"Swim for where?"

He nodded toward where the Azwans' ships were berthed. "Closest one's the Sea Skimmer."

"The Gek will pull us back."

"Up there on deck."

Both Azwans stood on the bow of the Sea Skimmer, dwarfed by the towering masts. They held their arms up, rays of sun flashing off their gold totems. S'ami must know any spell directed toward me might vanish. I didn't know how to prevent it or how he could help me.

And I knew I didn't want him to. I was going to end this.

I leaned back in the water, feeling the current catch me sideways and tug me along. I did a lazy backstroke, testing the Gek's reactions as much as the waves. The Gek resumed their darting and diving, giving the waves momentum around us without touching us. Valeo swam toward me, only to find the Gek flickering around us like a school of baitfish, bright and silvery and entirely too close.

I took another stroke, my injured wrist slicing the water as well as I could manage, watching as the two Azwans aboard their respective boats cast spells that danced in the air and fell uselessly around me. Apparently, my un-power affected the water, in much the same way as water could carry the aftershock of lightning bolts.

It dawned on me that I was assessing this like I was looking for a weakness, as though their use of magic had a soft spot or a fracture or a hidden tear of some sort. I thought of everything in the way a healer sees things— but these two men represented an infection whose only cure was amputation. They had to go. And only I could make them. Once they were gone, Nihil's influence on our island would fade, too.

So I pushed away from my city and all the people I ever knew, the girls who'd jeered at me and the boys who'd never noticed me at all. The same Grand Concourse I'd learned to swim in towed me out of the reach of every- thing and everyone I loved—the din of the market, the full-throated songs of sailors, the busy sick ward and the kindly healers who ran it. Back on shore, and moving far- ther away, was the mother who'd raised me to find my way in the world. She had given up that freedom for a title. She had made her choice, and I was making mine. Mami would be pacing and fretting, but someplace deep within her, she would know she could trust me out here.

And I felt her presence like a prayer, guiding my arms as I turned around in the water to swim away.

"Where by Nihil's nuts do you think you're going?" Valeo shouted above the waves and breeze and splashing lizardfolk.

I called over my shoulder: "Don't you want to see what the Gek want?"

"No."

I tried a different tack. "You're my guard. So come along and guard me."

Before he could protest, I flipped underwater and raced below the waves. I resurfaced only when my lungs demanded it, popping up many body lengths from the two ships and the arcing currents of increasingly bright, angry spells launched from their decks. The Azwans must have been manic. I grinned and enjoyed the surge of static that built within me as the spells dissipated in the water around me.

"Undoer has decided." A Gek bobbed next to me. A crest atop his head told me he was male, and his small size meant he was their equivalent to a teenager, like me.

I nodded. *For now,* I signaled with my one good hand. *Just for now.*

Valeo lurched in the water at some distance, Gek weaving around him as he struggled to evade them. I took stock of my misery. My wrist had stopped throbbing already but the brackish water stung the rope burns on my ankles. I shivered in the cool current. I'd lost my head wrap some time ago, Nihil knows when, and my loose locks dripped shamelessly down my back. My dress was ruined and clung in all the most immodest places.

My sandals were useless for swimming, and my toes were cold.

And yet I felt good—very good. The rightness of my actions settled deep inside me, like being tucked under warm blankets, tight and warm and cheering. Amidst all this chaos, my actions had made sense, and Valeo and I were alive, and I was finally going to get answers and perhaps find out my purpose in all this. The Temple and its horrors were at least temporarily behind me. I would find answers, and I would return—but whether it was to wield power or authority or what have you in S'ami's terms didn't seem likely, or even appealing.

Meanwhile, Mami and Babba were safe, and they'd see to my sisters. If they could claim I'd been captured by the Gek, I might not have to worry about the shame they'd face.

Yes, I felt good, and even my wrist felt better for being in the cool water. I dragged it through the current as I pushed on.

I turned to the crested Gek, treading water as I signed. "I'm a strong swimmer, but your swamps are too far for me."

He cackled a laugh. "We have logs."

The logs, it turned out, had been hollowed into canoes. The Gek took up crude paddles as we climbed aboard. Valeo clambered into my craft and wordlessly took up the paddle, shooing away any Gek who approached us. He gave me a disapproving look, then I turned to face forward as he quickly caught up to the lead canoe.

That felt right, too. I didn't want to go on any misadventure without my hulking, drooling dromedary of a bodyguard. And he could help me get out of trouble if I needed it. I was beginning to believe he could do anything and that nothing was beyond Valeo's strength and skill, but that was the foolish little girl in me, wanting a hero. Maybe he wasn't anything like a hero, but he was what I had, and he was tagging along.

# 24

*The insurrection began, as ever, as words; some whispered, some shouted, some spoken behind partitions, some delivered in impassioned speeches. The priests heard these words and did their best to cut the rebellion at its stem.*

*The priests scolded: How does one rebel against god? What tools and weapons could you wield against the Temple?*
—*from "The Fall of B'Nai," Verisimilitudes 13,*
The Book of Unease

We didn't head toward the swamps at all, but glided parallel to the shore as it wound southward. The shoreline smoothed out and the fens beyond the edge of the city gave way to stretches of rocky beach.

The remains of the swamp gaped at us blackly, a dreary, ash-covered place. I'd pictured the normal ruins of a forest fire, with scorched crowns and blackened boles in an uneven line. This devastation was complete. Sunlight streamed unfiltered across the skeletons and charred ghosts of a forest that should've been a thousand shades of green. Blackened, bony limbs bore silent testimony to the stilled cries and chirps and calls of all that had fled or died. It was a butcher's boneyard, dead and left to rot.

Neither Valeo nor I spoke or moved much, except to glance back at the charred landscape. The green crept back in slowly when we were far enough to measure the distance in what sailors call rowing lengths, or the distance a twelve-man crew could row in a hundred strokes. We had gone many dozens of rowing lengths before the shore was more verdant than not.

The Gek turned toward a spit of shoreline littered with volcanic rock as black as anything we'd seen in the swamp, but covered with lichen and moss. I waded ashore, my hair a knotted, ratty mess, my limbs still sore from swimming, my skirt stiff with drying saltwater. I was grateful for the heat of the midday sun and suddenly hungry.

Valeo plunked down next to me on a boulder overlooking the log flotilla as Gek shoved their impromptu craft ashore. On land, the fleet looked like a new forest growing sideways across the rocky beach.

"Now what?" Valeo said. He didn't look my way.

"We see what they want." I had so much more I wanted to explain to him, but I sensed it wasn't the time. He wasn't ready.

"We? There is no 'we' here. There's you."

Maybe I shouldn't have brought him along. Did he have to be so hurtful and demoralizing? It's not like I had set out to have some grand little adventure, as though I was oblivious to the danger. I tried to shake off my bruised feelings.

Why did I need him to like me? I didn't need an official, embossed seal that I'd passed his inspection. I cast him a quick, sidelong glance. Valeo had bent one leg and propped an arm on it, a casual pose that did nothing to hide his rippling muscles, now only thinly covered by his soggy togs. I looked away. My stomach growled, but I was too irritated to feel embarrassed or apologize. And honestly, I really didn't care if he knew I was hungry, of all things.

From the corner of my eye, I could make out Valeo gazing at the Gek as they scurried to lug the last of their canoes ashore. Just when I thought a calming silence had overtaken us, he cleared his throat.

"You know, if you go over to their side, I have to kill you." *What an idiot*, I thought. But I said, "Orders, I suppose," with a sigh.

He'd just get whatever eldritch power S'ami said I had and bring it back inside him—if the Gek let him get that far.

"Yep."

"And if the Gek kill you?"

"It's war." He shrugged. "Men die."

My stomach dropped inside me, and I swallowed back a sudden upsurge of bile. How could he be so blithe about his own death? I looked at him and pictured the arrow-riddled bodies of his comrades strewn across half my city. I'd run past their twisted limbs and pained faces, the unstaring eyes and bloody mouths. They cropped up in my head as I watched Valeo and his cool expression. Blood—I had seen a sea of it today, pooling along the cobblestones, forming a highway of dark bootprints along the wharf. I had run through others' blood today.

"How could you be so casual about this?" I asked.

"There is nothing casual about the way I fight." He kept his focus on the busy Gek.

"You're unarmed."

"I don't need weapons to kill you."

"That's reassuring." I stared out at the Gek again. It was a better choice than continuing the conversation. I wasn't going to melt into drippy puddles of tears in front of the Gek because the man who'd kissed me was threatening to kill me. The only answer was to act as if this sort of thing happened to me every day and force myself to let his ugly words slide past me.

Besides, how did he know if I was going to change sides? How about my side? Maybe there was a third side in this. I did have a side—and it wasn't the Temple's or the Gek's. But I wasn't neutral, either. My fleeting insights weren't congealing into actual plans, though. Some sort of breakthrough eluded me, even after all I'd been through. Was I a peace broker? An emissary? Was I looking for a different way to exile the Temple and restore harmony here? Bah. I couldn't think on an empty stomach anyway.

Fortunately, the Gek had a landing party meeting them, and a cluster of them scrambled up to us with reed baskets of food. I'd expected bugs and leeches and whatever else I'd seen Bugsy gobbling by our hearth, but the flat-woven platters contained fresh fruits and berries and dried fish. Valeo nodded gravely but took the food, as did I. They'd clearly expected us, or at least me, but whether they simply signaled ahead just before we got here or planned far in advance was impossible to gauge.

We ate in silence. Valeo cleared his throat again. I winced. What now?

"You shouldn't have saved my life," he said.

"Well, I did. And I would again." *So there,* I thought. *I'm better than you. And you know it.*

"So, what is this thing inside you? That picks magic locks and breaks spell-shields and does . . . other stuff."

I glanced over to see him staring at me. He was no longer pretending to be fascinated by the Gek, who appeared to be mostly done with their chores and were congregating on the tops of the beached canoes. I made a point of ignoring the question. He wasn't my mother—I didn't owe him an explanation—and the less he knew, the better. Maybe he wanted my power for himself, as S'ami had. A sudden fear seized me. What if everyone, knowing about my power and how it was obtained, wanted it for themselves? What if, among humans and Feroxi, I would forever have to watch my back? Whom could I trust?

Not Valeo, even. My power—whatever it was—was something he shouldn't have. No one should have it, not even me, but I felt a sudden pang of possessiveness. I could undo magic. I could understand tongues. The fallen star had singled me out, and I was meant to be here, watching the Gek, fully assembled on their logs as though at an amphitheater watching jugglers and acrobats. Only I was center stage.

What act did I need to perform, what role was I to take on?

Peace broker. I settled on that idea because it crash-landed into my brain first and stuck there. I could get the Temple to go and restore things the way they were before the Azwans arrived. I could keep an eye out so that our island became what it was supposed to be—a singular place where magic and nature coexisted in an uneasy truce, far from the Temple's ugly glare.

Yes, that sounded like a plan, or at least a goal. And it sounded lofty, too—something I could look back on, if I could pull it off. I was beginning to believe I could accomplish pretty much anything, and on a moment's notice, too. Who needed plans? I had a mash cat's instinct for danger and a crane's agility to soar above it all, didn't I? And a big, strong guard by my side, if he didn't kill me. I didn't think he would. He would've done so already, wouldn't he? So. Success was just a matter of us pooling our talents, such as they were.

I finished congratulating myself and turned back to our hosts, who'd gathered on shore. They numbered about a thousand, far fewer than I'd imagined. Maybe that's all that were left, or maybe the rest were out battling in my city.

"I wonder what they're doing," I said.

"Well, if you don't know, then I sure as Nihil's balls don't know."

"Does your mother know you talk that way?"

"My mother talks that way."

"It must be good to be queen."

"It has its benefits."

I was spared the agony of more barbs by a Gek chieftain, whom I recognized easily from his mighty crest, which stretched from roughly even with my shoulders to the top of my own head. It formed a natural crown and turned a vibrant crimson as he approached. The rest of him flushed to match.

"Undoer, you light the stars on our path," he said. "The sun itself bends its rays in your presence."

So they could speak figuratively. I hadn't caught that before, even with their prayers. I'd only heard their language as having crude, literal meanings, one-dimensional and weak. I'd have to rethink that idea. It wouldn't do to underestimate them, as fighters or as a people.

"You must forgive me," the chieftain said. "My nest-sister was our Shaman, and she was killed on the day of the Great Burning. We have none who may represent us to you, except for myself, if you find me acceptable."

With that, he bowed so that his crest pointed all the way down toward my navel.

So he was Bugsy's uncle, and I was sitting beside the man who'd killed his nest-sister. Once again, I felt the inadequacy of any word or signal I could give.

I held up my hands and signed my gratitude and something about his skin being as radiant as any star. I left out the part about who'd killed the chieftain's sister, but it did make me wonder where Bugsy would be. Was she here somewhere?

I signaled my question to the chieftain.

Pale blue streaks raced along his spine, a sign I took to be pleasure. Maybe I was getting good at this. *Yes,* he replied, *she has been taken somewhere safe to rest.*

"Translate," Valeo grumbled. "Please."

"They're happy we're here."

*"You're* here," he corrected.

I signed again. Before I demanded to know why I'd been dragged here, I asked after the Gek people: if they'd built new homes in the untouched parts of the swamp, whether they were in good health overall. I was polite, in other words; the chieftain would've sniffed out any insincerity even if I couldn't pull off the magnificent trick of changing my skin color with my mood.

"The Undoer must see with her own eyes," the chieftain replied. "You and your mate will follow."

My "mate" cast me a dirty look when I translated for him but picked himself up without complaint and held out a steadying hand for me, which I took. We followed the chieftain past the assembled Gek, who watched us with an unnerving silence, as unmoving as lizards in the midday sun, their stillness belying their unblinking gaze, which missed nothing. If I'd tripped or shouted or made some other unexpected move, I half expected to see all thousand of them dart away, tongues flicking, skins a camouflaged green.

A group of them went ahead and parted branches for us and the way was easier going than I had thought it'd be. We followed a well-worn path from the landing site inland, up toward a small volcano at the island's heart. Mount Meridiana, it was called, because it lay at the dead center of Kuldor's map. I wondered if the Gek would make us climb its steep sides, overgrown with jungle, steam rising in fat puffs from hidden vents. It wasn't the lava-blasting kind of volcano, like those that could be seen on calm nights along the distant horizon. This one belched sulfurous steam that reeked like rotting eggs, but otherwise it kept quiet vigil above the surf.

Without boots or sandals, Valeo had a harder time picking his way along the roots and rocks. The volcanic rock could cut like glass, and the state of his feet began to worry me. My sandals had miraculously survived my misadventures. I paused and ripped a long length of my skirt away. The Gek chieftain stopped to watch but said nothing. I ripped the material in several pieces. I gave them to Valeo, who was eyeing my bare calves. His face registered surprise.

"You'd better wrap those slabs you call feet," I said. "Or they'll be hashmeat before long."

He did as he was told, but the flimsy covering looked like it wouldn't hold him for long. He fell back in behind me, and I could sense he'd regained some of his confident bearing.

"Thank you," he grumbled.

"I worry about worms or infections," I said, by way of acknowledgment, but I was secretly pleased at his gratitude.

"Not about my feet," he said. "I meant the view of your legs. Usually, I'd have to pay to see that much flesh."

"You have no manners at all," I said before I could stop myself. "I did that to help you."

He chuckled. "It's helping, believe me, it is."

"This is serious. You could . . ."

"I know." His tone was suddenly grave. "Look, we both know only one of us is coming back from this little excursion of yours. If this is my last day, I want to enjoy a beautiful pair of legs."

I whirled around. "I would never let them harm you."

"And if I had to kill you?"

"The Gek would never—"

"They're fast, but not strong. I'm stronger." The stare he gave me was unreadable, part scorn, but part regret, too.

"Just tell me why."

The Gek, hearing my irritated tone, pressed in close around us and a dozen javelin tips appeared at Valeo's chest and back. Before he could say anything, I reached up and held a finger to his lips. I had to step on a boulder to reach his chin to plant a kiss, since he was still so much taller.

The javelins and spears retreated. *Mate,* I signed again and the chieftain shrugged and turned to continue. I clambered down from the boulder and Valeo fell in behind me, his face registering both surprise and amusement.

"I have the same troubles with my own mate," the chieftain said over his shoulder. "It is not always nest-building and egg-laying. You must be there for the thunderstorms as well."

I could swear the chieftain cackled as he said this. Valeo just grunted when I translated for him. The sound of rushing water grew too loud for conversation. The trail widened and we came to a wide clearing along a gentle part of the slope with Gek huts built onto the ground instead of in the trees. A waterfall cascaded and vanished into a mist-shrouded basin. Steamy vapor enveloped us and I couldn't tell which part of me was damp from steam or sweat. I tugged my hair into a loose knot, but it was a futile gesture against the humidity.

Gek poured around us and formed a ring, leaving only the chieftain, myself, and Valeo at its center. They seated themselves in low-hanging branches or on hut rooftops, or squatted on rocks or logs. This was clearly our destination.

The chieftain didn't wait long. I was right in assuming he was the boss; his crest stood higher than anyone else's, and his stature was upright and dignified. He reminded me, in his lizard-like way, of S'ami. Maybe all species had their self-important folks who put themselves at the middle of everything, carrying themselves with the same arrogant bearing.

The chieftain held up one bony hand and the Gek ceased their nervous chittering and turned toward us three.

"These are the salt baths," the chieftain intoned. He raised his arms toward the falls. "These waters pour from the center of creation itself and bring with it sacred salt from the very core of our being."

And sulfur, too, from the smell of it, and likely many other minerals. I kept listening and translating. Valeo was instantly transfixed, but probably not out of any curiosity for the Gek. He had his own reasons for wanting to know what was being said; one or both of our lives would depend on it.

The chieftain continued in his gravelly cackle, with even his clicks and snorts carrying an extra weightiness. "It is our sacred task to keep the salt bath from the Nothing Man, who twists all that is natural into what is not. It is why the lizards crossed the dark waters that separate this island from the larger lands beyond. We guard this place for all Lizardom, and for you drabskins, too, though you know it not."

Valeo nudged me. "What happens to this salt if Nihil gets to it?" Like me, he assumed there was only one Nothing Man.

I bowed to the chieftain and signed as best I could with one hand. He nodded and continued.

"The Nothing Man destroys all things at their core."

The Gek around us repeated the chant in unison. ". . . at their core."

"He changes the very nature of nature," chanted the chieftain.

". . . of nature," the crowd repeated.

I was beginning to hate religion of all sorts. Even the Gek followed a priest who caught them all up in rituals and mindless chants and conformity, just like everyone else I knew. If the chieftain said chop down all the trees, I wondered if they would.

Maybe *they* had burned their forest. Then again, Bugsy had been clear they hadn't. I wondered if she was in this crowd somewhere, but there was no telling them apart any longer, except for the one chieftain.

They had finished a few more chants along the lines of Nihil's awfulness and the chieftain again turned to the waterfall.

"The Nothing Man has turned these sacred waters against us," he said. "And you must take them back, Undoer. Else all creation will be poisoned against Nature, and all that crawls or flies or runs or swims across its surface will cease."

The chieftain continued like this, explaining all the ways the sacred waters were despoiled, but I couldn't be sure whether that was meant as some sort of religious metaphor, or if the waters were genuinely polluted somehow. I had an urgent curiosity to know, to see for myself, and to help them if I could.

"Is that it?" Valeo said, after hearing the translation. His voice held more relief than incredulity. "He wants you to do your hibbity-jibbity unmagic over the water and then we can go? That's great!"

He thumped me on the back.

"Get to it, woman. We can still get back in time for a proper supper."

## 25

*As close as eyelash to eye,*
*As near as teeth to tongue,*
*Unseeing, together lie,*
*Lips joined in silent song.*

*This hymn of loving*
*Springs from solemn space*
*Between being and becoming*
*As two, as one, embrace.*
*—from the song, "Between Us," by anonymous*

Valeo's thunderous approval aside, I couldn't tackle much of anything without rest. As soon as I realized more or less what the Gek were asking, fatigue washed over me. I hadn't slept since the previous night, and I'd already survived a battle, a swim, and a hike that day on a single meal. I couldn't expect the Gek to look me up and down and know, as a human healer would, that I was worn and scared and soul-achingly weary. They couldn't tell my moods except by scent, and I probably smelled too much like sea water.

The chieftain ambled closer to me and waved several other Gek toward us.

"You will do as we ask?"

I nodded, and then signaled my need for rest. I didn't care if I had to sleep on a log; every part of me felt as if it would melt into the ground. Within moments, Valeo and I had been hustled into one of the huts, where we found straw mats on the ground and crude blankets that bore the telltale floral designs of human make. Mami and I must've traded these to them more than a year ago. I again wondered how far in advance they'd prepared for my arrival, then shrugged it off as mere coincidence.

But it would be something to think about—when I woke up. I lay down, hoping for instant sleep. Valeo hovered in the doorway, inspecting the walls and ceiling for any camouflaged Gek. Satisfied we were alone, he stepped inside, positioned himself by the doorway and trained his watchful gaze on the Gek outside.

The lull of the waterfall did its trick, and I woke much later in total darkness with a weight pinning me down and a droning buzz in my ear. Valeo snored beside me, and the weight was his arm draping across my middle. I shifted, one tiny finger-width at a time, gently, slowly so as not to wake him, until I had turned over to try and study Valeo's face in the pitch-black. I wanted to memorize every sharp line and furrow, the scrap of stubble on his chin, the way his forehead protruded over his eyelids in that Feroxi way, and the dark smudge of brow. I could make out only dim shadows, though.

My heartbeat matched the steady rhythm of his breathing, and I had to keep myself from finding and tracing his jawline with my finger. I'd stared at so many sailors and dockworkers, wondering what happened on a marriage night. Then I'd learned much more about sex in a purely clinical way from the healers. I knew what a man and a woman did together and had imagined it, or tried to.

But this—this closeness. I hadn't thought about that at all, my body next to his, absorbing his warmth, savoring my skin's tingling. I thought of the song my father sometimes sang to Mami when he thought we girls were asleep.

*As close as eyelash to eye*
*As near as teeth to tongue*

I'd always assumed it referred to a married couple's bodies joining, but Valeo's nearness let my imagination open to other possibilities. This closeness—was it something he had also felt before he closed his eyes to sleep? Had the same thrill run through his skin as it did mine?

Was this what it was like to be married? I wondered if Mami lay against Babba every night with the same mix of curiosity and wonder, the same longing to touch and keep touching, dreading the morning and its glaring light. Maybe what Mami felt was so much more intense, after a lifetime of sleeping beside Babba, or maybe the feeling wore off after a few years. A man was a wondrous thing when there were no spears or swords at hand, no unkind words or brutish manners. I even loved the sweaty, musky smell of Valeo, and the way his arm lay over me, protecting me even in sleep.

Beneath his blanket, he was stripped to his waist. I could make out the tufts of black fuzz curling up his rippling stomach and across his chest. Since becoming a healer's apprentice, I'd seen any number of men's bodies, most of them old or sickly. I'd seen Valeo once before, sick in a cot, but this was different. I wanted to run my fingers through all that fuzz to see what it felt like. If I awakened Valeo with my fingers on his chest, however, I didn't think I could come up with an explanation that sounded even slightly chaste. And that mattered to me, even in the wild with the Gek thinking us already married. I wasn't married, and I knew that, and I would have to watch myself. I was in the wild, but I was a civilized woman.

Valeo's snore turned into a snort and he gave a start. Without opening his eyes, he pulled himself closer to me and nestled his face in my hair. Then he was asleep again, and I had my wish. There was no place to put my hands except on his chest, and I let them lay there, soaking in the warmth of his tawny skin. I wanted this moment to last forever, with all the pain and threats and heartache banished into the sheltering night.

I woke again just before the first rays of daylight, the spot beside me empty, Valeo's blanket neatly folded and set aside. Disappointment welled up within me, but what had I expected? He was a soldier, and he was likely back to standing guard and mentally reviewing the conditions under which he might let me live and safely return home, I decided bitterly. Any sort of comfort from the night vanished with the pale streaks of light streaming through the doorway, and my loneliness settled into a dull ache.

Whatever I decided to do for the Gek, I was in it alone. Even with him standing right beside me.

I sat up and rubbed my eyes. I had a sour taste in my mouth and I felt stale all over, as though I'd been left out too long and had begun to ferment. My rope burns were scabbing over and itched, and my skin smarted from sunburn and seawater. My wrist felt less acutely painful and had settled into a dull throb. It was just as well I didn't have a man around to see me looking like some flotsam the tides had tossed ashore. Time to improvise: I'd been raised to be resourceful, right?

I found a jug of fresh water the Gek had left for me and scrubbed my face. I tamed my hair into a knot at the nape of my neck and wrapped my blanket around my middle for a skirt. What was left of my shift served as a blouse. My slippers had dried out and were wearable, if a bit stiff.

Satisfied I'd made myself as presentable as I could, I stepped out of the hut into twilight, only to be struck by the soft glow of a thousand softly luminescent flowers. I'd noticed the lush flora only vaguely the previous day, but most flowers shut their blooms tightly each night.

Except for one.

At my feet and strewn all around me in the clearing lay hundreds of moonblooms, petals fanning from cactus branches, still reaching for the moons' last rays before the sun would send the petals into their daily hibernation. It was an odd time of year for moonblooms to blossom, but perhaps the volcano's unrelenting heat gave these delicate flowers a year-round chance at life. At one time, they'd been Mami's cash crop, with a pungency and purity greatly prized by people who knew something about nature and its ability to heal and restore.

But now, to me, they could be no more than flowers. Nothing in my life admitted to any more medicines or natural cures.

Still, Moonblooms had saved Valeo's life. I was momentarily back at Mami's old hearth, separating petals and dehydrating them, hoping we'd make a tincture or a tea in time to cure a Gek poison. Scores of Feroxi warriors had been stricken. And that was also the night I'd been taken away to the altar for the encounter with a demon that had eventually led me here, to this sheltered space with its mist and its moonblooms and its sweetly incandescent beauty.

Otherwise, my surroundings were as they had been the day before: the Gek were everywhere I looked, barely bothering to camouflage themselves, though many turned an instinctive green around me. I suppose I'd hide from myself, too, if I could. I was some sort of Undoer and I had to battle against feeling undone.

"You look nice, for someone in the middle of nowhere," Valeo's voice boomed from behind me. He must've been standing watch outside the hut's doorway. He had put his togs back on and had wrapped his feet in the sturdy blankets the Gek had provided us, held together with what looked like vines. I wasn't the only resourceful person here.

"Thank you, I guess. And, um, so do you." What passed for pleasantries on such an occasion? Nice day for some really vigorous blasphemy, you don't say. Why don't we return to my ravaged city so you can lead me off to jail?

"You're missing something, though."

What, a hot bath? Breakfast? Real clothes? I was missing a lot of things.

He held up a garland he'd made from tropical flowers, with more than a few moonblooms mixed in, and gently placed it on my head, tucking the strand under a few curls so it sat straight. I didn't know what to say, so I just stood there, a rock-sized lump in my throat.

"There. Now you look like you could be a Gek priestess. Just don't bite me."

"I can't change color like they do." What a stupid thing to say. I forced a smile anyway.

"Nonsense, you're turning bright red."

He didn't miss a thing. Curse him and all observant soldier types. "I think that's sunburn."

"Ah. Well. Before Spike gets back here, we have to talk."

"Spike?"

"The snakeman with the dozen scaly horns on his head. Spike. But we need to talk about you."

"You mean, you should talk. I can't tell you about my secret undoing powers because they're so secret, even I don't know about them."

He seemed cross, and I guessed that wasn't the answer he wanted.

"Don't interrupt, please. As soon as ol' Spike comes around, all these Gek run around like they're still on fire, so moments are wasting here. Look, I know you don't trust S'ami. But he's got a grudge against Nihil he's nursed for a long time."

"I know about his daughter." I wasn't going to sit through an apology for the man. He was lost in his own hatred, and better left there.

"Everyone knows about S'ami's daughter," Valeo continued. "It was pretty damn public. But that's not it. S'ami has known for a long time how to battle Nihil, but didn't have the power. You've got the power, but not the knowledge of how to use it, right?"

If I had been a Gek, I would've been a battle-ready red or a mortified gray, flower garland notwithstanding. "Where is this going, exactly?"

"I've been thinking—"

"That sounds dangerous."

"Stop it. I mean it. I told you the other night that everyone's tried to defy Nihil in one way or another. Everyone leads a double life around Nihil, and the closer you are, the more you need to be two people—the one who believes, and the one who wishes you didn't have to."

"That's not how I've lived my life, thank you," I lied. Valeo was speaking straight from my own soul, if there was such a thing. He was speaking the truth of my own life— what kind of life is it to worship a god you resented?

"Well, you're lucky you're still alive, then. And I'm hoping you stay that way."

"What about your plans to kill me?"

"I need proof you're the Undoer."

"So if I help the Gek, you'll kill me, even after saying yesterday you wanted me to do so in time for supper?"

He shook his head. "I'm lousy with explanations. Look, we have zero time. With proof you're this Undoer, I might have something to hope for. Everyone would, from the Crystal Desert to the Sunless Sea. Even if you can't defeat him, you could keep him in check, balance him out with your Unmagic. But it has to be our way, not yours."

"And just why is that?"

"Before I escorted you off and we went for that little swim yesterday, I got two separate orders: from one Azwan to kill you if you ran over to the Gek, and from the other Azwan to keep you alive no matter what. And you wouldn't believe which one wants you dead."

"S'ami."

His look of surprise told me I was right.

"Valeo, he has you duped. If you kill me, whatever power I have jumps to you, and then you bring it back to S'ami, who kills you and takes that power for himself."

"S'ami would never kill me."

"And Reyhim is my grandfather."

"I'm not joking."

"Neither am I. That's why he's the one who wants me alive."

I had only a moment's satisfaction seeing those bushy eyebrows rise in shock before the chieftain showed up again with a swarm of other lizards and my stomach grumbled at the sight of platters of food. The Gek, so far as I could tell, had no customs for hospitality and sharing a meal hadn't the same significance as it did among humans. So they gathered around to watch us eat as if what we were doing was strange and exotic, while the chieftain explained more of what they wanted from me.

As I translated, however, Valeo's face contorted, his overbrow furrowing as he picked at his food.

"This isn't good," he said.

"Shall I tell the chieftain the salad isn't to your liking?" I wondered if the Gek would feel insulted or just shrug it off as finicky drabskin appetites.

"No, what you're telling me. About this crack at the center of the world, or whatever bunghole on Nihil's ass this place is supposed to be."

I put down a succulent fruit I'd been peeling. "If you don't watch your language—"

"I'll watch my language when you have proper clothes to put on."

"I, at least, am trying to be civilized."

"I'm trying to keep us alive. And I'll say what I need to say if it helps me think."

I kept my voice as singsong sweet as I could make it. "Maybe you shouldn't attempt things that are clearly too difficult for you."

Instead of a verbal assault, he sighed. "Nihil love a fish-wife's tongue, as the saying goes. The crack. What's wrong with it and why on all Kuldor would it be Nihil's fault?"

I turned to the chieftain and asked him to repeat the part about some sort of impurity, or violation—the Gek chatter had multiple meanings, and it was hard, even with my quirky ability to understand them, to get the exact meaning down. What I did understand is that I had to see it, to *feel* it, he insisted. And the Gek felt they had already waited too long for me to experience this waterfall shrine of theirs and whatever was wrong with it.

All this I tried to convey to Valeo. I didn't actually consider him stupid, but his looks of confusion and anxiety only added to my own.

"You have to do this thing, and I have to make a decision about it," he said at last, not looking at me.

"Which Azwan to obey?" I asked. "Which one would you rather obey?"

He looked away. "Normally, I'd say whichever gets me in the least trouble."

"How brave of you." I nearly snorted in disgust.

Without looking at me, he continued. "Nihil took my father from me. He's taken any sense of home I ever had. I have no inheritance from that side, nothing but an empty title from my mother's people, who'd rather I'd never have been born."

He fixed a rock-hard stare at me, his deep brown eyes flashing with sudden fire. "So, yes, I try to stay out of trouble."

I clamped my mouth shut. How could I have known any of this? An empty title? Prince? How could he believe that with the way his men looked at him? His glower told me not to ask what he meant by his father, but I might get away with one question, if I put it delicately. I did my best to ask without any hint of sarcasm.

"Then why become a soldier?" I asked. "Isn't that the worst kind of trouble?"

"My life isn't worth much, but I'd rather not throw it away idly, if that's what you mean."

The hideous lump returned to my throat again, forcing my voice to a whisper. "Don't ever say that. Your life is valuable, of course it is. Very."

"You thought I was dead and your life went on just fine."

"No, it didn't. Nothing about my life will ever be fine again without you."

Valeo hesitated a moment, then leaned over and kissed my cheek. A few Gek chittered their approval, not understanding anything but that they'd witnessed a human mating custom, as best they understood it.

"Reyhim's the higher rank," he said. "And my life would be worth something to him if I brought you back to him."

He pushed away from the table and stood, towering over the Gek, who scampered away from the big man and his growly voice. Valeo ignored them and gave me a curt nod. "Let's do this, then."

He had included himself in that statement, which sent my heart cartwheeling. I reached up and touched the garland on my head. Some change had occurred in him and he'd decided I needed to live, and even the most stubborn, jaded part of my brain told me it wasn't just because he was avoiding trouble. No, I didn't believe that at all.

I was plenty of trouble for him, and he was looking for ways to keep it coming.

I almost dared a smile. Almost.

# 26

> But their cries, pitted against words of evil, fell
> as uselessly as raindrops at sea. Heretics slit the
> priests' throats, shamed their wives, and sold their
> children into slavery. They defiled their Wards
> with statues of their dead gods, who should've
> been long forgotten, and again worshipped beings
> that do not exist.
> —from "The Fall of B'Nai," Verisimilitudes 13,
> The Book of Unease

The un-rightness of Mount Meridiana hit me as a queasy
feeling almost the moment we set foot on the path to
its peak. I followed the chieftain and Valeo followed me,
and behind us came a procession of several dozen Gek.
By the time we'd clambered halfway up, the uneasy feeling became more like vertigo. It wasn't from the height.
Meridiana angled up sharply, but the Gek had long ago
molded a wide, grass-covered series of switchbacks that
should've made for gentle hiking.

I stopped every so often to figure out if I was truly lightheaded. I didn't feel or hear any buzzing or strange music or any fizzy static against my skin. That's how magic usually affected me. But this was deeper, as if something in my head and my lungs and stomach were all upside-down at once, and I couldn't quite right it or even catch my breath.

Near the peak, the chieftain stopped us. I realized I'd been watching his skin change hues in rapid procession, and he had taken on seven or eight overlapping shades at once, all in brilliant, tropical hues, as lovely as anything I might've embroidered, but in rings and spots that radiated in the sun. Around him, the rest of the Gek had done the same, so that a shimmering sea of colors swelled in waves around me.

"This is the sacred place," the chieftain said. He pointed a bony finger through a natural archway beneath a bower of trees. "See and feel, Undoer. See and *know*."

This was it, then—what I'd come to learn. I drew a shaky breath and ducked under the branches. I found myself in a wide, rocky clearing, where steam vented from several bur-bling pools of yellowish mud. The sulfur stung my nostrils, but fresh air wafted from the mountain top, too. After a few moments, I found the stench more bearable. Valeo followed me as I clambered over and around outcroppings of rocks. Nothing grew here, but the loss of vegetation was sudden, as if nothing had ever grown in this spot.

The baldness stretched a few dozen body lengths or so up to the jagged peak, but all the steam I'd associated with the volcano poured from the pools around me. The woo-ziness felt no worse than it had—at first. The air over the pools rippled as though super-heated, but it was a typical fair autumn day. Something burned and I cringed at the stench. Valeo placed a hand against my shoulder blade.

His unspoken support helped to steel me a little. My knees wobbled, and it wasn't from the vertigo. It was just plain fright. It didn't matter how much I thought I'd prepared myself for some sort of defining moment—I couldn't remember what I'd resolved or why or what I thought I was doing here. Something about a peace broker, something about there being three sides in this, about having my own side, carving my own role. Peace broker, peace broker. Think peace.

But there was only the wooziness and the wavering air.

Valeo leaned in and whispered. "Listen. They're praying."

I turned to see if the Gek were indeed praying as they had been on the wharf, but it was human and Feroxi voices that sifted across the breeze to us. I couldn't see anyone. The muted hymns kept coming, and I caught dawn prayers and evening ones jumbled together. A snatch of a Sabbath prayer wafted from one pool; a mourner's meditation from another.

Valeo strode to the largest of the pools and held a hand into the steam.

"They're safe enough," he said. "Probably could heat a nice bath."

Did he never stop being crude? "Valeo, this place is sacred to the Gek."

"Can they understand me?"

"Well, no, but—"

"Then I've committed no sacrilege."

I wondered if I would end up venting steam of my own. Instead, I joined him with a sigh. "There is something wrong here. You can hear voices. I can hear them. It's not something magical, then."

He raised one eyebrow in response. "So what do you hear?"

"You mean because I can understand them all."

"This big puddle of stink is talking to us in about six different languages."

"More." I held a finger to my lips. I needed a moment to concentrate. I caught nuances of Tengali, the Feroxi tongue Fernai, the common tongue, and perhaps Belai and a western dialect or two. The songs came in waves, with a current of sound lapping up from the steam and drifting away as another swept forward, back and forth, gentle but constant. The air rippled in time with the praying, carrying the steam's fine mist upward in soft spirals.

The muddy, steaming pits burbled up these voices and their muffled prayers, as if it had all welled beneath the surface for an age or so and could escape only in slow drifts. I had no sense, however, if these prayers had been uttered a century ago or this morning or this very moment, as we listened. It was all a confusing jumble. I wanted desperately to understand.

I had no answers yet; only more questions, always more. I would've kicked the mud in frustration if it would've done anything but get me dirty.

Valeo stuck his hand in the steam again, which parted around his palm and dissipated. That didn't prove much. Sticking *my* hand in would be the real test.

I was right. The steam parted clear down to my feet, forming two streams around my hand. The ground trembled faintly beneath me, and I glanced up at Valeo.

"A quake, you think?" he asked.

"It's only in my spot."

He picked up a rock and tossed it into the puddle. It splashed, but didn't sink. "Solid ground."

"Then it's not a sinkhole or a bog," I said. "I'm going to walk out there."

"Keep your sandals on. You don't want scalded soles."

Something my mother would say. I shot him a quizzical look. He chewed his lower lip and I realized he looked as worried and confused as I felt. I bit back a snotty reply and simply nodded at him. Keep my sandals on. Yessir.

The yellowish mud stuck to my soles with a splick-splack sound as I took careful, gingerly steps to the pool's center. It took long minutes to get used to the heat, but it stopped just short of scalding. Even so, I couldn't stay in it long. From deep within the mud, bubbles of air welled up beneath my feet, as if the ground itself would burst with me on top. But the steam and soft burbling kept on as usual, the distant, praying voices rising and falling without change.

"What do you feel?" Valeo scowled down at the ground near my feet.

I glanced around for the Gek but didn't see them.

"I'm not sure what I'm supposed to feel. It's just . . . I don't know. Like the air is very heavy around me."

"More than the humidity?"

"Yes, like it's pulsing upward."

And then the air burst. Phantasms poured up from the ground; faint outlines of people sobbing, throwing themselves in supplication, praying, pleading with hands clasped before tear-stained faces. They rose, glowing a pale mustard color from the mud. The murmured, formal chants of prayer services gave way to desperate pleas and shouted prayers.

As these ghosts sifted around me, their terror became my own. What if Nihil never forgave me? What if I'd taken on too much, sinned too broadly, strayed too far from the path he'd set out for me? I might never see my family again, never meet them beneath the fruitful boughs of the Eternal Tree or meet my grandmother.

My grandmother. I jolted back to reality. There was no Eternal Tree in the afterlife, and my grandmother—my heretical, exiled, executed grandmother—would certainly not be meeting me there. The flood of other people's grief swept me up with its raw, emotional force.

*Nihil forgive.*

*Please, gardener of the Eternal Tree.*

*Take pity.*

*Have mercy.*

*Kind Master, please.*

Prayers and supplications welled beneath my feet, venting in heaves and belches from the ground. The blunt, open neediness of so many nameless, ghostly souls built within my chest, down to my feet, up through my shoulders, my fingers, neck, ears—my whole body filled with the power of others' sorrow and desperation. I had to force it to stay down, pressing my entire being into the effort, sweat beading on my upper lip.

*Nihil*, they all thought. I heard this thought. It was the same, all of it.

*Nihil.*

*Please.*

So much desperation and desire, focused, singular, aimed like an arrow to the one being who could take all that raw sorrow and . . . do what?

"It's like a well," I said. "A well of prayers."

Valeo humphed, his gaze tracing the outlines of mourners and supplicants as they dissipated above his head. "A well is only a hole dug into the water table. So there is some underground table of prayers?"

"From which Nihil draws," I said, the realization hitting. "Listen, people's prayers—this is why he needs all of us to worship him."

"I don't get it. He stores prayers?"

"S'ami said Nihil steals power from the demons, but he has other sources, too, sources S'ami believes are irrelevant. Maybe he's wrong."

Valeo glanced at the sobbing phantasms and shook his head. "Not if he could see what we're seeing."

Prayers were that other power. And that power was more fierce and deadly than weapons, than witchcraft—than words, even. Here was proof, screeching out of the ground around me as my breathing gathered speed, panting as I took in some of that power for myself, pulling it in through my nose and mouth, breathing it all in. My brain sparked with sudden static, my senses becoming more acute: colors grew sharper, the outlines of objects more vivid. Beyond the sharp stench of the sulfur pits, I could make out the most delicate aromas of flowers and berries ripening. Then sounds: chirps and hums of a million insects, the Gek chittering and clicking their anxiety and curiosity. My skin prickled against the breeze as if I could feel every dust particle, every pollen spore beating against me one by one by the thousands.

A vibration in the air, so subtle, it barely moved, told me Valeo had spoken, even in the fraction of an instant before the words hit my ears.

"A prayer well. What thirst does he quench with our prayers, except our free will?"

"No, not quench." My mind raced ahead of me, making sudden connections as the powerful chants and pleadings swirled around me, nearly drowning out my voice. "This is his power. Millions of focused minds, all turned to him. When we pray, we know our belief can overwhelm us."

I was ranting, I knew it, but the words poured out as if they, too, had been suppressed beneath the surface, waiting to bubble up. "We fall to our knees, we prostrate ourselves, we stagger back to our feet, we cry and moan, we feel humbled, but hopeful, downcast, but redeemed. Don't we? Isn't that what it's all about, that next chance, that forgiveness, that hope that something larger, that someone, can save us from ourselves?

"What if you took all that prayer and its power and concentrated it by the millions, and aimed it, straight as a crossbow?"

"Are you saying you will? Or that you can?" I heard hope in Valeo's voice.

Could I? He didn't need the answer: I did.

I closed my eyes and stretched out my arms, feeling the power course through me in urgent waves. How could I shape it into something magical? And did I even want to?

I focused on the prayers and pleas swirling around me. I could feel them leaning in, pressing into me. I gathered the phantasms, circling my arms as if embracing them.

The power in my limbs surged, like I could climb a dozen mountains, like I could fly.

They prayed, and I caught their prayers. These were mine. I took their wishes and longings and I could do as I pleased. My fingertips crackled and sparks flew from my nose, eyes, and mouth. This was power. I could shape it, level the mountaintop, uproot trees, set the world afire.

Magic.

I opened my eyes and sighed, the extra strength immediately dissipating.

*This is how Nihil does it,* I thought.

And I didn't want anything to do with it.

My stomach curled at the thought, and bile leached up into my throat. I shuddered, a giant, involuntary shake that rattled me from shoulder to knees. I'd rather this magic kill me than master me—because I would be its slave, needing more and more and ever more, like a drug. You couldn't wield something like this; you succumbed to it and it owned you.

I wondered if Nihil was like that, a slave to what he'd created.

"Hadara, explain. You looked like you were spellcasting. Can you do it?" Valeo leaned in, but didn't step into the prayer well, as I was already calling it in my head. "If you can, it could change the world. It could . . ."

The martial gleam in his eye came from someone I should've recognized sooner. This was the real Valeo, not the one who made flower garlands. His every muscle tensed, his body coiled and ready to spring, hand hovering over an imaginary scabbard for a sword he must miss.

I made a fist. This is exactly what I had feared—that he envied me my power, or he'd fight me to use it. What would I do if he charged me and killed me?

"I won't. I will not."

To my surprise, he backed off. "No, of course not." He eyed me warily, hovering and alert, just a few steps further back.

"Can I trust you?" I already knew the answer; I needed to see if he knew it.

"No," he said. "You're a fool for even asking."

"And could you trust me with power like this?"

He hesitated, one eyebrow rising. He hadn't considered whether I could be trusted. Had he forgotten his mission so soon? But then, which mission had he chosen after all— to kill me or bring me back?

Then he popped his own surprise: "Do you trust yourself, Hadara?"

"Yes," I said, about as firmly as I've ever said anything. "If I did this—"

"You don't need to explain."

"But I do. I've fought my whole life, in one way or another, against magic. Am I going to use it now? It's more likely to destroy me than Nihil."

Disappointment and disdain rolled off him like the heat. "There are so many who would help you."

"They could be my priests, is that it? I'd need temples, too, and tithes and worshippers—especially those."

He paused. "And some way to keep them all in check, I suppose. So you'd need guards. A whole, huge system to make sure your prayer well was always full."

"So you understand?" I blinked in disbelief.

He stubbed the ground with one foot and stared at it, then shot a look at me that was hard to read. Was he angry? His tone was curt, brief, hard. "It's not tough to understand. You drag me here to this stinking pit and it's like the edge of salvation itself; everything most of the world has ever wanted. To be free of Nihil, to have someone loving and responsible and kind wielding this power instead. And you're pushing it all away."

Loving and responsible and kind? This was the flower-garland Valeo instead, though he hadn't dropped his coiled pose. But his words and their resigned tone told me this wasn't about seizing that power for himself.

"If I won't seize Nihil's power," I began, "I can try to at least cut it off."

A half-smirk stole across his lips, just a faint raise in one corner of his mouth. "Now, *that* would be a thing worth doing."

"Happy enough?"

The smirk broadened into a grin. "Seal it off forever? Make him the impotent, weak little despot that he is? Damn, yes."

I grew confused. He was again imagining far more than I thought I could do. I didn't want to fail him, and said so, in a fumbling, stupid-sounding way. I stammered what I thought I could do, how I could seal this up, perhaps, but if it was his prayer well, maybe it wasn't the only one? What if there were others?

He shrugged. "My commander always says we can only do what we can do—and that is the impossible."

"Meaning?" I had never liked his Commander.

He flicked his wrist toward the pool around me. "I know you can do this. Then I can take you home, if the Gek don't make you queen."

27

*I took the best of my followers and taught them to subdue Nature. I made them more powerful than drought, than flood, than sea currents and winds, than mountain or desert, or the body and its frailties.*
—*from Verisimilitudes 7,* The Book of Unease

The afternoon sun beat down on my shoulders and heated my knot of hair. I hunched on a boulder, defeated and angry, my chin to my chest, elbows on knees. I had been fussing all day at the mud pools, at times trying to suck the phantasms from the ground, at other times shoving them back down. I had no idea what I was doing and nothing worked. As soon as I walked away, the commotion had died down and the specters and noises faded.

The Gek had recovered some of their bravery and nosed around the prayer wells, as though scouting for evidence that I'd done anything, anything at all. They had accepted my explanations with a variety of excited chitters and croaks, with the chieftain praising the sunbeams lucky enough to light my path, or some such drivel. I didn't want a Temple of Gek and told him so. He had agreed, and the Gek had returned to skittering in a wide berth around us as they inspected the steam vents.

Valeo sat beside me, arms folded across his chest, lost in thought. Finally, he cleared his throat.

"You pulled out and stuffed in," he said. "There's no sideways or inside out or upside down way you could try to seal this?"

"No, no, and no."

"I'm trying to help."

I couldn't mask my irritation. "It's too big. It's like the whole world is in there."

"Would it harm the world, what you're doing?"

"How on Kuldor would I know?"

"Listen, hold on. There's no rush. I know I said get it done, but you don't need to be short about it. We can ask S'ami—"

"We are not asking S'ami."

"For a text or manuscript of some kind. He's the Curator of the Boundless Repository, remember? If there's so much as a scroll on this, he'll have seen it."

"A scroll? Of what, instructions?" The moment I said it, I regretted it. If Nihil's penchant for journaling was true and not a myth, likely something, somewhere, could help. Only a fraction of his writings made Scripture—even I remembered that from lessons. But I'd had so little interest in Scriptures as they were, I'd never been curious about what hadn't made the final cut.

And the only textbook, a true book, I'd ever seen had been the one on anatomy I used as a healer.

"That's it!" I said. "Thank you, Valeo. You're right. So right!"

"Glad to know it," he said. "Even if I have no idea what I'm right about."

"A text! My anatomy text. Look, my mind just made a huge leap, alright?"

"From anatomy to . . . ?"

"I'm a healer, right? I might be able to heal the prayer well. Not seal it, more like a bandage."

"What's the difference?"

I was already halfway out to the largest pool again, waving my arms madly, skipping across rocks and jumping in an attempt to get the phantasms started again. They cooperated, sifting up with the chanting and beseeching. Again, I let the power of their raw need course through me, only this time I didn't stop there. My mind reached down, far down into the ground to the hot, coursing veins of the volcano. The heat didn't touch me this time—only the sheer muscle of Kuldor's center welled up within me. The prayers and this volcano sharing an essential power was infinite and mighty.

The white-hot core of the mountain didn't merely hold the prayers, but also distilled them down to energy that rumbled through my body. I could use the volcano itself to repair the damage to its side, but I had to do it without converting this energy to magic. I had to resist that temptation. I had Valeo's confidence in me to bolster me, not to mention the Gek's obvious need for this.

But as I dug deeper, feeling around for the beginnings of the prayer well—where *did* it start? —I also felt the rest

of the island. I closed my eyes again and its rocky shoreline became my bones; the trees rising above the swamps
were my skin; and muddy water coursed through my rivers of veins. The fizzing I'd learned to associate with magic
sprung into my head with such force, I staggered backward. My footing would've been unsure, but my feet were
the roots and boles of trees. But all of it made me sick,
a dizzying, nauseating spin in my head that turned the
horizon into a wheeling storm of color. I parted my feet,
planted them more firmly, and kept exploring with every
part of me, swallowing back bile, closing my eyes against
the whirling scenery.

Beneath the island—far beneath—magic was at work.
The very soul of New Meridian had become corrupt and
black. Of course the swamp had burned—an unnatural
current had surged beneath its murky surface for genera-
tions, waiting for a spark to ignite it. The prayer wells must
be merely blisters where the infection surfaced first.

And where would it strike next? The force welling
beneath me was shifting water, lapping and eddying, swirling this way and that. I couldn't see any pattern to it.

"Because I impose the pattern."

My eyes jolted open and I shouted to Valeo, who
watched me from the boulder we'd been sitting on. "Did
you say something?"

"No."

"Did you hear a voice?"

"I hear lots of voices. All praying. Anything new?"

"Well, this one's more of a—" I stopped mid-sentence.
A tenor. Rich and pure, lilting and flawless.

"It is I, your Master."

Nihil.

Panic seized me. My feet froze to the spot, sticking in the coarse mud. I rubbed my palms against my makeshift skirt, which loosened and began to fall off. I clutched the cloth to my chest instead, stifling screams, which came out as short, shrill hiccups.

"You have come again," Nihil said. "And you will fail again."

What did that mean? I had failed—I would fail—I am failing! I sank into the steaming mud. The blanket sank into the mire with me. I was a mass of yellowish, stinking filth, small and terrified and unready. Nihil!

*I am a restless creature who flouts the prudent course.*

I don't know why the line from Scripture hit me. Amaniel was always reciting this one at me, telling me it described me from hair curls to toenails. The words poured out on their own, while my brain scrambled for something familiar and safe, but found only her odd scolding.

*Who seeks shadows instead of light, then would reverse myself.*

Nihil chuckled, his voice ominous and high.

*This I want, and then that, to take risks and then retreat, to settle down and still wander, to weave and then rend.*

I don't know why I kept at it, murmuring a bit of nonsense, perhaps the only verse I could ever recall. But *he* was here, or somewhere, and I grasped at something I knew he'd know.

*Do not begrudge me this urge or say that I am fickle. You are made this way yourself, after me.*

The invisible Nihil mocked me, his voice derisive, jeering:

"How clever to throw my verse back at me. You learned a thing or two this time, at least. But you are yet a useless, arid scrap of space dust, hurtling down uninvited, your comet tail comprised of vaporous promises and the blood of decent men. Why should I not begrudge you?"

I stopped my chanting. That was as much as I could remember, anyway.

But comet tail? Space dust? He thought I was the meteorite, and that the meteorite was a person of some sort, perhaps in the same way the Gek thought of it as wise and self-aware. I reflexively said my own name; I'd been saying it all too often lately, as a way of insisting that I wasn't some demon or space dust or anyone but Hadara of Rimonil.

"I don't care whose form you've taken," Nihil said, his voice sounding unimpressed. "You're going to leave there or I'm going to turn that island upside-down while you stand in the middle of it. That's more innocent blood on your hands, if you're even keeping track."

I glanced over at Valeo, who knelt on one knee by the side of the prayer well. I hadn't noticed him coming over here. Was he praying or begging or humbling himself to his god? I was shocked to realize he might be worshipping Nihil. I had to remember, yet again, how little I knew him.

I began to stammer, but Valeo caught my gaze and held a finger to his lips.

"Worthy Master, it is I, First Guardsman Valeo Uterlune, your servant and guard to your person. Do you hear me?"

"I do, I do." The voice sounded pleased. "A voice of sanity, calling from the mist. You will of course explain."

So Nihil couldn't see either of us, and we couldn't see him. I gulped air; and even the sulfur stink brought relief.

"The human female Hadara of Rimonil is here at the Gek's bidding, and I am here to see she does you no harm,

Benevolent Master," Valeo said. His gaze held mine in a lock, but his head shook, ever so slightly, as though to say I shouldn't believe his words, no matter how convincing they sounded.

I wanted to believe him. I wanted an ally and friend. I wanted his friendship. I nodded back. It was all I could do.

"Benevolent Master," Valeo continued. "Tell me your bidding."

"Is she possessed? What did the Azwan of Uncertainty say?"

"She is not possessed, so far as he is aware."

"Then get her away from this site and kill her."

Before I could react, Valeo had taken over, his voice more commanding than pleading. "And would not her eldritch powers then become my own, and would that not displease you, Greatest of the Great?"

"She has eldritch powers?"

Nihil's surprise caught both Valeo and myself off guard. How did he think I'd found my way into the unseen heart of the volcano? By digging through the mud? I knew my mouth was open in surprise, but Valeo gave me a cool look, as if reassessing the situation. He kept his voice even.

"You were not apprised of this, Most Worthy Master?"

Silence. The air wafted past, and I noticed the Gek had stopped their chatter. Could they also hear our exchange? Did it matter?

I was on my knees in mud. Valeo was about to tell Nihil about what powers he supposed I had. Valeo was judging what to say and how to say it, parsing his words so he could remain as neutral-seeming as possible, not giving anything away to Nihil—or to me? What chance was I taking here?

None.

And that last realization shook me out of my stupor.

Valeo couldn't pick my side. I wouldn't let him. I was in this on my own, and he was getting back alive, and I was sealing this stinkhole up before anyone said another word. Besides, it wouldn't take long for Nihil to figure out it was one of the Azwans who hadn't filled him in on my so-called eldritch powers, and I didn't think Port Sapphire wanted to be in the middle of that fight. And I suspected it would be big.

Quick. Something. Anything. I struggled to my feet. In my head, I yanked hard at the forces milling and churning deep beneath me, drawing mud and rocks and steamy heat to the surface as densely as I could imagine. I turned the fissures into gashes and then turned those into open wounds, letting all the pent-up prayers loose into the world. Lightning coursed through me, like an alarm horn, blaring its warning. I lit up like a hundred bonfires, building to a thousand stars. I began moving things around—rocks, mud, sticks, entire trees, parts of the hillside itself—making room for all that stored magic to dissipate into the air with every new and sudden explosion of steam.

This place had to be utterly, completely emptied of its contents and then permanently sealed, and Valeo and I had to leave. The top of the volcano began spewing steam as well, and the ghostly prayers rose from a din to a roar, growing in both volume and intensity, as if thousands and then tens of thousands of people shouted and wept at once.

"Kill her." Nihil's voice broadcast clear and distinct across the din. "Kill her now."

The force of the steaming, streaming voices had already blasted Valeo off his feet, though, and it had taken me this long to notice. I hesitated, just long enough for the roar to subside, long enough to peer through the yellowish gray fog to see Valeo had leapt to his feet again, unharmed, and long enough to make out the Gek scrambling in every direction as the ground gave way in ripples and undulating waves. The Gek were agile; they would be safe. But Valeo needed solid ground, something difficult to find.

I was sure Valeo wouldn't kill me, but I wasn't sure I could avoid killing Valeo.

"Stand behind me," I shouted. "It's the only way."

"Kill her!"

Damn Nihil. He'd heard me call to Valeo. He couldn't know Valeo had switched sides.

I let up my efforts, taking deep lungfulls of dirty air, coughing and wheezing out the dust and reek and rot of the vents I'd widened. Valeo wobbled and wove over the unsteady ground until he too was ankle deep in the hot mire with me. He grabbed me around the waist, steadying us both before either of lost our footing again.

"I hear and I obey, Master," Valeo shouted. "She is strong and hard to fight!"

Valeo did nothing but nod down at me.

"She is weakening," Nihil said. "Now is your chance."

I wasn't weakening, just resting. Valeo was safe. The Gek had scrambled to somewhere far below me, behind a covering of dense scrub and forest. I struggled to catch my breath and keep going.

I gave the magic beneath me one last tug with every last copperweight of strength I possessed. The ground turned liquid in every spot but ours, and the world went flying upward. Rocks, mud, steam, pebbles—it all sprayed skyward in a giant, backward rainstorm of debris that scattered far and wide. In the distance, the Gek shouted and called to each other, scrambling still further from my spot.

The last of the prayers and chants, the bottled-up devotion and longing and desperate need, belched forth in a final burst of white noise. I grabbed at some small portion of it and held it deep in my chest. I needed to make that seal, and knew no other way than to use the very magic I'd just let loose, the stuff I'd just sworn I'd never use.

Rocks clattered against my ankles, and even twigs and trees piled up, until debris clogged every fissure and the ground had moved back together again. Valeo and I were nearly knee-deep in debris. But it was working. Nihil's voice died away with the last phantasms and chants, whispering his final warning:

"Ah! You always make the same mistake. And you will always fail."

I shuddered and stood amid the mounds I had made. Similar mounds covered the other pools, which leaked steam but nothing else, nothing unnatural. Valeo stood and stared through slitted eyes, and I didn't want to imagine what he must be thinking. Let him wonder about what I'd done.

"He's gone," I said.

"I know." His voice was low and soft. "I suppose you had to do it your way."

The Gek returned, slowly at first, tiptoeing through narrow openings and picking their way with care. It took long moments for them to reach my spot, skittering around the reformed landscape, sniffing with their tongues, camouflaging against the sulfurous rocks. Some waved sticky fingers at me and were murmuring prayers to me. I cringed.

"Stop, all of you, stop," I said and signaled at once. "This is absurd. I'm human. Mortal."

The chieftain spoke up from beside Valeo. "You are the star, and you can no longer deny that. Even Nothing Man believes it to be so."

"We don't know what Nihil believes. I do know that I've rid this island of magic and it's time to go home. That is what I know."

It was true, about the magic being gone. I stepped out of the prayer well and inhaled. All I sensed was sulphur and steam. I stretched my arms to the sky, my feet rooted to the soil, and tried to sense something that didn't feel right, deep beneath the surface. Nothing.

The Gek began clamoring, bobbing and milling about and flushing all kinds of soft, happy hues. Many danced in place out of excitement, and their happy croaking and whistling spoke of feeling the absence of the magic. I felt their relief, too, though I was more wary about it. They obviously didn't know I'd used magic to stop magic. That bit of irony was going to claw at me until I solved the riddle, if I ever could.

Again, a sense of rightness poured over me. The air was fresh, the trees' roots in the forest beyond reached deeply down into the purity of the water table, the volcano before me gently slept, snoring out vapors. Life sang all around me, and none of it seemed unbalanced or off-center, as if some unseen force had tampered with it.

That feeling was gone, replaced by a sensation of openness, like the cool, fresh weather after a storm has passed. My surroundings seemed more crisp, clean, and bright. Tension eased out of my shoulders. I dusted off some of the caked mud, and let myself breathe in a little relief.

I still didn't know if this had been the only well of prayers or just one of many. I suspected it must've been important if Nihil had noticed and tried to make himself heard here. I wasn't sure how much magic it took to broadcast your voice halfway across the world. A lot? A little?

I let myself imagine that this well of prayers was the only one, since it's what I so desperately wanted to believe. There'd be no more swamp fires. Perhaps the two Azwans were back in Port Sapphire, trying desperately to conjure spells, not understanding why their gold totems no longer worked. I smiled. It struck me as funny, them conjuring and nothing coming. Then I noticed the Gek once again bowing to me and I frowned.

"No religion. No temples or priests or guards, Valeo, remember?"

He glanced at the Gek. "Or worshippers."

"Especially not those."

Valeo stepped away from the sealed-up pool, and we both motioned to the Gek to rise to their feet, as many were bowing and kneeling. They rose only hesitantly, casting their darting, furtive glances at one another, at their chieftain, and back at me. I signaled to them all, not just the chieftain. I wasn't going to play into anyone's notion of religious hierarchy.

"I am just like you. I am not a star and I didn't fall to Kuldor. I am not here to take the place of the one you call Nothing Man."

I went on. I pleaded with them for peace, to leave off attacking the human city they had come to hate in recent six-days and to set aside their loathing of us drabskinned folk to learn to live side-by-side again. I had wanted these things all along, but now I sensed I had the authority to ask for them. They listened and flushed scores of different shades. Their emotions ranged all over, from some obvious fear to dismay or anger or hope—it strained my knowledge of them to figure it all out.

Mostly, I was confused and afraid. Confused, as I'd used magic and I knew flat out I'd rationalized it away. Afraid, because I really had no idea what I'd done, if it would hold, and what might be happening in Port Sapphire.

So I sat down again on the boulder, Valeo on one side, the chieftain on the other, as Gek wandered around us. Someone brought gourds of fresh water, others carried platters of food. I chewed slowly, trying not to hear the chieftain's many questions, my eyesight blurred. I needed desperately to be alone and think through what happened and how and, most importantly, why.

Earlier, the weight of so many people and their expectations and questions and needs had felt tangible to me, like being scraped raw with rocks. I had met and exceeded them, I think, and they owed me some quiet time alone. Perhaps this was what being a leader really meant: not the privileges that Babba basked in, or the stature to make demands, but the sense that the burdens of the world had to be set down every once in a while, that the world could wait until my thoughts caught up to my actions.

I signaled to the chieftain, saying I needed to rest. Maybe that was partly true, though I wasn't tired. A few clicks and croaks later, we were on our way back down to the waterfall and its array of huts. Along the way, I took the time to describe to the Gek around me what I'd done and why, being careful to point out in my hand signs that I had indeed felt the need to use magic, after a fashion. I knew I wielded it crudely and that I obviously lacked Nihil's finesse, but I hated myself for having used it at all. I told them what Nihil had said, that it was a mistake and I would fail. That nagged at me, and I watched the chieftain closely for his reaction.

The chieftain whistled and croaked his agreement. "Nothing Man is right. He has you play his game and by his rules. These are his tools, the tools of the unnatural making. Your task is to unmake his evil messes, not to try to make them better or after your own fashion. But you are young as your people measure lives, yes?"

"I've only just come of age, Wise One."

"Yet you have already taken a mate. He is stout as a tree trunk, to be sure. We do remember a short span of days ago, however, when he killed us with great skill and no shame. The one you call Eater of Insects has little good to say of him."

"Is Bugsy here?" I was delighted at the mention of her name.

"She is with the rest of lizardfolk in a safe place. She has much she wants to teach us about your kind."

"Please tell her how much I love her and wish her well." I could only imagine the odd things Bugsy had observed from Rishi alone.

"Yes, this I will do. Now you must look to your rest and to your mate. I am not sure I trust him, but you do, and that's what matters. Otherwise, his body would be back in the drabskin nest cluster with all the others."

Valeo grunted as I softly translated. "Tell Spike I'll skin his scaly hide if he tries. Bare-handed."

"I will not."

Valeo wheeled on me. "Then tell him I don't answer to some toad-faced, slithering worm who barely comes up to my ass. And that nest cluster he talks about is full of the bodies of better men than him. Bodies he put there."

"Valeo—"

"So that he could drag you here. And now you're done and I'm taking you back."

We walked in silence after that, Valeo glowering, me wilting from being around too many people at once. When we reached the waterfall, I paused to wash the mud off me. It was a clumsy effort, as I struggled to keep some semblance of modesty with the sodden blanket wrapped around me, dirtying me again each time I scrubbed clean. Finally, Valeo retrieved one from a pile by a hut and he turned away while I bathed my legs and splashed my face. Except for worrying about him, I was at peace. I had won. I had a right to be pleased about that.

The chieftain watched me watching Valeo's back. "You are young, and we overestimated some things about you. You have made some mistakes, and these you must undo first, before you can fulfill your destiny."

I shook my head. "I don't know what this Undoer is, and I'm not sure I wish to be it. And I believe my job is done, no?"

"The poison you said you felt beneath the ground. Do you think it was only here?"

I turned to him. "I'm not sure, but I take it you do."

He nodded. "It is why lizardfolk came to this island at the Center of the World. This world is our Great Nest that is home to us all, even to your kind. We can sense in ways that drabskins cannot how the Nothing Man poisons it from deep within. This island was the last to be so touched, and therefore the most important to us. We had failed to guard it well enough."

I met his unblinking gaze with solemnity and chose my signaled words. "You envision that I will do for the Great Nest what I did here?"

"Yes, but you must avoid using the Nothing Man's tools."

"Is this the only such place that stored the Nothing Man's poison?" I asked. I had to know if this had been the only prayer well or not.

"His poison is vast and deep, beyond our understanding, but perhaps not beyond yours."

Well, that didn't help much.

I bowed, just as I did with Babba when I wanted to show deference and maybe hide my scowl. The chieftain seemed to see it as a sign of respect and bowed his own head in reply. I made my excuses and went into the hut where'd I'd slept the night before. His was just one piece of advice too many in recent six-days, and all the things I'd learned and done and heard were clamoring in my head at once.

Finally, I was alone. I could enjoy a few moments of solitude to sort my thoughts. I lay back down on the pile of blankets and stared up at the thatching overhead.

So somewhere, S'ami and Reyhim weren't spellcasting. Or maybe they were.

Was that important to me?

Or was it more important to see their red sails dipping back over the horizon so life could return to what it was before they came?

I no longer felt sure of the answer.

I couldn't stop all magic. The wellspring of it underground had been immense, and I'd tapped only a portion of it, if what the chieftain said was true. Trying to remember the enormity of that well felt too difficult. I couldn't restore the Gek's Great Nest to whatever they thought it should be. If I was the Undoer, it had to be on a local scale only. I had my home and my ways and customs, and the Gek had theirs. Becoming their Undoer would be no different than being their Azwan. The thought made me cringe. I was nobody's god or numen or high priest and I did not want to be.

I had come seeking answers, and again I found that more questions sprouted like mushrooms after a dark rain. Valeo fumed over dead friends back in Port Sapphire. I'd also know many families missing their fathers and brothers. I closed my eyes against the lump in my throat, but it didn't work. I had to return home and sort things out with the Temple of Doubt, with my parents, with my city. Each one of these was its own separate battle, needing its own strategy. Even if I could figure out what to say to my parents, what mess had I made with the Temple?

If they could still spellcast, I could still undo those spells. If they couldn't, I didn't know what to picture. A triumphant scene where I waved the crippled magic users off on their magnificent ships? A humbling scene where I magnanimously forgave them and let them leave peacefully?

I needed a plan. I knew I wasn't going to get a procession in my honor; I'd be lucky to avoid a jail cell, let alone the gallows. So whatever I said or did upon my return, it had to include some way to save my hide and convince the Azwans there was nothing more here for them to do.

Thinking this way made it sound so easy.

Small, local, doable. I had to focus on one task at a time, or one piece of a giant task, or it would become a massive, tangled ball, one I couldn't unravel. One foot in front of the other. Focus on what I could do. Breathe. In and out. One thing at a time.

I sighed, closed my eyes, and went over the day's events in my head a few more times, trying as hard as I could to be honest with myself. I fought not to gloss over the magic I had clumsily used or to rationalize it. I had had my reasons and excuses, but they were bad ones. There was one other needling thought that prickled me: what was it about that hunk of star or space dust that made Nihil and the Gek both think it still lived and made its home inside me?

What if it were there, not just as a few leftover powers, but as a thinking creature? Perhaps it was like the volcano, only dormant if seen from a distance, but venting its odd talents through fissures in my consciousness?

What if I were possessed after all?

28

*You have asked me to pass judgment on women's virtue, which I do with great reluctance, as each woman's circumstances differ. In the desert lands, a woman is worth barely the dirt displaced by her sandals. Among the giants, she is queen. And have I not taken a woman's form from time to time? I was modest in my dress and conduct then, and so shall you require it of my daughters now.*
*—from* Oblations 18, The Book of Unease

We set out with the sun only a little past its zenith, with the Gek again loading us onto their log canoes and paddling us against the tide toward the distant city. That gave me plenty of time to think of a counter-strategy to Valeo's terrible ideas.

He wanted to do all the talking, of course. He was sure he could've straightened things out with Nihil if I hadn't cut him off, so he would be in charge of a new plan. He didn't say what my part was supposed to be, but I imagined it was something along the lines of staring wide-eyed and stupid and hoping everyone pitied me. The fact that I looked exactly like the image of the wild, natural girl of rumor and gossip did not figure into Valeo's calculations. I would get as much pity as a disease.

He rambled on about handling this, about how S'ami clearly hadn't told Nihil everything and he could use that to his advantage, how I didn't understand the delicate politics between the two Azwans, how I should possibly act wounded or sickly or like it was all the Gek's fault.

Fortunately, I sat in front of Valeo in our makeshift craft and faced forward so he couldn't see my constant eye-rolling or my fuming. The logical part of me realized that Valeo didn't know he was describing the sort of idiotic and complacent girl who I'd once tried and failed to be. Just as I'd truly come to accept my differences, he was asking me to give that all up and play the baby-faced know-nothing and leave all the thinking to the big, smart, manly man.

After a while, I tried to shut out the sound of all his important plans and schemes and tried to let the canoe lapping against the waves lull me a bit. His voice droned on.

"And it might even save *my* neck, too," he said at last.

I picked up my head at this. I remembered the obvious relief in Nihil's voice after Valeo had announced his presence at the prayer well. I didn't think Valeo was in any danger. I didn't even turn to face him in the teeter canoe but shouted over my shoulder:

"You? You're the guard of Nihil's person, aren't you? Or whatever he calls you."

"I thought you cared whether I lived or died."

That brought my head around. "Don't you ever think otherwise. Of course I do."

"Well, act like it then."

I didn't like the angry look on his face. What did he mean?

"What do I have to do? I kissed you. *You* are the one doubting *me*. I should just toss you over the side."

He snorted. "Try it. Go ahead."

I made a growling noise and turned back around. Thanks to Valeo's robust paddling, we'd gotten far ahead of the other Gek canoes—too far for my liking. I glanced over my shoulder again, meeting Valeo's still-amused gaze, and then looked further back to see the other craft at least a full rowing length behind. Blast it. There was safety in a crowd, as Babba would say, and one canoe felt too vulnerable to me.

And then an idea pounded into my brain with the force of stone. I turned all the way around to face Valeo.

"Did you say there'd be search parties out for us?" I asked.

He nodded.

"How close do you think they'd be by now?"

He cocked his head and squinted. "You're serious? They're just up ahead."

I whipped back around. Sure enough, I could make out the tiny specks of people paddling toward us. I'd been so lost in my fog of anger and annoyance that I'd missed it.

That didn't give me much time to perfect my half-formed plan, but I had to try. I needed to time this just right, or at least make it look like it was timed right. The thought struck me that I had to convince three parties of three separate things in order to save both my own life and Valeo's: Valeo had to believe I was betraying him, the Gek had to think I wanted to go back to my people, but my people had to believe I belonged in the wild. Only in that way could I make sure that Valeo came out of this looking like he'd never harbored a single, heretical doubt in his thick head, and that I wasn't fully a heretic deserving of a hanging.

All the sweet, flattering things Valeo had ever said about me could be scattered on the next strong wind for all it mattered. He had to hate me, and it had to be real, or his comrades and commander would think he'd lost his head over some crazy witch. He may not feel he had much to lose, but I suspected otherwise. Sooner or later, I would have to wreck his life.

And it'd have to be sooner, rather than later, or, I realized with a gulp, I'd never work up the nerve. He was now envisioning his triumphant return with me and all the stories he'd weave to try and save our hides. It would likely mean whole new layers of lies.

I waited until the rowboats pulled close enough to see us. I had picked up a paddle in the bottom of the canoe and had joined Valeo's frantic paddling, as though I were also anxious to return. When the boats were too big on the horizon to ignore, I leaned forward and braced my knees against the sides of the canoe. I gripped the paddle for power rather than steering, adjusting my grip subtly so Valeo wouldn't notice any strange movement. I turned my torso ever-so-slightly so I could put my whole body into that paddle.

Then I whirled around and whacked the side of his head.

Valeo tumbled into the water with a yelp, but I'd already begun paddling toward shore as furiously as I could manage. Behind me, Valeo cursed and shouted. Then silence. A hand clamping on the side of the canoe told me I hadn't rowed fast enough, but we'd been traveling parallel to shore. As he reached for me, I dove into the water on the other side of the canoe and swam the short distance to the beach. I ran up the beach toward the Gek, visible in the distance in their tiny craft.

I couldn't look behind me to see whether the human boats were any closer. I'd dropped my blanket skirt and was running in my underclothes, my legs bare to the world. I didn't know I could run so fast, as I hadn't had many opportunities to do so. Civilized girls stroll politely. But I sprinted. Valeo caught up to me with a string of curses, the names he called me so vile and awful, they burned all the way down to my heart. I had wanted this be real, and it was, and I hated it.

I struggled to free myself from his iron grip. I kneed him in his groin and managed to briefly wriggle free to a new stream of his curses. This time he held me from behind, his massive arms folded across mine.

How I wish ears had lids, as eyes do, so I could've shut myself off from the vile flood of invective he poured into them: I was the worst sort of traitor, I'd taken his trust and smashed it, I was ungrateful and fickle and cruel, and a thousand other evil things besides. I continued to struggle and wriggle and kick in his grip, but I didn't utter a word. I wasn't going to fling hurtful retorts at him or engage in a shouting match. It would hurt me too much and, there wasn't a fiber in my entire body that could bring myself to say a single bad word about the man who'd risked his reputation, his career, and possibly his life to follow me out into the wild.

The first rowboats pulled up to shore and men dashed toward us. I fully expected them to raise weapons, which they did. I expected them to point those weapons at me, which they didn't.

They surrounded us. One of the men I recognized as a port inspector, one of my father's men. His name was Aleen, and he'd been a ship's captain before falling in love with a Port Sapphire woman and weighing anchor for the last time here.

"Let her go," Aleen said. "Or die, Feroxi bastard."

"You fool," Valeo fumed, gripping me harder. "I could wipe out all of you before you blinked."

Aleen raised a sword as the other men pressed in. "You rapist bastard. Now that you've finished with the daughter of our esteemed Lord Portreeve, we shall finish you."

Rapist? I wanted to laugh, but clamped my mouth shut and wriggled free of an astonished Valeo. The word had its effect on him, too, and he eyed me with an unspoken plea in his gaze. It seemed to ask "How far will your betrayal go?" We hanged rapists in Port Sapphire; I wished that had occurred to me when making my phony escape plan.

"You've come in time, Port Inspector Aleen," I said with as much gravity as I could muster, despite looking extremely ravaged and unchaste. "There's no harm done here. My fate brought me out to these woods, and this soldier wishes to bring me back. There's nothing else to assume by his actions."

Both Aleen and Valeo relaxed their stances. Valeo continued to stare at me, probably wondering what game I was playing. I wasn't sure, myself, since I was making up the rules as I went. Rule number one: keep Valeo safe. He only knew how to wield weapons; I was learning how to wield people. I only hoped I was getting better at it.

"So he hasn't tried anything?" Aleen asked. "And you wish to stay here?"

I shook my head. "I seem to have brought all sorts of terrible violence to our city, Aleen. This is all my doing. Aren't you safer if I stayed away?"

Valeo interrupted, "Don't listen to her—"

"Shut up, Feroxi thug," Aleen said. More men had joined him, and Valeo faced a sea of knives, pikes, and swords. He seemed more annoyed than afraid, though, and kept giving me hard, beady-eyed stares that made me shift uneasily and turn away. At some point, I realized something soggy was dangling in my eyes. I pushed up a few locks of hair to rediscover my wilted moonbloom crown, its petals now flaking around my shoulders and embedded in curls of hair. I brushed a few off in a futile gesture, but Valeo's makeshift wreath had stubbornly nested itself in my unruly mane. I wanted to cry from frustration and heartache and a sudden onslaught of irony.

Aleen gave me a weighty, solemn look that spoke of important matters.

"Hadara of Rimonil, there is not one soul in all of Port Sapphire who blames you for what's happened," he said. "The Azwans should've stayed in their far-away land and the meteorite could've stayed with the Gek, and we'd all have gone on just fine."

Valeo scoffed. "You couldn't possibly believe that. Have you any idea—"

"Once again, you interrupt, you stinking shark," Aleen said. "To the dark bottom of the sea with your kind. It's where you belong."

Valeo's jaw dropped. "You dare?"

"*You* dare. Our women are not for your plundering; this woman especially. You have dragged her from us, and we are bringing her back."

"Dragged? You think I dragged—"

The mightiest struggle that day turned out to be the one I had with myself to keep from bursting into peals of laughter. The two men argued over whose fault it was that the Lord Portreeve's eldest daughter was found on a deserted stretch of beach without half her clothes and in the clutches of an angry soldier. Valeo glowered and glared like fish could've wielded weapons more skillfully against him than this group of clerks and peddlers. But I hoped he also picked up on what Aleen wasn't saying: the city had no more use for the Temple of Doubt and had come around to my own sense of disgust. Perhaps they'd even felt some difference in the magic there—maybe there was no magic, if the prayer well had been sealed as well as I thought.

I would head home to a very different city.

But any mirth gave way to dread when Aleen spoke up again: "Your father needs you urgently, Hadara. It may already be too late."

"Too late for what?" My pulse raced. What could be wrong? I remembered he'd been wounded, but certainly

Leba Mara and the other healers would've helped him, right?

"We don't know, Hadara. Healer Mistress Leba Mara has said it's no longer in her hands, and you're rumored to have some strange power that could help him. We have nothing but that rumor to go on."

I didn't even take the time to reply. I ran toward the nearest boat and clambered in, men pushing off after me and climbing on board to help me row. I glanced back to see Valeo had taken over a boat and was rowing himself behind us. Every time his boat caught up to mine, however, the other men shoved at his boat with their oars. Some spat in his direction, others cursed in the local tongue. Valeo's face hardened but he kept on course, never letting his boat get more than a body length behind.

Further back, the Gek kept up their own rowing, making their steady way back to the city they'd left smoldering.

But I was no longer thinking about that, or anything. An image of Babba's bleeding body crept into my head and stuck there, and it was all I could do to keep breathing, keep breathing, as if just by inhaling I could speed the little rowboat along or pull it by an unseen cord. I had no idea what could be wrong, or if it was too late—if everything that mattered in my life would evaporate in smoke and dust.

I closed my eyes, but the tears came anyway. The shoreline crept past more slowly than ever as the flotilla of boats made their steady way back to the ruined city.

29

*Nature is malleable. There's nothing in nature I
cannot change, if I desire. This power I call magic,
and it comes from me. You may not wield magic
except by my permission.*
    —*Oblations 10,* The Book of Unease

A landing party greeted us by the boat launch, but Aleen
and the other men wouldn't let me out of the rowboat
until someone had fetched fresh clothes to borrow and
a comb for my hair. I changed behind a tree while they
stood guard nearby, hustling into a too-short dress and
a frayed head wrap. My clothes were mismatched, but I
looked presentable, at least. I thanked the men for taking
the time to help me where many simply would've stood
around and gawked.

"It is time to go," was all Aleen would say. He took my
arm and led me along the wharf, past the blackened skeletons of ships sunk low, the corpses of a mighty merchant
fleet still moored to the place they'd burned. I hadn't seen

Valeo go, but he must've sped on ahead to Ward Sapphire, as I didn't catch sight of him anywhere. There were no soldiers at all, for that matter, and I wondered what might've happened here after I'd left: had I really succeeded in capping Nihil's source of magic? Was there no more magic, and the Temple Guards had holed up with the perplexed and suddenly powerless Azwans?

But S'ami didn't look powerless when he greeted me at the Ward's mighty gates. He looked as proud and haughty as ever, with that way he had of looking down at everyone, even the giant guards around him. He wordlessly dismissed Aleen and the other men, who bowed and did the vomit-hands greeting as they always did, but with scowls instead of subservient looks. S'ami extended his hand to take mine, keeping it aloft like something precious he was holding up to the light. We strode like this through the compound, a row of soldiers to either side of us, while S'ami muttered softly in Tengali.

"I know you understand me, so I'll get to the point," he said. "Your father, as you've heard, is quite ill and we don't understand its nature."

"And you can't admit that to the public," I said.

"I'll talk. You listen. It would seem that your people consider your father the worthiest of all the men on this island. Yet if your father isn't worthy of Nihil's forgiveness and healing, it stirs up a swamp rat's den of doubts. And that is trouble Nihil never needs."

"How is my father?" I asked. If S'ami was talking in terms of Babba needing healing, then he must be alive. I clung to that lonely piece of hope.

"You shall soon see."

I didn't like the sound of that, but I had another urgent question. "Are you able to spellcast?"

S'ami cast me a sidelong glance. "Is there some reason I wouldn't?"

So he didn't know about the prayer well, just as Nihil hadn't known about my alleged powers. No wonder Valeo was so keen on secrets and lies; he was used to being around people who hoarded bits and pieces of truth like gold. I would have wondered whether I should be the one to explain to S'ami and ask what effects he'd noticed, if any, but we'd reached the sick ward, and Leba Mara flung open the doors as we approached.

Instead of her usual boisterous greeting, she looked ashen and reserved. I felt even more anxious as we were swept inside, healers pausing over cots full of the injured and burned, silently watching me pass. I realized they, too, might not be able to use magic and that healing would be difficult. I was less happy about the idea of that. S'ami ushered me to the same tiny room where'd I'd recovered from touching the egg, when I'd awakened to this nightmare of strange powers and stranger events.

I paused outside the door to take in the sound of weeping. The healers had resumed their business in the main part of the ward, and their bustling drowned out the sobbing voice inside the room, but I would know it anywhere. Mami.

My breathing grew ragged and I leaned against the wall for support. I had come too late. It was all over, and I had been out in the swamps on some ridiculous errand, seeking answers to questions I hadn't known how to pose, stirring up trouble, when the one person

I might've been able to help had died for want of my skills.

I stood before that door, damning myself for every waking moment of my life that I'd ever smiled or laughed, repenting every good feeling I'd ever had, punishing my wicked, ungrateful, selfish heart for its continuous beating while Babba lay dead.

"Why do you wait, child?" S'ami's voice had taken on a paternal tone.

"Because I'm too late, aren't I?"

"Do you have the skills to know that from here?" The surprise in his voice made me think I might be wrong.

No, it'd be wrong to hope. Mami sat on the other side of the door, weeping. Hope was an ugly thing. I hated myself, and I wanted Mami to hate me, too. I knew I deserved it.

S'ami slid open the door and I took timid, halting steps inside. Babba lay on the sick cot, his face pale, his hair matted on his uncovered head. His eyes were closed. As I drew closer, I could see his chest rising and falling, his breathing shallow.

But he was alive.

Mami saw me and reached for me. I kneeled on the floor beside her and let her hold me and rock me back and forth.

"Oh, blossom, there's nothing more they can do for him," she said. "Their magic's not working."

My eyes welled up. This couldn't be happening. What had I done? Maybe I hadn't awakened yet, maybe I'd gone to bed after that night I'd kissed Valeo—was it just two nights ago?—and I was dreaming, and this horrible scene could be rubbed from my eyes when I yawned and stretched and blinked into a new day. Any day but this one would do.

A raspy voice came from the doorway behind me. "He's been a good husband to you, Lia."

Reyhim edged his way forward to sit on Mami's other side but she didn't turn away from me.

"Lia, please," Reyhim said. "Let me be here for you. For all the times I wasn't."

"If it pleases you, Azwan," Mami said. The sudden narrowing of her eyes told me she didn't mean it. She didn't look at him.

The only benefit I could see to having both Azwans here was that it forced Mami to regain her composure. She washed her face in a basin by Babba's cot and straightened out her dress. As she did so, I took a closer look at my father. I wasn't accepting this. I wasn't going to remember forever that our last time together had been a scolding. There had to be something wrong, something to fix.

I touched his hand but pulled back at the sizzle of sparks it sent into me. Strong magic coursed between us in that brief touch. One of the healers must've tried to patch his wounds earlier. A patch of blood oozed from the side of his body that faced the wall. I tugged at the cot so it angled away from the wall.

"Hadara, what are you doing?" Mami said.

"I want to see the magic they used," I said. I may have patched up some hole in the world, but that didn't mean there wasn't plenty oozing around outside of it.

Reyhim cleared his throat, but S'ami spoke first. "There is ambiguity here to let her try."

Reyhim shook his head. "I remain the judge of that. Hadara, explain. Do you mean to undo healing spells, done with good intent, and to the best of a healer's ability?"

I hesitated. His voice had a practiced tone, but what was he getting at? I'd come too far to ask his permission for something he clearly needed me to do. "I want to examine the wound and the magic on it. I believe that's why you brought me here?"

It was S'ami's turn for the head shaking. "We've discussed it, although only briefly, given the circumstances. We're trying to decide if there are theological grounds for what you do."

Was I hearing things? The very same Azwan who'd winkingly had me undo a spell that made the original warehouse fire worse was now lecturing me about doctrine. My entire childhood had been spent memorizing absurd contradictions and endless, boring details of a fickle god's boring, endless life. That god had been crippled, as far as I knew, and either the Azwans hadn't been told or were lying.

Brave, resilient, clever Babba, who didn't have time any longer for the Azwan's uncertain ambiguous doubts, needed my unique help. Besides, this was my *father*. What other reason did I need? I reached for him, not knowing—alright, I'll say it, uncertain—about what I was going to do. I had nothing to lose, except the man who'd held his family together despite the odds against it.

But . . . but I'd had to use magic out at the prayer well. What if my un-doing also failed here? What if I had no other options here, too? What was I willing to do for Babba?

As my hands passed over Babba's chest, the sparks and streams of colors from the healing spells became visible to me. They enshrouded his entire body, weaving to and fro as if he'd fallen prey to some monstrous spider. It was hard to tell what was flesh and what was the electric weave of theurgy.

I had used magic with less reason than to save someone I loved. I could use it again. I had sworn not to, but who had heard that vow? No one. Maybe I'd made it rashly. Maybe there were times when the unnatural was necessary and right and good.

No.

I shook my head with such violence, it knocked my borrowed head wrap loose. I tucked in a stray curl and glanced over at Mami, S'ami, and Reyhim, crowded around me, waiting for me to do something spectacular and important. If I did cast a spell, how would I know what I was doing? I had nothing at my disposal unless I could somehow reach with my thoughts all the way to the sealed prayer well and back.

That sounded so impractical, given that it was empty. Besides, whatever type of power I wielded, it had to fit the task, not my feelings.

"I can undo all this magic, but I have no idea what's beneath it," I said.

S'ami grabbed my shoulder. "Don't do this. It can't be justified. There'll be no way to defend you."

Reyhim cleared his throat. "Tell her, Lia."

Mami caught my eye and held up her chin. "Hadara, do as your conscience dictates."

"And what of yours?" Reyhim said. "You lost your mother, who refused to help. Now you stand to lose your daughter for undoing such help."

Mami kept her eyes on mine, and they were steady and clear. "It's your choice."

My always-restless mind hit on something that might keep the Azwans at bay. "I'm a healer's apprentice, and I want to see how their spells are put together. I have a student's right to learn from my betters."

This had the benefit of being true.

"You promise that's all?" S'ami said.

I nodded, and he released my arm with a smug look at Reyhim that told me I'd again become a playing piece in their game of strategy.

"You're on your word," Reyhim said.

I spread my palms over Babba's chest and watched the rays of color leap to my skin. Babba's chest gave a lurch and he convulsed. I didn't move my hands, but kept them in place, watching. The bands of color unweaved beneath my palms. I could see the metallic blues and fiery copper of Leba Mara's spellcasting, and the yellow and orange sheens of one of the other senior healers. They danced under my palms. I sorted them as if untangling yarn. Faint music tinkled in my head, reminding me of a cantina heard from across the bay, inviting but indistinct. This was familiar territory, easy doings compared to what I'd seen out at the side of Mount Meridiana.

But what would lie underneath? I could be un-magicking my father to death. My hands held steady, even as my nerves frayed.

S'ami leaned in closer while Reyhim edged away. I suppose that told me something about their differences. S'ami cocked his head. "Tell me what you see."

"I see weaving and unweaving. I hear music, but also the sound of something fizzing, like static." I pointed to S'ami. "Your spells are in here, too. Your musical colors, they're all here."

S'ami shook his head. "I haven't worked on the Lord Portreeve."

"There are the Azwan of Ambiguity's pale grays, and some other hues. The high priest's, I think. When I separate the threads of light, I can hear different tunes." They were distinct, like the timbre of a voice or the fine lines on one's fingerprints. At least, that's how I tried to describe it to S'ami, who began waving his gold wisdom knot above my hands.

Did he not know about the prayer well, or sense that his magic had dried up? For a brief, panicky moment, I wondered if I'd failed after all, and if nothing had changed for spellcasters or even for Nihil. How would I know?

S'ami muttered in Tengali, in what I figured must be some sort of incantation. He mentioned seeing colors and light and dark, weaving and chaos and unweaving. Everything I'd said, he was repeating as an incantation, a lyrical stream of nonsense, the words strung randomly like children's play beads. Was that all there was to spellcasting? It seemed so simple. No wonder the spells appeared so frail to me.

"Can you see what I see?" I asked.

"I believe so," he said.

Reyhim pushed his way between S'ami and Mami, who'd been watching raptly, one hand stroking Babba's hair.

"I forbid this," Reyhim said.

"On what grounds?" S'ami didn't budge.

"This . . . undoing. I've seen enough."

S'ami remained cool. "I haven't."

Reyhim's voice dropped to a low growl. "There's no point to it. The man's dying. Let him be."

"I want to know why my spells are mixed in with the healer's."

"I'm ordering it stopped."

S'ami took out his totem and waved it at his older rival. "There isn't any further harm we could do to the Lord Portreeve. I don't see the point in halting our exploration, unless your real goal is to widow your daughter."

"She's not my . . ." Reyhim halted mid-sentence. He took a sudden interest in Babba's limp form, even as Mami's gaze shifted to Reyhim's bowed head. He didn't look up. With a sigh and a shake of his head, Reyhim backed away. He spoke in a language I recognized as Fernai. "You bastard. You blackmailing, backstabbing, ball-crushing bastard. You'll pay. Our Master will hear of all of this."

S'ami's reply came in Fernai as well. "I'm counting on it."

Reyhim pursed his lips and switched back to the common tongue. "I won't be witness to this perfidy, at least." Then he was gone, without so much as a parting nod to Mami or any of us.

For a brief moment, none of us spoke. Mami brushed her fingertips on S'ami's sleeve. "It feels like I ought to be thanking you for something."

"Not yet," he said.

He held up his totem.

"How is that still working?" I thought aloud. Too late, I clamped a hand over my mouth.

S'ami lowered his totem. "Meaning?"

I shook my head.

"Out with it, Hadara. What is it I should know?"

I looked down at Babba again. "Let me get back to this."

"I just defended you. I have defended you often. I am the reason you're not in a jail cell this very moment. Tell me. Was there something the Gek had you do?"

I told him. The words came out in haste, about the trip there, the prayer well, the confrontation with Nihil, all of it. I jumbled the order of events, prompting questions from both S'ami and Mami until I got the details right.

S'ami wanted to know what Nihil said.

Mami wanted to know what the Gek did.

"Look, let me help Babba first, please," I said. "Can't this wait?"

The two exchanged a look I didn't like, the ones I used to get as a child when two adults were exasperated with me. They'd formed some sort of instant alliance, which didn't seem fair. Then S'ami nodded and we both turned to the tangle of magic, only half-unknotted. With a few waves of his wisdom knot, S'ami made some of his colors visible so he and Mami could tell what I was doing, at least with his own spells. The colors were much feebler than I remembered, though. They were even feebler than the old ones that clung to Babba. That answered my question, then: the totem worked, and magic flowed, but diminished and pale.

Nothing about Babba's condition had changed, but Mami nodded vigorously when S'ami asked if she could see any of his work.

"Then your theory about the origins of the spells on your father were right, Hadara," he said. "There it is, my luminous talent laid bare where I didn't put it. This is indeed unexpected and I could probably make a case for your undoing it."

He suggested I try to find all his conjurations and separate them out singly. I didn't know how to do that. Babba moaned when I tried. I began to fret. Was Babba worse for my actions? Was I helping? What was I doing, exactly?

"Hadara, it looks like it's flowing into you," Mami said. She pointed at my middle. "Not just your hands, but everywhere. It's siphoning off of Rimonil and into you."

S'ami rubbed his chin, radiating frustration. "I was afraid of that. Whatever's dismantling Nihil's theurgy's coming from deep within you. And this Well of Prayers? And my weakened spellcasting? Whether you've set out to do so or not, you have quite clearly set yourself up as his rival. At least, I'm sure that's how he'll see it."

I scowled right back, but with frustrations of my own. "And what of your revolution now? Have you changed your mind? Or am I like the other Lord Portreeve, someone you discard when I can't do what you ask."

My hot words were met with S'ami's stare and his slow, careful reply. "If you were to ever face Nihil without my help, he would crush you. Don't doubt it. And I'll use or discard whom I like. There's a more urgent matter at hand than who governs a tiny port on a faraway island.

This particular portreeve's life is important to me strictly because it's important to you."

I gulped back the lump in my throat. "And because this faraway island would pack you back onto your ship and set it afire if he does die."

Mami managed a smile at that, which she hid behind a corner of her head scarf.

"The politics of this particular situation are indeed tricky, Hadara," said S'ami. "I must remember not to keep confiding important information to you."

I sighed. "If I undo anything, I don't know if he's alright underneath. Babba could bleed to death in front of us. He could be fine. He could be so enmeshed in theurgy that his flesh comes undone with the old spells. And even then, there would be his existing injuries. They're still there, and he seems to have lost a lot of blood."

S'ami stroked his chin.

"See if you can undo a spell at a time, and see what happens. If we can rid him of most or even all of it, I'll see if a new healing spell does anything for him," S'ami said. "My theurgy's much weaker now, thanks to your Well of Prayers, or whatever you called it. Even so, my weak spells are likely stronger than anything the healers here could provide. Though you'll step outside if it comes unraveled with you here."

"If we fail?"

"Then he dies, Hadara. But if we do nothing, he dies."

Mami leaned in. "Hadara, do not blame yourself if it doesn't work. This isn't your doing. Babba would want you to be brave. *I* want you to be brave."

"I know, Mami," I said. "But can't we try some sort of natural remedy? Leba Mara well knows how to stitch wounds and dress them, and you and I can make a poultice ..."

"And go directly to a gallows," said S'ami. "Neither I nor Reyhim could protect you at that point. It is this, or nothing."

Valeo had complained that I wanted to do everything my way, that in fact I *had* to do it my way. It was exhausting being right all the time. I took another look at Mami's tear-stained face and knew I'd pushed everyone's limits— mine, the Azwans, Mami's, even Babba's, to their breaking points. It was time to declare victory, however incomplete.

I nodded, unable to speak. I cleared my throat and tried to focus. I pulled back the blanket covering Babba and examined his naked chest. There was no bandage, not when the healers' arts were supposed to have wrapped some invisible, magical bandage on him. All I saw was a mesh made of nonsense, a hairy noise of confusion and turbulence darting without pattern or rhythm across Babba's body.

It probably didn't matter where I put my hands, I reasoned. So I lay them flat on his thin belly and waited. Nothing happened at first. My hands slid beneath the multicolored fabric of light and noise. I closed my eyes and imagined myself pulling on the threads, picturing the way the knots would disintegrate, impatient to do it quicker. Babba's moaning grew louder and more distinct, becoming shouts of pain and raw fear. He convulsed beneath my palms. But it was working. The fizzing built in the way it does before it bursts.

I thought I heard Babba say my name, but it sounded too faint beneath the crashing noise of the spells as they came apart in my head.

"Rimonil, love," Mami said. "Oh, love, open your eyes."

"Lia," Babba said. "The pain."

A light tap on my shoulder brought me to reality again. It was S'ami. "My turn. Quickly."

I backed up to the door. Despite being weaker, S'ami's magic hadn't changed from what I'd first heard on the wharf the day he came: sonorous, chiming, and clear. I spotted a few tendrils of color, just a few, snaking toward me along the floor and took another step back. The bright stripes withdrew until S'ami and Mami's bodies blocked my view of them. The magic had been making its way to me, as though it had a mind of its own and knew me.

Alright, I had some sort of eldritch power all my own, I told myself. It's as unsubtle as a thunderclap and about as easy to wield. It's not like the embroidery needles I could manipulate with such finesse. My un-magic was more like a hatchet, hacking at everything, or a bucket of acid, indiscriminate and coarse. I sighed. It wasn't something that would be easy to explain to people, especially to the man sitting up on his sick cot, hugging my mother, motioning for me, a pleading look on his drawn face. S'ami's spells had worked on Babba where others had left a knotty mess, adding one more mystery to the jumble in my head.

I'd have to solve those mysteries, if Nihil let me live.

# 30

*I shall take whatever form pleases me, for as long as it shall last. I am a man or a woman, a child or a grandfather, a giant or a human. You will worship me though I buzz like stingflies, or hide within the petals of a flower, or crawl through the soil under your feet.*

*You will bring your oblations to me whether I make myself seen within the Temple or hide, whether I wander among the peoples of Kuldor or swim beneath the cresting waves of the sea, whether I land in your nets or in your traps, whether you know me or not.*

*—From Oblations 8,* The Book of Unease

The morning horn woke me from a fitful night's dreams. I'd been soaring toward the marsh again, desperate for a place to land, sure I'd missed my mark somehow. Falling, crashing. Wet.

Panicking.

I struggled up from the hard, knotty wood of the cot I'd slept on. I was in a converted storage room in the sick ward: my jail cell. Outside would be a pair of thick-necked, unsmiling guards. I took a chance and jiggered the latch to get their attention. Locked, of course.

One of the guards slid the door open and peered inside. "Need something?"

"Dawn prayers?" I wanted to get out, if even for a short while.

"Not for you." The door slid closed. The latch clicked. I'd be stuck here while everyone else was in the exercise yard, stretching and greeting the day. I wiped drops of sweat from the back of my neck and looked around for a basin and towels. A wet cloth and some soap would wash away the night's foul humors. Someone had left a bedpan for me, too—crude, but it would have to suffice. I didn't think I'd be granted a trip to the bathhouse.

I could've used the Dance of Life. I looked and smelled and felt awful. Every part of me ached or throbbed or smarted. I flopped down on the cot again and regretted it. It collapsed beneath me and shed splinters of wood when I tried to right it. I gave up and nestled myself on the flimsy mattress. At least it was clean. Leba Mara ran a spotless sick ward. I could admire that. I liked her, trusted her, knew that if it were up to Leba Mara, I'd be out in the main part of the sick ward at my tasks.

But I was at the mercy of the Azwans, who'd had me escorted to my cell, or whatever I was to call it, without even a moment alone with Babba and Mami. I couldn't hug Babba for fear I'd undo S'ami's spell. I only got a last, over-my-shoulder glimpse of Babba's pained expression.

Maybe Mami would know enough about my plight to explain. Maybe he wouldn't worry too much.

Maybe the world was upside down and I was the only one right-side up. I yawned again. It sure seemed that way.

The latch clicked open and the orderly, Til, entered. He nodded toward the bedpan and basin. "Just here to clean all that up for you. Orders are to get you some hot water for a sponge bath."

I did a second take. Til grinned and added, "Not from me, silly. You can bathe yourself."

I returned his smile. "Good to know they trust me with *that*, at least."

He pretended to scratch his head. "Hmmm. Leba Mara says you're under arrest, but you're supposed to be treated nice and everything. What's going on?"

I shrugged. "I have a weird power to undo magic. I'm not sure how much I'm supposed to tell people."

"Is that why you went with the Gek? To undo something for them so they'd leave us alone? You know they're encamped in the marshes outside the city, yes?"

"I'm not surprised." I wondered what else they wanted from me. Maybe they were checking to make sure I got rid of Nihil for them. How could I do that from here?

"Yes, well, they've sent a peace greeting of some sort," the orderly said. "But your father was too sick to receive it."

One of the guards angled his head in the door. "That's enough of that. Do your business and get out."

Til and I didn't speak after that, except to thank him after he'd reassembled my cot and tucked the bedding together again. He left and reappeared with an empty basin, a jug of piping hot water, and some fresh towels. A satchel slid off his shoulder and landed at my feet.

"Azwan says to give you this." The orderly nodded at the satchel.

"What is it?"

He shrugged and held a finger to his lips and murmured. "Something big's happening."

"What?"

The orderly shrugged again and backed toward the door. "When we've mastered our doubts, our faith will be strong."

I shook my head. "My doubts are stronger."

The orderly made a sad half-smile. "Nihil's blessing on you then. I hope you'll be alright, Hadara, I really do."

With that, he turned and left, leaving me with luxuriantly hot water and a bubbly soap with a tangy scent that left my skin glowing and soft. I scrubbed away the grime of the last few days and thought about my conversation with the Azwans yesterday after I'd helped Babba.

It hadn't gone well. I'd started out talking to S'ami, who'd brought me outside on the plaza overlooking the sea, only to have Reyhim rush out in a huff, angry because he'd heard from First Guardsman Valeo that a magic well of some sort had been found and sealed. Valeo had done his duty—I couldn't blame him for that. He wasn't about to show loyalty to me after I'd run off at the last second and made him look like a violent, sleazy, rapey thug instead of a hero. That hadn't been my intent, but what did it matter anymore? He hated me, and I had to resign myself to that. I'd tried to save face for him and ruined everything instead.

And that's what I was thinking about, over and over again, while they argued and I tried to get the disquieting, creaking sound out of my head. It took long moments of staring around, trying to find the source of the sound, only to realize S'ami had seated me in the shadow of the gallows for all the doubtful souls they'd found unworthy. The creaking was the swinging of a single rope, the noose awaiting its next victim. How could I have let myself get so distracted that I hadn't grasped S'ami's unspoken message?

And then there'd been Reyhim, pacing with the energy of someone much younger, moved just by the force of his anger. There had been no word from Nihil on anything for more than a day, leaving him to believe that what Valeo had said had been true: that some essential connection to the source of magic had been severed. Yet both men could cast spells, if more feebly than before. They argued in Fernai, with Reyhim oblivious to the fact that I could understand him. S'ami didn't give that away, so I kept a straight, cool face, stared out at the ocean with my arms folded across my chest, and listened in.

Reyhim speculated there was another source of magic, and S'ami reminded him that Nihil pulled energy from the stars. To me, that meant the star people, some sort of numinous creatures who must be losing power more rapidly since the prayer well closed. What had I done? Had I made things worse? Instead of my own people on their knees to generate enough awe and terror to fuel Nihil, a distant, dimly understood species may die for his greed.

Could I get nothing right? How many more lives would be on my head before it swung from a noose? How much more blood would shed because of me?

As I listened in, I wanted to be sick. The nausea rose in me, jostling my insides, the bile searing the back of my throat as I forced it back down. My lungs sucked in deep, moist gulps of sea air, which helped clear my head and steady me. The two men argued so fiercely that neither noticed me panting or closing my eyes to block out my view of them.

Mercifully, the two men didn't last long before Reyhim sauntered off. That's how it always seemed to go: they'd argue until Reyhim gave up, regrouped, and came back for another round. I expected S'ami to continue some sort of conversation with me afterward, but he led me to my cell without another word. I suppose the view of the gallows said everything for him.

And that had been the last I'd heard from either Azwan until the satchel dropped at my feet that morning. The hot water for my bath felt soothing against my skin and hair, and a comb took care of the worst knots until my curls began to spring and sproing in their usual crazy way, drying quickly in the stuffy air. I could almost call myself refreshed afterward, if not quite calm. I decided to open the satchel to see what important thing might be inside. It held the shimmering, sunset-hued silk dress S'ami had given me for my Keeping Day. I found jewelry in there, too, bangles and beads and earrings and a headscarf made from lace so fine as to be nearly invisible.

I put everything on, with each new piece giving me more reasons to feel surprised and flattered. By the time I finished dressing, tiny bells tinkled faintly from ankle cuffs made of real silver, rings with iridescent stones gleamed from my fingers and toes. I found a small vial of infused oil and dabbed some on my neck and arms, savoring the warm, flowery perfume. I slid whisper-soft slippers onto my feet and a few bangles onto either wrist. My sprain from the other day had proved little more than a nuisance, not an injury. I felt pretty good, all in all.

I didn't have a mirror but I was sure I looked more beautiful than any other prisoner on the island, maybe in the world. I certainly felt the most beautiful I had ever been. I didn't know what big thing was happening, but I was certain it wasn't my execution. No one would care what I wore beneath a shroud.

Which Azwan had sent all this stuff? S'ami, I figured. He'd given me the dress in the first place. He seemed to have an eye for luxuries. I thanked him inside my head and could picture him nodding back. Maybe I was going to appear in public again, and S'ami wanted me to look spectacular for some reason. That had to be it, but for what reason?

I became aware of a low, sweet hum in the air around me. Magic. It didn't sound like anything I'd heard before, but it was distinct enough that I knew whoever was casting the spells wanted to be heard. I heard soft chimes and wooden flutes, warbling birds and the steady rhythm of the surf. It didn't pound your ears, demanding you listen, as S'ami's could do. It was more like the tempting aroma of a spicy dish, wrapping around you, calling you in. It teased, but it was persistent, impossible to miss.

The latch to the door unlocked and a guard slid it open. He made no move in or out and didn't motion me either. I peered into the corridor.

"What's going on?" I asked.

One of the guards answered. "Flutes today, instead of horns or drums. You can proceed at your own pace."

I had no idea what that meant and said so. The guard acted cross with me, like I had deliberately misunderstood.

"You're being summoned." He didn't embellish, so I was left to figure out where to go and how to get there. How did he know this was a summons and it was meant for me? Guards. They were under orders I wasn't allowed to know. It would've been nice if they at least pointed me in the right direction, but they didn't budge.

I decided to follow the music.

It led out and around and wound into Ward Sapphire's main yard, where dawn prayers would have already finished, but the usual flow of people was nowhere to be seen. Guards held positions on rooftops and at the Ward's wide gate. Smoke curled beyond the Ward's rooftops, the remnants of the battle from a few days ago. No battle cries or warring sounds broke through the soft music, which echoed across the empty space, growing more distinct and pleasant as I neared the sanctuary. Flutes, definitely. Reedy pipes, too, and the whistling of breezes through eaves, the creaking of trees in strong winds, the busy chirring of insects.

I didn't know what magic could make this music, but I felt it through every part of me. I could sense it with my toes even inside my shoes, or my fingertips, inside my belly or on the tip of my tongue. My body thrummed with this unseen force, inviting me forward. My un-magic wasn't undoing it or un-sensing it. It just was, and I was part of it.

Three guards stood at attention by the sanctuary's vast, carved doorway. The one in the middle was Valeo. He must've found or borrowed armor from someone, but I recognized his angry, black stare from beneath the battered brass helmet. His eyes focused on some point over my head and into the distance, as though I weren't headed straight for him. I turned to see that the two guards from the sick ward had followed me at a slow gait. They snapped to attention in front of Valeo, giving their chest-thump salute. He thumped back.

I gave him a long look over, wondering if he'd speak to me, give me some wink or hint. He continued to stare beyond me. It was nothing personal, I told myself. Whether he noticed me gazing up at him or not, his expression didn't change.

What would Amaniel say to all these stiff guards with their sharp weapons and sharper eyes? She'd know the right words. What were they? I took a deep breath and held it.

"Pious guardian of Nihil's person," I began. Valeo's gaze shifted to my face. "Would you please let me pass?"

Valeo edged to one side and I paused. The only things left to say all felt wrong.

I said it anyway, as softly as I could, hoping he, and only he, would hear.

"I know you don't understand why I did what I did," I said. "But I think I love you. Whatever else happens, please remember that."

And then I brushed past without another word. The two guards by the doors made no move to open them for me. I stopped, waiting to see if they would. I found myself staring at the intricate woodcarvings, taking in details I'd scarcely ever noticed. These had always been two vast doors to me. Maybe it was the tinkling music that made me pause and read the wooden panels. I could understand them without Amaniel's help. They portrayed the Six Hesitations, the very foundation of the Temple and all its tenets.

There was Doubt itself, a giant beast that gnawed at the mighty trunk of the Eternal Tree. Uncertainty was a blind and crippled man, stumbling along a rocky path. I ran my fingertips across Ambiguity, a thick bush of thistle rose, beautiful but deadly, perfumed and poisonous, its good and evil entwined together.

Incredulity was the beautiful wife who threw her jewels at her pleading husband, unsatisfied even with the best he could offer. I fingered one of the beaded creations around my neck, silently thanking S'ami again. Discord was at eye level on my right, the largest and most ornate of the panels, with warring serpents wrapped around a long sword stabbed through a pile of skulls.

Last would be Irreverence, the one I joked I understood the best. I'd never really paid much attention to the panel at the bottom of the door. I stole a long look at that last panel. It showed a woman smiling—or maybe she was smirking. At her back was a group of starving, skeletal people, their arms reaching toward her, palms outstretched, begging. The woman's hair flowed immodestly down her back, coursing and curling in sensual waves. In her upraised palms was a giant moonbloom.

This, then, was my grandmother, the other Hadara, the one who turned her back. Almost every day of my life I had walked past her and not noticed, not truly seen her, until I was walking in her footsteps.

I took a deep breath, chastened by what I'd finally had the sense to see. I opened the vast doors and was surprised to notice the shoe racks filled to overflowing. Sabbath had been before the battle, but perhaps it was being celebrated again today. I didn't think there were allowances made for wars though. We were many six-days from Winter Solstice, so it couldn't be a holiday. The racks should be empty, and so should the prayer mats within the sanctuary.

I left my new slippers in the racks, the guards following behind again. The inner doors slid open and I entered the sanctuary with its streaming light. The cavernous room was full, men to the left, women to the right, everyone kneeling in supplication on the many rugs, hands over their hearts, heads bowed and eyes closed. I stole forward, step by careful step, until the altar came into view.

I froze, hatred and horror creeping into my heart.

Two things I saw: Amaniel, lying naked on the altar, eyes closed.

And a wiry, white-haired figure seated on the high priest's throne beside her, thumbing through a careworn ledger.

Nihil.

# 3 1

*Know only this: you know me not. Seek me and
I may find you soon.*
    *Forget me and I shall find you sooner.*
    —*from* Oblations 1, The Book of Unease

He had to be Nihil. We didn't have any portraits or carvings of him, but everyone knew. The ageless face, the milky-white hair braided down his back. The thin, even features. The compact, spare frame. This was the body he'd inhabited for nearly two centuries, the eleventh in a line of human and Feroxi forms he'd invaded and taken for himself. Whatever mind had inhabited the body before Nihil was long gone.

    The music I sensed wasn't coming from him, though. It emanated from the mirror in back of the altar, and I realized that Nihil must still be in his home in a desolate place called the Abandoned City, clear across the sea and far from here. So who was this seated figure, lord of everything, calmly reading that awful ledger from the warehouse with all its names of the accused, while my sister suffered?

I held back for a while, becoming aware of the muffled sobs and moans of the people around me. The seated figure wore robes made of intertwining threads of light that seemed to ripple in time with the melody. The same beams meshed together to make the figure's skin and features. The closer I got, the clearer it became that this wasn't a flesh-and-blood man but a representation, a simulacrum or avatar that could sit and read a book and be a physical presence among us.

Without looking up from his reading, the simulacrum Nihil motioned for me to approach. Just a flick of his finger, subtle, but with purpose. No one else was in the aisle, so he must have meant me. I took steady steps forward—one, two, counting them, measuring them, not too fast or too slow, waiting for all of this to vanish like a fever dream.

Amaniel didn't look at me but I stared at her a long time, her back against the hard, tiled surface of the altar, her hair fanned out around her, a beatific smile on her glowing face. It wasn't hard to see why I'd been dressed with such ostentation, or the choice Nihil would have me make. I would make it. The Temple itself had been preparing me for this choice from the first time the schoolmistress had smacked Amaniel's arm instead of mine.

The simulacrum Nihil cleared its throat, but although the sound came from his figure, the music shifted from the mirror. The source of the spells must be on the other side of the glass. The Nihil that looked like he was here, but wasn't, cocked his head toward me.

"A rag doll in my image."

I grew confused. What rag doll? The one taken from our home by the soldiers? Rishi's little doll? This was what he cared about—and not the prayer well? My heart thumped harder inside me, to the point of chest pains. I had no idea what to say, so I said nothing.

He continued. "No remorse, then. If you were sorry, you'd be on your knees."

His voice sounded preternaturally calm, almost expressionless. I briefly remembered the flawless diction from the night I'd been brought here to what I'd thought was my death, the trilled r's and silky vowels.

I wasn't sorry, but I had Amaniel to think about. I tugged my skirt up enough to get on my knees and bowed my head.

"Much better," Nihil said. "Now, the rag doll. Plus all the other useless bits of profane nonsense seized from your people. Shall I spare you?"

I was being tried on the entire city's behalf, not merely my sister. I struggled to keep from fuming.

"Lord of piety, am I on trial for everyone, then?"

Nihil snapped the ledger shut. "Of course not. That would be barbaric, wouldn't it?"

"If it's your will, Fey One."

"My will. Is that what you think separates a civilized people from some tree-dwelling beasts? My will alone?"

If Nihil had been shouting, I could've handled that. I would've known how to respond. I'd have glared back or given him a cool, unfazed look or known how to keep my voice steady. But he was the chilly one, calm and droll and with a snide undercurrent to his voice that made me feel like the smallest person in the room.

Thousands of pairs of eyes were trained on my back, but all my beautiful clothes were melting away in my imagination and I was sure at any moment I'd be stripped, body and soul, before the world. I hated every item on me, down to the last jingling bell. I wanted to throw everything at Nihil's feet and grab Amaniel's hand and make a run for it. To where, I don't know.

Nihil rose and the music shifted again, with a few shrill notes emanating from the mirror. A small buzz sounded in my ears. I realized that strident note was coming from me, and every time I bristled or tensed, it grew louder and more distinct. My un-magic was working after all. If only I could figure out how to wield it with some degree of precision. What if it failed me, as it had out by the prayer well? For the first time since I'd realized I had this power, though, I had hope. Something deep within me, whatever it was, *wasn't* failing me.

"Tell me this, Hadara of Rimonil of my very own city of Port Sapphire," Nihil said. "What is it that separates the city from the jungle? A civilized people from savages? Tell me what you think my greatest gift to humanity might be."

I went for the answer I thought Amaniel might give. "Your theurgy, Master."

"So wrong. Then again, I was apprised of your limited achievement in school."

I hung my head, but not in shame. I was too angry for that. I may not have been the best student, but I'd never harmed anyone, ever. In a fair world, that ought to count for something.

"A little hint?" Nihil said. "Or we'll be here until my next incarnation."

"Yes, please." That's all I could manage without spitting.

"Alright. A hint. Sewers." Nihil seemed pleased with himself, crossing his arms across his light-clad chest.

"Master?" How I hated having to call him that. The word felt wrong on my lips.

"It's just a hint. Humanity one day stopped excreting in the same waters it drank from. You want to imagine why?" He leaned forward. "You're welcome, by the way."

He waved the back of his hand at me, a gesture I took to mean I should stand. I struggled to my feet, breathing hard, partly from fury, but also confusion and fear. I was being tested, just like in school, and failing again. The shame of it seeped across my face and burned at my ears and cheeks. So much more was at stake than a simple whack of the pointer, and I didn't know how I was supposed to have prepared for this. I'd never known.

"A stunning woman," he said. He glanced me up and down, nodding with approval. "At the first bloom of your beauty. A supple form, yours, with good teeth and radiant skin, the very model of health and vitality. An accident of fate, right?"

"I thank you for my many blessings, Cryptic Numen," I said. It seemed like the appropriate thing to say. Nihil nodded again and the corners of his mouth lifted almost imperceptibly. It was a cruel, knowing smile, with his pale brown eyes creasing at the corners. His voice carried a condescending lilt that made my skin prickle.

"Had I never come to Kuldor, do you know what you might've looked like?" Nihil asked. He didn't wait for my answer. "Starved and sickly, a pygmy, foraging for roots because you had to, not because you could get a few extra coppers for them. Married off at twelve, a mother by thirteen, dead by twenty. Yes, Nature's grand, isn't it? Certainly worth putting all your faith in."

So that's where this was going—to point out that my entire life had veered off course. My first instinct was to blame Mami for dragging me into the swamps, but I tamped that down. This had nothing to do with her. Behind me came the sound of sobbing and weeping. The entire city was cringing and mourning before the god who'd lifted us from our own filth and misery. If they'd been disgusted with the Temple yesterday, they were fully back in line today. All it took was a spectre of light floating in front of them to make every piece of self-respect and common sense dissolve.

I wondered if, somewhere, a new prayer well had formed and was already filling.

Nihil took a step forward and the air crackled between us. My un-magic again. I'd have to think of a name for it if I lived through this.

"Tell me why you unleashed the Gek on your own people," Nihil said.

"I didn't. I swear I didn't," I said. My words were so high-pitched and feeble I hated the sound of them. I stood trembling before my god, peeping like a lost crane chick. I had to find the Hadara who could wade into a swamp and climb a tree and paddle a canoe and make six different kinds of medicines from the same plant. That Hadara wasn't a bad person. That Hadara had done the world a favor by closing the prayer well, even if it hadn't done all that I'd hoped.

I had to believe that.

"Really. The Gek just happened to know where to find their new goddess." Nihil's face was impassive, but his eyes, or the simulacrum's eyes, never left mine.

I was stammering for a reply when I heard a quiet whisper, accompanied by a short, echoing note of S'ami's magic. I hadn't even thought to look for him in the crowd. "Don't answer him," the voice said. "Don't fight on his terms."

I shut my mouth. I had no idea what that meant, having never fought anyone.

Nihil's eyes narrowed to slits. "What did S'ami just tell you?"

"Master?"

"No one spellcasts without my knowing."

S'ami coughed from somewhere behind me. "If I may, Fey One."

"Later," Nihil said, his gaze returning to mine.

I trembled as our eyes connected. S'ami had said I'd be crushed if I faced him alone. But I had to try. I was old enough to marry, to learn a trade, to take my mother's place and run a household. I could answer for my actions, even if they were being twisted into something I didn't recognize. I silently thanked S'ami in my head for buying me that brief moment to compose myself and run my whirlwind mind through a few replies.

After all, I didn't have a reservoir of desperation and longing to draw from. I had only my upbringing, my sense of self, a faint hope that at least my parents still loved me, and a robust skepticism. All of that would have to do.

"Well?" Nihil asked. "Don't keep me waiting."

"The Gek are wrong, Master."

"About what."

"I can't and don't wish to take you on."

"Is that what they asked?"

"Not in so many words."

"It's what they want?"

This would go badly for the Gek, I realized. I couldn't give them up to save my own hide. I second-guessed myself. "*Are* they wrong?"

Nihil paused. "You think I should be *taken on,* as you put it?"

An already quiet congregation stopped moving. I felt like they were leaning into me, pressing against me with their silence and their anxious watching. Even the music had softened to a sweet hush.

"Should I want to?" I asked.

S'ami's voice rang in my ear. "Excellent. Turn it back on him."

"Stop coaching her." Nihil's face broke into a frown for the first time, his thin eyebrows furrowing.

"My apologies, Master," S'ami said aloud. "It's only natural to root for the novice. She meant no harm."

"Harm's been done." Nihil turned to me again. "Do you think this is about a rag doll? Or the ledger you stole—don't deny it. The fire, the battle, the wellspring, any of it?"

I tried to keep my voice to a whisper, but it echoed across the quiet chamber. "Apparently, it's something to do with sewers."

S'ami's laughter carried across the room, briefly blocking even Nihil's music. I waited for Nihil to strike S'ami dead, but he only gazed at S'ami without changing expression and raised the ledger above his head. It dropped with a sharp bang against the floor. He stood astride it and paused. I thought S'ami and I had an odd relationship, but to take this kind of liberty with Nihil was beyond imagining.

Unnerved and trembling, I stooped to pick up the ledger but Nihil kicked it away. In the moment his foot passed near my hand, the space between us sizzled. Part of his foot seemed to dissipate like smoke, with tendrils snaking toward me. I pulled my hand back and stood.

Nihil had noticed, yet his voice betrayed no emotion. His eyes, the avatar eyes, never left my face. Yet they seemed to look beyond me, like I were standing further back than I was.

"I believe I have already seen what this undoing does," he said, his voice smug. "Though pulling together a pile of rocks to plug a volcano struck me as very similar to magic. Wouldn't you say, S'ami, my Ear, my Azwan, my Defender of Doctrine?"

"Aye, now that you've made me aware of it, it does," S'ami said. "Which is why I called her a novice. Let her come and study properly, and we'll see what kind of priestess we can make of her."

I didn't have much confidence in myself, but I was absolutely positive S'ami didn't want me to follow him to the Temple of Doubt to attend seminary. He wanted my powers for himself, and having me close would be better than having me far. It was such an obvious lie that it made me realize that even with all of the advantages Nihil had over me, he lacked one important thing: the truth. Without it, he was dependent on whatever flattering, fawning nonsense people drooled at him.

I had the truth, or at least some of it. I had facts and decency and rightness on my side. I'd made a mistake, and I could admit it, at least to myself—something I doubted Nihil could ever do.

I reached toward Nihil. The buzz in my ears restarted like a swarm of sting flies, angry and excited, an unpleasant sound I wished would go away. I winced and held my hand steady as I continued reaching. If other spells had sparkled and fizzled in my hands, this one threw out electric arcs. Nihil's form lost its sharpness for a few moments, then refocused, as clear as ever.

I tried again, with the same result. My hand smarted, and my skin began to crack.

Nihil didn't flinch as his figure rewove any parts of himself that had frayed at my touch.

"Unimpressive," he said. "Unless you're not really trying."

"I don't want to be doing this." Maybe there would still be a peaceful way out, some way for everyone to save face.

"Perhaps I've pressed you too far. My Azwan seems to think so." His voice held a kinder note to it, but it was only that—one note, and not too convincing. I hoped he was almost done with me, but part of me knew otherwise.

"Please." My voice was a hoarse whisper.

"Alright, why don't you stand down, then. You've been put through much."

I bowed my head to him, fearful that this couldn't have been so easy, but hoping against hope that it was. "Thank you, Cryptic Numen."

Nihil crossed to where Amaniel lay on the altar.

"I trust you'll agree to offer your sister then in your stead. That seems fair, doesn't it?"

3 ב

They rejected me. They rejected the god of flesh
and bone, a god they could see and hear and who
lived among them.
— "The Fall of B'Nai", from Verisimilitudes 13,
The Book of Unease

I lunged forward. Nihil's question could not be answered
with words. I answered with action, grabbing at the appa-
rition again. Never mind how much it stung, I had to get
rid of him. Forget peace, then.

The simulacrum exploded in my arms and threw me
against the altar. I fell backward. The congregation gasped,
but quieted again as the music lifted in pitch and volume, which told me I hadn't gotten rid of Nihil. I'd only
a singed dress for my trouble. I waved off a wisp of smoke
and choked back a cough.

I stared up at Amaniel's feet. Nihil had no reason to do
this to her. My family had done so much for the Temple, my
sister believed so firmly in it, and this was our thanks—to

see my sister shamed and killed. Her, the true believer, who'd find some way to make this about selflessness and virtue instead of Nihil's bizarre demands and cruel appetites.

I picked myself up in time to see a cloud of colors emerge from the mirror and coalesce as another avatar of Nihil. A few short steps took him back to the altar to face me across my sister's body. Amaniel trembled at the site of him. She ignored me.

Nihil smiled his tight, mean smile again.

"Much better," he said.

"Better? I don't understand."

"I want to know what I'm up against," he began. "If you're motivated by saving your sister, that's easily handled. You only have to convince me there's nothing more."

Nothing more? I stared at him in disbelief. I stammered out my reply. "I-isn't that enough?"

He laughed. "An excellent reply. Honest. Heartfelt. Alright, your family can go."

I almost fell over from relief. The flutes took a laughing, cheerful turn and people all around me began shouting praise for their god. Some applauded. I'd passed whatever test he'd held for me. Or had I?

Out of the corner of my eye, I could see S'ami in the front row. His round face seemed anxious and closed.

Below me, Amaniel closed her eyes and scrunched up her face as if about to cry. I grabbed her hand to pull her to her feet. She shrieked, shrill and piercing, her back arching, and began writhing in agony. I let go, but her contortions continued. Scream after scream resounded above Nihil's terrible, happy songs.

"Stop it," I said. "You said she could go."

"Ah, about that," he said. "I just wanted to remove one very important doubt you may yet have about my hold over you. Say farewell to your sister."

I strode over and slapped the simulacrum. He struck me back, a hard blow that exploded sparks in my face and stung my skin. His fist vanished, then reformed.

Amaniel kept screaming.

I yanked away my headscarf. My hair tumbled free around my shoulders and down my back.

"You'd do that in my presence," Nihil said.

I didn't answer, but took the flimsy fabric and stretched it out as wide as it would go. I laid it gently over Amaniel's body. She tried to push it away. "Hadara, don't. It'll be over soon. I'll be blessed, too."

"It's alright, I know what to do now."

I crossed behind the altar, away from Nihil-the-representation, and down the short steps. A few more strides and I was at the gilded mirror, with its thousands of jeweled insects and their gleaming eyes. They weren't watching me: they were beautiful, like so much of what the Temple created, but they couldn't see; they were as blind as the Temple, too.

The Nihil simulacrum didn't turn to face me at the mirror, as I expected it wouldn't. It continued to face out at the congregation. The god making it move was staring through this mirror and didn't need to turn to see me.

I held both palms up and whispered to the real Nihil.

"I made a mistake at the prayer well," I said. "And I don't know how to fix it, but I can ask you for one thing."

The simulacrum spoke facing the congregation. "And what is that?"

"Let her go," I said.

"Or?"

"You know what I'll do."

Nihil sighed. "S'ami did say you were bright. Such a waste."

I heard another of Amaniel's screams, louder this time and more urgent, her voice rising in pitch and trailing off into a sob.

Both my palms met the mirror at once, feeling the coolness of the glass. I was figuring out how to work my un-magic, that it was tied to my emotions and I had to be angry enough to invoke it. Well, that wouldn't be a problem. Rage coursed through every part of me, pulling at that mirror, plucking its magic free and sending cracks up its smooth face. I pulled away in time to escape the thousands of shards that crumbled at my bare feet. My fingertips bled.

The music stopped.

The shouting started.

I glanced around. The simulacrum had indeed vanished. Men reached toward me, trying to break free of the crowds, their faces contorted in rage. Feroxi guards lined the aisles, pushing everyone back with their shields. Valeo positioned himself in front of the dais, holding a sword across the chests of several men. Just yesterday, I'd thought the crowd was on my side and against Valeo. Maybe I didn't have any power with people after all. I bit back a wave of disappointment and frustration and shook my curls loose around my shoulders.

Mami rushed up the dais and pulled Amaniel off the altar then tugged her to safety. Across from her, S'ami

shouted at the guards while Reyhim motioned for everyone to settle down. A guard left S'ami's side and picked up a
prayer rug, tossing it down beside me so I could cross barefoot over the broken glass. He escorted me to the Azwan.

I exhaled. "What now?" I asked S'ami.

"Patience."

With chaos unleashed around me, I didn't think I had
any patience to spare.

I pulled at S'ami's sleeve. "Tell them I had no choice."

"We always have choices."

"It was my sister."

"All these people have lost someone in recent days."

I hated when S'ami was right. "Tell me what to do,
then."

He patted my hand. "I'm already doing enough for you
by not instantly killing you."

"But Nihil's gone, right?"

I got a bemused look by way of an answer.

Across the room, Mami hugged Amaniel, envelop-
ing her in both arms, shielding Amaniel's nakedness from
the crowd, not looking at me. Angry, confused, terrified
women had left their segregated enclosure and swarmed
around the two of them, jostling and screaming. Mami
held fast, returning their fury with stoic silence, maintain-
ing her calm amid a roiling sea of madness. This was the
right thing to do. But I needed a signal from Mami, something. It seemed such a flimsy thing to hope for, just a look
amid all the reddened faces, but I had to know I had one
ally in the whole world, and that my mother of all people
hadn't shied from defending me when everyone else was
demanding my death. She glanced up, gave a curt, tight

nod, and pulled Amaniel closer in. That would do. I let out a burst of air that rattled with grief.

I buried my face in my hands, struggling to regain my poise despite the swell of furious worshippers. They'd been so fickle. Yesterday, they were ready to evict the Temple. Today, they were back to being blindly devoted.

My breathing grew ragged, until I couldn't tell whether the swell of emotions included relief or remorse or more terror. I couldn't tell anything anymore. S'ami pulled me into a loose hug, rubbing my back and making soft, reassuring shushing sounds. Reyhim's angry rasp cut through the noise.

"I'm going to tell these people to calm themselves. I can still conjure, that should reassure them."

"We should be getting them to higher ground," S'ami said.

"You don't think?"

"Hadara's left him no other choice."

My head shot up. S'ami gave me only a cursory glance before turning toward Reyhim, whose slow nod eroded any hope that somehow my ordeal had ended. Reyhim laid one hand on S'ami's shoulder.

"Despite our differences, it's been an honor, brother."

"The honor's mine, brother," said S'ami. "I shall die with dignity by your side."

"To the Eternal Tree, then."

"To the Eternal Tree."

I pulled away. "We're going to die?"

S'ami shrugged. "You're young. You cannot be expected to understand all the consequences of your actions."

"How? How does he plan to kill us?" Maybe there was some way to stop Nihil. There had to be.

S'ami and Reyhim had already walked away from me to direct the guards. Shields pushed the crowds back, back, until people burst out the sanctuary doors. Guards propped open the doors facing toward the bay to clear the sanctuary more quickly. S'ami steered me toward those side doors and motioned for Mami and Amaniel to join us.

Amaniel had someone's shawl wrapped around her torso and my hair lace draped across her shoulders. She gave me a puffy-eyed frown. She'd been crying.

S'ami shook a finger at her. "You mustn't blame your sister. You've been spared a terrible fate."

"Yes, Azwan."

Mami hugged her close. "Is there more to come, Azwan?"

"I'm afraid so. You'd best get Amaniel to higher ground. Is your husband in the sick ward?"

"Yes. My other daughter's with him."

S'ami scowled. "Get them as quickly as you can. Tell anyone you meet on the way to head for a bluff or a solid rooftop as far from water as they can find."

"May I ask why?"

There was a kindly, apologetic tone to S'ami's voice, one I wasn't used to hearing. "Our reasons remain our own, Lady Lia."

Mami paused long enough to hug me and then whisper in my ear, "Whatever happens, this will have been the proudest day of my life."

"But what about Amaniel, Mami?"

"I'm proud of her, too." Mami beamed down at a teary Amaniel. "My two bold girls."

With that, my mother and sister hustled out the main doors to the sanctuary and to whatever fate lay beyond. S'ami kept his arm around my shoulders and guided me out the side doors. We climbed up a grassy embankment where we had a flawless view of a gleaming, deep blue bay.

"Feel anything yet?" S'ami asked.

I shook my head. "Should I?"

S'ami dug out his totem and turned it over in his palm. "It's been getting weaker. Your well is indeed running dry."

"The prayer well?"

He nodded. "He's drawing on the power of his brothers and sisters among the stars, as I told you. But it's not enough, and it's far away and flickers in intensity. People and their prayers and their wants and yearnings and endless needs are very close, and constant."

"So what I did worked?" I couldn't believe it. I had been right after all. It might have been a small victory, but it was something.

"You would've made a fine priestess," he said. "Or revolutionary. A pity we'll never find out."

His words jerked me back to the present. "Why, what is Nihil going to do?"

"You know that answer."

"Punish me?"

"Your instinct is to leap in with the easiest reply. Reach further, Hadara."

I thought some more. "Is this really about sacrifice, or maybe vanquishing me? Does he believe the demon is alive somehow?"

"All questions you can answer for yourself."

Anne Boles Levy

I said nothing after that while I mulled what S'ami had said and tried to think matters through with some degree of calm. I'd reacted to Nihil in anger. Nothing I'd done had been level-headed or reasoned. But logic would not have saved my sister and there was no guarantee Nihil would've spared the city anyway.

There it was. Reason. Logic. Truth. I had to expect the unexpected, which then *became* the expected, until Nihil changed his mind again. This, then, was the heart of the Temple of Doubt. It's not that we were to have confidence in him, but doubt in ourselves. His whole hold over us depended on it.

But why? To generate prayers, that's why. When people caught themselves in a storm of self-doubt, the Temple provided them shelter. It was their rock, their sturdy foundation.

And it was all built on lies.

Whatever was about to happen, I had to stay in control—of myself, of my powers. I promised myself for Mami's sake, wherever she was right then. She'd defied the Temple all her life and kept her head and they'd left her more or less alone. I'd have to do the same, even if this was the last thing I ever got to do for anyone.

The sun climbed higher in the sky as we watched from the Ward's patio overlooking the bay. We waited for something to happen, but the Azwans said nothing, only gazing out at the deep blue waters. From far away, smoke from smoldering warehouses drifted above the battered skyline. It was hard to see through the haze that clouded the western half of Port Sapphire. Sea breezes swept the worst of it away from where we stood.

A throng milled around us, made up of priests and guards and worshippers who'd filed out the side doors with us. The gallows were still there, but the ropes and their hated nooses had been tethered to one side to keep from swaying. I couldn't spot Valeo and didn't want to make a scene looking for him. Everyone but the guards chattered at once or asked the Azwans this or that, but the two holy men kept their mute vigil over the bay. Both palmed their totems, S'ami rolling his over and over, waiting for some signal that took its time in coming.

I rubbed my toes on the paving stones and tried to hide my mounting anxiety. My stomach was tying knots around itself, and the jitters crept across my flesh. My head began to ache. Maybe that was only from the sun, or fear, or a mess of emotions that tumbled from a door in my head that refused to shut.

At last, from far across the city came rapid bursts of a horn. A guard murmured to S'ami, "That's a warning horn, Azwan."

"Find out more. Find out everything you can. Quickly."

My jitters reached a fevered pitch and began buzzing in my ears.

"Oh no," I said. "I recognize that."

S'ami stared at the totem in his palm. "I do, too."

"Is it starting?"

"Don't keep asking me questions to which you already know the answer."

I spoke through clenched teeth. "Is this a good time to tell you that I absolutely hate you?"

"As good a time as any."

"Well, I do."

333

"Save your strength. Something worse than me comes your way."

S'ami pointed toward the bay, where I saw only the tide winding its way out to sea.

I waited, waited some more, and waited yet more.

Until I realized that the waiting itself was the trap.

# 33

*Which of your gods can make it rain? I asked.
Which can make the ground shake or the moons
wax and wane?*

*Ba'l named the gods who made rain or tem-
blors or moonlight. So call on them to make
the ground shake, I said. Ba'l took up his staff
and prayed, and was met by silence. The people
moaned their disappointment.*

*I slammed my fist into the city. The walls
shook and crumbled and the people fell to their
knees. They shouted, You are our god! We shall
worship you.*

*I was satisfied, and spared them.*
*—"Nihil Converts Ba'l," from Verisimilitudes 5,*
The Book of Unease

Sandbars that hadn't been seen since the last triple full
moons cropped up as the tide receded. The sea was pulling back, revealing the bay's muddy bottom and swells of

stranded crayfish. Cranes and shore birds swooped in for easy kills and raced off again.

That was wrong, something I knew even without connecting it to the fizzing magic that rippled up and down my spine and rattled around my head. Nihil's music chimed faintly in the distance, and I scanned the horizon in vain for colorful rays of power or any other sign of his theurgy.

The guard S'ami had sent away came racing back. "The Gek are darting around the city, pulling people onto rooftops, Azwan."

"And people are letting them?"

The guard nodded. "It's as though they never fought."

"They haven't retreated toward their swamps?"

"No sir. That's the odd thing. The ones that aren't on rooftops are scrambling toward higher ground, where you sent the congregation."

Reyhim had overheard and nodded his head. "They know."

The guard pointed into the distance. "There, sir."

A ridge of water grew at the horizon. The sea that pulled itself back was pushing the ridge higher and higher. A moment later came the sound of a horn I'd been taught to memorize as a child. Three short bursts and three long ones, over and over again.

It signaled a tsunami.

Reyhim raised his voice. "It's time to pray. May Nihil redeem us, even now."

Either I acted, or we all died. It was that simple.

I clambered down the embankment to a dock for the city's many ferries, ignoring the nasty splinters that immediately found the soles of my feet. I concentrated on the receding tide, the evilness of it, holding back to give us only enough time to flee uselessly in the face of it, holding back death only long enough to mock us. Below me, the dock soared over empty sand; the sea had retreated too far for me to jump off safely.

I tried to ease myself over the side, but got tangled in rows of ropes and the waterwood buffer nailed to the docksides. I pushed against the bulky hunks of porous waterwood but only tiny crumbles broke off. The buffers were nailed in place to keep boats from bashing their hulls against the dock, but they barred my way. I tried to slide between them, but rusty nails jutting from the sides caught the seam of my dress. The fragile silk tore. I was getting used to ruined clothes. I tugged myself free and dropped a full body length into the sand.

Once I felt wet ooze between my toes, I closed my eyes again and tried to feel for the direction of the magic. The ridge growing into a mountain deep into the bay might not be the right place to run. If the magic came from somewhere else, then that was where I needed to be.

Nihil's trick with the mirror had taught me that.

Behind me, guards kept back the crowds. Their shouts and finger-pointing began to give way to chanting and praying. That was fine with me. They could pray all they wanted. I was the only one who could help them, and I couldn't expect so much as a thank-you for it.

The tsunami horn kept blasting and blasting, ringing clear across the city. Screams and shouts came from the farthest corners of town. Above all those sounds came the beating of drums, thousands of drums, crashing and pounding out unfamiliar rhythms. I remembered what the guard outside my door had said. Flutes that time, not drums or horns. This was all drums. I was hearing Nihil's war cry. Far out at sea, storm clouds gathered and whipped the ridge of water into a foaming frenzy. The drums added peals of thunder to their pounding beats.

I raced toward the music, struggling in my long skirt. I tied the hems in knots at either side above my knees and kept going. My feet landed on clamshells that tore them open and I raced harder, faster, as fast as I could manage, and it was nowhere near fast enough. The ridge of water was a mountain dozens of body lengths high and it began to slide forward, fast and angry and ugly, toward a helpless city.

I knew I was getting closer to the source of the magic but I wasn't a good judge of the distance. A hundred paces? Two hundred? The tsunami began closing fast. My lungs couldn't hold another breath, my chest hurt with every heave. I kept going.

Someone grabbed my left arm and dragged me forward. Valeo had me by the wrist, running and running, forcing me to keep up with his giant strides. He lugged some sort of wooden shield over his back but all that registered was the sudden speed with which we flew across the sand bars and shallows.

Valeo had me crossing the bay at a diagonal, something that was making our journey longer, but I couldn't manage enough breath to speak. The drumming resounded through me, beating against my ribs and into my head. Drums competed against drums, against the roar of the giant wave and the distant storm. My knees began to give out and Valeo yanked me up again and onward. My lungs nearly burst from the exertion.

The diagonal began to make sense. The magic that sparked and whirled in my head grew louder and more distinct. Something gold in the sand caught a ray of sun and glinted up at us. I pulled Valeo in its direction until I could see waves of color shoot all around it, beaming strong magic in every direction. Like all the other gold items wielded by magic users, it would be a talisman used to focus Nihil's power.

The tsunami would reach it before I did.

I lunged forward again, only to be lurched back. Valeo braced my entire left arm by his side and knotted a rope around it. He'd dropped the hunk of wood and it lay wedged into the sand.

"What. Are. You. Doing," I gasped.

"Catch your breath," he said. "Do it."

He'd obviously gone mad. I wasn't close to the object, but I could get closer. I had to try.

Then it was too late.

We dove into the wave as it thundered over us. I could hear the drums reverberating under the water and swam for the gold item. Maybe I could reach it before my lungs gave way. Some unseen force tugged me upward by my tethered wrist, away from my goal. I tried to wriggle free but the rope had wrapped around Valeo's thick thigh.

The air in my chest was running out. Pain stabbed through my lungs. I had to breathe. But I wouldn't get another chance at this. I turned and twisted and reached my right arm toward where the gold talisman had been, or where I thought it might be. Nothing was certain in the sea's determined darkness, not even up or down, except that I was being pulled away.

I reached and yearned and wanted and strove. I fought with the wave, feeling magic unraveling around me, the drums dissipating into hundreds of dull thuds, then dozens, then only a few solitary bursts of noise. A calm spot opened in my mind where soft, pale light poured through. There was no more magic, none.

I spun in empty space, the water pressing on every side, unsure where I was going or whether it mattered anymore.

# 34

*I left B'Nai in ruins, its cities and villages sacked, its pastures uprooted, its rivers rerouted. Those who surrendered their idols and swore fealty again to me, I let live and left their flocks, orchards, stores of grain untouched. All others fell beneath the swords and spears of guards, or to my unfettered wrath.*
*— "The Fall of B'Nai," from Verisimilitudes 14,*
The Book of Unease

I lay on my back, gagging. I had vomited water straight up into the air. It now dripped down from Valeo's chin. His open mouth pressed on mine, breathing hard down my throat, forcing air into my lungs. The kiss of life. My eyelids fluttered but I hadn't enough air or strength to tell him I could breathe on my own. I let him fill my lungs one more time, only half-believing that someone could insist so firmly on keeping me alive.

Valeo had dragged me up onto a hard surface, something floating.

Something. Floating.

I felt that something against my back, coarse and porous but wonderfully lighter than water.

Waterwood. I flopped to one side and Valeo pulled up next to me on a round hunk of dock buffer that he'd ripped off and tethered to both our wrists. It had bobbed back up to the surface, dragging both of us with it. This was what I'd thought was a shield. Every child in Port Sapphire knew how to make a wave-rider from chunks of buffer and float himself onto shore. Valeo's boyhood must've been filled with the same reckless adventures.

Rolling over, I could make out the flotsam and jetsam of what had been Port Sapphire's outer docks, or perhaps pieces of burned ships. Empty barrels bobbed past, and the occasional oar, then broken pieces of mast, some dragging lengths of sail spread like the soggy wings of some giant, crippled bird. From my weak vantage point, all I could do was crane my neck toward shore, which seemed farther away than it should've.

We'd been dragged further out with the receding wave and would have to wait for the current and our tired limbs to bring us back. But what city would I find when I returned? What would be left?

"The city," I gasped. And Mami. Babba. My sister and friends and cousins and aunties and everyone. The Customs House. Callers Wharf. What remained of my beloved home and the people I'd endangered?

"It's still there," Valeo said. "Mostly. A lot of people shaking fists from rooftops. Not sure if it's at us or Nihil yet, though."

That would have to do. I rested for long moments on my side, Valeo cradling me from behind, one arm over my middle. I folded my arm over his and entwined my fingers in his, panting, catching my breath. But who did I have to thank? What god had arranged this? Not the one I'd always worshipped. I was done with him. There was nothing out there but random fate and hard luck, from what I could see.

After a few moments this way, I realized I was clutching something unfamiliar, and that my fist was tightly wrapped around something I must've grabbed while still in the water. When I uncurled my fingers, my palm flashed gold. A huge totem of all three full moons glittered in my palm. It had come to me in some way I couldn't fathom. Yet.

Valeo roared his approval. "You did get it. Heh. S'ami didn't think you would."

"S'ami put it there?"

"Tossed it over the side before the Nomad's Grief pulled into harbor."

"Then he foresaw this?" I had trouble believing it. Just how much was S'ami capable of?

"Even he's not that talented. No, Nihil's sprinkled all of Kuldor with these things. New Meridian had gotten off free until we arrived. Keep kicking, we're almost there."

I gulped fresh air. "Just tell me why you helped me."

The look I got wasn't what I'd expected. Valeo scrunched up his face, his tone mock-serious: "Two reasons."

"They are?"

"One: I think I love you, too. And two? Apparently, it has something to do with sewers."

"Is that supposed to be funny?"

"Funniest damn thing I've ever heard. S'ami, too, from what I could tell."

"You're in on this, this scheme or whatever of his?" I nearly rolled off the wave-rider in shock.

Valeo pointed with his chin toward land. I looked up at the Temple rooftop, where a dark figure in amethyst robes waved his arms.

"Now do you believe?" the man called. "Now do you *believe.*"

I believed. It was a question that would ring with one meaning throughout a city that thought me a skeptic, a doubter. It meant something else entirely between two would-be heretics—make that three, if Valeo was included.

Did I believe in S'ami's demon, in his capriciousness and malevolence? In the need to rid my people of Nihil's fickle, fear-mongering self?

I believed. Oh, yes.

When I was ready, I turned over and we kicked and paddled with our arms to turn our makeshift wave-rider around. Valeo and I rode our flimsy waterwood craft across the waves, paddling and kicking toward a city more water-logged than we'd left it, but mostly safe. Many docks were gone, and more than a few houses. Chunks of boardwalk floated past us into the bay. In a short time, I felt certain, bodies would float ashore, too.

But I believed.

# 35

In the end, I had lost.

I even signed an official surrender, which let my family live and my city exist.

People without armies, S'ami had said, usually lose.

So I signed, and, a day later, Leba Mara was tying me in knots and changing my bandages, cheerful and oblivious. "It's a good thing I make my staff learn old-fashioned wound dressings."

Any spot on my body Leba Mara thought had any chance of oozing, itching, or bleeding was trussed up like a Solstice roast.

She wagged a finger in my face.

"Now, when I told you to help get rid of the Azwans, you know that's not what I pictured, right?"

I managed a smile. "I'll get it right next time, promise."

"There'll be no next time." Leba Mara's mock scolding gave way to a wistful look as her gaze wandered off to nowhere. "It'll be a nice send-off. Something for our bruised city to be proud of."

She sent me off to get my father with a stern warning that he wouldn't want to miss the spectacle, he being Lord Portreeve and all.

I found Babba outside chiding two workers lifting him in a sedan chair.

"Blossom, look at this crazy thing. They're trying to make me seasick."

Everyone was being studiously cheerful around me. I was pretty sure I'd have to yell at them all to stop. Things only got worse when the procession got underway. We were behind the Azwans and S'ami couldn't resist the chance to chatter in Tengali, pretending he was chanting some folksy tune from his homeland. Only the words were improvised and aimed at me.

The message spells had been so weak, he sang, the Azwans could barely read them. They'd been ordered back to the Temple of Doubt with as much haste as they could make. There would be an urgent review of doctrine, followed by an official period of healing. Priests must double their prayer services, both in number and length, until further notice, or Nihil's wrath would be upon them.

S'ami was more cheerful than I'd seen him in a while.

"How's our dearest human sacrifice?" he said in the common tongue.

That was the official story that the rest of Port Sapphire got to hear: I had run into the wave to spare my city and sacrifice my life. Nihil had accepted this noble gesture and, in his benevolence, *he* had lifted the tsunami. After all, I *believed* now. My doubts had been lifted, or so the priests told everyone. For certain, this time.

And here was the part that nearly undid me to agree: either I accepted this lie, or the Azwans took up permanent residence here, along with their guards. That is, except Valeo. He had been ordered back to the Temple of Doubt whether the Azwans left or not, as soon as a ship could sail. S'ami wouldn't tell me why or what trouble he faced or if I could board Valeo's ship with him to say good-bye.

I hadn't, in fact, seen Valeo since he'd saved me and the entire city. He'd vanished in a crowd of soldiers who had seemed to swallow him whole, and all I had was a single, backward glance from him and a wink. I had fainted then from exhaustion and had woken up in my makeshift jail cell surrounded by Azwans and priests.

That's when Reyhim, of all people, had described the terms of my surrender, as he'd put it. Mami had handed me the plume to sign the scroll. I had signed without crying, which was all the victory I got to claim.

And what good would it have done to cry? It wouldn't have changed anything.

The procession wound out of Ward Sapphire's gates, and I plodded numbly along, not really caring. From his chair above my head, Babba beamed happy faces at me, the kind of fatherly chest-puffing usually reserved for Amaniel. I wasn't Amaniel, and I hadn't earned that bursting-with-pride look, at least not the way Babba pictured it.

I had a headache. I couldn't think straight. All sorts of irritable, restless thoughts swirled inside me, along with a low, steady noise I couldn't shake. I couldn't sense any magic being performed around me, so it was dehydration or exhaustion or lack of sleep or a bout of prickly heat. Who knew? I didn't care. I wanted the send-off to be over and done and to be halfway to somewhere else.

We crossed Pilgrim Bridge to cheering throngs and made our way past the crowds along Callers Wharf. Along the burned-out rooftops, I spied a handful of Gek, keeping a silent vigil. I'd have to ask about the new peace accord. Mami, the only one who knew their language, had hammered it out on a bluff just north of the city and in desperate haste on both sides. Babba had recovered and accepted the treaty, insisting Mami was as much a lord as he. It had been the one highlight of recent days.

At last, we reached the Azwan's ships. Mami, Rishi and Amaniel were there, an overstuffed satchel at their feet. Inside would be my best dress. I'd told Mami to pack the one with the ocean theme, with all my neatly embroidered fish leaping across the rippling hems. I wasn't sure what other items of mine would be in there; I'd have to take inventory later.

Amaniel raced up and hugged me. I swirled her around and tugged at her head scarf.

"I'm going to miss you," I said.

"Don't cry. If you cry, then I have to cry, and I'm trying not to."

"Agreed. No crying."

"I'm going to miss you, too," Amaniel said, her eyes welling up.

Babba shouted at the men holding him up to set him down. He hugged us both at once as a crowd on the Customs House balcony shouted and screamed their approval.

We all waved up at them, Mami and Rishi, too.

Reyhim strolled over to Babba, shaking his head. "You're getting a better reception than us, your lordship."

"My apologies if it offends you, Azwan," Babba replied.

Reyhim chuckled. "House Rimonil's a force to contend with. Something in all those herbs you drink."

"Used to drink," Babba corrected. Mami shrugged.

When all the good-byes were done, a sailor shouldered the satchel and lugged it up the Sea Skimmer's gangplank. Reyhim put an arm around Amaniel and winked.

"Ready, pupil?"

"Ready, Azwan."

Reyhim led Amaniel aboard the ship that would take her to the Temple of Doubt and to learning and lore far beyond what Ward Sapphire's school could do for her. I detested how close she'd be to Nihil, but the idea enchanted Amaniel and neither Mami nor I could dissuade her.

I was being left behind but not forgotten. Leba Mara had given over my stuffy makeshift cell for a permanent room, where I could watch and be watched.

A pat on my shoulder told me S'ami was ready for his final words, which weren't likely to be brief. He gave me instructions for writing to him and how often and I was to record everything I could or couldn't do, and how long it took to master a new task.

"I'm not the scholar you are, Azwan," I said.

"Never mind all that. Jot it down and make sense of it later." He switched to Tengali but kept the same windy, nonchalant tone. "You've badly damaged him, you know.

It's been more than two centuries since all five Azwans have attended him at once, and that was some theological nonsense that history's forgotten. A real wound, this time, though sadly not a mortal one. He's also ordered extra prayers until Solstice."

"I know. You told me that part already."

"Ah, but it's worth repeating," he said in the common tongue. "Remember, doubt your certainties, and be certain of your doubts."

He patted my arm and that would suffice for a good-bye. Mami got a peck on the cheek and Rishi a pat on the head. Babba got the full embrace. That also drew shouts from the crowds. Babba could declare himself king of the city after this and no one would squeak about it.

The stomp-stomp of boots told us the soldiers were next. From all the hoopla, that was the crowd's favorite part, but not mine. Mami pulled me next to her and made me point out Valeo, which battered what was left of my broken heart. He didn't nod or look our way as he passed. I didn't expect to see him again. I didn't expect to be kissed by him again.

My chest ached, and a new pain burst into my head. A sob escaped. Just one. And then I bit down on my lip and let the tears stream. Mami handed me a handkerchief and I clutched at it like I was back out at sea and this flimsy piece of cloth was my only raft.

The Nomad's Grief had withdrawn to a dot on the horizon and I hadn't budged. The tears had by then dissolved into sobs, and from sobs into hiccups. I would never see him again. We loved each other, but our lives would stretch out along different paths.

Before my parents had left me in peace, Babba had said something about being glad to see *that* ship go, at least, and Mami had elbowed him.

"It's her first love, Rimonil."

"She's got a sack full of courting notes she never finished reading," Babba said. "A fine batch of men wait in that group—men who appreciate a woman's chastity, men who are gentlemen."

I sighed. It didn't seem worth correcting his implied insults about Valeo.

My sighing prompted Mami to give Babba a scornful look, but he returned her scowl with a smug smile. "Courting notes, Lia, that's the thing. She'll be a happy bride by spring."

They left with Babba teetering in the sedan chair and Mami ribbing him, Rishi darting around people's legs. The crowds dispersed and even the Gek withdrew as discreetly as they'd arrived.

I kept my eyes on the horizon, my head pounding, my vision blurred by tears. The irritating drone grew louder and more insistent. It burst like a flaming shot in my skull. I put both hands against my head and squeezed my eyes shut.

A woman's voice cooed to me. "I'm weak yet."

"May I help you?" I turned around, but there was no one there.

"You've been great help already," she said.

My head craned this way and that. There was no one on the pier but myself. My headache had cleared but I was hearing things.

"You're not hearing things," the woman said.

"What is that?"

"Here. Within you."

"What do you mean, within me?"

But I already knew. Even before she said the words, "In your mind, and in what you call your soul," I already knew.

"No." I backed toward the railing. This wasn't happening. I wasn't possessed. I couldn't be. No and no and no, no, no. I shouted at the sky: "I'm Hadara of Rimonil of Port Sapphire."

"Yes, you are. And so am I."

I whirled to face the bay. The crimson sails were gone. I clenched my teeth. "Come back, S'ami. Come back. Oh, dammit all, come back."

# Acknowledgements

You know your family finally gets you when your Facebook feed is flooded with selfies of your loved ones reading your debut novel. Thank you, Lanny and Debbie and Bob and D2 and Howard and Mel and Larry and Joyce and all your offspring, and all my cousins and Aunt Sandie (especially Aunt Sandie), plus assorted relatives, friends, and relatives *of* friends, and friends of relatives. I probably don't deserve you all, but you're stuck with me, and I'm glad to see you're making the best of it.

My children still haven't forgiven me for not including even one dragon or flying cat in my novels, but they're coping with it. Sorry, kids.

Special hugs to my mother-in-law, Shelly Levy, for raiding all the nearby Barnes & Noble stores for copies of *The Temple of Doubt*, and for being a good friend.

Not to brag or anything, but I have the greatest day job of all time. My students at BASIS Phoenix in Arizona are the smartest people I've ever met, and I'm grateful to them (and their parents) for schlepping to book signings, words of encouragement, retweets, Instagram likes, and turning in their homework on time and in complete sentences.

My head of school, Petra Pajtas, has given me space and time and a steady paycheck while I work out how to manage the alternate realities of teaching and novel writing.

My coworkers, particularly the world's greatest English department, inspire me every day and endure my creative messes. Sorry about that.

I am forever indebted to my agent, Regina Brooks, for talking me off the ledge when things get hairy and for her nonstop optimism.

My editor, Nicole Frail, once again led a crackerjack team at Sky Pony to put together the book of my dreams. Big high fives to Joshua Barnaby, Rain Saukas, Nicole Mele, and Kiley Wellendorf, for making it all seem easy.

Not every writer has their own personal SWAT team to raid their worst writing excesses and make short work of clichés and limp prose. My critique group—Tanita Davis, Sarah Stevenson, Kelly Herold, Sara Lewis Holmes, and David Elzey—save me from certain humiliation time and again.

As I write this, my husband is away on a business trip. I had to break the news to him via email that I actually ate broccoli today without wincing or holding my nose, perhaps for the first time in my entire life. Thank you, honey, for believing that miracles do happen, even this one.